With Lies and Magic

Chapter 1

The streets around the Tempests building were busier than usual. Feya sat on a small bench outside the Inn, nervously picking her fingernails as she watched the bustling dwarfs. Three weeks had passed since Angelus's defeat. Three weeks since Jakob was nearly killed just outside the city walls. Yavanna and Anna were still treating Jakob's injuries. He had sustained a lot of damage both externally and internally. Yavanna was amazed at how quickly Jakob was healing. Though, it would still take him time to be ready to head up the Broken Spear, Yavanna believed it was Gadreed's power that thwarted death. Aside from her outburst when Jakob discovered the charm, Ava hasn't left Jakob's side. Jakob's distant and standoffish demeanor visibly hurt the young elf. Still, she refused to be away from him. Feya had barely spoken to him since the charm incident. Since Ava revealed the Faeries feelings for him. Aside from the occasional greeting when she would bring him drink or food, Feya remained silent around her friend. She didn't want to come between Ava and Jakob anymore than she already had. Still, part of her was happy he knew but wished it could have been said from her own lips.

Feya watched as wagons passed by quickly. Some came uncomfortably close to the bench she sat on. She didn't comment on the reckless driving of the hasty dwarfs. She wished being hit by a speeding wagon would launch her back before everything had gone wrong. Instead, dwarves in the box seats screamed insults, somehow blaming the Faerie for the benches position. A powerful yawn struck Feya's ears as the door of the Tempest building opened behind her. She didn't need to turn to know Balin was exiting the headquarters. "Feya." Balin said through his yawn as he scratched his beard. The dwarf grunted as he stretched his back. "What ya doing out here by your lonesome? Gonna get slammed by one of these half-blind merchants out here." The dwarf eased himself around the bench, taking a seat next to the Faerie. Feya shrugged, holding the charmed necklace in her hands. Balin watched as his friend slid the charm into her pocket. She hadn't worn the necklace since Jakob found it hidden in his trunk. "Don't let it keep you down, las." Balin said, nudging Feya with his shoulder.

Feya sighed as she slouched against the benches back. "I know." She said softly, not looking at Balin. "It's just… embarrassing." Balin made himself comfortable on the bench, resting his arm behind Feya's shoulders. "I wish I could talk to him, but what could I say? Is there even a point in saying anything?" Feya whispered through heavy breaths. "I don't like how things are now. We have to climb a mountain when Jakob is healed. I don't like knowing I'm the cause of all this tension."

"Aye." Balin said, rubbing his mustache. "Is going to be a hard journey. Ava shouldn't have acted like an undisciplined child over such trivial matters." Feya rolled her head slightly to eye the dwarf. Even through his thick facial hair, she could see his wide smile. "Traversing a mountain is no place for love." Balin joked. "I lost me great love atop a mountain once."

"You?" Feya said in shock. She slowly sat up to face the dwarf. "Who was she?"

"Aye." Balin said, pursing his lips and nodding his head. "A real beauty she was. Marvelous shape. The perfect weight." Balin crossed his arms as he looked up to the sky. "And… she was so strong."

"What happened to her?"

Balin released a long breath, closing his eyes. "Fell off the side of a cliff." The Dwarf said softly. Feya opened her mouth to speak but couldn't find the words to say. Balin sighed, making Feya wonder what kind of woman she must have been. "Oh." Balin said softly. "How I miss that hammer." Feya closed her eyes, feeling a mixture of annoyance and humor. She pulled a strand of hair from the dwarf's beard as she was consumed with laughter. Balin couldn't hold his serious facade any longer and joined in her laughter. "Come las." Balin said, fixing his beard after Feya's assault on his whiskers. "Let us get away from these walls for a while and see the city." Feya nodded, thankful that Balin was still the same. She knew the only tension was between the three of them. The others were more focused on preparing themselves for the trek up the mountain.

Feya crossed the street cautiously as crowds and wagons passed the great speed. Balin didn't seem to mind the traffic. He crossed the street as though he was the only inhabitant in the entire city. Walking across the street with a proud dwarven strut. When a pedestrian or wagon would venture to close to him, Balin would sling insults and curses in his native tongue while puffing his chest. Angry dwarfs were not a rare sight in Murdok. At almost every shop, one would see dwarves in arguments over prices or the quality of goods. Despite the angry citizens, Feya did enjoy the city. The Great City lived up to the reputation and rumors she had heard long ago. Magic seemed to flow freely in the city's buildings. A familiar yet strange magic. Heat, water, and climate control were common magics in every building within the Great City. Still, Feya would often think back to the islands. She had been on the continent so long, remembering her Da and Ma's faces had become harder with each passing day. Even her memories of the village and her people were hazy and unclear. Feya slid her hand into her pocket, feeling the amethyst stones of her charm on her fingertips. It made her think of Jakob and that night at the festival.

Balin looked over his shoulders after a shouting match with a passing merchant. "You should put it back on, las." The dwarf said, turning back towards the street. "Jakob gave it to you. No reason to hide it."

"As I recall." Feya said. "It was both of you that gifted me this."

"Aye." Balin said, shoving a slow walking pedestrian away from his path. "I simply… wanted to move things along." The dwarf said, turning to wink at his Faerie friend. Feya smiled as she watched Balin continue his strut. She was embarrassed. Thinking she had hid her feelings so well, only to realize Jakob was the only blind one. She felt the cool feel of the chain and sharp edges of the amethyst in her palm. He had given her this. Proof he intended to keep his promise. She wanted to fly, and he wanted to see it happen. She slid the chain free from her pocket and slid it over her head. The metal was colder than she remembered against her chest as the charm sat just above her breasts. She could feel her magic flowing into the stones. It made her want to fly. Her wings fluttered, but she knew it was unwise. Fear-filled rumors were still told about Faerie. Cleansers camped just outside the Great City walls. Some were likely moving amongst the citizens of Murdok. She didn't want to draw attention to herself. She pushed her desires to of the sky to the back of her mind as she followed behind Balin. "Aye." Balin said, looking over his shoulder. "That's more like it." Suddenly the dwarf stopped and stared intently at the brick wall of a local remedies shop. "Feya." Balin said without turning to her. "I have concerns… about Bas."

"Of him turning?"

"Aye." Balin said. "I find it strange that he hasn't. I wondered if perhaps Yavanna, Anna, or even Hadriel has given him treatment for his ailment."

"No." Feya said, rubbing her chin with two fingers. "I don't believe anyone has seen to him medically. Hadriel hasn't been around, or seemed interested enough, to do anything either."

"Yet." Balin said with a heavy breath. He turned to her, crossing his arms, and puffing his chest.

"He seems to be improving." Feya breathed.

"Aye." Balin said, tugging his beard. "I think we should talk to Jakob about this. I'm sure he has much on his mind, but something aint right."

"I agree." Feya said, crossing her arms. Her face displayed her eagerness to speak with Jakob. Yet, it also showed her concerns about Ava. She knew the elf wouldn't leave his side. Especially, if Feya was to be part of the conversation. "Where has Elizabeth been?"

"Scouting." Balin grunted. "Off looking for a good place to begin the climb. She is searching for an area the Cleansers likely won't find us. Unfortunately, she has spent most of her time putting them in the ground."

"Should we go find her?"

"Aye." Balin said with a wide smile. "Not like I was heading anywhere in particular anyway. I was just trying to stop your streetside sulking."

Feya playfully shoved the dwarf, ordering him to lead the way to Elizabeth. "Thank you, Balin." Feya whispered. "You're a good friend."

"Aye." Balin said, puffing his chest and flexing his arms. "No better friend to have than a dwarf. Luckily for the lot of ya... ya got a handsome one as a bonus."

"I guess we are lucky a woman hasn't snatched you away from us." Feya laughed.

Balin puffed his chest again, resting his hands on his hip as he walked. "Aye. Any las would be lucky to have a man such as I. Perhaps Elizabeth will see what a catch I am, if she sticks around long enough."

"Is that so?" Feya asked, stepping beside her friend as she raised a curious brow. "Should I whisper good things to her about our master dwarf?"

"Bah." Balin barked. "No need for that. If the las can't see with her own eyes the quality of merchandise before her. a man forged to perfection. She be no catch of mine." Balin smiled as he looked up at the Faerie. "Besides, las. Ya got your own love issues to deal with."

"Thanks." Feya breathed, trying to hide her face in her hands. "You really are one of a kind Balin."

"Aye." Balin groaned. "Don't be forgetting it."

Carts and wagons lined the streets of the seaside city of Oothra. Citizens placed their dead in designated deposit sites while Oothra guards tossed the fallen Draugar and citizens into their carts. The Devil's minions appeared from nowhere. The Draugar horde focused their attention on the destruction of docks and ships, before assaulting the citizens. Oothra guards were nearly wiped out from the ferocity and numbers of the Draugar horde. Then, as quickly as they arrived, they perished. While the guards tossed the corpses of Draugar into wagons, Wise Women began roaming the streets, singing praises to the Gods for defeating the Devil's minions. A parade of young and beautiful women, all singing the names of Gods and Goddess's for striking down the Draugar. Citizens, quickly turning to anger, tossed a variety of stones, fish, and vegetables at the *Sisters*.

Kylo shook his head, watching one of the Oothra guards grab the oldest woman by the arm and toss her onto the pile of slaughtered civilians. *Typical.* Kylo thought. *Another group of radicals trying to force their beliefs, thanks to the misfortune of the moment.* The young man had spent most of the past year searching for a decoratively dressed man in a luxury wagon. A man claiming to be the fabled Savior of the realm. That is, until the day he found the wreckage of the wagon and what remained of the man scattered around a hillside. Kylo had found a few feathers near the wreckage. Angel feathers. It was clear to the young man that whoever the well-dressed man was, he was not the legendary Savior.

The parade of women began slinging insults and curses at the guards and angered crowd, damning them to the deepest parts of the Devil's realm. Kylo knew the Sisters all too well. Another cult similar to the Tempests and Cleansers. Groups who preyed on the weak by instilling fear or false hope over the Gods. Although, he had heard rumors that a branch of the Sisters paid a mercenary to kill an Angel. *They probably saw the truth about the Divine.* Kylo thought to himself, watching the youngest of the Sisters standing between the guards. *The Angel probably wanted to claim a few of their younger girls for themselves.*

"Oi, boy." A scratchy voice said from behind the young man. He turned and lowered the hood of his eggshell white robe. "Ye just gon stand 'round watching us load up the dead?" An old man said, looking up at Kylo with his only good eye.

"My apologies, sir." Kylo said, giving the man a wide smile as he combed his fingers through his red-gold hair. "I arrived in Oothra only a few moments ago. I'm surprised to see Draugar here… and in such numbers." The old man hissed and spat on the ground. "how were you able to defeat them?"

The old man scratched his exposed stomach through his tattered and stained shirt. "They aint our typical tourists." The old man said, rubbing his bad eye. "If ye ask them Sisters… was the Gods who struck down the Devil's minions." Kylo chuckled as he turned to see the Oothra guards arresting the eldest Sister, escorting them out of the city. "Ye look to smart for all that nonsense. Though, you do dress like one of them followers of the Gods." The old man said, glaring at Kylo with his yellowing eye. "You a Cleanser, boy?"

"No sir." Kylo said with a wide smile. "I am not one to follow organizations who wish to oppress others." The old man let out an approving grunt as he scratched his patchy beard. Dead skin and grime fell from the mans face. An unpleasant sight. Even more than the odor emanating from, not just the old man, but the city itself. "Tell me sir… how well do you know these waters?"

"Oi." The old man said with an enthusiastic grin. Kylo forced a smile, able to count the man's teeth with one hand. "Been fishing these waters me whole life. Made a good livin out of it."

Kylo placed his hands on his hips, pushing aside his robe to display his coin purse. "Seems I've found the right man then." The young man said. The old man gave a single nod with a half smile. "I'm searching for someone to take me to the islands. Does that sound something you would be capable of, good sir?"

The old man narrowed his yellowing eye to the white robed man. He spat on the ground before releasing a series of disapproving grunts. "Aint no one taking you to them isles, lad." The old fisherman hissed. "waters near them isles are cursed by the great sea beast Oothra." Kylo tilted his head, unfamiliar with the legend. He was a traveler of the world and considered himself well versed in the Divine, beasts, and folklore. "Oi." The old man said, stretching his back as he prepared to exit the conversation. "Oothra has sank many a ship in its day. Only when the islands come into view do the ships meet the great beast of the sea."

"I've never heard of such a creature." Kylo said, crossing his arms.

The old man grunted as he coughed. "Theres a reason we normal folk don't travel to the Faerie isles. Same reason the Gods wouldn't dare touch their soil." The fisherman coughed hard, spitting a mouthful of mucus and blood on the street. "Faeries have their own beasts to protect 'em from the Gods wrath since the war."

"Are you sure I can't persuade you, sir?" Kylo said, unclipping his coin purse.

"No." The old man hissed, knocking the purse to the ground. "No coin is worth me life, lad. Ye won't find a sailor in this city to take you to the isles." The fisherman took a limping step as Kylo knelt down to retrieve his coin. "I'll tell ya something, lad." The old man said, standing behind Kylo. "Don't be asking fold so openly as ya done me. Cleansers be roaming the city. They more dangerous than them Sisters, ya see."

Kylo nodded his understanding as he returned to purse to his belt. "I understand." The young man said with a smile. "I appreciate your time, sir."

"Don't know what business you think you got on them isles, but best forget it." The fisherman said, limping towards the pile of corpses. "Aint no good come from them Faerie. Best leave 'em to their islands and away from us decent folk."

Kylo sighed as he looked at the broken citizens of Oothra. He could feel the prying eyes around him. Watching him clip his purse to his belt. Angry glares from the Oothra guards were locked on him as they tossed the dead into wagons. Kylo stood out in the seaside city. Everyone was dirty, smelling of filth and fish. Days of cleaning the city from the Draugar horde has made the people of Oothra bitter. He stood clean and well-dressed on the blood-stained street, watching them sweat and work to rebuild their city. The young man reached into his robe pocked, pulling out a set of ten gold and silver rings. "Best I leave Oothra for now." Kylo whispered to himself as he slid the rings on their designated fingers.

It was the rings that guided Kylo to the city of Oothra. He could feel a growing sense of Devil magic and decided to follow. Unfortunately, he arrived too late, and the city was destroyed by the Draugar horde. He knew it wasn't the Gods that struck down the Devil's minions. The likely scenario was that someone, somehow, killed the Demon that summoned them. He knew Draugar turned to ash when killed unless their master was slain. Kylo tightened his fists, hoping the rings would detect the one who killed the Demon. The rings didn't react. *Perhaps they were killed during their battle with the Demon.* Kylo thought. *Or they are too far away now.* The young man quickly made his way towards the city gates, scratching his chin as he thought. He had hoped to be on a ship to the islands, but that was now out of the question. *It would be worthwhile to find whoever killed the Demon. It would make hunting easier… traveling with someone else capable of fighting Divine beasts.* Kylo shrugged, pushing the thought to the back of his mind as he slid his hands in his pockets.

A man was standing in the middle of the road just outside the Oothra gates. He was hooded with an unrecognizable face. "You there." The man said. Kylo stopped and turned to face the stranger. The man's cloak was black. He didn't see any markings of a Tempest or Cleanser, but his arms were bandaged from his wrist to his shoulders. "What happened to the city?"

Kylo looked over his shoulder towards the city gates before turning to the cloaked man. "They were attacked a few days ago." Kylo said with a shrug. "I only arrived a few hours ago... they did not seem too welcoming. If I were you, I would postpone your visit."

"You had nothing to do with the attack?" The cloaked stranger said, tilting his head to meet Kylo's eyes. The young man stepped back, seeing the glare through the shadow of the stranger's hood.

"No." Kylo hissed. "It also isn't wise to accuse people on the streets of such things." Kylo balled his fists as the cloaked man turned back to the city. He sent his magic into the rings, feeling the calling in his blood as a hunter of beasts. The rings rejected his magic, causing a nervous sensation to run up Kylo's spine. He swallowed hard as he looked at the stranger. "Best of luck to you with your trip to Oothra." Kylo said, ready to end the encounter with this strange man.

"Best of luck to you as well, sir." The cloaked man said, scratching his bandaged arm. "Enjoy your stay in Murdok."

"Murdok?" Kylo said, turning back to the cloaked man. The stranger never turned away from Oothra. "What makes you think I have business in Murdok?" The stranger shrugged and began walking towards the city. Kylo shook his head as he watched the man enter the city gates and vanish amongst the Oothra citizens. "What a strange man." Kylo whispered to himself. He sighed as he tugged at his collar. *Let us hope the next town has a decent Inn with good food.* The young hunter thought to himself. *Perhaps... even some decent women.*

Feya and Balin stood back several paces from the blood covered commander. Elizabeth pulled her spear free from the back of a fallen Cleanser as she screamed angrily at a Murdok guard. Insults and profanities were tossed between the black-haired soldier and the blond bearded dwarf. Feya sighed as she rubbed her temples. Elizabeth commented on the Dwarf guards lack of combat skills, while the dwarf made derogatory remarks about the soldier's mother. Elizabeth returned the spear into the Cleansers back with a thud, causing Feya to shake from the sudden sound. She stepped towards the angered dwarf, their argument only growing in volume the closer they stepped. Balin crossed his arms as he puffed his chest, laughing as he watched the pair argue. Feya attempted to ignore the quarrel, looking at a nearby path leading up the mountain. There were several bodies lying around the rocky path. *Cleansers no doubt.* Feya thought to herself. "Las has my hammer throbbin." Balin laughed. The Faerie covered her face, wishing she was back on her sulking bench. She sighed, noticing the signs with poorly painted writing near the Cleanser corpses. Threats. The Cleansers did not want anyone to attempt to climb the Broken Spear.

Being the place of legend where the Savior Child was born, Cleansers did not want anyone interfering with the mountain. Or, what remained at its peak. Unlike the Tempests, Cleansers are strong believers that the Savior Child was a sin against the Gods. As was anyone who still possess magic since the departure of the Gods. Feya scanned the area, noticing dozens of signs around the mountain paths. *There must be hundreds of them.* Feya thought. The dwarf guard glanced over at Balin and Feya, tossing his hands in the air as he walked away from Elizabeth. It was clear the Murdok guard had grown tired of arguing with a human. Especially since Balin was cheering her on from the side.

Elizabeth grunted as she pulled the spear free from the Cleanser. "Fucking dwarves." The soldier hissed, watching the blond bearded dwarf drag away bodies. "No offense Balin." Elizabeth said, wiping blood from her chest plate.

"Aye." Balin laughed. "We be a difficult bunch." He puffed his chest, flexing his arms as he eyed Elizabeth. The soldier handed her spear to Balin as she attempted to tie back her blood drenched hair. "You seem to have killed a good many of them." Balin said, watching the soldier tie back her hair.

"They keep showing up." Elizabeth said, turning towards the Murdok guards. "And our friends here aren't very skilled." Balin returned her spear, smiling wide through his whiskers. "It is going to be dangerous to head mountain if they keep popping up from nowhere." Elizabeth said, turning to Feya. She saw the Faerie holding her charm as she stepped over a fallen Cleanser. "They have heard rumors of a Faerie in the city. They want to find you." Feya swallowed hard. Her mind shot back to Madam Mallets Inn, where both she and Jakob were attacked by a pair of Cleansers. Elizabeth could see the discomfort on Feya's face and placed a supportive hand on her shoulder. "Hey." Elizabeth said, smiling confidently. "I'm not going to let anyone take you." Feya smiled and nodded at her friend. "Can't let you leave with this guy." Elizabeth said, gesturing to Balin with her chin.

The dwarf let out an awkward laugh as he rubbed his neck. "Aye. Ya might have too much fun with me if we were alone." Balin said with a wink, twirling his whiskers. Elizabeth closed her eyes as she smiled. If it wasn't for the armor… and blood smeared on her face… Elizabeth would look like the village beauty. Feya chuckled as she looked at Balin, understanding why he was so attracted to her. She is tall, fit, with beautiful black hair. Feya looked at the soldier's chest plate, realizing why so many races enjoyed the company of human women. "Perhaps we should talk to the Tempests and see if there is a way to deal with the Cleansers."

"Agreed." Elizabeth said, propping herself with her spear. "Feya." The soldier said softly. "Before our little... discussion, one of the dwarfs told me of a magic library in the city. They sell books on magic spells and are rumored to have some grimoire. Thought you might be interested."

"That would be wonderful." Feya said. "But what's the difference between a magical book and a grimoire?"

"I figured you would." Elizabeth said, smiling as she pulled a crudely rolled Dwarven cigar. Balin seemed even more impressed by the soldier as he watched her take a hit of tobacco. "Basically, magic books are just magic history and theory. Grimoires are rumored to have magic within them. You are able to learn a spell or type of magic from understanding the texts." Elizabeth took a long drag of her smoke, exhaling slowly towards the dwarf. She gave him a wink before continuing with Feya. "I figured you would enjoy something that could teach magic... since Kal passed. Something you and Jakob can do together again." Feya forced a soft smile, looking down at her charm. "Forget about Ava." Elizabeth shouted, wrapping her arm around the Faerie. "You two are close and both of you need to learn more magic. And if you ask me... you two are a better fit than the two of them. Just my opinion on the matter." Elizabeth said, tapping the ash from her cigar. "Has anyone seen Hadriel?"

"Gods only know where he is." Balin huffed. "He has not been much help since we arrived in Murdok. He will probably just fly off to the Broken Spear and leave us to climb alone."

"Can't rely on anyone of Divine blood, huh?" Elizabeth smiled.

"We can rely on Jakob." Feya said softly. "He is of Angel blood. I trust him."

"Aye." Balin said, nudging the Faerie with his elbow. "Trust the lad with me life. Takes a brave man to risk his soul with Gadreed. Which is why we should make sure he is at full strength before we head to the Broken Spear." Balin combed his fingers through his beard as he thought.

"Bringing those texts would be a good ice breaker for speaking to Jakob about Bas."

"What about him?" Elizabeth asked with a raised brow. "Is he showing signs of turning?"

"On the contrary." Balin said. "Old man seems to be getting better. Feya and I are curious as to why."

"We worry the change is coming." Feya said. "That this sudden burst of energy and wellness is the Demon's magic beginning to take over."

Elizabeth propped herself against Balin, rubbing her neck. "I doubt that. Maybe Kal's magic has been healing him all these years."

Balin shrugged but said nothing. Feya remained silent as well. She knew it was unlikely, after all these years, Sebastian would be suddenly healed by Kal's magic. Still, Feya hoped it was true. That maybe in her death, Kal had managed to heal her partner and give him a chance to be with his grandson a little longer. "that must be the shop." Balin said, pointing to a building on the adjacent street corner. "It's the only non-dwarf shop on the street."

"Very observant." Elizabeth said, smiling at the dwarf. "Yes, that is it. It is apparently run by an old man and his wife. The guards are growing tired of protecting them from the Cleansers."

Elizabeth opened the shop door, allowing Balin and Feya to enter the *Lost Arts*. The old shopkeepers gave greetings while stocking shelves and wiping down glassware. The old man turned, seeing the trio enter the shop. "Come in." The shopkeeper said slowly. His eyes widened as he offered Feya his hand. "Gods." The man said, shaking Feya's hand. "I haven't had the pleasure of meeting a Faerie before."

"Hello." Feya said awkwardly. She forced a smile and bowed her head, releasing the aging shopkeeper's trembling grip. "I am searching for books on casting elemental spells. Or a grimoire if you have any."

"What would a Faerie need with magical literature?" The old woman asked, stepping closer to her customers. "Or a grimoire for the matter. You Faerie still posses the Gods Resource."

Feya sighed as she looked into the curious eyes of the elderly shopkeepers. "Unfortunately." Feya said, gripping her charm. "We do not. We have been without magic for as long as the rest of the realm."

The old man looked at his wife as he scratched his balding head. The news of powerless Faeries confused the shopkeepers. "You don't say." The old man said. "I guess one mustn't believe everything they hear." Feya forced a smile, knowing the rumors and bigotry directed towards the Faerie. From gossip about their bonding to fear of their ties to dark magic. "Still." The old man breathed. "It is a shock to hear. Some of us prayed the Faerie would somehow return magic to the rest of the realm."

Feya softly laughed. It was the first time she had heard any kind of hopefulness of her kind from the continent. She thought back to Jakob's village where no one would even trade with her because of her race. Not until Jakob agreed to help her. She smiled softly, remembering that because of that, she had met him. *And in time fell I love with him.* Feya thought to herself. "Aye." Balin said, stepping between Feya and the shopkeepers. "We be on a quest to find the Savior and return this realms magic."

The shopkeepers passed fear-filled glances to one another. "One must be careful speaking of such things, master Dwarf." The old woman said. "Cleansers patrol these streets, despite the Tempests calling Murdok home."

"I noticed." Elizabeth said, wiping blood from her cheek with her thumb. "I've had the pleasure of meeting a few only moments ago."

"Come." The old man said, escorting Feya towards the counter. "We have many texts. Some predating the Gods War. I believe we have texts on the Savior himself, but I cannot guarantee its authenticity." Feya stepped towards the counter as the bell rang on the shop door. The old woman turned and greeted the new customers as Feya looked over her shoulder. The cloaked figures entered the Lost Arts shop. Feya felt Balin hand against her as she noticed the markings sewn onto each of their cloaks. A scroll with a dagger piercing its paper. *Cleansers.*

Silence filled the room as Jakob slowly opened his eyes. He carefully turned to stretch without irritating his injuries. As he moved, he felt another body next to him. The young man pulled back the blanket and saw Ava asleep next to him. Despite the tension between them, she had remained by his side through his recovery. She had apologized countless times for what she had done and said but had never done the same to Feya. Part of him had wished it was Feya lying next to him, waiting for him to wake up after his treatment. He had seen little of Feya for the past few weeks. Their separation had taken an unfamiliar toll on the young man. He was used to her being beside him, hanging on his arms, or simply falling asleep against him after a day of traveling. Jakob pulled the blanked back to cover Ava before running his hand along his stomach. He felt the scar from the lethal wound Angelus had dealt him. As his fingers felt the rough skin of his scar, a burning sensation flooded his stomach. It had been weeks since Angelus had fallen, but his body still remembered the pain. Jakob laid back on the bed slowly. Ava shifted closer to him, resting her head against his chest. He hovered his hand above her but decided not to touch her. The young man was conflicted. He enjoyed Ava's company and friendship.

Since her outburst, various thoughts had run through his mind. He thought about the time both he and Ava had spent together. Part of him questioned what it was they actually had together. Anna had shared her opinions on the matter, which angered the young elf. But part of him wished it was Feya next to him. He wanted to feel her warmth beside him. Hear her voice and just talk like they used to. The day couldn't come soon enough for Yavanna to allow him out of bed. The magical treatments both she and Anna had been performing were exhausting. It wasn't easy on the elf or Daemon either. He had suffered major damage to his organs from Angelus. They pair would drive themselves to exhaustion and magical depletion. The room became foggy, as if sleep was consuming him. Jakob shook his head, trying to remain conscious. He sat up, looking at the foot of his bed. A surge of adrenaline hit as he saw the figure standing at the edge of his bed. "Gadreed?" Jakob whispered as the figure expanded its four wings.

"Jakob." Gadreed said in Jakob's mind. Jakob was confused, he had not seen the Angel of War in their world before. He had only spoken with the Angel through thought or in the dreamscape. "Something dark is brewing in this city." Gadreed said. "I sense Devil magic at work. Old magic is here, and its source is not from your Daemon friend."

"What do you mean?" Jakob asked, trying to adjust himself in the bed. "Wouldn't there be old magic in the Great Cities?"

"Yes." Gadreed said. "The magic that flows freely in the Great Cities are not of Divine origin. I sense the power of the Basilisks still within these walls. What I also sense, is a power Devil magic." Gadreed turned, eyeing his sword sitting in the corner of the room. "Something sleeps in these lands, Jakob. Be wise in your use of my magic and blade." Jakob opened his mouth to speak but the Angel had vanished as quickly as he arrived. Jakob fell back against his pillow and sighed.

"What's wrong?" Ava groaned, still half asleep. She ran her hand along Jakob's chest and stomach. "Are you hurting? Hungry? Should I go get Anna?"

"No." Jakob said softly. He decided to embrace her. she welcomed it as she pulled herself closer to him. "I'm fine. It was just Gadreed."

"He spoke to you?" Ava asked, fully waking from her drowsy state. "Has he been speaking to you while you sleep?"

Jakob shook his head slowly. "No. He has been silent these past few weeks." Ava sat up, combing her fingers through her hair. Jakob smiled softly as he watched her. "You cut your hair." Jakob said.

"It was getting too long." Ava said. "It was running to far down my back." Jakob ran his fingers through her light blond hair, feeling her soft pointed ears. "You don't like it?"

"I never said that."

"But you hate me." Ava said, holding Jakob's hand as his fingers caressed her ears.

Jakob sighed as he looked into her emerald eyes. "I don't hate you, Ava." He said, looking at the broken expression she was giving him. "I just wish… you hadn't done that to Feya." Jakob said as Ava looked away. "She is our friend, and I don't like that she feels unwelcomed here." Ava turned to him with pursed lips. "She care too much about her. I made her a promise and I intend to keep it."

"I know." Ava said pouting. "I just…" the door to Jakob's room opened. Anna stepped into the room, tilting her head at the sight of Ava in his bed. Ava rolled her eyes and uncovered herself from the blanket, revealing she was fully clothed. "Nothing happened Anna."

"Good." Anna said with a smirk. "He is still healing and in no condition for the activities you two seem to enjoy." Ava scoffed and climbed out of the bed as Anna sat next to Jakob. The Daemon lifted the blanket to examine Jakob's injury. "It is healing nicely." Anna said. "Are you in any pain? Do you have any strange feelings from the magical healing." Jakob shrugged dismissively. "Don't act tough." Anna scolded. "If you are feeling anything strange, you have to let me know. Your body could have serious problems if we don't do the healing properly."

"Just cramps from lying here all day every day." Jakob said, smiling at the Daemon. "I don't think it would kill me to get out of bed every now and then."

"Yavanna might kill you." Anna said sharply. "She has been doing most of you healing and knows what you can and cant handle." Jakob sat back in the bed. Anna turned to Ava and sighed as she closed her eyes. "I'll speak with Yavanna and ask her if you can get out of bed for a while." Jakob smiled and nodded his head. "but until she gives the word… you stay put." Anna looked at Jakob with her scolding green eyes. He had noticed her horn getting longer and saw pigment changes in her eyes. *Her power is growing.* Jakob assumed. Slivers of yellow were showing in her once pure emerald eyes. "Has Gadreed spoken to you, Jakob?" Anna asked suddenly. Jakob tilted his head curiously. "I just… I feel the longer we are here… something just feels wrong with this city."

Jakob released a slow breath as he rubbed the back of his neck. "He actually spoke to me a few moments ago." Jakob admitted. "He said he sensed old Devil magic here. And he wasn't talking about you." Anna took a slow breath. Jakob noticed a soft tremble in her hands as she nervously picked at her fingernails. "Gadreed said we need to be careful when using his magic or the blade. He said something is sleeping nearby. He didn't tell me anything else."

Anna rubbed her temple and horn with her fingers as she fell into thought. Ava sat back on the bed next to Jakob, watching Anna pace through the room. "I don't know or remember anything sleeping near the mountains or the city." Anna whispered. She was growing frustrated as she tried to remember anything she could. The Daemon had regained a great deal of memories, but there were still gaps and confusion within them. 'Really my concern is the Devil magic.' Anna said, turning to Jakob. "I have had a strange feeling, even before we arrived in Murdok. It feels like someone is watching us. Someone of Devil magic."

"Do you think we are being spied on?" Ava asked.

Anna shrugged. "I don't know." The Daemon said, slouching her shoulders. "Something hasn't felt right since we left Graham."

"Maybe the artifact affected you somehow." Jakob said. "You said it was planted right."

"Maybe." Anna said, rubbing her chin. Jakob knew by her tone she didn't agree with his idea. The Daemon moved her hand along her jaw and up her ears. "Whatever it is, Gadreed senses it as well. So, we should be on guard. The Cleansers don't seem to mind patrolling, even with the Tempests here. Who knows what else is lingering in this city's streets."

"Don't worry." Jakob said confidently. "I'll defend this bed with my life if they decide to make a move."

"Very funny." Anna said, rolling her eyes. "You are in no shape to fight off a cold let alone a Divine being. Do not forget, Jakob." Anna said, turning to exit the room. "The more you use Gadreed the more of you he will take. You are in no condition to fight or use magic. If you summon him… you very well may shorten your time."

Jakob slowly nodded his understanding as Anna left the room. She slowly closed the door, eyeing her sister as the lock clicked. Jakob eyed the corner of the room. Gadreed's shield and sword were propped against the wall by the door. He was curious about the power that was held within the sword. Still, he remembered what Gadreed had told him when Balin delivered the blade. *Any manor of creature...* Jakob remembered the Angel of War warning. Beasts, monsters, and who knew what else would sense the power of the fallen Angel and come to investigate. The shield was an exhausting tool of Gadreed's already, he couldn't imagine the toll the sword would have on his body. *A tomorrow problem.* Jakob told himself. *No point in worrying about the sword when I can't even get out of bed.*

From what he could see through the window of his room, Jakob knew the sun was close to setting. The days seem to have melded together since Yavanna confined him to his bed. He closed his eyes as he felt Ava press herself against him under the blanket. He could feel her smooth skin against his side. Somehow, without notice, she had managed to remove her clothing as she climbed into bed. He smiled but pretended not to notice.

His feelings were conflicted and still had a lot to sort through in his mind. Jakob closed his eyes and could hear his grandfather strumming his lute in the next room. A common occurrence when the days were coming to an end. *At least he still seems to be feeling better.* Jakob thought as he faded into sleep. *Hopefully… I won't lose you Gramps. Like I lost everyone else.*

Chapter 2

The worship hall of the Temple of the Divine God was almost as cold as the weather just outside its walls. Dozens of rows of seats were empty and abandoned. Baren walls surrounded the worship hall that were once decorated with beautifully painted works of art. Shelves that once held the offerings of artwork made of marble, stone, and rare woods now stood empty. The Temple now stood as a representation of how the mortal world had turned away from their faith in the Gods. Gidione sat on one of the benched seats in the front row of the worship hall, looking at the rotted podium surrounded by broken glass. The Goddess sat patiently on the bench, watching the snow fall from the crumbled roof. Angelus had failed her. failed to find the Abomination or kill Gadreed's host. The son of the Angel of War seemed to lack his father's power or determination to succeed. Tedros was of no use to her. Her last remaining sibling only seemed interested in watching on the sidelines. None of the Gods seemed focused on finding the Abomination. Leaving the task to mortal cults or their Divine servants. Now, she was forced to contact the only Devil she even slightly trusted. She knew Devils enjoyed playing games with the Gods with their words. Lucile was the only Devil that might tell her what steps their kind had taken to find the child of two blood.

The temperature dropped intensely as Gidione felt a surge of Dark magic approaching. She turned to the doorway, not standing from her seat, waiting for the Devil to enter. Gidione felt a gentle pull at her white hair. She quickly shifted as her eyes met a red gaze looking at her. "Must you always make such entrances." Gidione hissed, coming her fingers through her hair. The Devil smiled as she sat next to the Goddess.

"one must make such an entrance." Lucile said, biting her lip and pushing back her flowing red hair. Gidione watched the Devil adjust in her seat, curious as to why she would wear such little clothing in this freezing environment. "When meeting with someone such as yourself." Lucile said, running her fingers along the Goddess's cheek. Gidione scoffed, shoving the Devils hand from her face. "Why would Gidione, sister of Kirames, summon me after all this time… in a church no less?"

"Information." Gidione said sharply, lifting her chin and leaning away from the Devil. Lucile pursed her lips as she eyed the Goddess. "What are the Devils doing about the Abomination?" Gidione asked, shifting in her seat. She gave herself what little space she could from the Devil and her prying eyes. "our Angels have seen little signs of your minions in the mortal realm."

"What would we need to be there for?" Lucile asked, biting her lip to reveal one of her fangs. "The mortals blame every tragedy that befalls them as our doing, giving us power from their fear."

Gidione stood from the bench, trying to distance herself further from the Devil. "Why is it every Divine being seems to downplay the threat of this Abomination?" Gidione hissed. "If he regains his power and those creatures return…" The Goddess paused as she looked at the rotted podium of the worship hall. The falling snow from the half-covered roof. "What was Kirames and Alvarome thinking? Creating such a creature." Gidione whispered.

"Please Gidione." Lucile laughed, twirling her red hair between her fingers as she watched the Goddess with lustful eyes. "Had you been male you would have had me with child centuries ago." Lucile slowly crossed her legs, revealing herself to the Goddess. "Or have you forgotten me?"

"This is no time for that." Gidione snapped. "Gadreed still lives within a mortal host. He and the mortals he travels with has slain Angelus."

"Kalross as well." Lucile said calmly. "You remember him, don't you?" Gidione remained silent as she turned to face the Devil. "But I have someone following the mortals." Lucile said proudly. "Though, they must be careful. There is a Faerie amongst them. A unique Faerie. Angelus nearly killed her... so I am told." Gidione scowled silently at the Devil after hearing of Angelus's ignorance. "Faerie blood spilled by Divine hands will awaken the King of Dragons." Lucile reminded the Goddess, crossing her legs once again. "What a ridiculous loophole to have in a spell that binds your enemy. You should be asking yourself what the Divine God and Ancestral Devil were thinking."

"Eeus... is not one for explaining herself since the Gods War." Gidione muttered.

"Neither is Ancestor Tor." Lucile smiled. "It would appear they each suffered lasting affects from using this worlds magic with their own." Gidione took a long breath and released it slowly as she rubbed her temples. "Perhaps they have done more harm to our kind when they bound the child and the Basilisks." Gidione quickly glared at the Devil, watching Lucile press her tongue against her fang. "Perhaps." Lucile continued, closing her eyes. "We just aren't powerful enough for this realm."

"Your mocking me."

"Am I?" Lucile asked, slowly opening her eyes. "Or am I speaking truth?" The Gods and Devil fear the child locking us away in our own realms." She shrugged her shoulders as her hair fell over one eye. "yet, that is not a death sentence."

"The Gods know your realm is just as ruined as ours." Gidione said. "That is why you were guided here."

Lucile laughed as she stood from the bench. "Guided here?" The Devil mocked. "Your kind invited us here to aide you in your futile war with the Basilisks. Tricking the mortals into believing the beasts were products of we Devils by the use of lies and magic." Lucile shook her head, still smiling at the Goddess. "Oh, my dear Gidione. Your kind are much more devious than even we Devils." Gidione roared with anger as her golden wings formed behind her. Divine writing began to appear down her arms as a circle of magic words surrounded her wings. Lucile mockingly pouted as she watched the Goddess's display. "Come now, Gidione. No need for tantrums. I agree the child would have been a problem. But honestly, do you truly believe is alive? The Devils have had beasts, Draugar, and Demons searching this realm for a millennium for him. Without his magic, he is likely dead. If he is alive and regains his power... he is likely to go mad and destroy this realm himself." Lucile stepped closer to the Goddess and caressed her stomach with her fingertips. "Then you Gods can swoop in and strike him down, becoming the heroes of the mortals once again." Gidione narrowed her eyes at Lucile as her wings faded. "Then..." Lucile whispered in Gidione's ear. Her breath was warm, and her hair smelled of citrus and cinnamon. "The game starts all over again. We send our minions out to torture and kill, and your Angels strike them down. We both remain powerful."

"So, this is just a game to you?" Gidione asked, taking in the Devils scent.

"It always has been, young Goddess." Lucile said. "You are much too young to know how long our kind have been playing this game. This is the only realm that has had its own Gods that were strong enough to push back against us." The Devil smiled as she wrapped her arms around the Goddess's waist. "In fact, they are strong enough to destroy us. This whole experience has been... Thrilling." Lucile moaned."

"What do you mean... this realm and its gods?" Gidione asked, shoving the Devil's hands from her waist.

"Sweet Gidione." Lucile said, pulling the Goddess by the hips. "The realm of the Gods you know isn't even your true home. We have been playing this game since the starts were young." Gidione shook her head in disbelief. She wanted to pull away, but part of her wanted the Devil's arms around her. "You believe Alvarome and Kirames broke some rule by being together?" Lucile chuckled as she slid her hand along the Goddess's body. "Tor and Eeus know each other very... intimately."

"You speak nonsense, Lucile." Gidione said, pushing the Devil away.

"Believe what you want, young Goddess." Lucile said, shrugging her shoulders. "You are always welcome in my chambers if you wish to... learn. But there is a secrete behind our little nephew... and I will discover it."

"And what do you think this secrete is?"

Lucile shook her head, leaning in to kiss the Goddess's cheek. "Sweet Gidione. You are but a baby bird, still too afraid to leap from its nest. You are not prepared for the truth of our kind."

Gidione stepped back from the Devil, summoning a portal to return her home. "You have been as useful as I thought you'd be." Gidione hissed before stepping into the ring of magic and runes. "Enjoy your game, while I hunt down this Abomination."

"Don't be a stranger." Lucile smiled, biting her lip as she watched the Goddess step through the portal. "I've missed the taste of you, my Goddess."

Panic and destruction filled the Lost Arts magic shop. The old shopkeepers screamed and hid behind a far counter as pieces of furniture and merchandise were tossed through the shop. The old man had attempted to rush his wife to the door, only to be met by the largest of the Cleansers. The other two, a man and woman, pushed and attacked Feya and the others. Feya leaped back from an attack by the striking Cleanser. She was wielding a thin sword and a small oval shaped shield strapped to her forearm. With a slight movement of her fingers, Feya summoned her pixies to incircle her. Her wings fluttered as she eyed the Cleanser woman. The woman steadied her stance as she released a curse, watching the pixies hover around the Lost Arts magic shop. The pixies stopped, she lifted her shield, but it wasn't large enough. Four met their mark, hitting the Cleanser woman on both legs, lower side, and upper shoulder.

Balin leaped towards the injured woman, grabbing a leg from a broken table as a weapon, striking her across the head. The woman groaned, grunted, and cursed in pain but did not fall. Elizabeth continued to hold off the other Cleanser while Feya's focus shifted between the woman and the one guarding the door. The commander's foe wielded two strangely curved blades. Elizabeth was forced to fight hand to hand. The shop was too small and there were too many people for her to utilize her spear. Balin rolled across the floor, preparing for another strike against the Cleanser woman. Feya focused and summoned a small magic circle around her left hand as she recalled the pixies with her right. All the liquid in the shop began to flow towards the magic circle around her left hand. As she tightened her fist, the liquid became a water-like whip with several pieces of sharp ice on its end. Feya swung her arm, slinging the whip of water and ice towards the Cleanser woman. The woman prepared to evade, Feya noticed and adjust her finger movements. The pixies flew through the air as the woman escaped Balin's attack. The whip slashed the across the Cleansers chest, allowing the pixies to end their conflict. The Cleanser woman groaned as she collapsed on the shop floor.

"That's one." Balin breathed, lifting the chair leg from the floor. He spat crimson on the floor as he wiped his thumb across his nose.

Feya nodded and turned to Elizabeth. The commander weaved through the Cleansers attacks, grabbing him by chest and tossing him across the room through the front window. The man roared as he stood from the ground, picking glass and splinters from his flesh. Elizabeth took the opportunity and grabbed her spear, tossing it through the shop towards the window. The spear hit with a thud. The man released a gurgled groan as he collapsed into the city street. "That's... two..." Elizabeth said through heavy breaths. "Now." The commander said, glaring at the large man still standing by the door. "Just the big one."

The largest of the Cleansers uncrossed his arms and popped his knuckles, stepping away from the door slowly. Unexpectedly, the large man rushed towards Feya. Despite his size the Cleanser was incredibly fast and agile. He swung a large blade that was hidden under his robe, grazing Balin's cheek and slicing through a display table. With a quick turn, the Cleanser kicked Balin in the chest, sending the Dwarf flying across the shop. The old shopkeepers panicked as the Dwarf's unconscious body slammed against the wall behind them. Elizabeth and Feya charged the beast of a man. The commander grabbed Balin's wooden weapon as Feya commanded her pixies to surround the man. Elizabeth slammed the piece of wood into the man's knee as he brought his fist heavily down against her temple. The Cleanser dropped from the pain, pushing Elizabeth's skull against the hardwood floor of the shop. The commander gritted her teeth as she tried to lift herself from the cold floor. Blood streamed down her head and began to pool on the ground beneath her.

Feya made a sign with her fingers, commanding the pixies to strike the Cleanser from behind. The large man screamed as the pixies pierced the man's side and back. Feya shoved her hand forward, forcing the pixies through the Cleansers body and imbedding them into the floor. "Godless... heathen..." The Cleanser huffed as he collapsed on the floor beside a beaten Elizabeth. "Are you alright?" Feya asked in a panic as she rushed to the commander's side. The dark-haired soldier nodded as she leaned against a broken bookshelf. "Balin?" Feya screamed. The old man stood from behind the counter, informing Feya that the dwarf was unconscious but alive.

The Faerie took a long breath as she looked around the demolished magic shop. She had come to find texts to learn, to be better for the journey ahead. To be better for Jakob. There was little left in the shop now. She watched as the old man helped his wife stand. The old woman rubbed her thinning hair at the sight of her shop. Elizabeth coughed blood, holding the side of her bleeding head. Another set of footsteps entered the shop. Feya turned instinctively to attack but was hit across the jaw by a powerful blow. The Faerie rolled several times on the floor, trying to remain conscious. She coughed, spitting up blood from biting her tongue. "Sorry love." A raspy voice said as she gasped for air. Feya looked up, seeing a shaved head man with a red braided beard. "Not me first choice of jobs but..." The man shrugged. "Coin is coin." Feya opened her mouth to speak but was quickly silenced by another fierce blow to the head. She felt her skull bounce against the hard wood floor of the shop as her vision began to fade. "And they are offering a lot for you, love." Muffled screams filled Feya's ears as the large man tossed her over his shoulder. Elizabeth reached for the Faerie as the stranger carried her out of the Lost Arts magic shop.

The man tossed her into a wagon that was parked just outside the shop's entrance and covered her with a blanket. Feya struggled to remain awake. Her head felt like the day after a long night of drinking. She reached for her head, realizing that the stranger had tied her hands and legs before placing her into the wagon. *When did he?* Feya thought, not realizing what was happening. *Why?* The wagon shifted as the man climbed into the box seat. "Get comfortable love. We got a few ours ride in front of us."

"W-Why?" Feya asked, closing her eyes. The pain in her head seemed to worsen whether her eyes were open or closed. "W-Why Cole?"

Feya felt the wagon jerk as the horses pulled off with speed. "Like I told ya and the lad before." Crimson Cole said dryly. "Coin is coin." He let out a long sigh as he turned the horses towards the Murdok gates. "I'm sorry, Feya. Got expenses and pleasures to pay for and they paying a great deal for an exotic like you."

"Why me, Cole?" Feya cried. "Why?"

Cole spat as Feya saw the city gates pass overhead. "Rumors been going around about a Faerie. Client wants him a Faerie for his... business." He turned and looked at the Faerie over his shoulder. "You're the only Faerie on the continent love." He lifted a piece of paper, revealing the details of the job. "Blue hair, blue eyes, fancy wings, and a purple charmed necklace." Feya's lips trembled as she looked at the parchment. Even more so when she saw the reward on the bottom. "A thousand gold pieces." Cole said cheerfully. "You're worth a lot, love. Won't have to take a job for at least a few months after this. Unless I get bored." The mercenary shrugged. Feya began crying for Jakob, burying her face into the blanket. "I'm sorry. Truly. It's just me job, love."

Sebastian cursed as he slammed a hammer against his thumb while repairing the wagons wheel. In anger, he tossed the hammer at the wagon wall, startling the horses that were tied nearby. The old mage took a long breath to calm himself as he looked at the two curious horses. Sebastian smiled from embarrassment, even though the horses were the only witnesses to his humiliation. He rubbed his chest as he knelt to pick up the hammer and nails. The mage continued his repairs, kneeling down to one knee as he looked under the wagon. As he was checking the various support beams for damage, he saw a pair slowly walking towards the Tempests building. Both were limping and mumbling curses. He stood, realizing the cursing dwarf was Balin. Balin and Elizabeth stepped around the wagon, blood and beaten. With a huff, the injured pair sat heavily into the Tempests bench.

"Gods hammer." Balin shouted as he gripped his chest. Sebastian rushed over, dropping his tools as he summoned a healing spell. "No time for that, Bas." The dwarf huffed, shoving the mages hand away. Balin took a long breath, closing his eyes tightly from the pain rushing through his body. "He got Feya." Balin said with a heavy breath. "Bastard took Feya."

"What?" Sebastian said, taking a step back from the bench. "What do you mean? Who? Where is Feya?"

Balin took another breath. pain and anger flooded his face as he tried to speak. Elizabeth leaned forward, gripping her spear. "Cleansers attacked us in a shop." The commander explained as she used her spear as a cane. Sebastian attempted to help the woman stand but she motioned him away. "We took out the Cleansers but…" Elizabeth's voice faded as she remembered the face of the man who attacked. "Crimson Cold came in the shop afterwards." Sebastian narrowed his eyes at the commander, confusion made his heart race in his chest. "Bastard nearly knocked me out. He did a number on Feya and threw her over his shoulder. He loaded her in a wagon and took off." Sebastian rubbed his chin as he processed Elizabeths tale. The commander reached into her pocket and pulled out a bounty. "He dropped this for us. Even wrote a note to Jakob on the back."

Sebastian took the paper and read the details of the job. They had described Feya perfectly but what drew his attention was the thousand gold piece reward. The old mage scoffed as he read the bounty before turning the page to see Cole's handwritten note.

Jakob,
My deepest apologies for taking your Faerie friend.
But coin is coin and I gots to make a livin'.
She will not be killed, my client intends to keep her alive.
Once I deliver her to him, you can find him in the city of Gosa.
Me clients name is Thrayn. You'll find him at his Pleasure Palace.

Be seeing you,
Crimson Cold

"Shit." Sebastian mumbled after reading the note. There were so many problems ahead of them if they were to go after Feya. Gosa was days away. Cole was a formidable mercenary. And… Thrayn. "Ava isn't going to like this."

"Aye." Balin coughed, still gripping his chest as he stood from the bench. "Bastard took her knowing we'd go get her back." The dwarf turned and walked towards the building's entrance. "I'm going to tell Jakob."

"Wait." Sebastian said, stepping towards the dwarf. "Jakob is still…"

"Fuck that, Bas." Balin huffed, puffing his chest despite the pain. "Feya is our friend and Gosa is at least a four-day ride from here. I know what he will say. The mountain can wait. Hadriel can wait. Feya is more important." Balin limped his way to the door. Sebastian didn't move, knowing he was right. He couldn't keep this from his grandson, and he knew Jakob would do anything to rescue Feya. He also knew he couldn't live with himself if he left Feya to the whims of Thrayn. The old mage shook his head and followed behind the limping dwarf. "Hope that wagon's ready to go Bas." Balin breathed. "Gon be a hard ride ahead of us."

Jakob repositioned himself in the bed as he read one of the books Kal had given him. He had been thinking about her a lot since being confined to his room. A soft smile crossed his lips as he read the texts. He could hear her voice in his head as he read the magical instructions as if she had written the book herself. Kal was an excellent teacher… and friend. Jakob closed the book slowly, wishing the elf mage had survived. He could only imagine what she would say about their journey so far. Ava rolled over, nearly knocking the book from his hand as she took over more of the bed. Jakob smiled as the elf released a nasally snore. He returned his attention to the book, after covering Ava with a blanket. The bed confined man opened the book, finding the passages Feya had studied about water magic. Reading the texts on magic circles and summoning water made him miss Feya more than he already did. She hadn't come to see him as often as he would have liked since Ava's outburst. He shook his head, pushing back those thoughts to focus on magical studies. Jakob knew he couldn't rely on Gadreed for every fight. The more the Angel of War's magic was used the more his own soul would weaken. He had decided to study as much as he could on the use of magic. The more he read the more he wanted Feya beside him. They used to study together, train together, just *be* together. *Feya seems to understand all this more than I do.* Jakob thought as he read. *She could explain this better than I understand it.*

The door swung open, slamming against the wall with a thud as Balin stepped into the room. "Jakob." Balin shouted, his face red with anger. Jakob noticed his friend was gripping his chest. A large bruise could be seen from his tattered shirt. "Feya's been taken. Captured by Crimson Cole for a bounty."

"What?" Jakob said, his voice trembling to a shout. He tossed off the covers and attempted to stand from the bed. Ava reached to stop him, but he slapped her hand away. As his feet touched the floor, he felt weakness in his legs from being in bed so long. Bracing himself against the wall, Jakob stepped towards the dwarf. "What happened? Where did he take her? Why did he take her?"

Elizabeth limped her way past Sebastian and Balin and handed Jakob the bounty Cole had left. Anna helped Jakob stand as he took the paper. He gave the commander a concerned look, noticing blood and bruises. Elizabeth nodded, a silent statement that she would be fine. Jakob turned to read the bounty. Elizabeth instructed him to flip over the paper to find the note Cole had written to him. Jakob's face turned red as he re-read every word of the mercenary's note. "We are going to Gosa." Jakob snarled as he crumbled the bounty. Balin smiled and nodded his approval as he puffed his.

"No." Ava shouted as she got out of bed reaching for her shirt. Sebastian coughed as he looked away from the undressed elf girl. "We can not go to Gosa." Ava said, her voice trembling with fear. "Not again."

"We have to." Jakob said, turning to Ava. "Thrayn has Feya… and I wont let him use her." Ava's face turned pale as she heard the dwarf's name. The dwarf who sold her body since childhood for profit. Ava closed her head and shook her head. "I am not going to abandon Feya." Jakob said. "I will not let her suffer…"

"Like me?" Ava screamed. "Let her see what it was like to live as I did. At least she will be alive. I'm not going to Gosa. Not again. Anna and I barely escaped the last time."

"Then stay here." Jakob said coldly as Anna helped him dress. "I'm not going to let anything happen to Feya. She is too kind and too important to me to allow it. And if you would really leave her to that life... perhaps it's better you don't come."

"Aye." Balin said, grabbing Jakob's trunk to load into the wagon. "I'll toss your things in the wagon before I grab my things." The dwarf said, resting his hand on Jakob's back. "Everyone, gather your things. We are going to get our Faerie friend back."

"Aye." Jakob said, smiling at the dwarf. "Gramps, could you grab the sword and shield?" Sebastian nodded and hesitantly lifted the weapons of the Angel of War before leaving the room.

Anna watched as the party departed to gather their belongings. She turned to her sister as Ava sat on the bed. "You would leave her with him?" Anna asked, not looking at her sister. She didn't want to look at her. Anna could imagine anyone leaving someone they considered a friend to someone like Thrayn. "You would condemn her to the same fate you endured... just because of some foolish relationship that, truly, you care nothing about." Anna's words became sharp. "Feya has so much respect for you, as does the rest of our crew." Anna shook her head. "If you would leave her... you don't deserve their respect. Or to be part of the good they are doing for this world." Anna never turned to look at her sister. She stepped out of the room, slowly closing the door. Before shutting, she saw Ava silently crying as she slid further onto the bed.

Hadriel stood by the Murdok gates, waiting for Jakob's wagon to approach. Yavanna had informed him that Jakob and his entire party had loaded up and disappeared, aside from the elf Ava. The elf had told Yavanna that Feya had been taken to Gosa by a mercenary and they planned to rescue her. Hadriel watched as Jakob's wagon made the turn onto the main road towards the gates. He knew they needed to be focused on climbing the Broken Spear. The Daemon summoned his wings as he stepped further into the street, knowing it was going to be difficult to sway Jakob from leaving. Balin noticed Hadriel and pulled the horses to stop. The Daemon and dwarf eyed each other silently as Hadriel made his way to the back of the wagon. Jakob pulled back the canopy opening and looked down at the fully displayed Daemon glaring up at him. "Leaving?" Hadriel asked, tilting his head. "Before we embark for the Spear?"

"I have to rescue Feya." Jakob said. "But I'm sure you're already aware of that."

Hadriel smiled and chuckled softly as he rubbed his chin. His wings extended for a moment before resting behind his back. "you would abandon our mission to save this realm... for a Faerie?"

"For Feya." Jakob said. "Yes. I would give up everything as long as I knew she was safe." Jakob leaned forward and looked into the Daemon's eyes. "Feya is important to this mission. If you can't wait for us to return with her, then just fly up to the mountain and grab whatever we're looking for. We can look it over when we get back."

"Aye." Balin shouted from the box seat.

Hadriel rubbed his chin and licked his lips with frustration. "You... mortals." Hadriel hissed, grabbing Jakob by the throat, and pulling him from the wagon. "You don't see the bigger picture. You don't think about the consequences of your actions." Hadriel lifted Jakob over his head before tossing him to the ground. "You think with your cocks and what benefits you in the moment. All the while the realm suffers for your lack of action."

"Feya is important to the bigger picture." Jakob said as he struggled to stand.

"You are Gadreed's host." Hadriel shouted. "You are the host of the Angel of War. We need Gadreed if we are to free the Basilisks and restore this world." Hadriel laughed as he watched Jakob stumble to the ground after standing. "Why? Why did Gadreed choose you, of all his lineage."

"Jakob." Ava screamed as she ran towards the wagon. The young man turned, seeing the elf carrying a sack of her belongings on her back. "What's going on?"

Hadriel tossed his hands in the air at the sight of Ava. "And here is another one." Hadriel said as Ava passed the Daemon to check on Jakob. "Is this one not enough woman for you for you to forget the Faerie? At least until we return from the mountain?" Ava narrowed her eyes at the Daemon. Jakob gently pushed Ava away as he stood and glared at Hadriel. "I will not let you leave, Jakob. Not when we are this close. Not when *I* am so close. I have been roaming this world for centuries trying to unseal my brother and bringing an end to this game of Gods and Devils. And I will not let you ruin this for some Faerie." Jakob snarled as he extended his hand towards the wagon. He felt a response before Gadreed's sword flew into his hand. "Do you plan to strike me down with your sword?" Hadriel laughed. Jakob tightened his grip. Divine words began to appear and glow along the swords blade. Fire engulfed the steel, flickering from hues of red, blue, green, and even black. Hadriel eyed the sword, realizing whose sword it was. "You test what you don't understand Jakob." Hadriel said, stepping back from Jakob and Ava.

"I am going to save Feya." Jakob hissed. "You can either get out of my way… or I will send you to the grave." *Jakob.* A voice echoed in Jakob's mind. *Hadriel is not worth the risk of using the sword.* Gadreed said. "I am going to save her." Jakob shouted, speaking to Gadreed. Hadriel tilted his head, watching Jakob argue seemingly with himself. *The Faerie is important, Jakob. I sense a familiar magic within her. Let me deal with Hadriel.* "No." Jakob shouted. "I will do what I must to save Feya." Jakob groaned as he felt Gadreed assuming control. "I… said…" Jakob's eyes rolled back as divine writing formed along his arm.

"Hadriel." Gadreed said. The Daemon stepped back, forming a protective circle around himself. "We are leaving Murdok and will return when the Faerie is safe."

"Don't be a fool Gadreed." Hadriel breathed. "We are so close. This was your mission."

"It still is. And the Faerie is important to the completion of this mission. You must trust me, Hadriel. I will not strike you, but if you try to stop Jakob…"

Hadriel scoffed and lunged at Jakob. The young man's eyes returned to normal as Gadreed released control. Jakob saw the incoming attack and swung the sword at the Daemon. Hadriel lifted himself into the air with his wings, avoiding the attack. The Daemon formed a magic circle as Jakob extended his left arm to call the shield. A strong magical wind struck Jakob as the shield attached itself to his arm. He lifted the shield, trying to form a protective barrier against the Daemon's magic. He was still weak from his battle with Angelus and unable to use the shields abilities without Gadreed himself. Ava kneeled behind him, panicking as the wind continued to push them with hurricane force. Jakob took several frustrated breaths as he felt his feet slide in the dirt. He knelt down, slamming the sword into the earth to anchor himself in place. A large crack spread across the street towards Hadriel. The ground shook and the crack split wider as flames shot towards the sky, burning Hadriel's arm. Ava ran for the wagon, not wanting to be caught in the potential fight that was brewing. Hadriel fell to the ground. Jakob roared, pulling the sword from the ground. The earth shook as the blade was pulled free. Screams of panic could be heard from every corner of the Great City. Tremors became more intense with each second. Suddenly, a thunderous noise echoed through the great city of Murdok. Hadriel turned and saw the Broken Spear crack and crumble. Clouds of dust, dirt, and smoke was all that remained of the once great mountain. "What have you done?"

A roar boomed through the air as the dust began to settle around the mountains. Jakob narrowed his eyes, noticing a shadowy figure within the dissipating cloud. Another roar shook the air as a tail cut through what remained of the dust clouds, revealing a large snake-like creature. The creature coiled itself around a nearby mountain before lifting its head over the city walls. The creature roared once again. Able to see more of the beast, Jakob noticed its head was a mixture of snake and dragon. It had several horns along its head and long dorsal fin running the length of its body. It had bright yellow eyes, but its skin seemed rotted or stone-like. "Gods hammer." Balin shouted. "What the fuck is that?"

Hadriel stepped back, nearly bumping into Jakob as he looked at the creature. "It's Senshe." Hadriel said, his voice cracked and trembled as he spoke. "Senshe the Taken." Jakob quickly turned to the Daemon. "The Basilisk of the Forests." Hadriel said, narrowing his eyes to Jakob. "He was the only Basilisk successfully turned into a Draugar. Hince the title 'Taken'."

"A Basilisk Draugar?" Jakob said as he backed towards the wagon. "how did they manage to… who took control of him?"

"What's it matter?" Balin shouted. "Get in the wagon, Lad. We got to get outta here… Now!" Jakob turned and ran for the wagon as fast as he could. Ava and Elizabeth helped pull him back into his seat as Balin ordered horses forward. Jakob watched from the wagon as the snake-like

Basilisk slithered into the Great City. Hadriel stood in the road, watching as building after building collapse under the weight of the massive creature. Sense lifted his head and opened its enormous mouth. A large star shaped symbol formed between his jaw as a stream of boulders and earth shot from the magical symbol striking the Great City.

"By the Gods." Sebastian said. "Is that… their magic?"

Jakob watched as Senshe slammed his tail into the city, causing a small mountain to form and destroy what was once a shopping district. Ava grabbed Jakob's arm, forcing him to sit fully in his seat. He turned to her with empty eyes. His face had turned pale, and he was beginning to sweat. "What have I done?" Jakob whispered.

Chapter 3

Kylo tied the last of the intricate laces of his pants, looking at the two women he had purchased for the night still lying in bed. The women would tease him by sliding the sheets further down, exposing more of their bodies for him to see. Kylo smiled, knowing the pair were only interested in taking more of his coin. He motioned for the ladies to stand and get dressed, it was time for him... and them to leave. the village he had stopped in was so small discovering its name was impossible. Kylo knew in a town so insignificant the only thing to be hunted here would be wolves or brown bears. The town did serve as a potential spot for raiders or even Cleansers to be lurking. The young hunter took advantage and watched the pair of women dress. By their expressions, they were ready to leave as soon as possible since he didn't want to offer any more coin. After sliding on their undergarments, the ladies grabbed their clothing and exited Kylo room. Kylo sighed as he watched the ladies walk down the hall towards the Inn's restroom. *What a shame I couldn't have stayed longer.* The young man thought to himself as he styled his gold-red hair with his fingers.

He was enjoying the freshly styled cut and shave he received from the Inn keeper. The Inn wasn't so much an Inn as a typical traveler would search for. It was simply a barber shop with a large enough upper floor for a bathroom and a bedroom. Kylo slid on his white robe and grabbed his sack of belongings and made his way down the stairs. After reaching the bottom step, Kylo looked out the window to see the two ladies searching for new patrons for the hour. *They were definitely worth the silver.* Kylo thought, smiling, and closing his eyes. *But now I must head out of this no-named town.* Kylo leaned against the counter, dangling his keys dramatically in front of the Inn keeper's wife. *What a vile looking woman.* The hunter screamed in his head as he looked at the balding, unbathed woman. "Tell me young lady." Kylo said, leaning closer to the woman. The woman smiled, revealing she had enough teeth to count on half a hand. "Where might the next… larger city be?"

"What might ye be looking for?" The woman asked while smacking her lips. "Where our whores not to your liking?"

"Oh, on the contrary." Kylo said, smiling wide at the old hag. "They were worth every copper." The old woman nodded, uninterested in the details. "I'm looking for somewhere that might… have remnants of the Gods War. Beasts or creatures… you understand.

The old woman chuckled. "Fancy yourself a slayer of beasts?" The hag said, smacking her lips. "Ye look to dolled up for slaying creatures from the War."

"I assure you." Kylo said, puffing his chest as he pulled at his robe collar. "I can be quite feisty in a brawl."

"If ya say so." The old woman shrugged. "Gosa is only a few hours ride from here. A day and a half on foot." The hag spat behind the counter and Kylo could hear a ting from a bucket. *Did she spit out a tooth?* The hunter thought as he fought against his disgusted expression. "Gosa got temples, a great forest where beasts are rumored to prowl, and of course… the Pleasure Palace."

"Pleasure Palace?"

"I knew that would peak your interest." The old hag laughed. "Thrayn provides… services to those who have the coin to afford it. Nothing is off limits. His word is law in Gosa. Basically, owns half the city himself. But his whores aint cheap like the two you bedded last night." Kylo tapped his lips with his fingers as he thought. "Who knows, maybe Thrayn has an Angel or Succubus there for you to… hunt."

"Sounds like the place to be." Kylo said, smiling as he slid a piece of silver to the woman. "I'll be off then."

"Do come back, young master." The old woman said with sarcasm as Kylo stepped through the door. The young man walked along the filth riddled street, winking at the women of the night he had become acquainted with. The pair rolled their eyes and continued calling for new patrons, ignoring the white robed hunter. He watched carefully where he stepped. The roads was littered with vomit, urine, and shit, both citizens and horses. Kylo quickly crossed the street, attempting to avoid a group of men trying to haul away a collapsed cow. *I wouldn't name this place either.* Kylo thought to himself. *Any name given would be too pleasant for this pit. Quality Whores though.*

The young hunter approached an elderly man that was struggling to climb in his wagon. The man's horse seemed well kept, compared to the others of the nameless village. "Good sir." Kylo shouted as he walked to the old man. "Might one ask a favor of someone as sturdy as yourself?" The old man turned, still unable to climb into the box seat. Various noises came from the man as he took a limping step towards the hunter. "Could I offer you some coin to take me to Gosa? I can pay you handsomely."

"Eh?" The old man said as he squinted his eyes. "Can't even get up in the box me'self." The old man said, turning to the wagon. "Might the young master wish to buy this old man's burden?"

Kylo smiled. "I can make an offer." Kylo began digging in his coin purse. "Does seven silver sound fair?"

"Oi." The old man said, taking the coin. "That'll be good for the wagon. Another eight for the horse."

Kylo took a long breath through his nose as he looked at the mischievous grin the old man was giving him. "A shrewd businessman, I see." Kylo said, forcing a smile. "You must be the head man of the village with skill such as yours." The old man tilted his head as he shrugged. Kylo handed the man eight more pieces of silver. The old man took the coin and slid them into his chest pocket. Without saying another word, the old man walked off, leaving Kylo with the wagon and horse. "What a strange old man." Kylo whispered as he climbed into the box seat. "Yet he fits in very well in this pit." The hunter tightened the reins and commanded the horse forward. The black and white mare tilted its head and neighed with frustration. Finally, the horse took off, nearly Kylo over in the box seat. "Bastard old man." Kylo shouted, hearing someone scream as the wagon left the village. "This probably wasn't even his horse and wagon." Kylo looked back, expecting to see someone in pursuit. Fortunately, the horse had already carried him out of town. "I guess if I did technically steal you fella, no body in town cared enough to stop me." Kylo said to the now calmed mare.

A man with a wooden crate on his back came into view after several minutes of riding. Kylo tugged at the reins, pulling the horse to a stop beside the walking man. "Good sir." Kylo said, giving the man a wide smile and he combed his fingers through his hair. "Might you know the way to Gosa?"

"Aye." The young man said, lifting the crate higher on his back. "Ye can head down this road until it forks. Then take the path on the right. Keep straight and Gosa is only a few hours ride from there."

"Many thanks, young man." Kylo cheered. "Might I ask why you are carrying a crate on your back?"

The young man looked over his shoulder at the box. "it's my wife, sir." The man said with a harsh tone.

"My sympathies for the loss of your beloved." Kylo said, trying to hide his curiosity through false sympathy. "Are you off to a family burial site?"

The young man shrugged. "Gonna toss what's left of her in the lake." Kylo blinked rapidly to keep his composure. "Caught my whore of a wife in bed with her own brother. Left his corpse for his wife to find while I toss mine in the lake."

"Well." Kylo said, snapping the reins. "Best of luck to you, young man. Hopefully, you next beloved will be more faithful." The horse pulled the wagon away from the corpse carrying traveler. "She better be more cautious as well, right big fella?" Kylo said to his steed. "What the hell kind of place is this?" Kylo said, continuing the conversation with the horse. "Filth and murder all around. Gosa better be a more sophisticated city. With proper Inn's, people, food… and whores."

The wagon suddenly jerked as it came to an abrupt stop, waking Feya from her sleep. She struggled to sit up and look over the wagon's wall. The small wagon shook as Cole stepped down from the box seat and tied his horse to a nearby post. Cole grunted as he scratched his back and stepped around the wagon towards Feya. She panicked and slid to the opposite side of the wagon. The Faerie tried to flutter her wings and realized the mercenary bound her wings as well. Cole stood at the back of the wagon, motioning for Feya to come to him. She shook her head defiantly and slid as far away as she could. "Don't make a scene, love." Cole grunted as he climbed into the wagon. "We are already here. Best you behave and be a good girl. Don't want nothing to happen to you."

"If you didn't want anything to happen to me, why take me then?" Feya hissed as Cole lifted her from the wagon floor. "Don't pretend you care what happens to me."

"I do, love." Cole whispered in his gritty voice. "Left a clue of where to find you with the dwarf and the feisty woman back at the shop." Feya's blue eyes shined with hope for a moment before she noticed several armed guards standing around the building they were parked in front of entrance. "Now play nice and behave. Don't give them a reason to kill you before the lad shows up to rescue you."

"Why even do this?" Feya whispered as Cole pulled her out of the wagon. "What was the point?"

"Like I said." Cole grunted, tossing Feya over his shoulder. "I didn't like the idea of taking you, but coin is coin. No one said I couldn't also set up your rescue while I get rich."

"You're a real bastard, Cole." Feya cried.

"Aye." The mercenary sighed. "That I know."

Cole carried Feya over towards the guards of the large building. There were no windows to see inside and each of the guards looked larger than the door itself. *Where did he bring me?* Feya asked herself. "Oi." One of the guards chuckled. "Look who we got here. Crimson Cole. Slayer of beasts and butcher of man."

"And bringer of Faeries." The other guard joked.

"Thought Boss wasn't thinking straight when he asked for a Faerie to add to his collection of whores." The first guard said, lifting Feya's wings. The Faerie struggled in Cole's grip, trying to escape the touch of the guard. "I guess if anyone could find a Faerie in this world it would be Crimson Cole himself." Feya could feel the guard's hands slide from her wings down to her legs towards her thigh.

She squirmed, holding back tears as the large man's fingers caressed her exposed thigh. "Hands off the merchandise." Cole snapped, turning Feya away from the guard. "Unless you want to learn why they call me Crimson for yourself."

The guard grunted but backed away. As large as the pair of them were, it was clear who would be victorious if they came to blows. The mercenary was known for his ruthless butchering of those he hunted. "Touchy when it comes to jobs and whores aren't you, Cole?" The first guard hissed, attempting to keep an air of bravado to mask his intimidation. "Very well. Come in. I'll tell Master Thrayn you're here with his Faerie."

"Thrayn?" Feya gasped, trembling in Cole's grip. "Thrayn?" Her mind called on the memories of Ava and Anna and the stories they had told her about the dwarf. How he had sold and used Ava's body for profit. Thrayn would sell any manner of pleasure as long as the price was right. Ava had once told her that the dwarf had allowed a client to kill the one, they bought. If one of his whores had grown past their usefulness, allowing a client to butcher and kill them wouldn't hurt the dwarfs purse. In fact, Ava had stated that Thrayn would encourage it, saving him the trouble of doctors and food for someone not worth the coin. Feya struggled against Cole, kicking, and flailing her arms. She was still pure and wanted to remain that way. Faeries save themselves for the one they are destined to bond with. She wanted to remain pure… for him. *I can't.* Feya screamed in her mind. *I can't do it. What would… how would Jakob look at me?*

Cole carried Feya into the building. There was a large sign hanging above the bar. *Pleasure Palace.* There were patrons everywhere, both men and women of every race. Hanging from the ceiling were cages with men and women stripped down to nearly nothing as bidding took place regarding who would have their way with them for the night. On the other side of the room were a pair of women and one man. They were chained by the neck as patrons bid on fulfilling their fantasies of killing a lover in the act of passion. Feya's heart began to race, and her head felt dizzy as several nude servers walked around the palace offering drinks and a few hours of passion for a set amount of silver. "Don't worry, love." Cole whispered as the guards went to fetch Thrayn. "You're a Faerie. You're valuable. It will cost a small fortune to have you. Might be days or even weeks before you have a buyer." Cole sighed as he sat Feya on a nearby stool and stood next to her for protection. Prying eyes locked on her as the mercenary sat her down. One curious man approached the Faerie, only to be halted by the massive man that was Crimson Cole. "It's just sex, love. Better to lose your purity than your life." Cole said, watching the shifty man walk away.

"No." Feya cried. "I'm not like that. I know who I want. I will not just give myself to someone just for a few coins."

"Aye. I know." The mercenary said as a dwarf approached with the guards following close behind. "Just behave yourself. Don't give them a reason to kill you… or rape you."

"I'm no whore Cole."

"I know." Cole breathed, looking at the Faerie with sympathetic eyes. "The lad will be here. Knowing him… he is already on his way."

Feya glared at the approaching dwarf. He had long slicked-back black hair, a long black beard with a single line of grey halfway down his stomach and was finely dressed. The dwarf slid off his dark blue jacket and handed it to his guard, revealing a luxury style green tunic. His black shoes were shined, and each had a golden metal toes and heels. "Crimson Cole." Thrayn cheered, forcing his hands together with a single powerful clap. Cole grunted as Thrayn grabbed Feya by the chin, forcing her to look at him. His brown eyes met hers as he examined her features. Thrayn pulled Feya from the stool, forcing her to stand. The dwarf pulled at her wings to make sure she was the real thing. His hand slid along her legs, thighs, and rear. The dwarf's hands moved up to her breast before Cole slapped his hand away with a grunt. The two guards stepped forward, but Thrayn quickly calmed them, knowing this was a business deal and that they stood no chance against the legendary mercenary. "By the Gods Cole, how do you do it? How does one find a single Faerie in this vast continent?"

"Experience." Cole grunted with a hard stare.

The dwarf laughed as he turned to one of the guards and gestured with his head. The guard scoffed as he reached for a purse on his belt before tossing it to the mercenary. Cole caught the purse easily and opened the purse. "Seems a bit light." Cole said, clipping the purse to his belt. The dwarf laughed and motioned for the guard to toss a second purse. "That's more like it." Cole grunted, giving the dwarf and guards a hard expression. "Going to be a long road to make back this coin Thrayn. Could of bought a few hundred whores for what you paid me for this one."

"Not so." Thrayn cheered. "This here… is a Faerie." The dwarf said, rubbing his fingers along Feya's cheek. "Not one person on this Gods forsaken continent can say they've known the feel of a Faerie. I bet she is untouched." The dwarf said, grinning maliciously at Feya. "I'll be charging seven thousand gold pieces for her first client."

"Seven thousand?" Cole laughed. "What fool would pay that much for a whore?"

"I am a dealer in pleasure, Master Cole." Thrayn smiled. "I do business with anyone and everyone. Poor, rich, and ridiculously rich." Thrayn pulled Feya by her blue hair, causing her head to sling back and look to the ceiling. "Kale." The dwarf yelled to one of the guards. The larger of the men walked over, holding a metal brace in his hand. The guard wrapped the collar-like brace around Feya's neck before snapping it shut. "Now." Thrayn said, releasing Feya's hair. "Incase this plaything knows the magical arts… this collar will keep her from having access to the gods resource."

Cole looked at the strange collar as Feya struggled against the steel bound around her neck. "How does one acquire such a device?" Cole asked.

"One must know the right people, Crimson Cole." Thrayn said, smiling at the mercenary. "They cost a small fortune. Even that thousand gold I paid you wouldn't purchase a collar of this caliber." The dwarf rested his hands behind his back and puffed his chest. "I have a fallen Angel in my possession and with the creator of these collars having fantasies of being with a Divine… I receive a substantial discount as long as she receives… her pleasures."

"You got an Angel?" Cole questioned, rubbing his chin. "And the Gods haven't seen fit to put you in a hole?"

"The Gods have forsaken this realm, Cole." Thrayn said as he smiled, revealing a golden tooth. "If I was capable of acquiring this Angel, he must not have been of importance to the Gods in the first place." Feya's necklace began to shine and levitate off her chest. The dwarf quickly grabbed the charm and pulled the chain off the Faeries neck, breaking the necklace. "What's this?" The dwarf questioned.

"Give it back." Feya hissed as she lunged for the dwarf. The larger guard grabbed the Faerie and forced her onto the stool. "It's mine."

"Oh. No, my dear." Thrayn said viciously. "You see. *You* are mine and what was your is now mine." The dwarf examined the charm, seeing the rune inside the tree shaped charm coated in amethyst. "A levitation charm." Thrayn said curiously. "Is this how you fly, Faerie? Has your kind truly lost your magic?"

"That necklace is mine." Feya screamed.

Thrayn sung his fist, striking Feya across the cheek "You will have to learn you place… whore. Whoever gifted you this… they no longer matter. You will find there will be several lovers in your future."

"I'm no whore." Feya hissed as she spat on the floor.

Thrayn leaned in close, allowing Feya to smell the whiskey on his breath. "You are now… little Faerie." The dwarf said as he snapped his fingers. The guards grabbed Feya by the arms and began escorting her to a back room. "Put her in the room those elf sisters used." The dwarf said, scowling at the hallway. He turned to Cole and had a curious smile forming across his lips. "Say Cole. You wouldn't have seen a pair of Elf sisters on your journey, have you? Both are blond with green eyes, and one is exceptionally beautiful. One of them was quite a money maker for me. I'd pay a great deal to get her back."

"Aye." Cole said, tilting his head. "Might've crossed paths with some elves fitting that description." Cole crossed his arms as he looked down at the dwarf with a face harder than stone. "How much she worth to you? Gonna be a long trip to get 'er."

Thrayn smiled as he combed his fingers through his beard. "So, you know where they are?" The dwarf breathed. "How about... a trade?" Cole tilted his head as he listened to the dwarf. "I know you are also a regular customer of mine. I know you know your whores and enjoy the... pleasurable side of life. I'll make you a deal. One that you would be a fool to deny."

"I'm listening." Cole grunted.

"You bring me the Elf sisters." Thrayn said. "If the frail one has perished then so be it. I need Ava at the very least. Bring me Ava... and I'll let you be the first to lay with the Faerie."

Cole tilted his head, rubbing his chin pretending to think. "You'd lose out on your seven thousand gold... just to get a single Elf back?"

"That elf made me a lot of money." Thrayn hissed. "I lost a small fortune when she took off. I'll put her back to work, recoup my losses." The dwarf smiled, revealing that golden tooth. "Then put her in the dirt for running off with her sister. Besides..." Thrayn shrugged. "Someone has to teach that Faerie how to properly work. Might as well be one of my... loyal customers."

Cole took a slow breath as he thought. "So, an elf whore... for a night with a Faerie?" Cole said with a smirk. "Easy enough. Consider it done."

"I'll consider it done when the elf is back spreading her legs to fill my purse." Thrayn snarled. "I'll give you two weeks. That will be enough time for me to break this Faerie of her temperaments and enough time for an... experienced mercenary to fetch an Elf whore."

"You got a deal." Cole said, offering his hand. The dwarf accepted the gesture, and the pair shook on the deal. "Just make sure the Faerie isn't damaged goods by the time I return, or I might have to reconsider handing you the Elf."

Thrayn nodded silently as Cole made his way out of the Pleasure Palace. The dwarf watched as the mercenary readied his wagon and climbed into the box seat. Thrayn sighed as he slowly turned to see the crowd of patrons making their final offers on the caged women dangling above them. "Kale." Thrayn said to his guard. "When the mercenary returns with the Elf… kill him… and bring me my property."

"It's Crimson Cole, sir." The guard said. "What if he comes back before the two weeks? He's good at what he does."

"If he shows and you are unable to outnumber him… then we keep our bargain." Thrayn said. "If we know he's coming, you and the others greet him with sword and spear but keep Ava alive. She has much to make up for."

The Great City of Murdok was filled with panic, destruction, and death as Senshe continued his rampage. The walls that once bordered the Great City had fallen under the weight of the giant serpent. The Tempests who were adept at magic tried to fight off the beast's assault to no avail. The magics used by the Tempests were no match against the immense power of the Basilisk. Hadriel formed protective barriers around the city, trying to find pathways that citizens could escape from. Still, his magic was no match for Senshe when his focus turned to the Daemon. The world had long forgotten beasts as large as cities. With each movement of his massive body, Senshe leveled block after block of the once thriving city of Dwarves.

Hadriel and the Tempests managed to evacuate several thousand citizens of Murdok during the beginning of Senshe's arrival. Unfortunately, that still left several hundred thousand still remaining inside the city walls. The Daemon knew that at least half of the population of Murdok had already been killed by the beast's arrival. Senshe was too large and too powerful to survive. Yet, he moved across the ground gracefully and methodically, like a cobra hunting its prey. *The beings that the Gods and Devils fear most.* Hadriel thought as he evaded a swift snap of Senshe's tail. The Daemon flew high over the creature's head and summoned his magic. A large magic circle formed underneath Senshe. Hadriel took a slow breath before releasing the magic, knowing it would kill whoever was still trapped in its barrier. The Daemon closed his fist, activating the circle.

A strong magical pull tugged at the Basilisk as the Daemon's gravity magic activated. Buildings and debris were pulled towards the ground. Senshe seemed unaffected by the power of the Daemon. The beast roared in anger as pieces of his stone rotten flesh fell from his body. Suddenly, the beast buried its face into the earth, pulling its body in behind him. "Shit." Hadriel cursed as Senshe tunneled his way away from the magic circle.

"Hadriel." Yavanna screamed as she was healing a wounded Tempests mage. "Where…" the ground collapsed from underneath the Elf mage. Both she and the surrounding city blocks fell into the depths of a giant pit left behind by the tunneling Basilisk. Hadriel quickly looked at the ground, watching the city street split and crack as Senshe continued to tunnel underground. An explosion of earth and debris shot from the ground as Senshe lifted his head free of the earth. A low rumbled growl echoed from the beast's throat as he opened his mouth to the Daemon. A magical star formed between the beast's enormous fangs as Hadriel attempted to evade the incoming attack.

In his panicked flight, Hadriel could sense a rise in magic. He dove straight down and screamed, narrowly avoiding a strong burst of energy shot from the creature's mouth. The blast shot past the city and hit the mountain range north of Murdok, crumbling several mountains before the blast subsided. Smoke and dust filled the sky, nearly blocking out the sun like a coming storm. Senshe rocked his head and displayed his dorsal fin as a show of strength. "So, you were a ruler of this realm." Hadriel breathed as he looked at the beast. "Who was powerful enough to claim you?"

A golden portal formed in the sky as three figures appeared through the ring. Hadriel took shallow breaths, realizing a God had arrived with two Angel's. "Fools." Hadriel hissed as he watched the trio fly towards the beast. The Daemon found a group of trapped civilians and used his magic to create a path for them to escape. He turned in time to see one of the Angels get devoured by the Forest Basilisk. Senshe shot his snake-like tongue towards the God, pulling him in like a chameleon snatching a fly. Hadriel took a slow breath, knowing the God was no more. The final Angel flew in a panic away from the beast. Senshe turned his head, eyeing the Angel. His eyes shined bright, interrupting the Angel's panicked screams, and turning him to stone. "Gods." Hadriel murmured as he watched the now stone Angel fall and crumble into nothing.

Realizing there was no stopping the Basilisk, Hadriel descended closer to the ground to flee. Using his magic, he made another clearing for the remaining survivors to escape. Countless dwarves ran through the opening as well as the few humans and elves that lived within the walls. "Well, well." A voice called from the ground under Hadriel. The Daemon looked down to see a tall red-haired woman looking up at him. He swallowed hard, sensing the intensity of her magic. "If it isn't Kirames's bastard son." The woman said venomously.

"What are you doing here?" Hadriel asked, landing several paces away from the woman. "What brings the great Devil Lucile to the mortal plain?"

The Devil smiled as she pressed her tongue against her fang and looked up at the Basilisk. "It would seem." Lucile moaned. "Someone found my pet." The Devil lifted her hand. It became red with magic as she snapped her fingers. In an instant, silence befell the land as Senshe stopped his rampage. The beast slowly approached the Devil, lowering his head obediently to Lucile. "Good boy." Lucile said, smiling as she pressed her hand against his scales. Hadriel took a step back, extending his wings for a quick escape. "What's the matter Hadriel?" The Devil sighed, not looking at the Daemon. "Are you in awe of the power I wield over this beast?"

"I didn't think someone who spends so much time on her back could tame such a beast." Hadriel hissed.

"Oh my." Lucile laughed. "What a sharp tongue you have, are you sure you are not a Devil?"

"Thankfully no." Hadriel snarled. The beast's lips quivered, revealing several rows of razor-sharp teeth larger than the Devil herself. Senshe tilted his head, allowing Lucile to climb his horns and stand on his head. "I doubt he will fit in your chambers, Devil." Hadriel mocked.

Lucile laughed as she caressed the Basilisks horn. "Oh, sweet Hadriel." The Devil smiled. "Senshe was here when the abomination was born. If anyone can find his scent, even after all these centuries, it will be my little pet here."

"You took Senshe when my brother was born?" Hadriel said, looking up at the Devil riding the beast.

"It wasn't easy." Lucile chuckled. "The birth of your brother would have been devastating to all nearby magical beings. Senshe used his body to absorb most of the power that was unleashed, protecting the Great City from being destroyed." Hadriel took a long breath, keeping a watchful eye on the Basilisk. "Poor Senshe was so weak after Alvarome and Kirames fled with the child, he was wide open for an attack from… a Devil like me." Lucile rubbed an exposed area of the beast's head where his skull could be seen. "I simply forced the Draugar toxin into him. Now, he is my pet. The only Devil or God who was able to best a Basilisk." Lucile cheered, singing her praises.

"You attack my brother with Senshe?"

"Who knows." Lucile shrugged. "Perhaps your brother will be of better use with the Devils. It was your kin who orchestrated this whole invasion, we were simply summoned here after the fact." Hadriel cursed under his breath as Lucile smiled down at him. "But who knows what would happen if he regained his power? I believe the Mortal Realm is incapable of surviving a being of three magics."

"Three?" Hadriel asked as he began to hover in the air. Senshe's eyes remained fixed on him, but Hadriel refused to meet the creature's gaze.

"He was born in the Mortal world." Lucile said sarcastically. "One must assume he is capable of both Divine magics and the magic of the Faeries. You of God blood fear the abomination because you think he would seal us all away back to our realms. We Devils do not fear such things. We could always find another Realm to rule."

"Then why stay?" Hadriel scoffed. "Why bother with any of this?"

"That is a much simpler answer." Lucile laughed. "Tor does not wish to abandon Eeus. Simple as that." The snapped her finger and Senshe obeyed, lifting his head high as he began to slither away from the Great City. "The game must go on Hadriel." Lucile shouted. "Let us see what part you play in the final chapter."

Chapter 4

Feya sat in the corner of the room she had been tossed in. The guards had stripped her of her clothes and possessions before shoving her into an almost empty room. There was a small bed made of recycled metal with a stain covered mattress. She also had a wardrobe with no doors or clothes, and a small table with one missing leg. The table was large enough to hold a lantern that had to be set on its far end to keep the table from toppling. The lantern was half empty of oil, it had become clear to Feya that Thrayn would not allow anything with magical properties in the room. She pulled the thin pink sheet off the bed to cover herself as she remained in the corner of her room. Sitting in the corner beside the bed felt like her only sanctuary. Guards would periodically open a sliding peep hole in the door to check on her. Some would tease and ridicule her, asking her to show them what makes a Faerie woman so special. She refused, remaining in her corner with the thin sheet as her only protector.

Feya knew that, eventually, someone would come and take her. For what, she didn't know but she feared the worst. She closed her eyes tightly to keep from crying, praying Cole was right. Hopefully Thrayn's price would be too high and give Jakob and the others time to reach Gosa before… The unlocking of the bedroom door startled Feya. She covered herself tightly, hoping a guard hadn't decided to take advantage of her vulnerable state. Her heart pounded into her throat and her blood felt hot as the door opened wider. A large man with a dirty apron stepped into the room. He was bald and missing an eye with a scar stretched from the top of his head to the bottom of his jaw. Feya cowered behind the table as the man stepped further into the room. The man knelt down near the table, giving Feya a toothless smile. He sat a plate of food on the floor near her feet, then stood and took a step back. "Is time to eat." The man said. Feya could tell he wasn't like the guards that had been harassing her earlier. The large man gestured to the plate. "Is Trung's favorite dish to make. Fish and carrot." Feya realized something was off about the large man by the way he spoke. "Oh." The big man shouted. "Me almost forgot. You need fork to eat." Feya assumed that maybe whatever gave the large man that missing eye and disgusting scar might have caused other damages. The man's feet were shackled but his chain allowed enough movement to perform tasks. "Trung never seen a Faerie before." The simpleton cheered. "I like your wings. They remind Trung of butterfly."

Feya forced a smile and pulled the plate closer with her feet, still covering herself with the blanket. "Thank you... Trung." Feya said cautiously. "Do you work here?"

The large man smiled and nodded his head. "Trung work in kitchen for Master Thrayn. Him good man to Trung. Me wish he was nicer to pretty ladies though."

"Me too." Feya whispered, grabbing the dirty fork Trung had placed on the plate. "He could have at least let me keep my clothes."

"Master Thrayn always take clothes when someone knew comes to work." Trung shrugged. The large man reached into his back pocket and pulled out a white stained shirt. "Trung shirt dirty... but pretty Faerie can have until she has new clothes from Master Thrayn."

Feya slowly accepted the reeking shirt, stained or not, at least it provided her with cover from the peering eyes of the guards. "Thank you, Trung. You are very sweet."

The man smiled and clapped his large hands. "Anything for a Faerie." Trung cheered.

"Trung, you oaf." A guard shouted from the hallway. "You are supposed to drop off the food and go. These whores aren't for conversations."

Trung pouted and slowly walked towards the door. "It not nice to call ladies bad names Kroll."

"Shut your yap and get back to the kitchen." Kroll shouted, slapping Trung across the back of the head. "You got more whores that need feeding and Thrayn is waiting for his supper." The guard slammed the bedroom door and clicked the lock. The peep hole door slid open, revealing the glaring eyes of the guard Kroll. "Don't go thinking you can trick that simpleton to get you outta here, Faerie." The guard laughed. "Many have tried. Yet, they all end up on a pike." The peep hole closed as the guard made his way down the hall. His footsteps growing fainter with each step.

Feya sighed and began eating the fish and carrots, instantly missing Balin's cooking. She thought back to their campsites and how picky the dwarf was with his seasonings and temperatures. Feya smiled, remembering the pride in Balin's eyes as he would watch everyone eat the meals he prepared. Her smile faded as she wished she was back with her friends, back with… Jakob. "I should have told you." Feya whispered to the flaking overcooked fish. She spun a carrot around her plate with her fork. "I should have told you during the festival." Tears slid down her cheek as she finished off the unseasoned fish and carrot. *Coward. I'm such a coward.* She screamed in her mind. *If I get out of here… I'm going to tell you myself.* Feya removed the sheet and slid on the dirty shirt Trung had gifted her. She was sure that Thrayn or the guards would take it once they noticed, but she didn't care. Even this filthy shirt gave her a sense of safety. When returning the sheet to the bed, Feya noticed scratches along the old headboard. She ran her finger along the headboard, realizing the scratches were drawings. A child's drawings. Small pictures etched into the wood of two small elf girls holding hands with a crudely drawn tree and flower. Underneath the drawn girls were names with a heart around them. *Ava. Anna.* Feya's lips began to tremble as she thought back to her friends. *This is where they lived as children.*

The bedroom door unlocked once again. Feya turned to the door and backed into the corner of the room. A large guard opened the door and stepped aside for Thrayn to enter the room. The dwarf raised a brow at the sight of the Faerie in a stained shirt. "I see Trung was here." Thrayn laughed as he rubbed his beard. "Keep the shirt." The dwarf grinned, motioning for a woman to step into the room. The strange woman was wearing a form fitting dress that revealed more than Feya was comfortable with seeing. "This is Miss V. She will be taking your measurements for your... uniforms."

The woman named V stepped into the room, grabbing Feya by the stained shirt. "Take this dreadful thing off, darling." The woman commanded with a thick accent. "We must make you beautiful." In one swift motion, Miss V had managed to pull the shirt off, revealing Feya's body. "Then... we work on your conversation. You can make money with both your words and your body, darling."

"Conversation?" Feya asked, covering her chest with her arms.

"Yes, darling." Miss V said as she ran her fingers along the Faeries stomach. "Patrons do not get the luxury of talking to us free of charge. Many can't afford our... pleasures, so they pay for our attention."

"I don't want to give anyone anything." Feya whimpered. "I haven't..."

"I am aware of Faerie standards." Miss V said, feeling Feya's legs and thighs. "After your first time... it will not be so bad. One terrible lover after another."

"I will only give myself to the one I love." Feya hissed as her body shivered from Miss V's touch.

"Then you better love whoever has coin." Thrayn scoffed, crossing his arms, and puffing his chest. "I aint in the business of matchmaking."

"A little privacy." Miss V said, turning to the dwarf and guard. "Prying eyes make for a fidgety body. Be gone with you. I will get what I need and find her some clothes." Thrayn huffed and ordered his guard to leave. He followed close behind, slamming the door closed as he exited the room. Miss V sighed as she pulled Feya's arms away from her breasts. "Do behave, darling. You don't want to suffer punishments."

"How can you work for him?" Feya murmured, looking away as the woman felt her breasts and side.

"I don't work for him, darling." Miss V said with a heavy breath. "He owns me. I am no longer called on for duties of coin, so I prepare and train his other goods."

"I'm not merchandise." Feya hissed, glaring at the woman.

"I'm afraid you are now." Miss V said, handing Feya the dirty shirt. "I have never seen a Faerie in person. It pains me to see you in a place like this. As it does with all young ladies."

"Then why stay?"

"I have no other choice, darling." Miss V sighed. "I was sold to Thrayn as a child. After several escape attempts when I was older…" Miss V turned and lifted her dress. A large scar ran from her thighs up to her stomach. "I was doused with boiling water until and violated with whatever the guards could find until I was no longer useful to clients." The woman lowered her dress and gently caressed Feya's cheek. "I feel this isn't going to be your home forever, darling." Miss V whispered as she looked at the door. "A Faerie on the continent is sure to be missed. Even if that is not the case… someone could offer to buy you from Thrayn." Feya remained silent as she looked into Miss V's broken eyes. "I will have your clothes by tomorrow, darling." Miss V said. "I will also bring you some clothes for sleeping. I will not let these perverted guards have their way with you with their eyes."

"T-thank you." Feya whispered.

"No need." Miss V said as she walked towards the door. "I pray the Gods watch over you Faerie… and bring you freedom from this hell on earth."

"Feya." The Faerie said as Miss V reached for the door. The woman turned, tucking her dark hair behind her ear. "My name is Feya."

Miss V smiled and nodded her head. "Victoria." V said. "It is a pleasure, darling. I will be seeing you soon."

The woman opened the door and walked into the hallway, locking the door behind her. *The Gods.* Feya thought. *They would rather see us dead.* The Faerie made her way to the bed and covered herself in the sheet. The bed was rough and hard. She thought back to their campsites and the Inn's they stayed in during their journey. Feya closed her eyes, letting the tears fall from her eyes as she thought about her friends. *Is it worth it?* She asked herself. *Is it worth saving me? Jakob could still find the Savior. Anna could remember his name and free the Basilisk and his magic. I'm nothing. Just a Faerie who wanted to fly.* She reached for her charm then remembered the dwarf had taken it from her. the gift she was given by Jakob. The gesture he had given to her to keep his promise. *I'm not worth it.*

Kylo rolled across the dirt road, narrowly avoiding the Arachnes's razor sharp leg. The half woman half spider creature continued her assault, slamming her spider-like legs against the ground towards the young hunter. Through all his travels as a hunter, Kylo had yet to see a living Arachnes. Until today. The creature had ambushed him from the trees, knocking him off the wagon and killing his horse. The spider woman had cocooned the horse in a thick web and hung it from a nearby tree, then turned her focus on the hunter. Kylo continued to evade incoming blows, attempting to slide on his rings between each attack as he rolled. Finally, the creature halted her assault and began scurrying around him. The Arachnes was fast, but he was still able to slide on his last ring. He felt magic flow through his body as his sense heightened. He could feel the vibrations on the ground when the spider walked, hear her breathing, and even her heartbeat. He turned, avoiding one of the creature's arms. Making a sign with his hand, he drew a line in the air. Suddenly, the creature's arm was severed above the elbow and fell to the ground. A pool of purple blood surrounded the severed limb as the Arachnes wailed in pain.

The hunter smiled, feeling his father's magic flowing from the rings into him. *Astaad, Slayer of Beasts. Angel of the Hunt.* An Angel bred for killing and hunting. A lone predator, always searching for stranger and stronger prey. He imagined the rush his father felt during his own hunts. Kylo could feel his heart race with excitement. He had read in his father's journal about the Arachnes, but he assumed his father had driven them to extinction. The spider woman hissed as venom spewed from its mouth. Kylo slammed his fists together, pressing each ring against the other. "Divine Snare." Kylo screamed. The spider woman was lifted by an invisible snare, pulling her into a tree. The beast snarled and hissed as it struggled against the unseen trap. Kylo grinned as he drew another line in the air. The beast's head was severed and fell to the earth, followed by its grotesque body. The hunter leaned in close and pulled a fang free from the half woman's mouth. "Another trophy." Kylo said, smiling as he examined the tooth. "Chose the wrong traveler today, wouldn't you say Miss Legs?"

The hunter sighed as he looked at what remained of his wagon and lifeless horse dangling from a tree. He combed his fingers through his red-gold hair, sliding the fang into his cloak pocket. "Oi." A voice yelled, pulling Kylo's attention away from the hanging horse. A man stood several paces away, wearing a dark cloak and had bandaged arms. Kylo cracked his neck and sighed, realizing the man was the stranger outside of Oothra. "You're a slayer of beasts?" The stranger asked.

"Aye." Kylo said as he styled his hair. He tilted his head and turned to the stranger. "Strange to see you again." Kylo said, resting his hands on his hips. "I thought you'd still be digging through corpses back on the coast."

"My business is elsewhere." The stranger said, crossing his arms. The mans presence gave the hunter an uncomfortable feeling.

"Oh?" Kylo said cheerfully, rubbing his thumb against his rings. "And what business is that? I find if more than a coincidence we have crossed paths again."

"Indeed." The stranger said, tilting his head. His hood prevented Kylo from seeing his face, but the young hunter's uneasy feeling continued to boil. His father's rings improved his magical abilities and senses, but he could not sense any Divine magic from the stranger. Though, the rings gave him a feeling of... pain, failure, and desperation. "There has been an interruption." The stranger said, not looking away from the hunter.

"Interruption?" Kylo said with a wide smile. "That sounds inconvenient."

"Indeed." The stranger snarled, causing a shiver to run up Kylo's spine. He swallowed hard, not letting his guard down around the stranger. "Someone has been taken, preventing necessary events that must be done to save this world."

"I'd say that is quite the inconvenience." Kylo smirked, eyeing the stranger. "But what does that have to do with me?"

"You are a Nephilim." The stranger said. Kylo narrowed his eyes at the man, calling on his father's magic. There was no response from the rings, which only increased the hunter's nervousness. Kylo licked his lips, unsure of what was happening or who this man was. "I have a job for you." The stranger said. Kylo took a long breath, feeling slightly at ease from the offer.

"Oh." Kylo smiled, putting on his air of arrogance. "Well, if you know I'm a Nephilim, then you know we are not cheap to hire."

"Indeed." The stranger said. His typical response had begun to irritate the young hunter. *Who is this person?* Kylo thought to himself. "Since your kind are... rare." The stranger said with a strange smirk. "I need you to retrieve someone. Is that within your capabilities, Son of Astaad?"

"How do you know my father's name?" Kylo hissed, losing his composure as his face turned red. "Who are you?"

"That is not important." The stranger said, looking over at the corpse of the Arachnes. "Coin speaks better than words in this world, I've learned."

"Indeed." Kylo said, mocking the stranger. The bandaged man didn't seem to take notice of his mockery and stepped towards the spider woman. "What is the job?"

"A Faerie." The stranger said as he examined the corpse. Kylo raised a brow, curious as he stepped closer to the strange man. "In Murdok there was a party of adventurers looking to unseal the Savior child. This Faerie was part of this group." The stranger knelt next to the spider and turned his head to Kylo. "A very important part." The man's voice became low and cold, as if he was infuriated and personally insulted by the situation. "A mercenary took her. I need her returned. Unharmed and untouched."

"So, I am to find the mercenary?"

"No." The stranger said quickly. "The mercenary has delivered the Faerie to a dwarf named Thrayn. He is the owner of the Pleasure Palace in Gosa."

"What a coincidence." Kylo chuckled. "I was just on my way to the Pleasure Palace."

"Indeed." The stranger drawled mockingly. "I need her liberated from the grip of the dwarf and returned to a man named Jakob Crenshaw."

"I hear Thrayn has a reputation." Kylo said. "It won't be easy to free her from such a… reputable establishment."

The stranger tossed a coin purse at the hunter. Dozens of coins spilled from the cloth bag along with several strange colored stones. "That is worth twenty thousand gold." The stranger said, turning back to the spider. "It will cost a small fortune to pay to be alone with her. you will not use her. you will not touch her. you will take the opportunity to free her."

"Then how much is the bounty?" Kylo asked, lifting the purse.

"Whatever is left." The stranger said. "When I see you again, I will gift you another purse of equal value."

"And I am to just take your word for it?" Kylo laughed. "Who are you anyway? How did you come about this coin?"

"I am but a vagrant." The stranger said. "A traveler of this world." The hunter clicked his tongue as he jingled the purse. "The boy Jakob." The stranger continued, standing away from the spider. "Is the host of Gadreed. The Angel of War. He travels with his grandfather, Sebastian. There is also a dwarf, a warrior woman, and a pair of elves in his party. One of them is a Daemon."

"Hmm." Kylo huffed. "Sebastian Crenshaw… one of the Tempests mages? I have heard stories of him and his elf partner."

"Indeed." The vagrant said. Kylo's face soured at the man's typical response. "Can you complete the job?"

"Easily." Kylo said. "But what is to stop me from just spending this coin at the Pleasure Palace on myself?"

"Me." The stranger said, his voice filled with venom and rage. Kylo's rings sent signs of danger through his body, causing his hands and joints to ache.

"Very well." Kylo said, swallowing hard. "Am I to return to Murdok?"

"The city is in ruin." The vagrant said, stepping towards the hunter. "A sleeping beast has awakened and is under the control of the Devil Lucile. Jakob has fled the city and is on his way here."

"Then why not just let them deal with the Faerie?"

"The Faerie." The stranger snarled as he approached. "Must not be touched. Must not be harmed and must not be killed."

"Alright." Kylo said, his voice cracking slightly as he stepped back from the vagrant. "I'll fetch this Faerie… for double what's in this bag." Kylo narrowed his eyes at the stranger, smiling wide.

"Very well then." The man said, shocking the hunter. "Forty thousand gold for the safe return of the Faerie. Plus, whatever you manage to keep from your transaction with the dwarf." Kylo nodded nervously. "There is a small village a few miles from Gosa. You can purchase a horse and wagon there." The stranger handed the hunter a large diamond. "This will buy you a fine steed and a luxury wagon. You will need to play the part if you want a chance at having access to the Faerie."

"How in this Gods forsaken realm do you have such wealth?" Kylo asked, feeling the weight of the diamond.

"I am but a vagrant." The stranger said, turning away from the hunter and making his way into the forest. Kylo watched, stunned, as the man disappeared into the thicket of the woods.

"That wasn't much of an answer."

Balin climbed into the box seat from the back of the wagon, ready for his shift manning the reins. Sebastian welcomed the change in shift, it had been hours since their last switch. Jakob had insisted on a continuous ride without stops, unless the horses needed to rest. The group was just starting their second day of riding and the journey was proving difficult for the old mage. The dwarf sat heavily on the bench next to Sebastian, rocking the wagon. Balin reached for the reins, grunting, and yawning as he wrapped the leather straps around his wrists. Sebastian nodded his thanks, knowing the dwarf had just woken from a midday nap. The old mage turned to look into the wagon's canopy and saw Jakob and the elf sisters asleep on the far bench. Elizabeth was still awake, rewrapping her injuries after her fight with Crimson Cole. "Fate seems against us, Bas." Balin said as he snorted. "Seems every time we take a step forward; we must take two steps back. Blasted Gods probably laughing at us atop their thrones."

Sebastian leaned back in the box seat, trying to find a more comfortable position. He was tired, but not enough to go to sleep. "It does seem that destiny isn't on our side." Sebastian said. "But Kal used to tell me; if you focus on what could have been, you will miss what is right in front of you." Balin turned to look at the mage, clearly too tired for thinking. "Meaning." Sebastian smiled. "Perhaps we were not supposed to climb that mountain. Perhaps there is something we are missing... something that Feya will find only in Gosa."

"Aye." Balin yawned. "I just hope she is alright. Those bastards better not touch her. Can't be saving the world without our Faerie."

Sebastian took a slow breath as he looked at the angry dwarf. "Let us not plague our minds with such thoughts. We will save Feya. I am sure of that."

"Aye." Balin said, seemingly more awake at the moment. The dwarfs' face became still and hard. Sebastian took notice and tapped on the dwarf's shoulder. Balin took a long breath through his nose to calm his nerves and turned to the mage. "What do you think befell the dwarven city? What do you think happened to Hadriel... the Tempests?

"The Gods themselves were no match for the Basilisks." Sebastian said. "So Gadreed says. Unfortunately, my friend, it is likely the Great City is lost... as are the Tempests who operate there." Balin grunted and leaned back in his seat. "But there was nothing we could have done. Feya must be our priority."

"Aye." Balin nodded. "I'm glad the lad agreed with me on departing when we did."

"I don't think Jakob would ever abandon Feya." Sebastian said with a grin.

"Aye." The dwarf agreed. The pair sat silently for several minutes in the box seat, watching the road and a few passing clouds. "Tell me something, Bas." Balin said suddenly. Sebastian turned his attention from the various clouds and looked at the dwarf. "You'll have to excuse my lack of… sensitivity on the matter but… how are you not dead?" Sebastians eyes opened wide as he raised his brows. "I mean… Kal was keeping you from turning into a Draugar. I assumed with her passing… things would only worsen for you. Yet, you seem to be as spry as when we first met."

"A valid question." Sebastian said, rubbing his chin as he watched the horses. "Considering everything, I should have turned by now. I know the infection is still within me. I feel it in my blood." The old mage sighed. "I don't know, my friend."

"Is it possible Kal's magic is still protecting you?"

"No." Sebastian said quietly, rubbing the back of his neck. "Our level of magic is unable to counter Devil magic or last beyond our own life. When she died, her spell died."

"Perhaps it is Gadreed." Elizabeth said, peeking her head from behind the canopy cover. The commander climbed into the box seat, sitting tightly between the mage and dwarf. Balin puffed his chest and flexed his arms as the soldier took the seat next to him. "The War Angel is protecting you with his shield, isn't he?"

"No." Sebastian breathed, shaking his head. "Gadreed did not offer Kal and I protection like the others."

"Aye." Balin said, looking at the soldier through the corner of his eye. "Might need to see if touching the sword will grant me even greater strength." Balin laughed, displaying his muscled arm to the commander.

"You carried the thing back from that old dwarf's forge in Murdok." Elizabeth said, smiling at Balin. "I would think if it was going to do anything… it would have done it then."

"Aside from summoning a sleeping beast you mean." Balin breathed. "But Jakob has activated the sword, perhaps now it will offer some of Gadreed's power." Balin turned his head and looked at Elizabeth, admiring her fair skin and dark hair. "The shield didn't offer you protection… maybe the sword will."

Elizabeth shrugged, resting both her arms along the back of the box seat behind the mage and dwarf. "I think I'll survive without the Angel's blessings."

"Brave and beautiful." Balin said, winking at Elizabeth.

"Careful now, dwarf." Elizabeth said softly. "Don't make attempts at beasts you can't properly tame." Balin let out an eager chuckle as Sebastian coughed in his hand, reminding the pair he was still sitting in the box seat. "I say take it as a blessing." Elizabeth said, turning to the old mage. "Maybe this mission has bound you to Jakob's destiny in freeing the Savior."

"Gadreed thinks otherwise." Sebastian said, forcing a smile as he awkwardly looked up at the sky.

"Who cares about a ghost?" Elizabeth scoffed. "He died long ago. it isn't up to him who lives and dies."

"Aye." Balin said. "Just… let us know if you star to feel more… Draugar-like." Sebastian laughed and agreed. "We are still a few days away from Gosa." Balin huffed. "If I get my hands on Cole, I'll…"

"Easy big boy." Elizabeth said, flicking Balin with her finger. She gave the dwarf a large smile, pressing her tongue against her teeth. "Don't go in halfcocked. You'll get us all killed. He isn't someone to take lightly." Balin grunted, puffing his chest out once again. "We have to make it to Gosa alive to rescue Jakob's little love bug." Sebastian and Balin gave curious looks to the commander. She was unusually playful considering the events that had unfolded over the past few days. "What?" Elizabeth asked with a shrug.

"I think things are a little more complicated with our young friends." Sebastian said, trying to hide his smile.

"Nothing complicated at all." Elizabeth said plainly. "There is a difference between fucking and love, old man.

"Aye." Balin said, raising a brow to the commander. "I'm surprised some grand knight hasn't snatched such a lass as yourself for themselves."

Elizabeth shrugged. "Maybe…" The commander said, leaning closer to the dwarf. "They just weren't good at shaggin." The dwarf blushed and began playing with his beard. "Anyway." Elizabeth said with a sigh. "They will figure things out eventually… as long as we rescue Feya in time."

"We will." Jakob said from his seat in the wagon. All three of the box seat occupants quickly turned, surprised that the young man was awake. "I made her a promise and I intend to keep it."

"I'm sure you have much to talk about as well." Elizabeth said from over her shoulder. Jakob remained silent, not looking away from the wagon's floor.

"I'm coming Feya." Jakob whispered to himself. "I'm sorry I wasn't there to protect you. It wont happen again. I'll never let you go again." Jakob leaned back, resting his head against the wagon wall. He closed his eyes, trying to calm his racing mind. Ava remained silent, pretending to still be asleep lying in his lap.

Feya sat tied to a chair in an observation room with Thrayn and two guards. The small room was connected to one of the many Pleasure Rooms of Thrayn's establishment. The dwarf had pulled the Faerie from her room and forced her to sit and watch through ha false magical wall. From the observation side, the group could watch and listen to the goings on inside the pleasure room as if they were in the room itself. The guests in the actual pleasure room were blissfully unaware that Feya and the others were watching and listening to everything. Whenever Feya would try and turn away, one of the guards would force her head forward to watch. There was a man in the room with two women he had bought for the night. Thrayn had ordered her to watch and *take notes* of what is expected of her at the Pleasure Palace. The man in the room was in the act of making love with one of the two elf girls he had purchased. When he wasn't engaged personally, he would force the pair to continue with one another as he whipped and cut them with various belts and blades.

"You are lucky, Faerie." Thrayn said, not taking his eyes off the client. "You are too valuable to let someone beat or cut. All they will be allowed to do to you is talk and fuck. No bruises. Not cuts."

Feya swallowed hard as she watched one of the elf girls bite a pillow, trying not to scream as the man cut her upper thigh as he entered her. "You're sick." Feya snarled. "How can you do this to people?"

"I do nothing." Thrayn said calmly. "It is them who are the sick ones."

"You don't believe you are responsible for any of it?" Feya hissed, turning towards the dwarf. The guard Kroll quickly forced her head forward as the man rejoined with the other elf girl he hadn't cut. She didn't want to watch and see what he was doing. She shifted in her seat, feeling her bottom tighten from watching what the man was doing to the poor elf girl. "You imprison people and sell their bodies… and you don't believe you are as sick as your clients?"

"My property owes me debts." Thrayn said proudly. "Or they owe debts to others that would claim their lives. I rescued them in exchange for their services."

"Debts they can never repay." Feya said.

"Usually not." The dwarf smiled, looking at his many rings. "You are one of the few that I… sought out." Thrayn said, turning to Feya. "A Faerie on the continent. Now that is something unique and exotic."

"I'm not property." Feya hissed, tugging at her restraints.

"Yes." Thrayn said dryly. "You are." He snapped his fingers, and the guards lifted the Faerie from the chair. "Take her to the baths." Thrayn said, not looking away from his client. "Miss V will have her washed before she tries on her new clothes."

The door to the observation room opened before the guards could carry Feya out of the room. A grey-haired dwarf stepped into the room and gently bowed his head to Thrayn. "I apologize for the intrusion, Master Thrayn." The old dwarf said, eyeing the bound Faerie. "But I have urgent news." Thrayn sighed and stood from his chair to face the old dwarf. "A great beast has awakened in the mountains of Murdok." Thrayn took a long breath as he adjusted his many bracelets and stepped towards the aging dwarf. "The Great City has fallen and I'm afraid… we have no word on your son's evacuation."

"What?" Thrayn hissed through gritted teeth. "What sort of beast could bring down the Dwarven city?"

Feya felt her heart race in her chest at the news. *Murdok has fallen? Does that mean Jakob…* "According to some survivors." The old dwarf said. "A great serpent burst from the Broken Spear. An undead abomination that is now under the control of a Devil."

"A Devil?" Thrayn questioned. Feya felt tears forcing their way through her eyes. She knew Jakob was still injured and she didn't know how they would have escaped an attack from a Devil. "Devils haven't been seen in our realm in…"

"They have." Feya shouted. "Your mercenary kidnapped me while on a mission to bring back the Savior." Thrayn narrowed his eyes and scowled at the Faerie. "My friends and I were traveling to the Broken Spear with a Daemon who knows how to unlock the Saviors magic." One of the guards shook Feya in an attempt to silence her. "We killed and Angel and a Demon." Feya screamed after the shaking had stopped. "You are too worried about coin to realize the danger our world is in."

"Take the Faerie away." Thrayn ordered his guards. "She will learn to use her mouth for more than just spewing nonsense and fairy tales."

The old dwarf stepped aside as the guards carried the flailing Faerie from the room. The grey-haired dwarf slowly closed the door and turned to Thrayn. "What if she is right, Master Thrayn?"

Thrayn slapped his ringed hand across the old dwarf's cheek. "Do not heed warnings from whores." Thrayn snarled. "Where is my son, Niko?"

"As I said, Master." Niko said, rubbing his cheek. "There has been no sighting of him. Many traders escaped the assault and waited at various checkpoints you assigned for emergencies… but he never arrived."

"Send them back." Thrayn ordered. "And you go as well. Find. My. Son."

"As you wish, Master Thrayn." The old dwarf said, bowing his head.

Thrayn stood in the observation room as Niko made his way slowly out the door. The pleasure dealer took several long breaths as his mind fixated on his son and the fall of Murdok. "Kroll." Thrayn shouted, summoning the guard just outside the room. Kroll stepped in and looked down at the dwarf. "Get that fool out of the Pleasure Room. Shut down the Palace… I'm in no mood for these scum tonight." The guard nodded his understanding. "If they ask for a refund… offer them your blade." The guard smirked and nodded once again. Thrayn sat back in his chair, rubbing his black beard slowly as he thought. Kroll stepped into the Pleasure Room, pulling the client off the girl and tossing the naked man into the hallway. Thrayn pressed his hands against his mouth, ignoring the screaming and protest coming from the Pleasure Palace lobby. "Where are you Ratrek?" Thrayn whispered. "You better not be…" The dwarf covered his face as his emotions overwhelmed him. He could do nothing but sit… and cry.

Chapter 5

No light could find its way into the chasm. The city had collapsed and fallen into the many tunnels dug by the great beast from the mountains. A dwarf moaned in pain through the darkness, interrupting the silence of the pitch black. Yavanna turned her head towards the sounds of pain, unaware of how long she had been trapped under Murdok. The elf mage was exhausted after using her magic. When she woke from her fall, she had found her leg trapped and crushed underneath remnants of the Tempests building. Knowing there was no other way to free herself, Yavanna made the difficult choice to remove her leg, using what little magic she could muster to close the wound. The dwarfs' pain filled groans rang in her ears against the deafening silence of the chasm. "H-H-Help." The dwarf yelled. The elf mage didn't respond, breathing had become painful. The air was thick, and she didn't know how much longer they could last in whatever hole they had fallen in. "S-Someone... please." The dwarf pleaded. Before the street collapsed, Yavanna had been attempting to heal the injured dwarf. She knew there was no point in trying to find him, there was nothing she could offer. She was drained, tired, and weak. The elf mage wasn't even sure her leg was properly treated after the amputation. All there was to do now was wait for death. "Madam mage?" the dwarf whimpered. "Did... are you alive?"

Yavanna closed her eyes and sighed. "Yes." She said softly, her voice quietly echoing through the darkness. She could hear the dwarf laugh softly in a panic, happy not to be alone in the pitch-black chasm. "What are your injuries?" Yavanna asked, leaning against a crumbled wall.

"I-I can't feel my legs." The dwarf said. She could tell by his voice he was in tears. "Me hand is broken." Yavanna heard the dwarf trying to crawl towards her. The elf sighed before humming a song from her childhood, allowing the dwarf to find her through the blackness. Near the end of her song, she could hear the dwarf approaching, dragging his body with his only good arm. Yavanna extended her hand, grazing the dwarfs. The dwarf panicked at her touch but quickly realized he had reached the mage. "P-Please ma'am." He pleaded. "Can you heal me?"

Yavanna shook her head instinctively, though the dwarf could not see her. "No." She said with a heavy breath. "I'm afraid I have depleted my magic when I amputated my leg."

"Oh." The dwarf breathed. She could hear him pulling himself closer to her, propping himself against the same crumbling wall. "We are going to die down here." He said, his voice cracking from fear.

"What's your name?" Yavanna asked softly. "You are not a regular at the Tempests building."

"Ratrek." The dwarf said, crying in his unbroken hand. "Your Miss Yavanna, right?"

"Yes." Yavanna said. "You are new to the Tempests?"

Ratrek sighed as he wiped his face with his hand. "I'm not really a member." The dwarf said. "Some of my father's men found one of your amulets and gave it to me. I was sent to spy on the Tempests and try to find a Faerie that my father was searching for." Yavanna said nothing as she took a long slow breath, feeling the dust filled air in her lungs. "He wanted the Faerie for his Pleasure Palace." Ratrek continued. "Said if I brought back a whore so valuable, I'd have access to my accounts again... and free my beloved."

"You're Thrayn's son." Yavanna said.

"Aye." The dwarf cried. "I'm sorry, Miss Yavanna. I just… Father was cross with me and…"

"It doesn't matter anymore." Yavanna said coldly. "We are going to die."

"I don't want to die, ma'am." Ratrek cried. "I aint ready for it."

"We never are." Yavanna breathed.

"was what the Angel was saying true, ma'am?" Ratrek asked. Yavanna turned to him, still unable to see through the darkness. "About the group the Faerie was with. Are they really going to free the Savior?"

"He isn't an Angel." Yavanna sighed, looking up to the ceiling. "He is a Daemon. He is half God half Elf but… yes. I believe Jakob and his group are gong to bring him back."

"You think they survived the beast?" Ratrek asked.

"They weren't in the city." Yavanna said. "Feya, the Faerie, was taken, probably by your father. They left just before the attack to go rescue her."

"Oh." Ratrek huffed. "I guess my father didn't believe I could bring him the Faerie."

"It would seem not." Yavanna said.

"This is the punishment the Gods must feel I deserve." Ratrek whimpered. "All the things I did to those whores… this is the revenge of a Goddess."

"Still calling them whores doesn't seem to be a good way to atone." Yavanna said dryly. "Why did Thrayn send his own son to spy on the Tempests?"

Ratrek wiped his face with his one good hand. "Said I was damaging his merchandise." The dwarf said. "I would use the whores… girls, I mean, for my own pleasures, even when clients were in the Palace."

"Doesn't seem to be a good enough reason to send you to us." Yavanna said. "He knew if we discovered you as a fraud we would have killed you on the spot."

"Aye." Ratrek said. "But a few months before I left… I began to favor a woman named Elva. She was one of my father's top earners but… I fell in love with her." Ratrek blew his nose and spat on the ground. "I told father I wanted her for me own, to take her off the clients list, but…"

"Now you are here… in a hole." Yavanna drawled. "I get it." The pair sat in the darkness, mostly silent after Ratrek's confession. The only noise interrupting the silence was the whimpering and occasional outburst of crying from Ratrek. The booming of battle had stopped what seemed like hours ago. *Did you run Hadriel?* Yavanna thought to herself. *Or were you stupid enough to think you could win against that beast?* Yavanna knew the Daemon was arrogant and full of himself. Yet, in his time at the Tempests, he had shown compassion towards the citizens and the members of the Tempests. She prayed that he survived. Prayed that Jakob and the others made it out of the city. And… she prayed that Feya would be unharmed when Jakob and the others found her. She knew Thrayn's reputation and knew the innocence of the young Faerie.

A sudden vibration shook the underground chasm. Dirt and debris fell from the ceiling onto Yavanna and Ratrek. The dwarf began panicking, screaming for the great beast to return to whatever hell it had come from. A think line of light shot down through the blackness as another vibration shook apart the ceiling. The smell of air rushing into the chasm forced the elf to smile as she inhaled. "Yavanna?" a voice called from the small opening of the chasm ceiling. A magical ball of light floated down into the chasm and cut through the darkness like the sun. Yavanna covered her face, shielding her eyes from the blinding light. "Yavanna? Come on, you couldn't have died on me so easily."

"We are down here." Ratrek screamed as he struggled against the crumbled wall, frantically waving his only working arm. "Please sir, we are down here."

The once pitch-black chasm was pierced by a glowing figure as he floated to the base of the chasm with golden wings. Yavanna pulled her hand away from her face, knowing the familiar voice coming to her rescue. "Hadriel." The elf mage breathed. "I don't think I've ever been this happy to see you."

"The feelings mutual." The Daemon smiled, offering her his hand. "I see you have lost a leg worth of weight."

"Shut up and get us out of here." Yavanna hissed, trying not to smile.

"As you wish." Hadriel said, lifting Yavanna into his arms. "Do not worry dwarf, I'll be right back. Can only carry one of you at a time." Hadriel tightened his grip around the elf as he flew towards the chasm ceiling. The moon was high, but its light was still blinding as Yavanna reached the surface. "Who's the dwarf?" Hadriel asked as he gently sat the elf on the crumbled street.

"A spy." Yavanna said, rubbing dirt from her eyes.

"Should I leave him down there then?"

"No." The elf said softly. "Bring him up. He can take us to Feya." Hadriel tilted his head curiously as he looked at the injured elf. He placed his hand on the stump of her leg, feeding his magic into her to complete the healing. Yavanna moaned as the pain vanished from her body at Hadriel's touch. "He is Thrayn's son. The one who had her taken. He will make good leverage if Jakob isn't able to get her." The Daemon nodded and dropped back down into the hole. Cheerful praises were sung by Ratrek as Hadriel slowly brought him back to the surface. Hadriel sat the dwarf beside Yavanna as the dwarf continued to praise the Daemon. The elf looked at the sleek black hair of the dwarf and the many rings on his mangled hand. *He looks just like his father.* Yavanna hissed in her mind, remembering the many elf girls she had lost in her life to Thrayn's Pleasure Palace.

"Thank the Gods you arrived." Ratrek said. "I thought we were going to die down there."

"You still might." Hadriel smiled venomously at the dwarf. Ratrek swallowed hard as he looked at the vicious glare the Daemon was giving him. "You see." The Daemon said, tapping his fingers against his lips. "Your father taking Feya is what caused this devastation." Yavanna narrowed her eyes as she looked at the golden winged Daemon. "Her dearest friend is immensely powerful and in his rage of her begin taken, he accidentally summoned that monstrosity from the mountains." Hadriel knelt down next to the dwarf. Ratrek leaned as far back as he cold as the Daemon looked deep into his eyes. "Now, you are going to take us to your dear old dad. You are going to give us Feya…. And Yavanna and I may just heal you. Or… I can simply throw you back into the hole. What do you say?" Ratrek turned back to look at Yavanna. The elf mage had an evil expression across her face. Slowly, he looked at the Daemon and nodded his head as quickly as he could. "Good boy."

Anna sat in the box seat next to Jakob, aggressively rubbing her eyes. She had used a great deal of magic on Jakob's wound, but that was not the reason for her exhaustion. The young man was only a few treatments away from being completely healed and his treatments didn't require much magic. What was bothering the Daemon was an excruciating headache she had been suffering since fleeing Murdok. Jakobid looked over at Anna, who was still rubbing her eyes, and noticed her horn had grown longer. What was once a small bump on her head was now protruding over her hair nearing the back of her skull. Anna lifted her hands to her forehead, seeing Jakob eyeing her instead of the road. She gave him a crossed look, causing him to quickly turn his attention back to the road. "Sorry." Jakob muttered, tightening his grip on the reins. "I-I was just noticing your horn."

The Daemon lifted her hand to the horn, rubbing her fingers along its length before reaching the point. "It's disgusting." Anna said with a scowl.

"I don't think so." Jakob said. Anna rolled her eyes and continued rubbing her temples. "C-Can I ask why you only have one horn?"

Anna shrugged. "I don't know." The Daemon said softly. "Probably because I'm a Daemon and not pure-blooded Devil." Anna leaned forward and turned to look at Jakob, shielding her eyes from the sun. "I would chop it off... but it would just grow back."

"Don't... do that." Jakob said nervously. "No need to mangle yourself." Ava peeked through the wagon canopy. Jakob and Anna nodded to the elf as a greeting as Ava sat on the bench nearest the box seat. "What is causing your headaches?" Jakob asked. "You've been having them a lot lately."

Anna sighed as she closed her eyes, protecting them from the sun. "Something... powerful has come to this realm. Something... familiar." Jakob passed glances between Anna and Ava before returning his gaze to the road. "Hadriel said that Senshe was *Taken*." Anna said. "I think whoever turned him into a Draugar has come to claim him."

Jakob took a slow breath as he thought about the large beast from the mountain. "A Demon wouldn't be strong enough to turn a Basilisk." Jakob said, knowing the answer. Anna shook her head slowly. "A Devil then." Jakob said in almost a whisper. "Just another problem to add to our journey."

"The Basilisk itself was a problem." Sebastian said from the wagon. "If its master has leashed him... there is no telling what destruction will come."

"How could a Devil claim a Basilisk?" Jakob asked. "I thought all this happened because the Gods and Devils couldn't best them."

"I... don't remember." Anna said softly, looking at the horses. "Why... why were we supposed to go to the Broken Spear if Senshe was asleep there?"

"Perhaps he was what you were supposed to find." Sebastian said. "If he remained asleep, it is possible touching him could have unlocked more of your memories."

Jakob sighed. "And I fucked it up." The young man said, gritting his teeth. "Gadreed told me not to use the sword unless I was willing to deal with the consequences." He shook his head as Anna turned to him. "But I... I just couldn't let Hadriel stop us from saving Feya."

"Aye." Balin shouted from the back of the wagon. "Blasted halfling should have understood and stepped aside. The damned War Angel tried to warn 'em."

"He's right, Jakob." Ava said. Jakob and Anna turned to look into the wagon where Ava was sitting on the nearby bench seat. The elf was rubbing her chest as if she was missing jewelry. She reminded Jakob of Feya and how she always played with her charm. Worry filled his soul as he looked at Ava, thinking of what might be happening to the Faerie. Every minute she was in Gosa was another minute someone could harm or touch her. "We have to save Feya." Ava said, slouching her shoulders. "What is happening now is what was supposed to happen. At least, that's how I choose to see it."

"Aye." Balin said, rubbing his whiskers. "When we get to Gosa, we gon..." The dwarf was silenced as Jakob pulled the reins, forcing the horses to stop and shaking the wagon. Everyone in the wagon was tossed from their seats. Anna grabbed ahold of Jakob to keep from falling as Balin cursed, peeking from the wagon canopy. Jakob narrowed his eyes, as did Balin, at the figure standing in the road. "Gods Hammer." The dwarf hissed through gritted teeth.

A large man was leaning next to a wagon parked on the side of the narrow road. His head was shaven, and he had a braided red beard. The man stood straight as he tossed whatever he was eating onto the road. Pulling his cloak open, he exposed a long sword. "Oi." The raspy and familiar voice called to them. He crossed his arms after gesturing for them to approach. "Best we talk, lad. Got much to discuss."

The wagon shifted suddenly, and Jakob noticed Elizabeth rushing towards the mercenary. "Cole." The commander shouted as she readied her spear. "I'll kill you."

Jakob jumped from the box seat, grabbing his stomach as his feet touched the ground. His pain wasn't as bad as it was back in Murdok, still, the memory of Angelus's blade and the pain he once felt rushed through his mind. Balin followed close behind, brandishing his axe. Cole slowly stepped towards the party with his arms still crossed. Anna stood in the box seat and summoned a pair of small magic circles around her hands. The mercenary lifted his hands dismissively to the approaching party. "Oi." Cole chuckled. "No need for all that."

Elizabeth closed the gap between her and the mercenary, resting the point of the spear at Cole's throat. "Tell me why we shouldn't leave you as a corpse on the road, Cole."

The mercenary smiled wiled, revealing his yellow teeth to the commander. Slowly, he pushed the tip of the spear away from his throat and turned to Jakob. "The Faerie is in Gosa." Cole said with a raspy voice. "Got an arrangement with Thrayn so she won't be touched till I get back." Jakob tightened his grip on Gadreed's sword. He wanted to cut down the mercenary. He wanted to see him dead in the street. As his magic began to flow into the blade, he could feel Gadreed's touch, calming his mind and the blade. "Thrayn wants them elves your traveling with." Cole continued, pointing to Anna and Ava. "Says I can have first go with the Faerie if I bring 'em back."

"And you think I'll let that happen?" Jakob hissed. "You think that…"

"Calm your tits, lad." Cole laughed. "I left ye the bounty and where I was headed didn't I?" Jakob took a long breath, his anger growing as the mercenary spoke. "I came so we can devise a rescue of the Faerie."

"Why?" Balin shouted. "Why did ya even take her?"

"Got paid a lot of coin, dwarf." Cole said with a shrug. "It's just business. You understand." Balin puffed his chest and grunted as he lifted his axe. "I don't want the Faerie staying with Thrayn any longer than necessary. I say, you let me take the elves back to Thrayn, then, we ambush 'em and rescue the Faerie." Cole shrugged again, resting one of his hands on the hilt of his sword. "Maybe kill Thrayn in the process." The mercenary smiled. "I bet your elves would love to see him dead."

"And we are supposed to just trust you?" Elizabeth shouted, still gripping her spear. "After you attacked us and took Feya to that… that."

"Aye." Balin said, stepping next to the soldier. "Your word doesn't seem valuable at the moment, Cole."

The mercenary turned his head to Jakob, smiling as he saw the vicious scowl the young man was giving him. "Want to cut me down, lad?" Cole said with sarcasm. Jakob could feel his arm twitching as he pulled his hand away from his sword. Cole smiled and tilted his head. He reached into his cloak and pulled out a large coin purse. He tossed the purse to Jakob. The young man looked into the sack, seeing the bag was filled with gold and silver. "Got a thousand gold in that purse." Cole said. "Think of it as… insurance. You keep it till we free the Faerie. Then I want it back."

"Feya is worth more than a thousand gold Cole." Jakob said, angrily strapping the purse to his belt.

"Aye." Cole grunted. "To you maybe. But to me… coin is everything. If I give you my word… and me coin… you know I'll be keeping my promises." Jakob turned to Balin as they gave suspicious looks to one another. "So." Cole said, crossing his arms. "We got a deal?"

"What's in it for you?" Jakob asked. "There is no coin to be gained by rescuing Feya."

Cole shrugged his large shoulders as he looked up at a passing cloud. "Maybe I be getting soft these days. Don't think that Faerie deserves to be in a whore house." Jakob tilted his head, glaring at the mercenary. Cole smiled then chuckled to himself as he looked at the young man and his party. "You've made me coin every time we've met, lad." Cole said with his raspy voice. "Think of this as... repaying my debts."

"You got a plan?" Jakob asked.

Cole nodded as he smiled. "Aye. Thrayn wants the elves." The mercenary said. "But that one." He said, pointing to Feya, who was peeking through the canopy. "Is the one he really wants."

Feya sat at a benched table trying to adjust her feet to a more comfortable position. Her legs were shackled to the floor making her movements limited and noisy. Feya sighed at the sound of chains scraping the floor with every movement. A young brown-haired woman looked up from her tray of food and looked at her curiously. The woman gave Feya a sympathetic smile. The woman's tray was filled with slices of meat, potatoes, and a steaming bun. Feya's, however, was filled with something she was not sure was even edible. Her punishment for her outburst in the observation room. The woman sliced her bun in half and slid a piece of beat between the bread, handing the food to Feya. The Faerie nervously accepted the offered food, devouring the buttered bun down quickly before a guard could spot her. "I'm sorry, las." The brown-haired woman said. Her accent reminded Feya of Bralin's. "It's typical for Thrayn to... break the newcomers." The woman sighed and shrugged her shoulders. "At least he doesn't seem to beast you like he did the rest of us."

Feya struggled to swallow the meat filled bun, drinking half her cup of water in a single drink to sooth her throat. "At least the rest of you aren't in chains." Feya said, pulling her feet to make the chains scratch the floor.

"We know our place." The woman breathed. "We know the punishments for… wanting something.' Feya tilted her head as she pushed the tray of slop away and looked at the woman. The brown-haired woman smiled wide at the Faerie. "My name is Elva. I wish I could have met a Faerie under better circumstances but… It's amazing to meet you."

Feya tried to flutter her wings, but Thrayn's guards had bound them with weighted rope after she had received her new clothes. "I'm Feya." The Faerie said softly. The woman closed her eyes and smiled. Feya could see scars and burns along Elva's arms and neck. "Where did you get those?" Feya asked, pointing to the scars.

Elva hid her arms under the table, nervously biting her lip. "I don't think you will have to please those clients." Elva said. "Master Thrayn see you as too valuable for it."

"So, a customer gave you those?" Feya asked. Elva nodded without making eye contact with the Faerie. Feya took a long breath as she looked at the woman. She was beautiful, as was most of Thrayn's *merchandise.* "Why hasn't anyone tried to escape… or kill the bastard?"

Elva looked around the room nervously as she held a finger to her lips to silence Feya. "Don't speak so bluntly of such things." Elva whispered. "Thrayn is worse than the clients, Feya." The woman leaned forward on the table but kept her distance as not to draw attention from the guards. "There were two that escaped. Master Thrayn was, and still is, furious. Word has it he hired the mercenary that brought you in to catch them."

"Anna and Ava." Feya whispered.

"You know them?" Elva gasped softly, still scanning the room for movement from the guards.

"I traveled with them. Our group is on a journey to…" Feya paused, looking at the woman, she didn't know how much she should say. She didn't know who she could trust. "We were traveling together." Feya finally said, deciding the details of their journey were irrelevant to Elva.

"Thrayn will kill Ava." Elva said coldly. "He has spent a small fortune trying to find her. I hear one of his guards had spotted her in Graham but was too terrified of the man she was traveling with." Feya smiled as her thoughts turned to Jakob. "Rumor has it the warrior killed a Draugar and travels with a powerful ban of warriors and mages."

"I know." Feya said with a heavy breath. she looked up and saw the woman's eyes were wide with curiosity. "I remember when it was just me and Jakob. Then his grandfather and his partner arrived." Feya couldn't stop herself from smiling as she thought back to the early days of their journey. "Then we met Balin, a dwarf. He is an amazing cook and really good friend. Then we met Anna and Ava and decided to keep them safe after escaping this place."

"Unbelievable." Elva said. "I'm glad to hear the sisters are alive and well. Anna was such a shy little girl. Ava sold herself in whatever way Thrayn demanded as long as Anna remained untouched." Feya nodded, watching a guard pass by the table. The guard stopped behind Elva and leaned over the food crusted table. He pointed to the tray of slop and pushed the food towards Feya. The Faerie glared at the guard. Suddenly, the guard tossed the tray at Feya, covering the Faeries face and chest with gruel. "Stop it." Elva screamed, slapping the guard's hands.

The guard grabbed Elva by the hair and pulled her face to his crotch. "Be quiet whore. Or I'll fill your mouth where ye can't speak." The guard laughed and looked at Feya. "Maybe the Faerie could use a lesson in how to please a man... since she is still pure after all." Feya grew angry and tried to summon her magic. The collar began to glow and tighten around her neck. The large guard laughed as Feya tried to fight against the tightening brace. "Oh ho." The guard chuckled. "I didn't know you'd be into that little Faerie." The guard said as his laughter continued. The large man slammed Elva's head against the table before continuing his rounds around the Palace.

"I'm sorry." Feya said, rubbing her neck.

"No." Elva said, seemingly unfazed by the guard's attack. "It is a common occurrence. It wasn't you."

Common occurrence?" Feya asked, wiping the slop from her face.

Elva nodded slowly. "Yes. Most of us are used to the guard's abuse. Even their nightly *Check in's*." Feya scowled at the thought of the guards preying on sleeping women. "Like I said. You are valuable. I'm sure Master Thrayn won't let you endure what the rest of us have to."

"Do you not want your freedom?" Feya whispered. "Do you not want to fight or escape?"

Elva smiled softly as she shrugged. "I thought I was going to be freed once." She said. "I fell in love, and he loved me. He asked Thrayn to take me off the client list. That he wanted me, and we were to be together." Her smile slowly faded as she looked into Feya's blue eyes. "I thought it being Ratrek... that I had a chance."

"Who is Ratrek?" Feya asked. "Someone willing to buy you from Thrayn?"

Elva shook her head. "No." She said, picking at her fingernails. "Ratrek is Thrayn's son." Feya wanted to stand in shock, but the shackles prevented such movements. "I know what your thinking... but he isn't like his father. Well, he was, until we met and..." Elva shrugged as a smirk crossed her lips.

"What happened?" Feya asked. "Why wouldn't Thrayn give you to his son?"

"He said Ratrek was damaging his merchandise." Elva sighed. "He cut off his funds and accounts. Then, he sent him off in search of... you, Feya." The Faerie released a breath she didn't realize she was holding as she looked into the woman's pain filled eyes. "He was told he could have his life back... and me... if he brought home the Faerie."

"But Thrayn hired Cole." Feya said, louder than she intended to.

Elva nodded. "Thrayn didn't believe Ratrek could do it. He was right, apparently." She cried softly. "Ratrek was supposed to pose as a Tempests member. I think Thrayn wanted him caught… or to just give up and come back begging." Trung walked out from the kitchen and began ringing a bell. Everyone in the dining hall stood and began heading back to their assigned rooms. Feya watched, still shackled to the floor. "It's time to turn in.' Elva said as she turned away from Feya. "We have work in the morning."

Feya watched Elva follow the crowd of Thrayn's men and women until she was out of the dining hall. Trung lumbered over slowly, brandishing a ring of keys, and smiling wide at the Faerie. "Hello again, Faerie." Trung said giddily. "Trung haven't seen you lately. Did you like chicken?"

"I wasn't given chicken." Feya said dryly as Trung attempted to unlock her shackles. "I was given this." Feya said, pointing to her slop covered shirt.

"Oh no." Trung gasped. "That no good." The shackles became loose and Feya felt her ankles becoming free from the chain. Trung leaned in close to whisper to the Faerie. "Trung bring Faerie friend a bun after bedtime." Trung said with a wink. Feya could smell the fowl on his breath as he spoke. Still, she forced a smile and gently patted his cheek. "Don't tell guards or Master, Trung will get lashes."

"It will be our little secrete." Feya said, still forcing a smile. "You won't get in trouble… my friendly chief." Trung smiled wide as a guard called Feya over to him. The simpleton waved enthusiastically as the guard shoved the Faerie towards the door and escorted her to her room.

In this world that was once filled with beauty and life was now barren. Only the Great Temple of the Divine God had any sign of the former glory that was once Elysian. Outside the temple walls were only deserts, storms, and fires. Life on the Gods world of Elysian had long gone extinct since the Gods selfishly stole their worlds magic, killing all life on their world. Gidione walked along the white stoned path that lead towards the Great Temple of the Divine God. From the pathway, the Goddess looked out towards the apocalyptic landscape. Her thoughts returned to her meeting with Lucile and her claims that the worlds the Gods and Devils now rule were not the first to be claimed by their kind. Gidione couldn't help but wonder how many worlds had met the same fate as Elysian, if what Lucile was telling the truth. *Was this to be the fate of Earth?* The Goddess thought to herself. Gidione sighed, pushing the thoughts of Lucile and her conspiracies to the back of her mind. She turned and looked down at the Angel escorting her to the temple. "Had Eeus summoned many of our kin lately?" Gidione asked curiously. It was uncommon, so she thought, for the Divine God to receive guests at her private temple.

"No." The Angel said plainly without looking at the Goddess. He stayed silent as they approached the temple gate. Gidione looked up at the beautifully crafted temple. Perfectly placed stones along the walls. Lush flowers and greenery everywhere. Masterfully carved wood with intricate designs along the gate's boarder. It seemed so misplaced in this dying world. "There is a situation happening on the Mortal world." The Angel said after a lengthy silence. "The Divine God believes you might be able to… handle the situation." Gidione raised a brow at the sudden pause from the Angel. It was uncommon for an Angel to speak so plainly to a God or Goddess. The gates opened slowly, revealing a wonderfully decorated chamber. The Angel stepped into the temple, not allowing the Goddess to enter first.

The Angel led the Goddess through the worship hall towards a room in the back of the large chamber. As the Angel opened the door, he lowered his head and gestured for Gidione to enter. The Goddess slowly stepped into the room. Sitting by a large stained-glass window, sat the Divine God herself… Eeus. The Angel stepped in behind Gidione and dropped to one knee without lifting his head. Gidione stepped forward, gently bowing her head to the Divine God. "Divine One." Gidione said as she lifted her head. "It is an honor to be summoned. How may I serve you?"

Eeus didn't move or acknowledge the Goddess or Angel. She sat motionless, looking out the window at the dying world she ruled over. The Divine God sighed and brushed her ghost white hair behind her ear. Gidione noticed how Eeus seemed feebler, sickly even. The magic she had used, along with the Ancestral Devil, must have taken a toll on her. Still, Gidione wondered why, after a thousand years, the Divine God was still suffering from the spell. Eeus turned her head slightly to look at the Goddess. Her eyes were emotionless and looked devoid of life. "A problem has arisen in the Mortal Realm, Gidione." Eeus said softly through heavy breaths. The Divine God turned back to the window, resting her chin in her palm. "Lucile." Eeus breathed. "She has reclaimed her pet… Senshe."

Gidione tilted her head curiously as she looked at the Divine God. "B-but." The Goddess mumbled. "The beast sleeps within the mountains."

"Something has awakened it." Eeus said with a heavy breath. "Something powerful. Whispers are filling the skies, Gidione. Of a Faerie roaming the continent. Daemons. Mages." Eeus sighed and turned to the Goddess. "And Gadreed." Gidione swallowed hard as she listened to the Divine God. "It would seem the Abomination has allies. They seek to unseal his power and awaken the Basilisks." Eeus slowly stood from her chair, her arms and legs trembling as she stepped towards Gidione. The Divine God was much shorter than the rest of their race, but her power was without question. "Even when I was at my full strength… I was no match for Shinrahn and his army of beasts. Now…" Eeus took in a long breath as she rubbed her boney chest. "We would surely fall if the Abomination regained his power."

"What would you have me do, Divine One?" Gidione asked, bowing her head.

"Lucile must not be allowed to play her games while the Abomination still breathes." Eeus said. "We, the Gods and Devils, need the Mortal Realm to keep our resource flowing. We must return to order. As we once were before Elysian."

"You mean… coexist with the Devils?" Gidione asked, watching Eeus slowly pace through the room.

The Divine God slowly turned to Gidione and nodded her head. "It is the order of things, Gidione. The Devils create chaos, and we create order. Both parties gain power from belief and fear. A symbiotic relation. Balance. Order."

Gidione licked her lips nervously as the Divine God sat back in her seat. "Forgive me, Divine One, But… is this world meant for us to rule?"

Eeus took a long breath and scowled at the Goddess. "We. Are. Gods." The Divine God hissed. "We do not fall to… beasts. We are the rightful rulers of existence itself. We will conquer as many worlds as it takes, until we find the world that is destined to sustain us. This world is filled with magic we do not understand, which is why it must become ours." Eeus began to suffer a coughing spell after angrily speaking to the Goddess. "Do not forget what you are, Gidione. We are rulers. Of everything. Beasts included. Though, I would see them dead than subservient." Eeus grunted as she leaned back in her seat. "Emanuel." Eeus said to the still bowing Angel. "You are now assigned to Gidione. Deal with Lucile and these… allies of the Abomination."

"Yes, Divine One." Emanuel said, finally standing from his kneeling position. "My Goddess, where shall I begin?"

Gidione turned to the Angel and narrowed her eyes. Emanuel looked strong and determined. Traits she wished Angelus had inherited from his father. She looked at the Angel remembering Angelus's mistakes as her face contorted into a scowl. "Murdok." Gidione said. "See if you can determine where Lucile and Senshe went… and what reawakened the beast in the first place."

Chapter 6

Feya adjusted to a more comfortable position in her bed. She had been confined in her room for what felt like days. In truth, it was probably only hours, but the lack of windows or any way to pass the time in the small room she was unable to be sure. Every few hours a guard would pass by the door and glare at her through the peep hole in the door. Some would mock her through the door, others would try to catch her changing or using the bucket Thrayn had tossed in the room as her toilet. Even when the guards would scream and taunt her from the other side of the door, Feya would ignore them. She had adapted, even become used to the guard's constant unintelligent insults. Feya knew that keeping her locked in the room was likely one of Thrayn's attempts to break her. The attempt failed, Feya welcomed the solitude. Even with the harassing guards every hour, the Faerie knew she was safe. Every minute Thrayn wasn't trying to break her gave Jakob another minute to rescue her. she knew he was coming. Deep in her heart, she could feel him pushing his way towards her.

The Faerie looked around the tight quarters of the room. She felt cramped as if thrown in a prison cell. *How did Anna and Ava live like this for so long?* Feya thought as she imagined two young girls living in the Pleasure Palace. It was hard for her to imagine someone keeping two little girls trapped in this room, only pulling them out for someone to abuse. The idea that someone, or multiple someone's, paid for a night with a little girl. A child. *How could someone allow such things to happen to children?* Feya thought. *I'll have to ask Thrayn, before I send my pixies through his heart.* The unlocking of the bedroom door broke Feya from her thoughts of revenge. She turned, without getting up from the bed, and looked at the guard. "Time to get to work, Faerie." The guard said, grinning as he eyed the bed. Feya's heart began beating out of her chest, but she didn't show her misery. She refused to let the guards, or Thrayn, break her or see her weak.

Miss V gracefully entered the room, ordering the guard away with a waft of her hand. The large man grunted and mumbled as he exited the room, leaving Miss V with the Faerie. "Do no worry, darling." Miss V said calmly. "You will not be performing acts of pleasure today. The bath needs a good cleaning. I have volunteered you to help me tidy up the place for the day." Feya sighed, still lying on the bed. Miss V stepped closer and lifted her shirt, revealing a fresh cut along her stomach. "You were meant for other duties today, darling." V said coldly. "I paid for you with punishment. Do not disregard the generosity I have shown you."

"Why did you?" Feya breathed, looking at the woman's scarred body.

"Because I tire of seeing young women lose their purity to the scum of this world." Miss V whispered as she knelt beside the bed. Feya's eyes met V's and she could see truth in them. Feya nodded and stood from the bed. "Good girl." V said, assuming a more authoritative tone as the guard reentered the room. "Elva will be joining us as well. As will Arys." Feya nodded again, not wanting to speak in the presence of the guard. "Kroll." Miss V said as she passed the large man. "Feya and I will fetch Elva. Have the Angel sent to the baths." Feya tilted her head as she listened to Miss V. her thoughts went to Angelus and the many times they escaped death at his hands. She wasn't prepared to see another Divine servant. Not here. Not with no way to escape or defend herself. "Come." Miss V said, pulling Feya's wrist. "The baths must be cleaned before supper, darling, or you won't be eating."

Thrayn stepped out of the Pleasure Palace and walked towards the guards that had summoned him. The pair of guards pointed to a luxurious wagon and beautifully groomed horses tied off near an Inn across the street from the Palace. Thrayn watched curiously as a tall red-blond haired man spoke with someone outside the Inn. The man was well dressed, well groomed, and seemed to be flaunting a great deal of coin. Thrayn grunted, his way of ordering his guards to fetch the wealthy looking man and convince him to spend his coin at the Palace. The guards nodded their understanding and made their way to the neighboring Inn. The pair of guards crossed the street, forcing passing wagons and horses to stop as they continued on towards the wagon. They watched as a young boy brought the wealthy man a bucket of food for his horses. The man joked with the lad and laughed at his own words as he tossed a gold coin to the young boy. "Oi." One of the guards yelled as they approached the wagon. The young boy looked at the guards and ran back behind the Inn. The red-blond man turned slowly to look at the guards. "Excuse us, young master." The guard said with a raspy voice. "Master Thrayn would like to invite you to his Pleasure Palace. We've tasty food, soft beds, and the most beautiful women."

The wealthy young man tilted his head as he looked at the guards curiously. "Oi." The other guard said. "Or if it be men ye fancy… we've them too."

"Oh my." The wealthy man said with a wide smile. "You two are quite the salesmen." The man combed his fingers through his well-trimmed hair. "I do fancy soft beds and tasty food. Having beautiful women is definitely a must have as well."

"Aye." The first guard said. "We've plenty of those. Most beautiful women in the world come to work for Master Thrayn."

"Hmm." The young man said, tapping his fingers against his lips. "There are beautiful women all around these lands." He said with a shrug. "If I am to spend my coin on a lady… I would fancy something… exotic."

"Got some of the most beautiful elf girls your eyes ever seen." The second guard said with a wide grin. The young man shrugged dismissively. "Got an Angel as well… if you are interested in a man."

"An Angel is very exotic." The man said, still tapping his lips. "But should I risk the wrath of the Gods on such a piece."

"Got a Faerie." The second guard said with a hint of frustration in his voice. The young man dropped his fingers from his lips and tilted his head. The guard smiled as the first guard slammed his fist against his shoulder. "She's a fine young Faerie. Blue hair. Petite. And…" His smile stretched from ear to ear with a vicious grin. "She be pure."

"I say." The young man said. "A pure Faerie. Untouched?" The guard nodded. "Well." The young man said, tossing a gold coin to the Inn keeper. "I will have to change my booking to the Pleasure Palace… if I can host a Faerie for the night."

"Aye." The second guard said. "What be your name, young master? So I can give a proper introduction to Master Thrayn."

"Kylo Astaad." The young man said as he began walking with the guards. "Heir to the Astaad smithing empire. I must say, I came to Gosa for excitement. Who would have thought I'd find a Faerie to spend my time with?"

"Aye." The first guard said. "Have to talk it over with Master Thrayn first. The price is nonnegotiable for the Faerie if he agrees to let you 'ave her. as my friend said… she be pure."

"Oh, I'm sure." Kylo said, smiling as he closed his eyes. "To be with a Faerie… let alone a pure Faerie… she'll be worth every copper."

"She'll cost more than copper, young master." The first guard said.

"Of that… I am sure." Kylo said, watching a black-haired dwarf approach him from the Pleasure Palace. "You must be Master Thrayn." Kylo said, bowing his head slightly. "It is a pleasure to meet you. You have quite the salesmen here."

"Aye." The dwarf said, crossing his arms and puffing his chest. "Our accommodations speak for themselves. I'm sure a man of your stature would enjoy our best offers. Luxury room and bed. Private menu, and a vast choice of pleasures."

"Oh." Kylo said softly. "No need to go on sir. Your lads here have already sold me on your accommodations." Thrayn nodded and smiled at his guards. "I would like one of your finest beds, large enough for two of course." Thrayn nodded and smiled at the young man, adding the cost of his visit in his head. "Your lads here have sold me on an exotic young lady you have." Thrayn let out a curious grunt as he eyed his guards. "Yes, I think we can do business, Master Thrayn. I only require your finest bed and board, a delicious meal for two, and… that beautiful Faerie you have."

"Oi." Thrayn shouted, looking at his guards. The dwarf coughed in his hands as Kylo narrowed his eyes to him. "My apologies, young master. The Faerie is off the market for the time being."

"Oh?" Kylo said, tapping his finger on his lip. He turned to the guards who were nervously rubbing their necks. "I do have coin, Master Thrayn." The dwarf swallowed hard as he looked at the heavy purse dangling from the young man's belt. "Would we not be able to make a deal? How much will you be asking for a night with the Faerie? When she becomes available."

"Seven thousand gold." Thrayn said dryly. "I know the price is high, but you see…"

"Oh, no." Kylo said, chuckling softly as he looked at the dwarf. "A pure Faerie would be worth every copper. I will make you an offer, Master Thrayn." The dwarf licked his lips and narrowed his eyes at the young man. "How about this." Kylo said, tapping his coin purse with his right hand. "If you allow the Faerie to be mine for the night, along with your luxury accommodations, I will pay you fifteen thousand gold."

"You must take me for a fool, young master." Thrayn said, scowling at the young man. "What kind of man would pay such a price for a night with a Faerie?"

Kylo sighed, rubbing his hand along his coin purse. "A man who haven't much longer in this world." Kylo said. "You see, I am the last heir of the Astaad's and I seem to suffer from a disease of the heart. My family's wise woman says I have only months to live. I decided to travel and experience all I could... before my soul is to be welcomed by the Gods." Kylo wiped away a fake tear as he lifted his purse from his belt. "Would you allow this poor soul the chance to enjoy his final days selfishly? If you'd like, I could purchase another, perhaps an elf woman to join us for the night as well."

Kylo placed one of the blue and purple coins in the dwarf's hand. Thrayn bit and examined the coins before looking up at the young man. Thrayn smiled as he slid the coin into his vest pocket. "Aye." Thrayn said, pinching the end of his beard with his fingers. "What kind of provider of Pleasure would I be to deny a poor soul his final wishes?" Kylo bowed his head gently to the dwarf. "You two." Thrayn said, barking at the guards. "Fetch Miss V and the Faerie. Have her ready for..."

"Kylo Astaad." The young man said, lifting his head.

"Have the Faerie ready for Master Astaad. She will be his company for the night at supper." The guards nodded and grunted their understanding as they entered the Pleasure Palace. "Now." Thrayn said, still pulling at his whiskers. "Let us settle your balance... before you choose your elf girl and see your room."

"After you." Kylo said, gesturing to Thrayn to lead the way. The dwarf nodded and led the young man into the Pleasure Palace. *This Faerie better be worth me risking my neck, vagrant.* Kylo thought as he entered the Palace. He followed behind the dwarf, passing several half naked men and women in the lobby. As well as several armed guards. Thrayn was stopped by another client stumbling through the lobby drunk. The dwarf began cursing at the patron as Kylo examined the room and its many guests. He narrowed his eyes at a figure sitting on the far side of the room wit ha topless elf woman in his lap. The man was wearing a hooded cloak, with bandaged arms. *Fuck me.* Kylo thought, recognizing the vagrant. The cloaked man nodded at Kylo and returned his attention to the elf woman as she escorted him into a private room. *Maybe I won't be alone after all.*

Feya sat in the smallest tub of the Palace bath while Elva scrubbed her back with a soap bar and sponge. Arys the Angel sat on the side of the tub, facing away from the Faerie as she was bathed. Miss V began pouring scented oils into the water as Feya cried in the tub. Arys turned his head slightly, hearing the Faeries cries from behind her hands. "Do not cry, young one." The Angel said, turning to Feya, averting his eyes from her body. Feya looked through her fingers at the Angel. Arys was kind and respectful to everyone in the Pleasure Palace. The Angel's wings were severed, and he wore a magic restraining collar like Feya. "You must learn to leave yourself when you work." Arys said softly. "It is the only way you can remain… you, after being used so many times."

"Arys is right." Elva said, scrubbing Feya's arms with the sponge. "The first time… is always the hardest."

"I am no whore." Feya cried. "I wanted… I wanted Jakob to…" Feya stepped and looked at the others helping her bathe. She took a breath, realizing that no one in the Palace wanted this life, yet, they tried to comfort her. "I'm sorry." Feya said from behind her hands. "I know this life wasn't what any of us wanted."

"True." Arys said, turning away from Feya as Elva began washing her chest. "Not a day passes that I do not wish the Divine God would strike me down and free my soul."

"How did you end up here?" Feya asked as she uncomfortably spread her legs for Elva to continue washing. "I'm sorry, I shouldn't have asked." Feya said as the Angel remained silent.

Arys turned his head slightly and forced a smile. "It is alright, young one." The Angel said. "Would you believe me if I told you a Succubus sold me to the Master?" Feya shook her head in disbelief. "The tale is true." Arys said softly. "Like the fool I am, I fell in love with a Succubus. One night, after a passionate time with one another, she called on a Demon that was lurking in the shadows. He severed my wings and the pair bound me with chains." Arys sighed and softly chuckled to himself. "As a joke, they sold me to the Master, and here I have been ever since."

"It would seem those of Divine blood are no different than us mortals." Miss V said. "Depravity, deception, and betrayal seem to partner with every race and gender."

"Very true." Arys sighed. "The worst part is… I wish to see her one last time. To forgive her."

"You would forgive her?" Feya asked as Elva began pouring water over her body, rinsing her free of soap. "I could never forgive such a betrayal."

"Love is… foolish." The Angel laughed. "I turned my back on the Divine God to be with my love." Feya looked at the Heartbroken Angel. He was different than Angelus. Kind, compassionate, thoughtful, a far cry from the murderous son of the Angel of War. "Would you agree, young one?" Arys asked the Faerie. "You hope that the man you love will storm through the door and pull you free of the pleasure prison."

"He will come." Feya whispered. "Even if…"

"Does he feel the same for you?" Arys asked. Feya shrugged, wrapping a towel around her body. "For you to have such feelings for him... I doubt he doesn't feel the same." The Angel said, smiling as he turned to Feya.

"I agree with Arys." Elva said. "You told us about the charm, about your journey, I know he feels the same. He will come for you."

"He already has someone." Feya muttered.

"Ava." Miss V said. "Ava may be... talented, but love is not a field she has experience in."

"She is still my friend." Feya said. "I will not be the reason she gets hurt."

"You are too good for this Gods forsaken realm, Feya." Elva said, drying the Faerie's hair.

The door to the baths opened slowly as an elf woman peeked her head inside. The elf searched the bath before spotting Feya and the others. Quickly, yet quietly, she tiptoed her way towards the bathing group. "Miss Feya?" the elf woman asked, looking at Feya. The Faerie nodded. "The... client I just served asked me to relay a message to you." Feya tilted her head curiously as the others turned their attention to the elf. "He said the man who you are to serve tonight... is not going to hurt you." The elf woman turned to the door, checking for any signs of guards or other patrons. The elf swallowed hard and licked her lips nervously as she turned back to Feya. "My client introduced himself as... a simple vagrant. He said you would understand."

Feya's eyes shot open at the title. "Christopher." Feya whispered. The Faerie combed her fingers through her wet hair, causing her towel to fall off her body. Arys quickly turned away, coughing in his hand from embarrassment. "I knew it." Feya mumbled. "They are coming."

"Do you see now, young one." Arys said, handing Feya another towel. "Love is... foolish." Feya turned and smiled at the Angel as she accepted the offered towel.

The elf girl smiled wide as Feya turned back to her and nodded. "The vagrant man was remarkable." The elf said, turning to Miss V. tears began flowing from the elf's eyes down her cheek. "Miss V." she said, her voice trembling as she spoke. "He bought my freedom from Master Thrayn. I am to gather my belongings immediately."

"What?" Miss V said. "I-I can't believe it. Mira… I'm so happy for you. Why did he…"

"He said if I agreed to pass this message on to Feya then he would insure I was set free."

Feya chuckled as she dried her body. "His name is Christopher." The Faerie said. "He is a strange man. I have only met him once I think… but he is someone you can't forget."

"It would cost a small fortune to buy our freedom." Elva said. "What kind of vagrant…"

"As I said." Feya interrupted. "He is a strange man."

"Let us get you dressed." Arys said, looking through a stack of clothing. "You will want to look your best when you walk out of here."

"Same goes for you, Elva." Miss V said. "Feya's client has asked for an elf to accompany Feya. If they are going to escape… I believe you have earned this opportunity."

The room was eloquently decorated. Beautiful curtains with a matching rug. Soft bed and sheets fitting for a lord. The furniture was clearly dwarven made. The woodwork and designs could have only been fashioned by someone who dedicated their life to the art of craftsmanship.

The room had its own private bath with a copper tub. There was even an iron enchanted stove used to control the room's temperature next to the bed. From the runes she could make out, Feya knew the stove could heat or cool the room, simply by adding one's magic.

After several minutes of pacing around the room, Feya decided to sit on the side of the bed next to Elva and wait for the client. She continuously adjusted her clothing. They were uncomfortable, tight, and too revealing. Elva placed her hand on her back as Feya took a calming breath. *He is not going to hurt me.* Feya told herself. *Christopher is here… or, at least he is part of my escape.* She prayed it would be Jakob that entered the room. She wondered what she would say… or do if it was, but Christopher was mysterious. It was likely a mercenary or someone he could use to pull off whatever plan he has. Still, Feya believed Jakob would be waiting for her. waiting to swoop her back into the wagon with the others, take her in his arms, and leave Gosa.

A gentle knock came at the door as a red-blond man stepped in. Feya took another deep breath as her body tensed at the sight of him. Elva took her hand gently as she stood to greet the client. The young man smiled wide as he saw her and the elf and greeted them with a bow. Carefully, he stepped into the room, holding a large tray with three plates of food. He shut the door with his foot and walked towards the bed. "My name is Kylo." The client said, handing Feya one of the plates before giving Elva her own. The Faerie looked at the masterfully prepared meal Kylo had just handed her. she was used to slop and bread. This plate… had a large steak, steaming potatoes, seasoned greens, and a buttered bun. The young man even pulled a bottle of wine from his cloak pocket, giving the two girls a wink as he set it on the side table. "I must say." Kylo said, setting his plate on the bed. He held a finger up to his lips, silently telling the girls to remain quiet. The client rubbed his thumb against his ring, drawing a sign in the air as he pressed his finger to his eye. His right eye began to glow green as he looked around the room. After a few moments, he blinked, and his eye returned to normal. "Sorry ladies." Kylo said, smiling wide. "I had to be sure that we are not being watched or that there are no prying ears." Feya nodded, as did Elva as Kylo sat on the bed. "Now." Kylo said, tapping his hand against Feya's thigh. "Let us eat as we discuss getting you two out of here."

"Who are you?" Feya asked as she nervously took a bite of her potatoes. "Why would you help me?"

"My name is Kylo, as I said before." The client smiled. "As to why I am here." He said, taking a bite of his steak. "A man hired me to free you from this whore house and return you to your friends in Murdok." Feya watched the man as he continued to eat and speak. He seemed to enjoy the steak, finishing the meat before eating anything else on his plate. "I was given a considerable sum of coins to gain access to you, and I will be paid equally when I return you to your friends."

"Christopher?" Feya asked.

"Is that the vagrants name?" Kylo asked, looking up from his plate. "He is a strange person, but he seems to have riches and a man needs coin to survive." Kylo ate a large spoonful of potatoes before continuing. "I am a hunter by trade. I hunt creatures and beings that do not belong in this realm."

"Monsters?" Elva asked, nibbling on her food. Kylo smiled and winked at the young elf as he nodded.

"You are not human." Feya said, taking a bite of her greens. Kylo's face took on a shocked expression as he eyed the Faerie.

"You've a good eye, Miss Feya." Kylo said with a wide smile. "I am a Nephilim. My father was Astaad the Angel of the Hunt. My mother was human." Kylo motioned for Feya to get closer to him as he spooned potatoes into his mouth. "Come closer." He said, his mouth filled with food. "Let's deal with this collar." The hunter rubbed the bottom of one of his rings with his thumb and drew a line in the air. Instantly, the collar was cut and fell to the floor. Feya took a long breath, feeling her magic flow freely through her body. "It's good to see you Faerie still wield your magic." Kylo said, taking another bite of his plate.

"No." Feya said. "I was taught how to use magic from a teach I had during my journey."

"Strange." Kylo said chuckling as he ate. "I didn't think Faerie's would need to be taught to use their magic." Feya tilted her head curiously as Elva continued to nervously eat. Kylo saw the confusion on the Faerie's face and sat his plate on the bed. "Did the spell even reach the islands?" Kylo asked. "The spell that forced the Basilisks to sleep and seal the Divine magic from the child?" Feya shrugged. "My father was a hunter. The only beast he was unable to best… was the Basilisk. When the Gods and Devils cast the spell. He protested and defected from the Gods, but I had no idea that the Faerie were affected."

"Why wouldn't we be?" Feya asked. "Everyone on the mortal world lost their magic when the Gods retreated."

"Has the memories of the Faerie been lost as well?" Kylo laughed. Feya didn't understand what he found amusing. "By the Gods." Kylo said, continuing to laugh. "Eeus really did a number on this world didn't she?" Kylo sighed and combed his fingers through his hair. "Feya." The hunter said, resting his hand on her thigh. "The Gods have their Angels. The Devils have their Demons and Succubus." He looked into her eyes and gave a single nod. "Basilisks have their Faeries."

"What?" Feya said, standing from the bed. Her plate of food fell to the floor, launching potatoes and greens along the bedside. "What are you talking about?"

"What are either of you talking about?" Elva asked, looking between the pair. "Basilisks? You mean… dragons?"

Kylo nodded to the young elf, giving her a wide smile and wink before turning to Feya. "As I said, my father was a hunter. An Angel who dedicated his life to finding stronger prey. He was never able to best a

Basilisk. So, he devoted himself to understanding them. The Basilisks fed their magic into this world. Just believing they exist fuels their power and they return it to the earth. Faerie maintain this realm, helping the mortals of this realm live in harmony with the great beasts and nature itself." Feya nearly collapsed to the floor as she stepped away from the hunter. Elva watched on, confused, failing to understand what the pair was talking about. "When the Basilisks were put to sleep, my father refused to slay them. If he was to keep his pride as a hunter, he would not hunt a sleeping beast."

"But." Feya said, trembling. "That can't be."

"Wait." Elva said. "So… Faerie are Divine?"

"Let us not get your brains wrapped around irrelevant topics yet. We have to get you out of here and I haven't the faintest idea as to how." Kylo leaned back on the bed and stared at the ceiling. "I can tell you more from my fathers journals after we manage to leave Gosa."

"Is… is Jakob waiting?"

"Who?" Kylo asked. "Oh. Right. The boy I am to return you to. No. He is still in Murdok I believe. The vagrant was pretty vague."

"But Christopher is here." Feya said. "Is he going to help?"

"Who knows?" Kylo shrugged. "Last time I saw he was shacking with an elf woman."

"He bought her freedom." Elva said in almost a whisper. "She only had to tell Feya that you weren't going to hurt her."

"Crafty, isn't he?" Kylo laughed. "No. I'm not going to hurt or touch you, Feya. As beautiful as you are… I will not defile someone such as you." Kylo turned his head to face the Faerie. "Unless…"

"No." Feya snapped. Kylo laughed and sat up from the bed. "How are we getting out?" Feya asked, glaring at the hunter.

"I'm only joking, Feya." Kylo smirked. "Remove that scowl from your face, your scaring your friend." Kylo stood from the bed and began pacing through the room. "We could go simple and jump from the window. You have your magic back and I have mine."

Feya thought about that idea. It was simple. Too simple. "What… what about the others?" Feya asked. "They don't deserve to be here either."

"Sorry, love." Kylo said. "Wasn't paid to bring down Thrayn's business. "Only to bring you back. Freeing your elf friend is something I wasn't planning on, but I had to entice the dwarf to let me get to you."

"What about Arys?" Feya asked. "He is an Angel. If you free him…"

"No." Kylo said quickly. "I don't feel like dealing with an Angel and finding a way out of the city." Kylo stepped towards the window and realized it was an illusion. He cast a spell, revealing that the room was made of solid walls. The window, and likely all the other windows, were simple runes to hide the true appearance of the building. "We would have to bring down the wall if we were to simply leap from the room." Kylo laughed. "But I don't think that would bother you much." Kylo tapped his fingers on his lips as he thought. "How strong are the guards? Do they use magic?"

"I have never seen the guards use magic." Elva said, standing from the bed. "But they are strong. They are brutes."

"I can hold my own." Feya said, crossing her arms and narrowing her eyes to the hunter.

"So, going out the front is out of the question then."

"Why?" Feya hissed.

"You didn't give me an acceptable answer." Kylo said, smiling at the Faerie. "Can't collect my reward if those guards manage to catch or kill us."

Feya and the others passed the time with small talk, filling Elva in on the details of the Basilisks, Gods, and what all she learned on her journey. Kylo would periodically press his ear to the room's door and walls, listening for anyone who might be approaching the room. He knew Feya was a valuable asset for Thrayn, and the risk of being interrupted was high, despite the large purse of coin he had paid. The young hunter would pass flirtatious offers to Elva, offering to take her with him on his travels. The elf girl seemed tempted by the offer but would reluctantly decline his proposal.

In the later part of the evening, they had decided that once the Palace had become silent, that would be the time to make their escape. Feya watched the hunter curiously as he mumbled strategies to himself as he paced. She was still thinking about what he said. The idea of Faerie's being somehow connected to the antient rulers of this world was still impossible for her to believe. *How could he know this anyway?* Feya thought to herself. Kylo had refused to talk more on the subject until they were free of Gosa and Thrayn's Pleasure Palace. Kylo lifted his hand, gesturing for the girls to get onto the bed. Feya unbuttoned a few buttons of her top as Elva removed hers completely, incase it was Thrayn or one of his guards coming to check on them. The hunter removed his cloak and shirt while unbuttoning his pants as heavy footsteps could be heard coming to the door. A large fist began banging against the door. Kylo stepped heavily across the floor as he made his way to the door, a simple ploy to act frustrated by the sexual interruption. He reached for the door handle, combing his other hand through his hair. Kylo cracked open the door, sighed, and opened it fully to reveal Trung in the hallway.

The simpleton pushed a small cart into the room, filled with cheeses, berries and wine. "Might I ask what is with this interruption?" Kylo said, resting a hand on his hip as he watched the simpleton. "I have paid more than a fortune for a night of peace with these ladies."

Trung lowered his head nervously as he looked at the hunter. "Trung sorry, Master Astaad." The large man said. "Trung just thought Faerie friend would like the treats Master Thrayn sends to his fancy clients."

"Does the Master often send the kitchen help to deliver such pleasantries?" Kylo snarled, causing Trung to slouch his shoulders.

"Enough, Kylo." Feya said, rebuttoning her top. "Trung has been good to me since I've been here."

"Faerie is Trung's friend." The large man said. Kylo rolled his eyes and crossed his arms. Feya stood from the bed and took a square of cheese from the platter. She smiled as she took a bite of one of the various cheeses. "Does Faerie like cheese?" Trung asked. Feya nodded and took another square, offering a piece for Elva as she slid on her top.

Kylo sighed and locked the door. He passed the large man and grabbed himself a square of cheese and the bottle of wine. "So." Kylo said, sitting on the bed and popping open the wine. "If the Faerie is your friend… perhaps you will help us then." Kylo said, tilting his head as he bit into the cheese. Trung smiled wide and nodded his head. Kylo looked at Feya as she gave him a single nod. The hunter turned to Elva, who also gave a nod of approval before he turned to the simpleton. "I plan on giving Miss Feya and Elva here their freedom. Will you help?"

"Trung will help. Trung will help." The large man said, clapping his hands loudly. Feya and Elva quickly instructed the man to remain silent and listen. "Sorry." The simple man said.

Kylo huffed as he slid on his shirt, eyeing the large man. "Here." Kylo said, handing Feya one of his rings. "Put this on whatever finger it will fit and keep your fist tight when we start. If it slips, the spell will break."

"What spell?" Feya asked, sliding the ring on her finger."

"Let your magic flow through to the ring and draw a semi-circle in the air. Then draw a line through it." Feya nodded and obeyed. As she finished the aerial image Kylo had instructed her to draw, Trung suddenly stepped back and began looking around the room. "Very good." Kylo smiled, looking at Elva. "You are quite adept at magic. I'd expect no less from a Faerie."

"Where did Miss Faerie go?" Trung asked, still looking around the room.

Feya looked at her arms, confused by Trung's question. "She is invisible." Kylo said, still looking at Feya as through he could see her. "A particularly useful spell for hunting. It won't last long… so once we start, we will have to move quickly." Feya felt the ring slip on her finger and Trung quickly turned his attention to her. "If the ring slips the spell is broken." Kylo reminded her. "You must keep the right tight in your hand."

"So, what's the plan?" Feya asked.

"Our friend Trung here is going to be key." Kylo said, smiling at the large man. "He will leave the cheeses and wine here. You will simply sit on the cart, and we will walk you as close to the exit as possible."

"And I'll be invisible." Feya said.

"Well, you'd look rather silly if you weren't." Kylo said, causing Elva to giggle. "Is there an exit besides the front, kitchen man?" Kylo asked the large man. Trung nodded. "Good. Then we will go out the least busy side of the Palace."

"Front always quiet at nighttime." Trung said. "Trung likes to sit in lobby cause it nice and quiet."

"So, the front is our safest way out?" Elva asked.

Trung shrugged and picked at his thumbs. "Master Thrayn stays in his office sometimes. Him may see."

Kylo patted the big man's shoulder as he leaned against him. "Tell me something, young man." The hunter said, rubbing his chin. "Have you seen a cloaked man with bandaged arms in the Palace?"

Trung nodded again. "Oh yes." The simpleton cheered. "Him gave Trung a gold coin to send cheese and drink to Miss Faerie. Him also buy Mira from Master Thrayn. Him good man."

"Is he still here?" Feya asked.

"Him in room with Mira." Trung said, rubbing his neck. "Miss Mira packing now with bandaged man. Trung going to miss her but think Mira going to be married."

"Doubtful." Kylo said. "So, he is still here." The hunter said, turning to Feya. "He is waiting for our move." Kylo paused for a moment before turning back to the simpleton. "Did he say when he was leaving? Did he say anything?"

Trung nodded once again. "Bandaged man says he is leaving soon." The large man shrugged, still picking his thumbs. "Him say him going to…"

A loud explosion echoed through the Pleasure Palace. The sound of stone, wood, and glass splintering and shattering on the lower levels shook the entire building, knocking everyone to the floor. Kylo quickly stood, as Feya helped Elva to her feet. Running for the door, they heard screams and patrons running in a panic. Smoke began to flow up the stairwell. "Looks like it's time to go, ladies." Kylo said, looking back into the room. "He really is a strange man." Another explosion boomed, shaking the floor of the luxury suite.

Feya felt the sensation of falling. She looked down and saw the floor had collapsed from underneath her. Kylo quickly grabbed the Faerie by the wrist and pulled her back into the doorway. Trung fell through the floor, landing two levels down into the lobby. Elva hung onto the bed, trying to pull herself back into the room. The bedding slipped, causing the elf girl to fall down into the lobby next to Trung. "Elva." Feya screamed. "Trung." The simpleton groaned and stood slowly, rubbing his back as he stepped towards Elva. "We have to get down there." Feya said, looking at Kylo. "You said you'd free Elva too."

Kylo sighed and nodded his head in frustration. "Can't leave a pretty lady in a pit like this I suppose." The hunter smiled. "Can you fly?"

"No." Feya murmured. "Thrayn took my charm. It is what let me fly."

"Oh." Kylo said, rubbing his face in his aggravation. "We will have much to discuss if we survive this."

The pair began their descent through the open floor until the reached the lower level, carefully climbing and leaping from floor to floor. Trung was still standing where he fell, holding Elva in his arms. The young woman was unconscious but alive, groaning in pain with each of Trung's movements. As Feya stepped towards the large man, after descending to the lobby, she noticed a piece of wood protruding from his lower back. Before she could offer him help, Feya was forced to turn around and come face to face with the guard Kroll. The large man wrapped his massive hand around her throat as he tried to ready a collar. Feya resisted and kicked at the guard until his head rolled off of his body. Feya gasped and stepped away from the headless corpse, seeing Kylo with his rings glowing. "Time to go Feya." Kylo shouted, his face stern and cold. Feya nodded, stepping over the fallen guard, and running towards Elva.

Guards and patrons were launched across the lobby from a powerful burst of energy. Thrayn shouted from behind a counter before noticing Feya and the others attempting to flee. "Faerie whore." The dwarf screamed as he drew a dagger from his boot. "This is all your doing." The room became still, and the air seemed to be absent. Feya and Kylo began struggling to breath. The dwarf was reaching for his throat, gasping for air that his lungs couldn't absorb. Trung collapsed to the ground, dropping Elva, and coughing as he struggled to breath. A cloaked man with bandaged arms walked into the lobby with the elf girl Mira. He turned to Feya and Kylo, snapping his fingers, allowing air to flow back into their lungs. Kylo grunted angrily as he took a long breath.

"Save them." Feya shouted to Christopher, pointing to Trung and Elva. The vagrant looked at her with cold eyes then glared at the pair lying on the floor. "Now." Feya demanded, seeing the hate and anger in the vagrant's eyes. A look she had only seen from one other… Angelus. The bandaged man's eyes shined with murderous intent. He snapped his fingers and Trung and Elva began gasping to catch their breath.

Feya ran to Elva, helping the young elf stand from the debris covered floor. "You are needed elsewhere, Feya." Christopher said coldly. Feya turned and glared at the vagrant. "You and Jakob are too important to the fate of this realm. Do not waste your time on those who will not survive the coming war."

"Shut up." Feya screamed as Kylo lifted Elva onto his back. Trung grunted as he stood, still reaching for his back where the wood had pierced him. "When the Savior comes, he will fight to save everyone, not just the useful."

Christopher took a long breath through his nose as Mira hid behind him. "The Savior will do what is necessary to insure this world remains free from the tyranny of the Gods games."

"Games?" Feya questioned.

Christopher gestured with his head towards the exit. "Come." The vagrant ordered those who could stand. "Jakob will be looking for you."

Feya and the others quickly followed Christopher as he blew apart the entrance wall. Feya could see guards, patrons, and those forced to work for Thrayn dying from asphyxiation on the floor. She quickly shook her head, grabbing Christopher by the shoulder. "Free them." The Faerie ordered. "They do not deserve to die like this. They are slaves to him."

"I do not know who belongs to who." Christopher said dryly.

"Then free them all." Feya snarled, looking into Christopher's eyes. The vagrant sighed and tuned to the people on the floor. He snapped his fingers, allowing air to freely flow into the lobby once again. Thrayn began coughing as he struggled to stand from his hiding spot behind the counter. Christopher ordered Feya and the others to exit the palace as he turned to face the dwarf.

Thrayn staggered as he stepped into the center of the lobby. "Who the fuck are you?" the dwarf hissed as he spat blood on the floor. Chandeliers and portraits fell from the palace's walls, along with pieces from the upper-level floors. "Why me? Why my business?"

"I am but a simple vagrant." Christopher said, looking at the dwarf from across the room. "I think it best if you leave Faerie's off your service menus from now on… Master Thrayn." Christopher turned towards the destroyed wall and stepped out of the Pleasure Palace. Thrayn collapsed onto his knees as he watched the vagrant leave with his most valuable merchandise.

A guard quickly rushed to his side, offering to retrieve the Faerie and bring back the head of the stranger. "I can get 'em Master." The guard huffed, trying to catch his breath. "Got three men with me to…"

"No." Thrayn shouted, watching the group walk towards Kylo's wagon. The dwarf swallowed hard as the vagrant turned one last time to the Palace. Thrayn could feel a vibration shaking the building. "No." He whispered. "You wouldn't make it out the door… before he killed us."

Chapter 7

It had been centuries since Gidione stepped foot in Onitara, the realm of the Devils. The Goddess studied the grand hall of this unnamed temple as she made her way to the private chambers. The dark dreary walls, stained glass windows, and lack of décor was nothing like the Gods temples back on Elysian. Nothing like her own temple back home. Stepping into the private chambers of the temple, Gidione found it strange that Lucile's private room was so vibrantly decorated while keeping the rest of the temple dismal and grey. These thoughts of Lucil's taste in design were meant as a distraction. A way to keep her focus away from the glaring eyes of the undead beast nestled along the temple's walls. Lucile's claims during their last conversation had intrigued the Goddess, drawing her to Onitara to ask more questions. She knew asking the other Gods would bring no answers about their history. Most of her kind brushed her curiosity and ambition away, claiming it was merely a faze from her youthfulness. Gidione wanted to know more about this *game* Lucile spoke of and know how many realms had fallen to their actions. Eeus's words had only added fuel to the Goddess's curiosity.

Gidione swallowed hard as the snake-like beast eyed her with each movement she made. "Sweet Gidione." Lucile said, biting her lip as she entered her private chamber. Lucile clicked her tongue, sending Senshe away. The beast slithered through the temple gate, coiling himself around the temple in its entirety. "What brings you to my chambers, my Goddess?" Lucile said mockingly.

Gidione scowled as she watched the beast's eye shine brightly through the stained-glass window. "How does that thing fit in this temple?" The Goddess snarled.

"Senshe can alter his size." Lucile said, eyeing the Goddess. "But he can only get as small as you just saw. He takes up most of the temple, but he is an obedient serpent." The Devil combed her fingers through her crimson hair as she stepped towards the Goddess. "You have yet to answer my question, Goddess."

"Its name is… Senshe?" Gidione hissed. "Disgusting."

"Dangerous… you mean." Lucile said, pressing her tongue against her fang. "Senshe is capable of slaying Devils and Gods." The Devil boasted. "And." Lucile smiled. "He seemed quite fond of working with your sister Kirames."

"She is no sister of mine." Gidione shouted. The large beast rocked its head as it exhaled heavily against the temple. The force of his breath caused boards to creek and windows to shake, shocking the Goddess. Lucile laughed as she shook her head. "Kirames betrayed our kin and the Divine God. I am loyal to my Divine and our cause."

"And what is your cause?" The Devil smirked.

Gidione balled her fists in frustration as she looked between the Devil and the beast. "To bring balance and betterment of our realm."

Lucile lost herself in laughter at the Goddess's words. "Betterment of our realm?" The Devil joked. "Do you still not understand, Gidione? This is not our realm." She turned to the beast as it shot its reptilian tongue through the air. "It is theirs." Lucile sighed as she stepped closer towards the Goddess. "Oh Gidione, so young and naïve. Do you know why Tor and Eeus try and forbid us all from roaming the mortal realm?" Gidione watched as the Devil circled her like a wolf preparing to strike its prey.

"Our realm is lost. Not the home you know. Not Elysian. Not Onitara." Lucile slid her tongue along the Goddess's neck, causing a shiver to run down Gidione's spine from the familiar touch. "Addilan." Lucile whispered. "The true realm of both our kin."

"What are you talking about?" Gidione murmured.

Senshe hissed as it released a yawn before burying himself in the ground to rest. "According to our elders, Addilan was a wonderous world. Both Devil and God drew power from the mortals. Until… the mortals turned away from their faiths and superstitions. Eeus fled the realm in search of a new world to rule. Once it was found, we Devils followed. Again, and again this process repeated. When Onitara fell, your kin found Elysian. Then… they destroyed it before our game could continue. Now, we are here, on Earth." Lucile looked at the now sleeping beast then smiled at the Goddess. "A world with its own gods. Gods that outmatch any Devil or God to date. Even the Ancestor and Divine."

"If what you say is true, why would we not simply go in search of another realm?"

"Your sister." Lucile smiled. "And my brother, of course. Alvarome and Kirames wanted to… take over the role of Ancestor and Divine. To take control of the game." Lucile laughed softly, looking at the grey and black ceiling. "They wanted to find a world with no deities. A world where both Devil and God can rule together. Tor and Eeus refused to leave a world like earth. So much magic. So much potential." The Devil said, displaying her fists mockingly. "So, our dear brother and sister decided to have their child after Eeus linked our fate to this toxic world. A being capable of using Devil, God, and Earth magic. Use him to seal us away from this world and usurp the thrones of our race together." Lucile shrugged. "That's the story you wanted to hear, am I right, my Goddess?"

"And how would…"

"So many questions." Lucile said, biting her lip. "If you would like to discuss more… you will need to earn your answers." Gidione tilted her head curiously as Lucile's red eyes locked onto hers. The Devil stepped towards her bed, untying her top and revealing her breasts to the Goddess. "Come, my Goddess." Lucile said as Gidione licked her lips. "It has been too long since we have shared breaths."

As Gidione stepped closer to the Devil, their lips met, and Lucile quickly removed the Goddess's robe. The Devil tossed the Goddess onto the bed and explored her body with her tongue. "Why do you Devils not seek the abomination?" Gidione ask as she slid herself free of her remaining clothes. "From what you say." The Goddess continued as the Devil continued her exploration. "The Abomination is a threat to all of us."

Lucile moaned as Gidione turned her on her back. "Do these questions excite you?" The Devil asked, pulling the Goddess's lips to hers. She released a low moan as the Goddess's finger found her. "Tor is confident in the stolen magic they used to seal his power." Lucile said, squirming from the Goddess's touch. "Sealing his potential away, forcing the beasts to sleep, trapping their subordinates on the islands." Lucile laughed cheerfully before Gidione's lips met her breasts. "The child is alone, and no mortal can unseal his power. If they did… we Devils would not be part of the war your kin wish to wage."

"So." Gidione said, straddling the Devil, running her fingers along Lucile's stomach. "Devils are cowards."

Lucile laughed softly as she grabbed the Goddess by her waist. Gidione moaned as she felt the Devils magic touch her own. "We are wise." Lucile whispered. "We know very well that this world does not want or need us." Lucile ventured with her hand as Gidione moaned, untying her hair. "Tell me… my Goddess, why would Eeus want this world?" Gidione was unable to answer as Lucile continued to feed her magic into the Goddess. "Divine are unable to feed of the magic of this world. Eeus had to spread lies and alter memories in an attempt to feed our magic into this world."

"This world." Gidione breathed. "Is filled with magic. If we…"

"There is no claiming the magic of this realm." Lucile whispered, scraping her fangs against the Goddess's neck. "It is toxic to our kind. You have seen Eeus, yes? Tor is no better. This world is not meant for us, and the more you venture their the more you will weaken."

"Then…"

The Devil pulled the Goddess underneath her, sliding her tongue down her neck to her breasts. "Then." Lucile moaned. "Your dear sister… was right."

"What?" Gidione shouted, shoving the Devil off of her. Lucile smiled but began to pout, sliding her hand along her hips. "You would rather Alvarome had ruled over Tor?"

Lucile laughed, rubbing her hand along the Goddess's stomach. "Of course not." The Devil smirked. "It was I who told the Ancestor of their plot and that Kirames was with child." Gidione took a long breath as she sat up in the bed. Lucile slid behind her, wrapping her arms around her naked form, resting her chin on the Goddess's shoulder. "Alvarome couldn't lead the Devils." Lucile said softly. "We feed off fear and he was too kindhearted. He was always more like your kin than ours." Gidione sighed, feeling the Devil's breath against her neck. "I agreed with him, though." Lucile admitted. "Tor and Eeus are too short sided. Stubborn. Too weak to bring us to a world of balance. Look at them now." Lucile said, pulling the Goddess's gaze to hers by the chin. "Weak. Cripple. By a magic they cannot harness. Yet, they will not abandon this realm. Eeus is too stubborn. Tor is too in love; they will be the end of our Divine race if they do not either leave this realm… or manage to kill off every beast in it."

"You think we can defeat them?" Gidione whispered.

"Of course not." Lucile said, pressing her lips against Gidione's. "They are the true rulers of this realm. That is why the Devils need a new Ancestor. Someone strong. Ruthless. Willing to do whatever it takes to preserve our people." Gidione pressed her forehead against Lucile's, feeling the base of the Devil's horn against her flesh. "Someone who is capable of taming a beast."

"You?" Gidione murmured as she pulled away from the Devil. "You plan on overthrowing Tor? Assuming control?"

"Is it not obvious to you?" Lucile smiled. "Tor was never fond of me, but revealing Alvarome's plan gained me his favor, and a little trust. But when I was able to tame Senshe, turn him into my obedient pet, all of our kind recognized my strength. Now, there is a divide amongst the Devils. Who should rule? The one who follows the Gods aimlessly to oblivion… or the woman who took Senshe of the Forest." Gidione swallowed hard, feeling a tremble through her spine as she bit her lips. She realized while the Gods and Devils were preoccupied with the Abomination… Lucile was plotting and gaining support for her mutiny. The idea of Lucile becoming the new Ancestral Devil sent fear through the Goddess, but she also felt excitement for reasons she didn't understand. Gidione reached for the Devil, allowing their tongues to meet once again as Lucile pulled the Goddess's long white hair. "Perhaps." Lucile said, gripping Gidione's hair tighter around her palm. "You should be more… ambitious as well. How strong our people would be… if we ruled together, what do you think… my queen?"

"You are insane." Gidione breathed, unable to resist the Devil any longer. "The Abomination will be the end of us all. Even you."

Lucile smiled as she kissed her way down the Goddess's stomach to her thighs. "The Abomination." Lucile laughed. "I will make an ally of him, and he will be another tool for me to use to secure my rule."

"You *are* insane, Lucile." Gidione breathed. "He will kill you. He will end us all. Banish us to our crippled realms forever."

"You and your kin are too short sighted, my Goddess." Lucile whispered before tasting the Goddess. "You will see soon enough, the war Alvarome predicted is close. You will need to choose a path yourself." Lucile said. "Eeus will not be able to protect any of you… and if there is no Divine… there will be no Gods."

The campfire and smell of roasting fish was a welcome change for Feya. It brought back memories of traveling with Jakob and the others. She was grateful to no longer be riding in the wagon, Christopher had ridden the horses hard since leaving Gosa. After several hours of riding, the vagrant finally decided to make camp. Deciding to make camp brought relief to Elva and Feya after listening to the hunter complain about the entirety of their escape. The hunter complained about Christopher's methods of escaping the Pleasure Palace, to the way the vagrant was driving the wagon.

Feya had remained silent during their ride, even while Kylo and Christopher set up camp. Elva and Mira followed Christopher around the camp like lost puppies, knowing the vagrant was powerful enough to protect them from any threat. Christopher didn't seem to mind, offering the elf pair each one of the larger fish he had managed to catch. Feya remained focused on the line of questioning she had for Kylo. The hunters claims that the Faerie were somehow connected to the Basilisks was still unbelievable to her. Christopher suddenly grunted, pulling Feya's attention away from the dancing campfire. He gestured to a large tent, a silent offer for the girl to claim it for themselves.

Kylo returned from the small lake just through the woods with a bucket of fresh water. The hunter sat the bucket next to Feya before sitting beside the fire. Feya reached into her pocket and pulled out the ring he had given her back at the Palace. Kylo nodded and slid the ring back onto his pinky finger. "You have been silent for many hours now, Feya." Christopher said, sitting beside a tree to rest his back. "Were you harmed at the Palace? Were you touched?"

"No." Feya breathed. "I just wish we could have saved the others."

"We saved the two elves and your simple friend." Kylo said, ladling water into his mouth. "Do you still have him fishing at this hour, vagrant?" Christopher grunted without answering the hunter. "Something on your mind Faerie?" Kylo said, seeing Feya's cold expression.

"You said we Faerie are to the Basilisks as the Angel's are to the Gods." Feya reminded the hunter.

"Indeed, I did." Kylo said, smiling ear to ear. "It baffles me that you do not know this, and… that you do not use the magic of this realm."

"Well, I don't." Feya hissed. "And I can't." She turned to Christopher as he adjusted his sitting position. "You told us you had no magic." Feya snarled at the vagrant. "What power was that you used at the Palace?"

"I do not possess the Gods resource." Christopher said softly as Mira took a seat next to him. "I have spent my life studying this worlds natural magic. The magic of the Basilisks… and Faerie."

"So." Feya said, watching her fish slowly cook. "It's true."

"I am rarely wrong." Kylo said, still smiling wide at the Faerie. "I read about the Faerie in one of my father's journals. He talked about the great power the Faerie wielded. That they were a difficult prey like the Basilisks themselves."

"Prey?" Feya snarled.

"Yes. Prey." Kylo said, combing his fingers through his red-gold hair. "My father was Astaad, Angel of the Hunt."

"Was?" Christopher asked, tilting his head to look at the hunter.

"Yes." Kylo said softly, watching the fire dance along the logs. "Father hated the idea of forcing the Basilisks to sleep. He knew the spell wouldn't be as… powerful as the Gods hoped for. Still, he refused to hunt a defenseless prey."

"I do not believe the Basilisks would have been defenseless." Christopher said as Mira rested her head in his lap.

Kylo chuckled as he turned to the vagrant. "As my father learned." The hunter said, his voice filled with pain. "Astaad sought a way to reawaken the beasts. To have the ultimate hunt once again. He traveled and trained for centuries before I was born. When I was about fifteen… he found one of them still awake." Feya took a long breath and turned to Christopher. The vagrant's face was still and hard as he caressed the elf girl's cheek as she slept. *Does he know?* Feya thought. "A red beast with the breath of fire. My father fought… and died." Kylo smiled as he rubbed his rings. "The crazy part is that the beast returned my father's body to my mother while I was hunting. She told me the beast spoke to her and prayed for my father, promising his soul would be at rest with…"

"Thanatos." Christopher said. "The Dragon of Death and Carrier of Souls." Kylo slowly turned to the vagrant, as did Feya. "The Basilisk Astaad faced was Akirakesi the Fire Bringer. A powerful being and a prideful hunter himself. He saw your father as a proper foe and showed his respect to your mother by returning him to her."

"You seem to know your dragons." Kylo said through gritted teeth. "In fact, you seem to know a great many things." Christopher shrugged, turning his attention to the cooking fish. "Why did you hire me to save the Faerie? You seemed more than capable of it alone."

"Because I cannot take her to the others." Christopher said, tossing a purse towards the hunter. Kylo opened the purse and saw several coins made of gold and various other gems. "Your payment, as requested." Kylo swallowed hard at the sight of the riches. "Feya." Christopher said. "The time of the final war is coming. I do find it strange that you do not possess the power of the other Faeries but ask your questions and I will answer them truthfully and to the best of my abilities."

Feya looked at the vagrant for several moments as she thought, growing more confused with each passing second. Christopher was a vagrant but seemed to be much more than that. He was powerful and wise. He knew the truth of the world, despite the lies mortals have learned to believe. "Are the Faerie truly one with the Basilisks?" Feya asked. Christopher nodded, seemingly disappointed at her question. "Why do the Gods and Devils never go to the islands?"

"Because they cannot defeat the Faeries." Christopehr said plainly. "For the Faeries on the islands still possess the magic of the Basilisks."

"That can't be true." Feya said. "I have no magic and no one besides the elders of the islands have basic magic."

Christopher shook his head slowly. "You are not from the islands, Feya." The Faerie shook her head in disbelief. "The memories you have of your home are planted by Shinrahn. The Dragon King. You were created by the Dragon King for the purpose of unlocking the Saviors magic and releasing the Basilisks." Christopher tilted his head and took a slow breath. "You believe you to be of the water tribe, yet you do not have blue skin, your ears are shorter, and you do not have webbed hands and feet. You and Jakob are the key to unsealing the magic the Gods locked away. Events predicted long ago are now unfolding." Feya continued shaking her head as the vagrant spoke. "The blood of Gadreed reigniting his mission, a Faerie traveling the continent in search of magic, the Daemon's of Kirames and Alvarome guiding you… this was all predicted centuries ago."

"You know a great deal indeed." Kylo said, rubbing his chin." I bet you claim to know where the Savior is."

"Yes." Christopher said, not taking his eyes off Feya.

The Faerie stood quickly, glaring at the bandaged man. "Where is he? Why haven't you told us before?"

"I cannot tell you." Christopher said. "It would be too dangerous for you to know. As I said before, if you find his name, he will come."

"If… if what you say is true… why can't I use Basilisk magic?"

"It would have been too dangerous to send a Faerie with their abilities to the continent." Christopher said. "Mortals are led to believe it is the fault of the Faerie that magic is gone. You would have been a target. More than you already are. If you cannot even fly… you would not have been seen as a threat. You were powerless… like the rest of the mortals."

"This whole story seems ridiculous." Kylo said, wafting his hand in the air. "It seems such a roundabout way to get anywhere."

"Indeed." Christopher said. "The game of the Gods has destroyed many realms and worlds. For whatever reason, they have decided to keep their claim to this world. Factions are forming in their ranks and discord is keeping them distracted. The ones who sealed away the mortal's memories, the Basilisks, and the Savior, are growing weaker."

"The Divine God?" Feya asked.

"Indeed." Christopher said. "And the Ancestral Devil. They are still weak from the spell using earth magic and grow weaker by the year."

"If they die…" Feya whispered. "Will the Gods and Devils leave?"

Christopher shrugged. "It is unclear. Gods and Devils rely on one another to feed their mythology to mortals. The Gods thrive on praise and worship while the Devils feed off the fears of mortals."

"I am aware of the *balance* the Gods and Devils believe in." Kylo said. "Father wrote about his history in the other realms in his journals."

"Can we defeat them?" Feya asked. "Do we even have a chance against a Divine?"

"Yes." Christopher said. "The mythology mortals believe is untrue. Gods and Devils are only immortal on worlds whose magic they can control. Basilisk magic is toxic to Divine races, leaving them mortal on this plain. That is why the Gods and Devils send their Angels and Demons to do their work in this world. They fear death. They fear the Basilisks."

"You spin quite a tale, vagrant." Kylo scoffed. "One might believe you are Divine yourself." Christopher looked at the hunter through narrowed eyes. "I sense no Divine magic in you… but my father's rings seem weary of your presence."

"I am simply more powerful than you.' Chirstopher said coldly. "I have mastered a magic that your father was unable to hunt." Kylo rubbed his jaw as he looked at the vagrant. "Do you have any other questions, Feya?"

"What are the Basilisks?" Feya asked. "I know it is said they are the original rulers of this world, but what are they?"

"In simple terms." Christpher said, pulling his fish from the fire. "They are dragons. Each filled with magic that feeds this world. Senshe of the Forest, Oothra of the Sea, Akirakesi of Fire, Materna of Fertility, and countless others that keep this world in perfect balance. One must simply see a Basilisk and know it is real for their magic to freely flow. By simply existing they are all powerful. It was the invasion of the Gods that disrupted the beauty and peace of this world."

"You really are a strange person." Kylo smiled as he took a bite of his fish. "If what you say is true, I would love to see how it all plays out."

"You have your place in this journey as well, son of Astaad." Christopher said, causing the hunter to pause. "You will find Jakob and the others and join their quest."

"You think so?" Kylo mocked. "Perhaps you are not as wise as you seem."

Feya stood silently as she watched the two men bicker about history. Kylo continued expressing his doubts to the vagrant while Christopher calmly answered his questions. The Faerie looked at the bandages along Christopher's arms and the bandage wrapped around his forehead. She thought back to Jakob and when Gadreed would assume control of him. How Divine writing appeared on his arm. She thought of Anna and how her horn had begun to grow as her memories were unlocked. Feya took a long breath, stepped around the campfire, and confronted the vagrant. "I have one more question." Feya said sternly. Christopher took a bite of his fish, nodding his head. She thought hard about her question, feeling foolish for what she was about to ask. "What is your name?"

Christopher looked at the Faerie curiously. Kylo laughed as he swallowed his fish, waking Mira. "I thought you two were acquainted." The hunter joked. "Did you not exchange names? How rude."

"Shut up." Feya snarled, glaring at the hunter. She slowly turned back to Christopher who remained silent. "You say you know where the Savior is. You say you can't tell me where he is." Feya said. "You are always bandaged but I never see blood. So, tell me, what is your real name?"

Christopher sighed and tossed the bones of his fish into the fire. "Feya." The vagrant said hesitantly. "I am but a vagrant. I was given my name by…"

Feya pulled at the bandage on Christopher's head, revealing a circular wound with a partial bone protruding from his skull. Christopher snarled and pushed the Faerie away as he covered his head with his hand. "What is your name?" Feya shouted. Kylo stood, seeing the vagrant's injury. Mira looked at Christopher with shock filled eyes as Elva stuck her head through the tent from curiosity.

"I…" Christopher said through gritted teeth. "I do not know."

Kylo stepped beside the Faerie, extending his hand towards Christopher's head. The vagrant slapped his hand away and stepped back as he wrapped the wound with his bandage. "Holy shit." The hunter said, smiling as he turned to the Faerie.

The air felt heavy and thick as Gosa came into view. Ava glanced behind the wagon from Cole's box seat, checking to make sure Jakob and the others were following behind them. Sebastian was in control of Jakob's wagon, giving Ava a single nod, reassuring her that they were not going to abandon her. Ava sighed and turned back to face the city she so desperately never wanted to see again. Cole scratched his neck and spat to the left of the wagon. Ava grunted in disgust, checking her bondage to ensure it was still loose enough to escape. She had to play the part of a captured runaway. There was no knot, a rope was simply wrapped around her wrists with the end sitting in her palm for a quick escape. "Still got that dagger I gave ya?" Cole asked, glancing over at the elf. "Might need it if ye decided to kill the dwarf yourself."

"I've got the dagger." Ava said, rolling her eyes. She lifted her skirt, revealing the knife strapped to her thigh. She quickly lowered her skirt, realizing the mercenary was interested in more than just the dagger. "Feya better be safe." Ava hissed. "You'll end up as dead as Thrayn will if something happened to her."

"Aye." Cole laughed. "I imagine the lad would see my head on a pike if something happened to his little Faerie." Ava hissed and rolled her eyes. Cole chuckled as he tightened his grip around the reins. The mercenary groaned with annoyance as several city guards approached the gates as they drew closer. "Strange." Cole said softly. "Not used to seeing so many guards." Ava slouched in the box seat, recognizing some of the guards from her time at the Pleasure Palace. "The Dwarf's men are in force as well." Cole said suspiciously.

"Holt." One of the city guards yelled. A tall slender woman with a bright silver badge on her chest. "What business do you have in Gosa? Where are you traveling from?"

"Murdok." Cole grunted. "Got business with Master Thrayn. Suppose to meet 'em ye see." Ava felt her skin turn cold at the dwarf's name.

"You know them?" The guard asked, pointing to Sebastians wagon.

"Aye." Cole grunted. "Those be my men. Thrayn has a job for us ya see."

The city guard narrowed her eyes at the mercenary as she spat on the ground. She turned to the pair of guards with Pleasure Palace insignias on their chest plates and tilted her head. One of the male guards looked up at the wagon, noticing Ava in the box seat and nodded to the city guard. "Very well." The woman said, backing away from the wagon. "Don't be surprised if Thrayn isn't… as welcoming as usual. Had a bit of an incident." Ava felt her heart skip for a moment as fear filled her mind. *What did Feya do?* Ava thought. *I know Thrayn had to of put a collar on her.*

Cole grunted his understanding and led the horses onward into the city. Ava began picking at her nails as they approached the turn that led to the Pleasure Palace. All the nightmares she endured began flooding her mind. All the men that used her body, even as a child, she began to feel them again. She could feel their hands on her body, making her feel filthy and worthless. The women that paid to torture her as revenge for their husbands paying for a night with her. The beatings and ridiculing that Thrayn and his guards enacted on her after every act of defiance. The innocent eyes Anna would give her when doodling on the walls and furniture. Every memory struck her mind at once, making her chest and head burn. Cole tugged on the reins and the horses made the turn. Ava closed her eyes tightly, then opened them to see a peculiar sight.

The Pleasure Palace still stood tall, decorated with stained glass windows, and finely stained wood with golden trim. Ava's eyes remained wide as Cole slowed the horses to a stop. Cracks ran up and down the building walls. Part of the second and third floors were destroyed, and the main lobby entrance had been blown out. "W-what happened?" Ava whispered, sliding her hands free of the rope.

"Cole." Jakob shouted as his wagon pulled alongside the mercenary. "Change of plans?"

"Aye." The mercenary said. "Something went down here. Something bad."

Jakob jumped from his wagon, followed by Balin and Elizabeth. Anna climbed out of the back of the wagon as Sebastian grabbed his staff. Ava remained motionless in Cole's box seat, looking at the crippling building that had once been her prison. A familiar voice broke through her despair. *Thrayn.* She looked through the fallen wall of the lobby to see the Dwarf arguing with city guards. She felt a hand on her thigh, and quickly turned from fright. Jakob was beside her, offering his hand to help her down. "Jakob." Ava whispered, taking his hand. "I don't want to be here."

"I know." Jakob said, brushing her hair behind her pointed ears. "But we have to find Feya." Ava nodded and turned slowly to the Pleasure Palace. Elizabeth handed Jakob his shield as she passed. "Perhaps a direct approach?"

"Got a lot of guards, lad." Cole said, strapping his sword to his side. "A lot… of guards. City too."

"Scared mercenary?" Elizabeth said, giving the large man a curious glare. "I'm not." The soldier said, turning to face the Palace. "Not after what I saw Jakob do in Murdok."

"Aye." Balin said, puffing his chest as he placed his axe on his shoulder. "Our Feya is in there and I aim to get her out."

"Aye." Jakob said. "Let's go talk with Master Thrayn.

The group made their way across the guard filled street. Every guard seemed too preoccupied to notice the armed party approaching the Palace. A black-haired dwarf kicked a plank of wood as he stepped through the opening in the lobby wall. "Bastards." The dwarf screamed at the guards following behind him. "When I get my hands on them, I'll…" The dwarf stopped mid-sentence as he saw the group of warriors approaching him. "Cole?" The dwarf said, his voice cracking from nervousness.

"Aye." Cole grunted. "Brought your…" He turned to Ava who was eyeing him with a vicious glare. "Your girl."

"And a few others I see." Thrayn said nervously as the guards stepped in front of him. "What is the meaning of this, Cole? We had an arrangement."

"Aye." Cole said, crossing his arms. "We did. But… I'd rather remain on my friend's good side. So, we came for the Faerie."

Thrayn scoffed and started laughing as he rubbed his chin. The guards drew their swords, but quickly stepped back as Elizabeth readied her spear. "A foolish move." Thrayn said, still rubbing his chin. "Do you not see the guards? The city?" Thrayn puffed his chest. "Gosa belongs to me, Cole. You do not make threats… or back out of deals with me."

Jakob drew his sword, sending his magic through the hilt. The blade became engulfed in multi-colored flames. Divine writing formed along Jakob's arm as he stepped closer to the dwarf. "Where is Feya?" Jakob said pointing the blade at the dwarf's throat. "If you have harmed her."

Guards began to circle the group, each drawing their weapons and preparing to jump to Thrayn's defense. Sebastian tapped his staff against the ground three times, causing a domed shield to form over them. The guards began slamming their swords, hammers, and axes against the shield, but they couldn't break through. Thrayn stepped back, bumping into one of his guards. Elizabeth grunted and shoved the spear into the guard's chest as Balin tossed his axe, killing the last of Thrayn's defense. "Wait. Wait. Wait." Thrayn said, dropping to his knees and lifting his hands. "I don't have the Faerie." Thrayn said.

"Liar." Ava screamed. "I know him. He would never let someone so… valuable escape."

"You did." Thrayn hissed as he glared at the elf. "Ungrateful whore. You had a home. Food. Clothing. All you had to do…"

"Was sell my body." Ava screamed as tears slid down her face. She lifted her skirt, pulling the dagger free and holding it to the dwarf's throat. "You piece of shit." Ava screamed as Anna ran to her side. "I will watch you die… by my hands."

Thrayn laughed as the blade was pressed against his flesh. "Do it then, whore." The dwarf smiled. "Then you'll never find your Faerie." The blade slid along Thrayn's neck, causing a small sliver of blood to slide down Ava's blade. The black-haired dwarf shoved Ava away and reached for his boot. In a swift motion, he pulled an exquisitely decorated knife from his shoe and shoved it into Ava's side. "I planned to kill you after you made me some gold." Thrayn hissed. "But I think I…" The dwarf began screaming as an axe sliced through his elbow, severing his forearm from his body. Ava grunted and pulled the blade from her side. Anna placed her hand on her sister, sending her magic to close the wound. "Shit." Thrayn screamed, watching the guards frantically try to break through the barrier.

"Enough.' Balin barked, lifting the axe from the dirt. Blood dripped from his steel as he shoved the dwarf onto the ground with the head of his handle. "It's clear Feya isn't here and it's clear it wasn't your choosing. She is free. You are no longer useful."

"No. No. No. No." Thrayn pleaded as he held the bleeding stump of his arm. "She… she was taken. A customer. Rich. Young. Gold-red hair."

Jakob shoved his blade into the earth and lifted the bleeding dwarf from the ground. Fire shot from the ground around the blade. Divine writing appeared within the purple and green flames that danced around the steel. Thrayn looked into the young man's brown eyes and felt fear. Hate. Anger. Murder. All of those emotions could be seen in the gleam of the young man's eyes. "How did she escape? Who was this man?"

"Astaad." Thrayn screamed as the fires shot higher around them. "Kylo Astaad, but it wasn't he who destroyed my Palace." The dwarf screamed, flailing in Jakob's grip. Jakob narrowed his eyes to the dwarf as a bright light began to shine in his eyes. Thrayn's face turned pale from fear and panic. The guards surrendered their attempts at rescuing their master, running away from the power displayed by the murderous young man. "It was a man. Wealthy but looked like a beggar. Bandaged arms and head. Probably a soldier or crippled guard."

"Christopher." Anna said, lifting Ava from the ground.

"Where did they go, Thrayn?" Ava said through gritted teeth. The dwarf looked at the once innocent little girl he had held captive. He struggled to breath as he saw the horn protruding from Anna's head as magic began to encircle the Daemon. "You wouldn't let them leave without an idea of where they went."

"I don't know." Thrayn screamed as Jakob tightened his grip around his throat. "He was a monster. Nearly destroyed my Palace." The dwarf trembled as he remembered the encounter with the strange man. "He used magic like I've never seen. He took away the very air. Shook the earth. He must be a dark mage. I never saw a magic circle. I never saw him do anything."

"Oi." Balin whispered to Jakob. "I thought Christopher didn't know magic."

"I didn't think so either." Jakob said, glancing down at his friend. "But Christopher is strange, and clearly been hiding a great deal from us."

"He's the one who took off with the Faerie and two of my whores with the rich man.' Thrayn said, sobbing in Jakob's grip. "He even paid for one of the whores to be free. The Faerie took one of my cooks with them."

Jakob tossed the dwarf on the ground and pulled his sword from the earth. The flames stopped immediately as Jakob sheathed the blade. Sebastian lowered the barrier as Elizabeth stood on his flank. Ava stood silently as she watched the dwarf who was the source of her torment struggle on the ground. Anna placed her hand on her sister's shoulder. "Ava." Jakob said softly. "Whatever you want to do… I understand."

Ava looked down at the panicking dwarf and took a step forward. All her memories, all her pain, continued to flood her soul as she looked at

Thrayn. The dwarf was screaming curses and insults at the elf. She didn't hear any of them. All she heard were the echoes of her torment. The destruction of her childhood. The only words that rang clearly in her mind was *Whatever you want to do.* She knew what she wanted to do. She wanted to feel the heat from his blood dripping from her blade. She wanted to watch the life leave his eyes as he looked at her… his prize whore. Revenge for all the men and women he allowed to force themselves on her. Ava's vision faded. All she could see was the faces of every man that forced her to look at them as they forced themselves inside her. *Elven whore, slut, property, trash,* every demeaning title given to her by the filth of this Gods forsaken world.

The echoing voices began to become clearer with each heartbeat. "Ava." A muffled voice called out to her. "Ava." She could feel her hands trembling. Warmth began to flow up her hands, wrists, and elbows. "Ava." Anna said, her voice breaking through the fog of her mind. Anna began shaking Ava's shoulders, forcing her back out of her mind. Ava blinked rapidly to clear her vision. Thrayn was lying underneath her, motionless with a look of shock on his face.

"Ava." Jakob said, kneeling down beside her. Ava looked at him with tear filled eyes before looking back down at Thrayn's lifeless body. Her hands hovered in blood. Her dagger plunged into the center of his chest. *I killed him.* Jakob lifted her from the ground, her eyes never looking away from the lifeless dwarf. "Ava?" Jakob said as Ava released a breath she didn't realize she was holding.

"It's over." Ava whispered. "It's over." She looked down at her bloody hands before turning to Jakob. "Let's go get Feya." Ava said, smiling at Jakob. 'I have a lot to say to her… and apologize for." Jakob nodded as Ava turned to face the Palace. "I need to check Thrayn's office first. Then we can go."

Chapter 8

The fabric of the tent was thin enough for Feya to see the moon high above the campsite. Christopher had given her his cloak to use as a pillow while Kylo gave the elves his blankets. Thoughts of Jakob and the others ran through her mind, keeping her from sleep. She could hear Kylo still questioning Christiopher while Trung attempted to join in the conversation. It was clear that the vagrant had no interest in entertaining the simpleton. *He would have let him die.* Feya through to herself. The face Trung and the others had made as they struggled for air still haunted her. *Did the others?* Feya thought back to the baths. *Did Miss V and Arys…*

Trung began to snore and mumble in his sleep. She smiled, hearing the simple man talk about fish and buns as he dreamed. Kylo announced loudly to Christopher that he had grown tired of the conversation and was going to sleep. He had spent several hours prying for information from the vagrant, yet, Christopher refused to give direct answers. "Jakob." Feya whispered, as to not wake the sleeping elves. "I'm safe. Kylo and Christopher are going to bring me back to you." She sighed as she closed her eyes, trying not to cry. "I'm sorry that… that I love you. That I caused you so many problems with Ava. I'm… sorry I was stupid enough to get captured." Feya folded Christopher's to be more comfortable. She could smell him on the fabric. She could *sense* the magic he had used at the Pleasure Palace. "Who is he?" Feya whispered, pretending she was talking to Jakob as she looked at Mira deep in sleep. "He… He claims to not know his name. He knows Basilisk magic. His arms…" Feya took a long breath as she rubbed her face. "No. I'm just not thinking straight. Faeries being one with Basilisks is hard enough to believe." Feya pulled the blanket over her head as she welcomed sleep. *Could he be… the Savior?*

As sleep began to consume her… "Feya." A voice whispered in the deepest part of her soul. She tried to open her eyes, but they were heavy. "Feya." The voice repeated. The voice was familiar. Powerful. Dangerous. *Gadreed.* "Do not wake." The Angel of War said. "If you wake, our connection will be broken. I am speaking to you by your connection to the shield." Feya said nothing. She couldn't say anything. Only listen. "Murdok has fallen." Gadreed said. "In his anger of your capture, Jakob drew the sword and my magic spilled into the earth." Feya could feel her heart racing in her chest. *Is Jakob alright?* Feya thought, hoping the Angel could hear her. "Yes." Gadreed said. "Senshe, Basilisk of the Forest was awakened. Long ago, he was turned Draugar by the Devil Lucile. The Devil had returned and claimed her beast. A potential power struggle amongst the Devils could spark war on earth before the child is unsealed."

What? Feya thought, remembering the warning of discord amongst the Divine Christopher had spoken of. "Jakob and the others are in Gosa. The elf girl has slain the dwarf, and they now are searching for you." *Ava… killed Thrayn?* Feya questioned in her mind. "Yes." Gadreed said. "Kylo is the son of the Angel of the Hunt. You will be safe with him. Is the other still with you?" *Yes.* Feya said in her mind. *Christopher is with me, but… Gadreed… is he?* "Yes." Gadreed said hesitantly. "I tell you this only because I need you to gain information from him." Feya could feel her heat trying to burst from her chest after her realization. "He will not travel with you, but you must learn where Anna must go to unlock more memories. He has been observing your progress and knows his only chance to be free is you and Jakob."

Then why does he not travel with us? Why wouldn't he join us? Feya asked the Angel. "The Gods and Devils know of your quest. Lucile has her own game planned for Christopher. It is safer for him to continue whatever it is he is planning on his own. Go to him… now, ask for locations of Alvarome's artifacts. I will reach out to you again."

Wait. Feya screamed in her mind. *Where is Jakob and the others? We left Gosa and…* "Talk to the Savior." Gadreed said. "Have Kylo escort you wherever he sends. We will meet with you there." *But… I am only a few hours away.* "Feya." Gadreed said softly. "You must speak with Christopher. He will sense when Jakob is close. He can smell my blood in him… and he will flee." *I don't understand.* Feya thought. *He is powerful with earth magic. If he fought alongside us…* "He would be discovered, and the Gods would send their Angels in force. Eeus is desperate for his death and the Savior does not trust all who travel in your party."

Feya's eyes shot open and Gadreed's voice ceased to speak. She sat up, realizing Elva and Mira were missing. Wrapping herself in a blanket, Feya exited the tent. Trung slept against a tree, snoring, and mumbling in his sleep. Kylo was sleeping by the dying campfire wrapped in his cloak for warmth. Christopher… was gone, as was the elf girls. Feya frantically searched the camp before realizing a parchment was stabbed into the tree Trung was sleeping under. Feya took a breath, pulling the knife from the tree to retrieve the parchment.

Feya, I cannot accompany you any further. I have taken the elf girls and will be providing them with shelter and coin. You are to head to the Great City of Nupross. Go to the Lake of Endless Fog. Prove to the waters that you are a Faerie. Remember the name Meer.
Safe travels Faerie.
- Vagrant.

"What?" Kylo hissed, angrily styling his hair as he read the tattered paper left by the vagrant. "Bastard. He wants us to go to Nupross? But... your friends are only half a day's ride from here." Kylo handed the parchment back to the Faerie. "This is ridiculous." The hunter screamed, kicking what remained of the campfire. Feya stepped back from the raging hunter. Trung loudly yawned, still struggling to wake from his long sleep. The large man stood from the ground, scratching his exposed belly as he continued to yawn. "I say we go fetch your friends, show them the note, you all head to Nupross, and I can be on my merry way."

"No." Feya said, narrowing her eyes at the hunter. "There must be a reason Gadreed doesn't want me to be with Jakob and the others yet." Feya sighed as Trung stepped closer to check on her. She smiled and nodded to the simple man as he adjusted his shirt. "I told Gadreed we were heading to Nupross last night. Jakob and the others should be heading there as well." Feya shrugged. "If we keep a steady pace... maybe they will catch up."

"Tell me something, flightless Faerie." Kylo said, crossing his arms and raising a brow. "What purpose would I have for going to Nupross? I hunt that which doesn't belong in this world."

"Exactly." Feya hissed. "Who knows what we will encounter on the way to Nupross. There could be creatures from the war. Demons. Angels. Anything. Isn't that what you hunt?" Kylo nostrils flared as he took a long slow breath. "We have run into a number of beasts and Divine on our journey." Feya said softly. "I... we could use your help." Kylo sighed as he rubbed his chin. "What if we find a Basilisk? Or... free the Savior? Wouldn't that be something worth seeing?"

"My father said it was distasteful to hunt something when it's not at full strength." Kylo huffed. "But… it would be something to see the beasts that bested my father."

Trung continued to scratch his bulging belly as he looked curiously between the pair. "Trung don't know who Goodread is." The simple man said through a loud yawn.

"Gadreed." Feya corrected. "He is the Angel of War. He lives inside of my friend Jakob."

Trung laughed as he rubbed his eyes. "Faerie silly." Trung said. "Angel can't live inside friend."

"He does." Feya said, not wanting to recount her entire history to the cook. "If it makes you feel better Kylo, I can pay you for taking me to Nupross." Feya said sarcastically.

"No need." Kylo shrugged. "If I join up… all I expect is to be fed, bathed, and preferably we rest in towns with… lovely ladies." The hunter said with a wink. Feya rolled her eyes as she turned to pack away the tent. "Nupross is a five-to-seven-day ride. If we aim for seven… your friends are likely to catch up." Feya nodded. "Don't bother with the tent." Kylo said. "We can leave them our own note. Hampshire village is the closest settlement. We can… stop there for something to eat and buy supplies. If your friends are coming, we will likely see them before we depart."

"Trung can come with Faerie friend?" The simple man asked as he picked at his nails. "Master Thrayn will be mad at Trung if he come back with no Faerie."

"Of course, Trung." Feya said, not wanting to tell the simple man that Thrayn was dead. "Maybe you can help my friend Balin when he cooks."

"Trung good cook." Trung said proudly. "Master Thrayn always like Trung cooking."

"And what do you plan to do with him if a beast or Divine show up, Faerie friend?" Kylo asked, sliding on his cloak.

Feya thought silently to herself as she slid on Christopher's cloak and lifted the hood. It was still hard for her to wrap her brain around the idea of Christopher... the Vagrant... being the Savior. "We put them down." Feya said. "Like we have done with every other threat that has come our way." She reached for her charm, remembering it was gone. Still lost in the Pleasure Palace.

"You must fill me in on your adventures." Kylo said. "And this Jakob who was powerful enough to wake a sleeping beast."

Sebastian and Balin loaded their weapons into the wagon while Jakob dealt with the head of the city guard. The Gosa guard was opposed to letting the elf sisters enter the palace after cutting down Thrayn, but with only a few words, the guard backed down from the young man. Sebastian wondered what his grandson could have said to make the entire guard stand down after witnessing Thrayn's murder. Yet, part of him didn't want to know. He had seen firsthand what Jakob was capable of and the display of power he demonstrated with Thrayn was enough to terrify the guards. Sebastian thought back to Murdok's destruction. As powerful as everyone thought Gadreed was, no one expected Jakob to be able to wake a Basilisk.

Balin grunted as he leaped down from the wagon. Sebastian smiled as the dwarf cursed while brushing off his shirt. "The elves haven't come out yet?" Balin asked as he walked around the wagon, impatiently waiting to continue the search for Feya. "Wonder what Ava is searching for."

"I don't know." Sebastian sighed. "I'm sure it brings back painful memories for the two of them just being here." Sebastian saw Ava and Anna walking through the palace lobby. Several of Thrayn's *employees* stopped to greet the elf sisters, grabbing their hands, or embracing them with hugs. A tall man followed behind the elf sisters as they exited the Palace. Sebastian tilted his head curiously, realizing the man... was an Angel. "Oh dear." Sebastian said, combing his fingers through his thinning grey hair. Balin turned and scoffed at the sight of the collared Angel.

Ava and Anna approached the mage and dwarf with the Angel following close behind them. "Balin." Ava said softly. "This is Arys. He is an Angel that was bound to Thrayn." Balin puffed his chest as the Angel gave the dwarf a gentle bow. "There is a collar on his neck suppressing his magic... would you remove it?"

"Are you mad, las?" Balin shouted, his face turning red as he eyed the Angel. "After what we have been through with the last bastard Angel, you expect me to just let this one regain its power."

"I apologize for the actions of my kin, young dwarf." Arys said, still bowing his head.

"Keep your apologies, Angel." Balin scoffed. "Can't risk you lashing out at those of us your *kin* seem to be anxious to see in the dirt."

Ava took a long breath and stepped closer to the dwarf. Arys placed his hand on her shoulder, stopping the elf from confronting Balin. "I understand." Arys said softly. "I would not be quick to trust an invader either." The Angel said, stepping forward. "Thank you for freeing us from Thrayn, my little elf friends." Arys smiled as he turned to Anna. "No longer the little elf cowering in her room, I see. You are not truly an elf are you young Anna."

"No." Anna said. "I am the daughter of Alvarome. I'm a Daemon."

Arys smiled, running his finger along the Daemon's horn. "So, you now search for the Savior. The one to seal all Divine back into our realms."

Anna nodded. Arys turned to look at Jakob, who was still standing near Thrayn's body with the city guard. His eyes were glowing, and the Divine writing had appeared on his arms. "Gadreed still lives." The Angel said, rubbing his wingless back. "It would seem the Angel of War is not constrained by the laws of life and death."

"Jakob is Gadreed's blood." Balin said with a huff. "Got incredible strength and power. Best remember that, Angel." The Angel smiled and nodded his understanding.

"Gadreed was always good to me when I was young." Arys said, looking back at Jakob. "When the Divine deemed him a traitor and ordered his execution… I was cast out for voicing my opinion."

"They didn't bother cutting you down?" Balin said, crossing his arms.

"I still had uses." Arys said, looking down at the dwarf. "I wandered the world after the calamity. The mortals saw me and still believed the Gods were watching over them. Even though I wandered due to exile."

"Calamity?" Sebastian asked.

"Yes. That is what the Divine call the day your Savior was born." Arys said. "When the Abomination was born, it was made clear that Kirames and Alvarome intended to assume control of our races." Arys sighed as he turned to face the old mage. "Not all of us believe we should be here… in your world. It is a plague to us. The magic of the Basilisks is incompatible with our Divine magic."

"So why stay?" Sebastian asked. "What purpose would you have to be here if the Basilisks are too powerful, and their magic is toxic?"

Arys shrugged. "I was never privy to such information." The Angel said. "But I know the Divine Eeus was made ill from the spell that changed this world. As was the Ancestral Devil."

"Ava." Jakob said, approaching the group cautiously. "Who is this?"

"An old friend." Ava said calmly. "Yes, he is an Angel, but he is no threat."

Jakob glared at the Divine being before turning to Balin. "Gadreed said Feya is headed for Nupross." Balin lowered his arms as his eyes widened. "He spoke with her. she is traveling with a Nephilim named Kylo Astaad."

"Astaad?" Arys said, rubbing his chin. "The Angel of the Hunt bore a child? I had no idea."

"Angel of the Hunt?" Jakob asked, looking up at the Angel.

"Yes. Astaad was a great hunter. The best even." Arys explained. "When the Gods and Devils collaborated to stall the Basilisks, Astaad refused to hunt them." Jakob tilted his head as he turned to Balin and his grandfather. "Astaad is a man of pride. He would only hunt that which gave him a challenge."

"You said the spell that *stalled* the Basilisks." Sebastian said. "What did you mean?"

"The Gods knew that the spell would not be permanent." Arys said. "Divine races know nothing of Earth magic. When the blending our magic with earth magic, we did not know if it would even work. Some of the beasts still roam these lands. Unseen by mortals until the day the Savior is unsealed."

"Why do they not attack?" Jakob asked. "Demons and Angels still roam the earth. Wouldn't they want revenge?"

"They wait." Arys said softly. "When the Savior is unsealed... they will, once again, be unstoppable." Arys shrugged as he looked at the elf sisters. "But for now, they only focus on protecting the Faeries." Jakob took a breath and stepped closer to the Angel. Arys looked around at the confused faces of the group and nodded as he thought. "I see." He whispered. "Gadreed has not told you."

"Told us what?" Jakob said, resting his hand on the hilt of his sword. "What do you know, Angel?"

"It is like this, young warrior." Arys said. "There is the Divine God, who created the Gods to serve her. Eeus then created us, Angels, to be the servants of the Gods." Jakob's nostrils flared as he listened to the Angel's tale. History of the Divine race told firsthand by a Divine being itself. "Tor, the Ancestral Devil, created his Devils as Eeus did with he Gods. Then Tor created the Demons and Succubus to function as servants for the Devils. Minions of Chaos and lust to fuel their power."

"What does that have to do with the Faerie?" Balin barked, puffing his chest, and crossing his arms.

"If I may?" The Angel said, bowing his head and smiling at the dwarf. Balin rolled his eyes and nodded, gesturing for the Angel to continue. "Shinrahn, the Dragon King." Jakob's eyes opened wider, remembering the name from one of Feya's stories about the islands. "Shinrahn is their Divine or Ancestral being. He created the Basilisks. Each Basilisk is focused on one of Shinrahn's magics. Each Dragon created their own servants to aid them in keeping the world in balance. Peace and order between the Basilisks, Mortals, and natural world. The Faerie. Each Basilisk created their own *tribe* of Faerie whose magic reflects the Dragon they serve."

"So…" Jakob said, looking at the ground as he thought. "Feya… should know the magic of the Basilisk she serves."

"Indeed." Arys said. "Has she not used her magic in front of you?" Jakob shook his head, as did the rest of the party. Jakob explained to the Angel how Feya was ignorant of magic until Kal had taught her. How she had come to the continent in search of magic and the ability to fly. "Strange." Arys said, tugging at his collar. "The spell used to stall the Basilisks was ineffective against the Faerie. They retreated back to the islands where Shinrahn's power still protects them. The reason the Divine races have not touched the islands… is because the Faerie are still capable of using earth magic."

"That… That can't be." Anna said. "Feya can't even fly without the charm Jakob gave her."

"Then she is different." Arys said. "Something about her is not like the others. Not only in appearance, but in magical capabilities. What tribe does she come from?"

"Water." Jakob said, showing the Angel his shield.

Arys bent down to read the protective runes along Gadreed's shield. "Hmm." The Angel said. "Very strange. This rune with Feya's name… it does not say water. But… it is unfinished. Do you see these markings beside her name and title?" Jakob turned the shield as he and the others examined the writing. "These markings are part of various titles. They are unfinished so I do not know what they mean." Arys stood straight, rubbing his hand along his wingless back. "I'm surprised she claims to be of the water tribe. She does not have blue skin or webbed hands and feet."

"Blue skin?" Balin scoffed. "Webbed? What?"

"The Basilisk Oothra is the ruler of the Seas." Arys said. "Her Faerie are capable of body transformations as to swim alongside their Dragon. Feya does not resemble any Faerie I have seen in my years in this world."

Jakob stood silently as he thought, rubbing his hand along the shield over Feya's name. Narrowing his eyes, he looked up at the Angel. "If we release the collar… will you travel with us and tell us all you know?"

Arys bowed his head. "It would be my pleasure." The Angel said. "But… if it makes you feel safer, you may keep my collar on. I understand you see me as a threat, and I do not wish to hinder your journey."

"Why?" Balin asked. "Would you not gain favor by kill us or the Savior?"

"Possibly." Arys shrugged. "But… I believed in Gadreed. I will honor his kindness and help you fulfill his mission for as long as I can." Jakob tilted his head, giving the Angel a curious look. "I am weak, young ones." Arys said. "I have been on this world for so long its magic has caused irreversible damage to my being. I do not know how long I can help you. The closer we get to the Savior, or even if you manage to unseal him, I do not know if I would survive."

Jakob turned to Ava. The elf girl smiled and nodded to the young warrior. "Very well." Jakob said. For now, the collar stays on. I'll let Balin be the judge of when it's to be removed… or if Gadreed has an opinion on the matter." Jakob turned to his grandfather. "Where is Elizabeth?"

"Buying supplies." Sebastian said. "She seems to have made it her responsibility these days to insure we are properly stocked."

"Anna. Ava." Jakob said, turning back to the elf sisters. "Go grab Elizabeth with Balin. Gramps and I will finish readying the wagon with…"

"Arys." The Angel said, bowing his head once again to the warrior.

"Arys. Right." Jakob nodded. "Tell her it's time to go. We are headed or Nupross."

The Sisters were the last survivors in their village of Marion. The village had served as the main settlement of their Commune *Divinity*. Marion was now in shambles as fire raged, leveling every shop and home. The only remaining structure was *Divinity*. A large multi-level stone church the Sisters used to worship and live. The building was not without its share of damage. A large serpent with the power of the earth itself was wrapped around the church walls. The thirty followers of the Sisters watched on their knees as their Wise Women were tied to steaks. A handful of Demons and Several Succubi seemed to enjoy the task of stringing up the elderly women. "Tell me… Sisters." The Devil woman said as she twirled her red hair in her fingers. "Where are your Gods? Why do they forsake you so? Here I am…" The Devil smiled, lifting her taloned hands in the air. The large serpent lifted its head as it took notice of the Devil. "Destroying your sacred village. A village that has devoted itself to the glory of your Gods. Yet… they do not strike me down."

"Fowl Devil." One of the Wise Women screamed from her steak. "You will soon learn… the power of the Gods is…" The Devil snapped her fingers, ordering the great beast to devour the screaming Wise Woman. Panic spread through the young Sisters still watching in horror as the beast fed on the bound woman.

"I grow tired of this world and its ignorant mortals." The Devil hissed. "I think the time has come." The Devil said, turning to her troops. "For all Divine to accept that this world is a lost cause. And…" Lucile smiled, pressing her tongue against her fang. "We might as well strip these beasts of their worshipers before we go." Cheers were sung by the Demon's and Succubi as they praised Lucile's name. Lucile snapped her fingers once again. Senshe tightened his snake-like body around Divinity, crushing the building underneath his massive form. "Each of you." Lucile said as her followers gathered around her. "May take these young ladies and enjoy them for yourselves." The Devil smiled as the young women began screaming and pleading for release. "Do not kill them." Lucile said. "No reason they cannot spread the word of their coming extinction to the rest of the world. Leave the old hags to the beast… he deserves a snack."

The Demon's and Succubi laughed as they separated the thirty Sisters. Senshe uncoiled his body and slithered towards the steaked Wise Women to fee. Lucile watched as her follower's beat and assaulted the defenseless young women. Pleasure filled her as she watched Senshe slowly devour the remaining Wise Women. Every scream from the old women and the pleading cries from the humiliated Sisters fille her with joy and lust. "You are disgusting." A voice said from behind the Devil. Lucile smiled, recognizing the trembling voice behind her.

"You didn't stop me, my Goddess." Lucile said, looking over her shoulder at Gidione. "They are your most devout followers… even though you are not their true God."

"Why not just kill them?" Gidione hissed. "At least show them some mercy."

"Devils are not known for mercy." Lucile smiled. "They will live and the tales they will tell will bring a new fear through this realm… fueling our kin." Lucile turned back to her follower's who were still tormenting the young women. "They will whisper my name in the ear of every woman as they violate them. My power will grow exponentially." Lucile turned back to Gidione and flexed her wings. "They will know the evil that is the Devil Lucile. I will become even more powerful. Gather more followers and finally rid myself of that fool Tor."

"I cannot let you do this." Gidione said as her wings formed behind her. "The Divine God has ordered your games to stop." The sight of the Goddess's wings caused Senshe to turn his attention towards the Divine pair. The snake seemed to snarl as he slithered closer to the Devil. Gidione glared at Lucile, keeping the serpent in her focus. She could feel the beast's power. Feel his anger and bloodlust. "You should return home to Onitara." Gidione said, trying to ignore the growing serpent. "Before I am forced to stop you."

Lucile laughed as Senshe's head hovered over her. "Onitara is not my home, little Goddess. It was but one stop on a journey for more power. Tell me…" Lucile said, stepping closer to Gidione. The serpent's head followed, tilting slightly to keep the Goddess in his sight. "Why would Eeus, in all her wisdom, send you? The most naïve of the Gods." Lucile laughed as her wings folded in behind her. "Too young to know our history. Too ambitious to prove her worth after her sister's betrayal."

"You betray your own people." Gidione hissed.

"Tor has betrayed our people." Lucile said calmly. "So eager to follow his lover that he would doom us all to extinction for a world we cannot possibly rule." Gidione's heart raced as Senshe opened his mouth, exposing his massive fangs still stained by the blood of the Wise Women. "Do you really not understand the position our race is in Gidione?" Lucile said mockingly, as if speaking to a child. "We feed off the fear of mortals. You feed off their praise. Still, we need the magic of the world to keep our immortality." The Devil shook her head. "The longer we stay... the more mortal we become." Gidione took a breath as the Devil began pacing around her. "Surely you have noticed this. Elysian and Onitara are dead worlds. We have been in this world for over a thousand years. Yet, we grow weaker. Mortals can strike down Angels, Demons, and magical beasts." Lucile stopped behind the Goddess, wrapping her arms around her, grazing her stomach with her taloned fingers.

"Eeus will fuel our power until we take control of this world." Gidione said, pulling away from the Devil. "Tor will do the same for you."

Lucile chuckled as she tapped her lips with her fingers. "I sense doubt in your words, my Goddess." Lucile smiled. "You have seen her, the Divine God, haven't you?" Sickly, paranoid, and weak. Tor is no better." Lucile stepped past the Goddess and looked up at Senshe. "You know these creatures have done wonders for this world. They have found the perfect way to keep balance and order. We must do the same in a world that can properly feed us... but this is their world."

"You sound as though you side with the beasts that have killed so many of us." Gidione snarled.

"I am." Lucile said, turning back to the Goddess. "I agreed with Alvarome and Kirames. It was time for us to leave, even before the war. Once the Angel Mela fell to the Faerie, it should have been made clear."

"Mela?" Gidione asked. "What does she have to do with anything?"

Lucile chuckled. "The story the mortals believe is that Dark Mages sacrificed Mela to summon us Devils, but you know as well as I that isn't true. Mela, The Bringer of Death, and bride of the Angel of War, was struck down by the Faerie." Lucile looked up at Senshe as the beast snorted. "A single Faerie." The Devil said. "Tor and Eeus sent many of our kin to their deaths against the Faerie when we first arrived. But when their masters appeared… it was made truly clear we were outmatched. We grew weaker through the centuries. Even while the beasts slept, we could not strike them down."

"Enough Lucile." Gidione shouted. "You wish to turn me against my own, my Divine, I will not turn as my sister did."

"I have learned much from my little spy." Lucile said, biting her lip. "An Angel has joined the ranks of the mortals that search for the Abomination. Arys." Gidione silently gasped as her eyes darted in every direction. "And the child of Astaad. It would seem the bloodline of the Gods has chosen their side. The side of the Abomination. Have you considered… our nephew is the key to, not only restoring this world, but saving our race?"

"You speak madness." Gidione said, her voice trembling. "You do not know what the Abomination is capable of. What if he aims to doom us? Destroy us."

"Which is why I said we must make an ally of him." Lucile smiled. "If he sees the Gods and Devils turning against the two that have caused all these problems, perhaps he will see reason." Lucile stepped forward and placed her hand gently on the Goddess's cheek. "Why not go see them for yourself?" Lucile smiled.

Gidione swallowed hard as she looked into the Devils red eyes. "I would be forced to kill them." Gidione said. "I cannot defy my Divine."

Lucile bit her lip as she leaned in to kiss the Goddess's cheek. "Lilith wouldn't allow that to happen." Lucile whispered. "I still have uses for those mortals. They… will lead me to our nephew and to the salvation of our people."

Hadriel carried the deer he had hunted back to camp. Since the fall of Murdok, Hadriel and Yavanna had searched for Tempests survivors. They had found hundreds of trapped civilians and a few dozen Tempests bodies. In the rubble of their building, they had only found one survivor. Yavanna had managed to stabilize the man but was still unsure if he would survive. The Daemon wanted to go in search of Jakob and the others, despite the fear of facing Jakob's wrath once again. Seeing the power he displayed with Gadreed's sword was concerning. The fear of Jakob losing control again had now become a worry for the Daemon. Ratrek cheered as Hadriel sat the deer near the campfire. The dwarf quickly volunteered to butcher and cook the meat. Yavanna glanced over but quickly turned her attention to healing the wounded Tempests mage. "You seem frustrated." Yavanna said, not looking at Hadriel. "More so than usual."

The Daemon sighed as he sat by the elf mage. "We need to leave and find Jakob." Hadriel said. "You saw what happened. Lucile has taken Senshe. We have been here too long already."

"The people here need our help." Yavanna said. "We can't just abandon them. There could be more survivors… and I have to wait."

"They need you maybe." Hadriel mocked. "I could go find Jakob and get them back on track… and what do you mean wait?"

"How could you get them back on track?" Yavanna asked, covering the Tempests man with a blanket. "He won't stop until he finds Feya."

"Then I help them find her." Hadriel hissed.

"Seems like something you should have done from the beginning."

Hadriel scoffed, looking away from the elf mage. "Why have we been sitting here? What are you waiting for?"

Yavanna sighed as she pulled at her ear. "I must wait for Grandmaster to return." The elf mage said. "He always comes to the Tempests building. Surely, he has heard of the attack on Murdok and is on his way here."

"Grandmaster?" Hadriel chuckled.

"Yes." Yavanna said. "He was here just before Jakob arrived. He is powerful and he too is searching for the name of the Savior."

"You have had me playing hero in this rubble… just to wait for your boss?" Hadriel screamed, standing beside the elf. The Daemon combed his fingers through his white hair in frustration. "You Tempests have been useless for centuries, and I see that hasn't changed today."

"You don't understand." Yavanna hissed. Ratrek glanced over nervously at his arguing rescuers. "Master Christopher… is powerful and has been watching Jakob's progress closely."

Hadriel opened his mouth to argue as Ratrek tossed the first piece of meat over the fire. The flame was extinguished. Only the half-moon lit the forest, leaving them in the dark. Vibrations shook the ground under their feet for several minutes. Hadriel grabbed Yavanna as the elf began to topple over. The campfire suddenly reignited, revealing the wounded Tempests mage and Ratrek had vanished. Yavanna looked around frantically and noticed a piece of the dwarf's shirt was buried in the dirt. "What happened?" Hadriel said with a trembling voice. "Where…"

"Master Christopher." Yavanna said, looking near the campfire. Hadriel turned to see a man with a shaved head. His arms were bandaged, and his forehead was bloody. "Master Christopher, Senshe… he has…" Christopher glared at the elf mage, forcing her to be silent.

Hadriel swallowed hard, becoming nervous at the sight of the stranger. "Why did you not go with them?" Christopher asked the Daemon. "Why did you allow him to level Murdok?" Hadriel's anger overtook him as he displayed his power to the stranger. He took a step forward, ready to confront the strange man. The man tightened his fist, and the Daemon was drug into the ground. Only his head remained above the dirt. Christopher knelt down above the Daemon. Hadriel began to panic as the man's eyes shined bright as he glared at him. The stranger's left eye shined as blue as the moon, while his right shined as red as the fires of hell. "The Faerie is too important to have allowed her capture." Christopher said softly. "I have seen to her freedom, and she is on her way to Nupross as we speak. As is Jakob and the others."

"So, he found her." Yavanna breathed.

"No." Christopher said. "It would not be safe for her to travel with them at the moment." Hadriel looked up at the man with an expression of confusion. "Feya is with the son of Astaad. Once they meet, the Nephilim will know who the imposter is amongst their group."

"What?" Hadriel said, struggling to free himself. The Daemon was unable to move, unable to lift himself free of the earth. "What are you talking about? I have seen their party, there is no…"

"A Succubus travels amongst them, taking the form of a mortal." Christopher said. "Your short sightedness has blinded you to it."

"What happened to the dwarf and the human?" Hadriel asked as he struggled to turn his head to Yavanna.

"Buried. As you are." Christopher said coldly. "They are not needed and were in the way." Hadriel could see the fury in the eyes of the stranger. "Lucile plans for war while you play in ruins. You two are going to the Temple of the Divine God." Christopher said.

"And why would we need to go there?" Hadriel asked.

Christopher stood and snapped his finger. The ground opened and the Daemon was set free. "There you will wait for the Goddess Gidione. She has been spending a lot of time in this realm. Her knowledge of the Gods and their texts will be needed."

"You think a Goddess will help us?" Hadriel mocked. "What could we possibly need with her?" Christopher said nothing as he watched the Daemon pull himself from the hold. Hadriel narrowed his eyes at the stranger, brushing dirt from his clothes. "Who are you?"

"Does it matter?" Christopher said as he looked at Yavanna. Hadriel looked at the bandages along the man's arms. Christopher turned his gaze quickly to the Daemon. "I am but a vagrant."

"I doubt that." Hadriel said, smiling at the stranger. "Your magic… is not Divine. Are you a Faerie?"

"You were on the islands." Christopher said. "Why would you ask that?"

"I was on the volcanic island." Hariel said, crossing his arms. "No Faeries there. Didn't want to be seen, you know. They might have killed me."

"Indeed." Christopher said as he walked over to where the Tempests man was buried. He placed his hand on the soil and the man's cloak lifted from the dirt. Christopher stood and shook off the cloak before sliding it on and lifting the hood. The dark cloak became a light shade of yellow as the Tempests symbol faded away. "Temple of the Divine God. Gidione." Christopher reminded the pair. "She will not agree to collaborate with you… but do not give her a reason not to trust you."

The campfire was extinguished and reignited a moment later. Hadriel sighed in frustration as he saw the vagrant had vanished. Hadriel turned to Yavanna who seemed unfazed by the encounter. "Who the fuck is he?"

Chapter 9

Feya and Kylo passed the days by exchanging stories of their travels. The hunter shared what he knew about the Faerie and the Basilisks from his father's journals but made it clear that Feya was the first Faerie he had ever actually met. Feya had demonstrated some of the water magic Kal had taught her to the hunter. He was impressed by her magical display, only to tell her he would be more impressed if she displayed her natural earth magic capabilities. During one of their stops in a small town, Kylo purchased the Faerie a new set of daggers. Feya ignored the more obnoxious side of Kylo's personality. His desire to hunt and slay beasts like his father did not bother her. his view on coin and women was a different story. Every morning after they had made camp or slept at an Inn, Feya would find the hunter paying his women of the evening. The Faerie was happy that Nupross was only a few hours away. Both Feya and Kylo had agreed that, once in Nupross, it would be best to leave Trung with some coin and send him on his way. They had made the attempt at one of the smaller villages, but there was little work and even less food.

Feya needed to reunite with Jakob. Their mission was too important, and he needed to know that Christopher... the strange vagrant... was the Savior. She doubted he, or the others, would believe her. *Hopefully Gadreed tells Jakob as well.* Feya thought from the box seat of their wagon. Kylo suddenly released one of the reins and lifted his hand. He pulled on the reins, causing the wagon to come to an abrupt stop. Feya turned to protest, but Kylo placed his hand over her mouth before she could speak. He pulled the wagon break and climbed down slowly. Taking cautious steps, he made his way to the front of the wagon. Feya watched the hunter as he tilted his head to each side of the road. Trung groaned as he rubbed his head after bumping it against the wagon wall. Kylo held up a hand, commanding them to be silent. Feya calmed the simple man before climbing down from the wagon herself. She pulled back Christopher's cloak, giving her easy access to her new daggers.

The Faerie looked to each side of the road as Kylo remained in the center. On each side of the narrow road were fields of grass as tall as the hunter. A landscape of blue and grey grass as far as the Faerie could see on either side. Feya narrowed her eyes as she watched the hunter slide his rings on his fingers. He turned to her and gestured to the right with his head. Feya swallowed hard and looked in the ordered direction. Up a small hill in the distance, she could see the grass sway and bend as if something was traversing through the thicket. She unclipped her daggers from her belt and readied herself. Kylo made a strange gesture, imitating how Feya used her pixies, and shook his head. Silent instructions not to summon her magic yet. Feya nodded her understanding then turned to the wagon. Trung was still standing and rubbing his head as he watched the pair in confusion.

The hunter grunted and pointed to the large man, ordering him to sit. Trung scratched his head and laughed at the angered man. Feya softly motioned for Trung to sit but heard movement coming from the grass. Whatever was wondering through the grass on the hill… had heard the large man laughing. Kylo drew a line in the air then shoved his palm forward, cutting a path through the blue-grey grass… but nothing was there. Feya tightened her grip on the daggers, hoping to sense any hint of magical energy. She couldn't sense anything. *Perhaps it isn't a magical beast.* Feya told herself.

The grass began to rustle and bend again as whatever was hiding scurried through. The air became still as the movements stopped. Feya tilted her head towards the grass and could hear whimpering. Not a wounded animal. *A child?* Feya questioned as she listened. The Faerie slowly made her way towards the hunter, who was watching for movement. "Kylo." Feya whispered. "I hear a child."

"I know." The hunter said, shocking the Faerie. "But something else could be out there. If we go into the grass… it could attack from anywhere."

"What about the child?" Feya whispered harshly. "We can't just leave it out there to be a feast for whatever is out there."

"Would you rather us be its meal?" Kylo hissed as he narrowed his eyes to the Faerie. "I'm sorry but… we can't afford to die right now." A small voice called from the grass. Cries asking for help from what sounded like a small boy. Feya turned to the hunter and saw his eyes widen as he looked over her. She turned to see Trung standing by the grass, pulling handfuls of the blue-grey blades away, searching for the child. "What is he doing?" Kylo snarled through gritted teeth. The simpleton stepped into the grass in search of the pleading child. After several heartbeats, Trung stepped back out of the grass holding the injured child in his hands. The young boy was bleeding from his head, and he had a large gash down his arm.

"What happened to you?" Feya asked the boy as Trung approached them.

The boy wiped his eyes with his blood covered hand as he looked at the Faerie. "There was a monster." The little boy said with a trembling voice. "It was big and destroyed my home."

"A monster?" Feya asked. The boy nodded. "What kind of monster?"

"It was a big snake." The boy said. "Bigger than my house." Tears began to fall from the boy's eyes. "Everyone is gone." The boy cried. "The Sisters prayed… but why didn't the Gods help us?"

"Sisters?" Kylo asked, stepping next to Feya. "Are you from Marion?" The boy nodded as he wiped away his tears. "I don't know of any beasts that are giant snakes." Kylo said to Feya.

"Do you remember anything else?" The Faerie asked the little boy.

"A woman with batwings." The little boy said. "Mommy called her a Devil… before the snake…" The boy began crying as he remembered. "Before the snake ate her. I hid in a wagon, but someone took the wagon, and I ended up here."

"Looters must have taken the wagon after the attack." Kylo whispered to Feya. "Marion is a long way from here. They probably found him and dumped him here."

"Trung." Feya said. "Take him to the wagon. When Jakob catches up, Anna can heal him."

"Another passenger?" Kylo said, sliding his rings back into his pockets.

"He needs help." Feya hissed. "We can find him somewhere to go when we get to Nupross." Feya escorted Trung to the wagon as he carried the boy. The Faerie tried to comfort the trembling child. Kylo sighed and followed behind them until they reached the wagon. The hunter climbed into the box seat and began styling his red-gold hair. Feya followed Trung to the back of the wagon as he placed the young boy into the wagon. Feya climbed into the wagon and covered the child in her blanket after wrapping his arm with a piece of cloth. It only took seconds before the little boy was asleep. Trung climbed back into the wagon, rocking it back and forth with his weight. Feya climbed out of the back after covering the child. She closed the canopy, keeping the sun from waking the sleeping boy. As she tied the final string, she heard horses and wagon wheels. She turned to see who was approaching. Her face turned pale as her eyes met the man in the box seat of the incoming wagon. "Jakob?"

Jakob leaped from the wagon before coming to a complete stop. Feya instantly fell into his arms as they embraced. The young man held her close, sliding his fingers through her blue hair. He could feel Feya's tears as she kept her face pressed against his chest. "Feya." Jakob finally said, reluctantly pulling away from her and looking into her ocean blue eyes. "I found you."

Feya smiled, pulling Jakob close once again. "I knew you would." Feya said, her voice muffled as she buried her face against him. The Faerie was quickly pulled away from the young man and lifted into the air. She could feel large arms hugging her stomach and laughed as Balin sat her back onto the ground. "I know you wouldn't leave me either Balin." Feya smiled, turning to the dwarf.

"Aye." Balin said, puffing his chest. "No one messes with our Faerie." The dwarf said, stroking his beard.

"Are you alright?" Jakob asked. "They didn't…" Feya shook her head and smiled. "Good. I'm… I'm glad nothing happened to you."

"Thanks to these two." Feya said, gesturing to the wagon. Jakob watched as a red-blond haired man stepped down from the wagon. "This is Kylo." Feya said as the hunter approached. "He is a Nephilim, and a hunter of beasts. The big guy in the wagon is Trung. He worked for Thrayn but kept me fed." The large man quickly untied the canopy and jumped from the wagon as he saw Ava and Anna walking towards the Faerie.

The elf sisters were shocked to see a familiar face from the Pleasure Palace. The large man picked up the elves in his arms as he embraced them. Ava awkwardly patted the simple man as he sat them back onto the ground. Feya met Ava's eyes and forced a smile, not knowing how to approach the elf. Ava rushed towards her and wrapped her arms around her neck, pulling her into a long embrace. "I'm so sorry Feya." Ava cried.

"I'm so sorry for… for how I treated you." Ava whispered. "Can I ride with you to Nupross?"

"Oh… of course." Feya said. "Anna, there is a little boy in our wagon. He needs help." Anna nodded and followed Trung to the little boy. "I'm so happy to see everyone." Feya said, looking at Jakob. Jakob's wagon shifted and a large man stepped from the back. Feya gasped as she saw Arys giving her a gentle wave. 'I can't believe Arys came with you." Feya smiled.

"I killed Thrayn." Ava said as a soft smirk crossed her lips.

"Well." Feya said, smiling at the elf.

"I think it best we head to Nupross." Sebastian said from the box seat of Jakob's wagon. "If we want to get there before nightfall." The old mage smiled as he looked at Feya. "It is wonderful to see you Feya. Balin has been preparing a menu for when we find you and I aim to have him prepare it." The dwarf puffed his chest with pride as he stepped back towards the wagon.

"I'll ride with Anna and Feya." Ava said, looking at Jakob. The young man looked at Feya then to Ava. "I told you… I have a lot to say to her… and I want to do it privately."

"Well then." Kylo said. "I guess the ladies are commandeering my wagon, so I'll tag along in yours, young Jakob. I'd like to know more about your Gadreed situation."

"Very well." Jakob said, shaking the hunter's hand. "And you can tell me more about the Angel of the Hunt."

"Jakob." Feya accidentally shouted. Everyone turned to her. Elizabeth chuckled as she walked from Jakob's wagon to Feya's, carrying her sack of belongings. Feya waved at the soldier to hide her embarrassment as Kylo eyed the commander. "It's about Christopher." Jakob tilted his head.

"Did the vagrant die?" Balin asked, rushing back to the conversation from the wagon.

"No." Feya said, picking at her nails. "Christopher… is the Savior." Everyone was silent. Balin coughed and rubbed his throat as he awkwardly looked at Jakob. "I know… I know it sounds ridiculous, but he is the one who hired Kylo to rescue me. he was there to help free me and he used magic." Jakob and Balin looked at one another before turning back to Feya. "Powerful magic."

"Not Divine magic either." Kylo added.

"Gadreed." Feya said through ha heavy breath. "Gadreed told me as well. That Christopher *is* the Savior."

"I… I don't understand." Jakob said, turning to his grandfather who was rubbing his chin in thought. "Why didn't he come with us? Why not help us?"

"Gadreed said that we are being hunted by the Divine." Feya said. "That the Savior wouldn't risk traveling with us in case we fail or get killed."

"But…" Jakob stumbled to say.

"I am the son of the greatest hunter the Gods have ever had." Kylo said. "I can sense all Divine magics." Kylo shook his head. "I could not sense his magic… but I felt his power. My rings." Kylo said, showing Jakob his collection of magical rings. "They could feel his power as well… and they feared it. My father was only bested by one type of beast. The Basilisks. I believe this vagrant Christopher knows their magic and the magic of the Faeries."

"Faeries?" Balin said. "So, what the Angel said is true."

Kylo turned to Feya and smiled. "I'll explain all I can on the way to Nupross." The hunter's smile faded as he watched Anna and Elziabeth in the back of his wagon. "She is of Devil blood." Kylo said sternly.

"Yes." Feya said. "That's Anna. She is a Daemon. Christopher's sister and Alvarome's daughter."

"And the other?" Kylo asked with narrowed eyes.

Everyone looked at one another with confused expressions. "That's just Elizabeth." Feya said. "Her uncle… died back in Grahm. So, she joined up with us."

"Hmm." Kylo huffed. Elizabeth's eyes met the hunters and she quickly looked away. Kylo clicked his tongue as he turned to Jakob. "Let's get to Nupross." The hunter said, his expression becoming more cheerful than suspicious. "Got to find an Inn, A bath, and some women."

Ava rolled her eyes and pulled Feya towards the wagon. Kylo laughed as he followed Jakob towards his own wagon. "Will you be joining us?" Jakob asked. "To unseal the Savior's magic and free the Basilisks?"

"It would seem so." Kylo smiled. "We are heading to the Great City of Nupross. We are going to visit the forbidden lake. The lake of never-ending fog. Something interesting is bound to happen."

Four Demon's stood at the gate of Lucile's temple in Onitara. Each Demon had a single braid in their hair that wrapped behind their ear and draped over their shoulder. The braids were dyed red with blood, representing their loyalty to the Devil Lucile. The Demon's were large, even by Divine standards. The four looked down at the Angel standing in front of them that was demanding entrance into the Devil's temple. Two Succubi sat in a large window looking down at the Angel, whispering insults to one another. Emanuel took a slow breath and flared his nostrils as he looked at the guarding Demon's. "I demand an audience with the

Devil Lucile." Emanuel snarled, causing one of the Succubus to laugh out loud from the window. "By order of the Divine God and the Goddess Gidione, I demand an audience." The ground began to rumble as the Angel spoke. A large tail dropped to the ground from the right wall of Lucile's temple. Emanuel looked at the slithering tail, following its trail up to the temple's peak. He narrowed his eyes as he saw the head of the creature. "So, this is Senshe the Taken." Emanuel said, meeting the creature's gaze. "A simple snake."

"Then strike him down." One of the Succubus shouted from the window with humor. "Show us the might of your race and strike down what your Divine fears so greatly."

Emanuel watched as the creature exposed his fangs. His front two fangs were twice… maybe three times taller than the Angel himself. The large gate to Lucile's temple slowly opened, revealing the Devil herself on the other side. Emanuel scowled as he looked at Lucile in her transparent red dress. "Stand down boys." The Devil said as she sensually rubbed her Demon's chest. "Gidione's little pet won't cause any trouble… that Senshe can't manage quickly." The Devil gestured with her chin for the Angel to follow her as the Demon's stepped aside. Emanuel looked up at the Succubi who were biting their lips and giving him a gentle wave as he entered. "Has Gidione become so cross with me she has sent you instead?" Lucile asked as she turned gracefully to the Angel.

"I am here of my own accord." Emanuel said, tilting his head. "Tor and Eeus have given strict orders for both Gods and Devils to remain in their realms. What has ignited this act of rebellion in you Lucile? The Abomination must be…"

"Silence Agnel." Lucile said, twirling her fiery red hair in her fingers. "The Abomination is of no concern to me… as I have explained to Gidione. Saving our race is what we must focus on." The Angel crossed his arms and narrowed his eyes at the half-dressed Devil. "Eeus and Tor are dooming us, Angel." Lucile said harshly. "Surely you feel the decay in your immortality… or are you too young to know how powerful you truly can be?" Emanuel took a slow breath, knowing the Devil spoke true about their power. "This world." Lucile said, shaking her head and pointing to the window high on the wall. Emanuel turned and saw the Basilisks eye peering into the chamber. "This world is theirs. Their magic strips our power and their mortals have lost faith in you Gods."

"So, you plan to strike fear?" Emanuel asked. "Rekindle their faith in the Gods?"

"No." Lucile smiled, placing her hand on the Angel's cheek. "I aim to rekindle their fear in the Devil Lucile." Emanuel shoved the Devil's hand from his face and stepped back. "I will become more powerful, rally the Devils, and overthrow that old fool Tor. I will bring the Devils back and we… and the Gods will find the perfect world in which to rule."

"Eeus will never agree to such things." Emanuel hissed. "The Divine God is…"

"Just as foolish as Tor." Lucile interrupted. "She is weak and will only continue to weaken. The Basilisks will be freed, the Abomination will awaken, and we will all be doomed." Emanuel scowled as he listened to the Devils words. "But." Lucile said, holding a finger up to the Angel. "If I control the Devils and say… Gidione assumes control of the Gods." Emanuels face turned red with each word the left the Devil's lips. "We can find a world in which both our kin can rule. The perfect world. With balance and order. The way these magnificent creatures have ruled this realm."

"Tor will have your head for even speaking such words." Emanuel said.

"Will he?" Lucile mocked. "I have been incredibly open here on Onitara about what needs to be done. Alvarome and Kirames did the same. The only difference is… I am stronger than my brother." Lucile leaned down to face the Angel. "And if my nephew joins me… there is nothing Eeus or Tor could do to stop me."

"You would awaken the Abomination?" Emanuel said, stepping back from the Devil. "You would doom us… for temporary power?"

"Temporary?" Lucile laughed. "You Gods are too short sighted. You do not see the big picture. The spell is breaking. The Dragons will awaken once again. The mortals will unseal the Abomination." Lucile shrugged. "We simply need to make him an ally. Eeus and Tor are the true villains in this realm. They are the ones who brough war and corruption to the earth, locked away his power, forcing him to live amongst this world being forever hunted."

"Gidione will never turn on the Divine." Emanuel said, crossing his arms and puffing his chest. "She is more loyal than her sister."

"For now." Lucile said, smiling as she pressed her tongue against her fang. "What of you, Angel? How many of your kind were forced to fight a foe that the Divine God knew you could not slay? I do this for my kind. The ones who fell to the only Gods our race has never been able to defeat."

"And where do you see this… perfect world?" Emanuel asked.

Lucile smiled. "We will have to wait." The Devil shrugged. "We wait on Elysian and Onitara. As you know, we are unable to search for other realms, since our power has depleted since the war."

"And what makes you think we cannot defeat the beasts or their Faeries?" Emanuel asked, tilting his head curiously.

Lucile's smile widened, knowing she had swayed the interest of the Angel. She looked out of the window, gesturing for the Angel to look with her. He obeyed. "Go fight him then." Emanuel quickly turned to eye the Devil. 'Senshe was gravely weakened when I turned him. Now, he would be the weakest of the Basilisks. Weaker than even his Faerie. Test your might against him. Even when I found him… he nearly killed me before the infection took hold."

Emanuel sighed and rubbed his chin as he looked at the angered beast outside the temple walls. "How will you convince Gidione?" The Angel asked.

"With the help of a Daemon." Lucile smiled.

Chapter 10

The Nupross guards were not what Jakob and the others had expected. Several men and women with simple leather armor greeted them with hard stares and stern faces. Nupross was a human dominated city. No other races lived inside the Great City's walls. Not for prejudicial reasons as Jakob and the others realized, only the strong and *proven* were welcomed in the city. Each guard was lean but muscular with half shaved heads and intricate braids. Feya and Ava stood behind Jakob as a woman with a scarred face approached, shoving the guard he was speaking to aside. "What brings ye to Nupross, travelers?" The woman said in a thick accent after spitting on the ground. "Don't see many… nonhumans wishing to visit the city of the proven."

Feya gripped Jakob's arm as the woman eye her with her sapphire eyes. "We wish to visit the lakes." Jakob said, keeping his eye on the scarred woman. The woman's blue eyes never looked away from Feya, twirling her blond braids between her fingers. The Faerie slid behind the young man, hoping the guards prying eyes would focus on Jakob.

The scarred woman scratched her ear as she cleaned her teeth with her tongue, sliding her attention to Jakob with narrowed eyes. "Do you now." The woman said with a vicious smirk. "Names Gweneth. Captain of the Guard and three times Proven."

Gweneth turned her head and eyed Feya. Jakob took a step forward, sliding the Faerie behind his back. "You keep saying that word." Jakob said, looking down at the slender captain. "Proven how?"

Despite Jakob's approach of their captain, the other guards didn't make a move. Seemingly unthreatened by the party attempting to make entry into their city. "It's how one earns their stay in these walls." Gweneth smiled as she looked up at Jakob. "One does not simply *live* in Nupross. You must be worthy of Nupross." Gweneth shouted as she extended her arms. Her guards began slamming their fists against their shields as they chanted battle cries. "Centuries ago." Gweneth said, seeing the confusion on Jakob's face. "Nupross was raided by Demons. Only we humans refused to give up our homes. Our city. Our way of life. We fought the Devils minions until the fled, but not before the Draugar were unleashed on our eastern wall." The guards slammed their fists against their shields once again. "We sealed off the eastern side of Nupross. Many brave souls ventured into the abandoned streets, seeking glory or death against the Draugar." More fists against more shields echoed through the still Nupross air. "To this day, we judge our people by *The Trial*. You train, you learn, then you venture into the forgotten city within our walls."

"You send your people to fight the Draugar?" Sebastian said, rubbing his chest. Jakob looked at his grandfather, still concerned about the day he too would turn. "Your young. Do you aim to destroy your people?"

The Nupross guards slammed their steel against their shields while chanting. "You must survive the Trial and become Proven." Gweneth shouted. "Show our Chief that you are worthy of being Nupross. You traverse the streets. Slay the Draugar. If you survive the week, you return to the gate and are given your mark and your braids. If you fall… your soul keeps watch of the city from the Fog as your body prepares to test the next to be Proven."

"So, you send them to their deaths." Anna said, eyeing the other guards and seeing their scars, markings, and braids.

"We Nuross build our strength by climbing atop our dead." Gweneth said. "May a thousand fall for the strong to climb higher." The captain turned to her guards and gave a single nod. The guards stepped aside, giving the impression of permitted entrance. "You wish to visit the lakes?" Gweneth said, smiling at Jakob. "The Lake of Endless Fog, I assume." Jakob took a slow breath as he looked down at the captain. "You must Prove yourself… before we allow you to touch such sacred ground."

"Jakob." Ava whispered harshly. "It's suicide." The elf eyed the captain before turning back to Jakob. "What if something happens… like Murdok?"

"We have to." Jakob said through a heavy breath. "Very well. We will prove ourselves."

"It has been nearly two hundred years since a nonhuman has participated in the Trial." Gweneth said, looking at Balin and the other races. "And it will be a first… that a Faerie has participated." Gweneth turned to Anna as she gestured for the group to enter the city. "Or… a Daemon." Anna swallowed hard as Gweneth examined her horn from a distance. "Who was your Devil parent, Daemon?"

"My name is Anna." The Daemon hissed. "Alvarome was my father."

"Father of the prophesied Savior." Gweneth said, nodding her head. "Then you must be powerful, and we hope to have great tales of the dead you return to the grave."

"You are not bothered by a Daemon?" Jakob asked.

Gweneth motioned the group on, walking with them through the city gates. To everyone's surprise, the city was masterfully crafted and well kept. The Nuross natives seemed hardened and only interested in combat and glory. The Great City was more beautiful than any other village or city Jakob had seen. Even the master craftsmen of Murdok would have been in awe of the human dominated city. "We do not fear the Gods and Devils as the rest of the world does." Gweneth said. "We welcome them only as challenges to test our strength. We have bested Demons and Angels, preparing for the day that the Divine reignite their war. Nupross will not fall, and we will prove that even the almighty races can fall to the hands of mortals."

"A bold statement." Kylo said. "You must have powerful mages in your ranks as well."

"We have no need for magic, Nephilim." Gweneth said, shocking the hunter as well as the others. "We have dealt with your kind as well. Using nothing but our pride and our might. What other mortals could say they have been hardened as us Nupross. When the season of storms come, the sky herself show us her ferocity."

"Season of storms?" Balin asked.

"Three months." Gweneth said. "Three months of relentless storms, lighting, snow, ice, heat, and fire." The captain looked up at the clear blue sky as she led the party further into the city. "The sky shapes us, hardens us, like a smith forges a blade."

"Aye." Balin said, looking at the great buildings of Nupross. "How has your city remained standing all these centuries?"

"The Great Cities were built to stand the test of time." Kylo said over his shoulder.

"Untrue." Gweneth said. "Nupross has fallen a number of times to the Season of Storms. We rebuild, we endure, we grow stronger."

"Sounds like a living hell." Arys said, rubbing his neck.

Gweneth turned to look at the weakened Angel and smiled. "Oh no, Angel." The captain smiled. "Hell would be too soft for us Nupross." Gweneth turned and pointed to a large building across the stone street. "You will lay your head at the Inn. We do not have regular visitors, aside from merchants, so take your pick of rooms. I will speak with the Chief, and he will ready the Trial." Jakob nodded to the captain. "Enjoy your stay in Nupross, travelers. May you find victory on the battlefield… or in death."

Jakob turned to the others, gesturing with his chin for everyone to head to the Inn. Elizabeth led the horses towards the Inn, tying them off near the trough. Trung pulled the second wagon next to Elizabeth. The simple man struggled to keep the horses under control, but the commander was able to calm them as she tied them off. "I don't see them welcoming our two friends." Elizabeth said as Jakob passed. "The simpleton cannot survive this environment and the child will be forced to be Proven when he is older."

"I know." Jakob said, rubbing his chin as he leaned against the wagon. "I didn't expect the citizens here to be so…"

"Human." Elizabeth said with a smile. "I've heard stories of Nupross. People call them savages. Brutes. They seem to be living better than most." Elizabeth said, looking at the architecture.

"Those who manage to live." Jakob said with a sigh. "Suggestions?" Jakob asked, looking at the commander and his grandfather. Balin stepped in beside Elizabeth as Anna, Ava, and Feya went in search of rooms.

"We should take the child and… Trung to the village we passed a few hours back." Elizabeth said. "Those who are needed should stay for the Trial and head for the Fog."

"Is that wise?" Jakob asked.

"Aye." Balin said, stroking his whiskers. "Elizabeth is right." The dwarf said, crossing his arms and puffing his chest. "The child needs medical attention… and a home. Trung would only slow us down."

"I am inclined to agree." Arys said. "And with this collar." The Angel said, pulling at his neck. "I fear I too would be a hinderance in your trial."

"You're not just trying to escape, are you Angel?" Balin said with narrowed eyes.

"Not at all." Arys said, bowing his head. "The Village is only a few hours away. If the Trial is to be set for tomorrow, or possibly longer, I shall return in time to be Proven."

"I will take them." Elizabeth said, looking at Jakob. "I can ride us there faster than the simpleton and I will make sure the Angel comes back. Whether he wants to or not."

Balin took a long breath as he tugged at his beard. "But we could use your skills in the Trial." The dwarf said, not wanting Elizabeth to depart.

"I believe I can have us back before then." Elizabeth said, biting her lip and winking at the dwarf. Balin's face turned red as he twirled his whiskers in his fingers. "I couldn't bare to be gone from my little dwarf for too long."

"You jest at me, woman." Balin said, his smile widening. "You make it back and I'll show ya I aint nothing to jest at."

"Oh, I'm sure." Elizabeth said, winking at the dwarf before turning to Jakob. "If we all stay, it is likely they will force the Angel and Trung to take part. Trung will die and I don't want to deal with a Draugar Angel."

"You think so little of me, warrior." Arys said, tilting his head at the commander. "I was a mighty soldier in my time."

"Your time has passed." Elizabeth said coldly. "You do not even have your wings, Arys." Elizabeth turned to Jakob and sighed. "This is all Christopher's doing right? You have dealt with him more than I have. You and the others need to get to the Fog. If there is something there… It will likely only be you to find it."

"I should go with Elizabeth." Sebastian said. Jakob turned quickly to his grandfather with a disapproving look. "I may seem better… but we do not know my true condition. It would be best to keep Arys and allow me to go with the others."

Jakob looked at his grandfather and saw the fear in his eyes. A small city filled with Draugar. Filled with reminders of his fate. A fate that no one can predict. Sebastian forced a smile to his grandson and Jakob did the same. "Alright." Jakob said. "Gramps and Elizabeth, you two will take Trung and the child to the village. We will participate in the Trial. If you make it back while we are in the Trial, see what you can learn about the lakes."

"You heard him, big guy." Elizabeth said, looking at Trung sitting in the box seat. Trung smiled from his lack of understanding. "Keep a bed warm for me." Elizabeth said, rubbing her hand along Balin's shoulder. "Better not die out there."

"Aye." Balin said, his voice trembling. "Best believe we dwarves know our way around a battlefield… and a bedroom." Elizabeth laughed as she climbed into the box seat next to Trung and took the reins. Balin untied the horses as Sebastian climbed into the back of the wagon with the child. Jakob and Balin watched as the wagon made its way back out of the city. The Nupross guards seemed uninterested in the departing wagon, laughing as they passed through the city gates.

"Splitting up again?" Kylo said, peeking around the doorframe of the Inn. Jakob turned, noticing the hunter's curious expression as he watched the wagon. "I think we should talk, Jakob." Kylo said, looking at Balin and Arys. "In private."

Feya shook off the dust covered linens of the Inn's bed. It was obvious that Nupross doesn't receive visitors. There was no one to distribute keys or even accept payment for the rooms. Feya assumed even the merchants only stopped in Nupross for quick sales and purchases before leaving the city with haste. The Nupross natives were a hard and unwelcoming people. It was easy to understand why outsiders didn't come to the Great City of Lakes. After dusting off her bed, Feya began cleaning the rest of her room. She had chosen a room on the second floor next to the stairs. she didn't want a lower-level room, thanks to her time at the Pleasure Palace. The stairs were old, and every footstep seemed to echo through the entire multi-level Inn. This gave her a sense of safety, knowing when someone was approaching her room.

Her mindless cleaning was simply an act to keep her body moving while her mind thought back to Ava. It was nice seeing her and it was even better that she greeted her with such a warm embrace. During the wagon ride, Ava apologized for her attitude and outbursts back in Murdok. She also apologized for stealing her charm in a fit of jealousy. In her pocket, wrapped in cloth, Ava had returned the charm and chain. The elf had found her necklace, along with her pixies, in Thrayn's office. Seeing the charm had brought Feya to tears during their ride to Nupross. Feya paused her cleaning and held the amethyst charm in her hand, enjoying the cold feeling of the chain.

The topic of conversation that had left Feya feeling torn… was what Ava said about Jakob. During his recovery and with Feya's capture by Cole, Ava had been struggling emotionally. The idea of returning to the Pleasure Palace had filled the elf with fear. When they arrived in Gosa, and she felt the heat of Thrayn's blood on her hands… the long fear that had plagued her soul vanished. In her moment of clarity, she realized the truth. A truth that Anna had told her… and Feya. Ava cared about Jakob, but she didn't love him. He was a good man to her and protected her. keeping her from the clutches of the dwarf that would sell her body. Feya was silent as Ava talked to her in the wagon, but the words she said before the guards approached still rang in her mind. "It is you he loves, and you need to tell him."

Ava had given her blessing to Feya, but the Faerie didn't know how to handle the situation. She had told herself back at the Palace that she would confess everything to him. Her love. Her desire to be bonded with him.

Now that the opportunity was there, she didn't know why it seemed so hard. Perhaps she thought he would deny her before, using Ava as an excuse. Now, there was a chance he would accept and want the same. The idea of him loving her as well sent fear and excitement through her. *Now is not the time.* Feya told herself after realizing she had been cleaning the same window for several minutes. *Not with the Trial coming.* She sighed as she looked out the window. Jakob was standing underneath her window speaking with Kylo.

Footsteps echoed from the stairs along with the sound of a crate being dragged across the floor. A gentle knock came from her door as it slowly opened. Ava stepped into the room with Anna, both pulling their clothing crate into the room. Feya smiled and welcomed the sisters as she saw Balin go in search of his own room. "Brought you your clothes.' Ava said softly. "Thought you might want to change out of the Palace's attire." Feya smiled as she looked down at her clothes. She had all but forgotten she was still wearing the outfit from Kylo's *session.* A far too revealing top with an uncomfortably short skirt. "You pull it off well though." Ava said with a smile.

"Thank you." Feya said, feeling her face turn hot. "I'm not use to showing so much… skin."

"I bet Jakob enjoyed it." Ava said. "Have you spoken with him yet?" Anna turned to her sister with a soft smile, happy that Ava had grown past her pettiness and jealousy. Feya shook her head as she pulled at one of her ears. "Nervous?" Ava asked. Feya nodded silently. "Don't be, Feya. Jakob loves you. If you want, I can make it clear to him."

Feya laughed softly as she looked out the window to see Jakob. "I don't know how to tell him." Feya admitted. "I have never… wanted someone before. I ran through it so many times in my head back at the Palace… but now that he is here…"

"Do it when you feel it is right." Anna said. "No need to feel forced."

"What is Kylo and Jakob talking about?" Feya asked, still looking out the window.

"I don't know." Ava said, stepping towards the window. "I know your hunter friend thinks highly of himself." Feya turned to Ava with a wide smile. "He seems to think of himself as a gift to women."

"He's taken notice of you then." Feya laughed.

"He has tried." Ava chuckled. "I told him by bunkmate will be my sister. I have no need for his company."

"His love seems more transactional." Feya sighed. "Always looking for good food, soft beds... and lovely ladies. But I still think he is a good man."

"well, he can search elsewhere." Ava said, leaning her head on Feya's shoulder. The pair stood by the window, trying to decipher what Jakob and Kylo were discussing. "I really am sorry, Feya." Ava whispered. "I wish I could go back and change my actions. I have done so much to protect myself and Anna... I shouldn't have seen you as an obstacle. I'd like... I'd like to really be friends."

Feya wrapped her arm around the elf girl as her wings fluttered softly. "I never had a sister before." Feya smiled. "I'd like to have two." She said, looking back at Anna. The Daemon smiled and joined in the embrace. "I'm just glad that we got a fresh start. Thrayn is awful."

"Was." Ava said. "He *was* awful."

Jakob listened as Kylo seemed to talk about everything but whatever he genuinely wanted to say. The hunter voiced concerns about the Trial, about the Angel Arys, or what could be waiting for them in the Fog. Jakob propped himself against the wall of the Inn and crossed his arms, waiting for the Nephilim to get to the point of their secret conversation. Kylo smiled as he noticed Jakob's growing frustration and combed his fingers through his red-gold hair. "I see you are not one for small talk." Kylo said. "I am new to this motley crew and do not want to offend… but should I get straight to the point?"

"That would be ideal, yes." Jakob shrugged. "We need to get prepared for whatever this city is going to throw at us. The Trial isn't my only concern here. The people seem just as dangerous."

"I agree." Kylo said, rubbing his chin as he looked around the empty street. It was clear that most Nupross natives lived further into the city. The only buildings near the city gates were the Inn and a few empty shops. All masterfully crafted but still unused. "How well do you know your party, Jakob?" Kylo asked.

"Very well." Jakob said. "Until now. We have some fresh faces. Including yours."

Kylo laughed as he pulled his rings from his pockets. "These were my fathers. They hold his Divine power as the Angel of the Hunt." Jakob looked at the rings, Kylo even allowed him to hold and wear a few of them. Jakob could feel the power of the Angel in the rings, but their power paled in comparison to the Angel of War. "With these rings, and my father's blood in my veins, I can sense all Divine life." Kylo explained. "I knew before seeing her that Anna was a Devil Daemon. I can sense Gadreed's blood in you and your grandfather. Along with the power of your shield and sword." Kylo shrugged. 'Arys… obviously an Angel just by appearances."

"Yes." Jakob said with a heavy breath. "All things that I am aware of."

"Elizabeth." Kylo said, his eyes narrowing at the young man. "You say she joined you after your… dealings in Graham. How certain are you?"

Jakob grew impatient with the hunter." What do you mean?" Jakob asked, taking a step towards the Nephilim. "It is obvious she joined us. She has been traveling with us for some time now."

Kylo shook his head. "The woman who rode off with the wagon… is not a human, Jakob." The hunter said, biting his lip nervously. "She does not smell human. Her stench is familiar. I do not understand how Anna has not noticed. Or Gadreed for the matter." Jakob dropped his arms and tilted his head as he listened. "I believe." Kylo said. "The Elizabeth you met in Graham… is dead."

"What?" Jakob hissed in anger.

"Listen to mc Jakob." Kylo said, his expression was hard, and his eyes seem to gleam with concern. "You and your crew have been blind to this, and it would seem her volunteering to leave was an opportune moment for her. Elizabeth…" Kylo said, taking a long breath. "Is a Succubus. They have the ability to take the form and retain the memories of those whose life they drain."

"You think Elizabeth is a Succubus?" Jakob said, rubbing his head.

Kylo shook his head. "I do not think… I know." The hunter pointed to the ring Jakob was holding. "Wear this when she returns if you want proof. The ring will allow you to see the truth. When Elizabeth returns… you will see her form as I have."

Jakob looked at the ring as he slid it on his finger. "You're sure?" Jakob asked nervously. Kylo nodded. His thoughts went back to Elizabeths constant disappearing from camp or venturing into cities in search of supplies. *Did you know this, Gadreed?* Jakob asked in his mind. The Angel didn't respond. *Your silence is answer enough.*

"I will not spread this to the others." Kylo said. "You are their leader, and it is not my place to make that call. I just wanted you to know that the Devils seem to have an interest in you and what you are doing."

"If she is a Succubus." Jakob said, still looking at the ring. "Why not just kill us? If we are to unseal the old magic… it doesn't make sense to keep us alive."

"It must be the Devil she serves." Kylo said. "The Devils are a fickle bunch and seem to have their own ways of thinking. Perhaps, they too are interested in the Savior."

"For what?" Jakob asked, shrugging his shoulders. "He is as much a threat to them as the Gods."

"I have never had the pleasure of dealing with a Devil." Kylo said with a smile. "Perhaps, traveling with you, I might get the opportunity."

Balin sat on an overturned bucket hammering his axe against his anvil. He had tossed his belongings in a room near Feya's. knowing she was back relieved the dwarf, but his sense of failure back in Murdok still haunted him. Had he been stronger, faster, more alert, perhaps Cole couldn't have taken her in the first place. Those were the thoughts that still stained his mind. Part of him hated that the mercenary had managed to scurry away, but he knew it was more important that Feya was safe. He slammed his hammer against his axe, wishing the steel was Crimson Cole. He slammed the hammer against the steel again, taking out his frustrations out on his axe. "Bloody Bastard." Balin shouted as he brought his hammer back down against the axe. A crack broke through the steel, chipping the tip. Balin's nostrils flared in anger. Not with his now ruined weapon, but at his sense of failure in Murdok. In his anger, he tossed the axe to his side and set the hammer on the anvil.

The dwarf stood and let out a grunt of frustration. He stepped into the Inn, shouting to those who could hear him that he was heading into town. Arys heard and acknowledged his leaving with a bow. Balin stormed off, venturing further into the city of Nupross. In a city defined by their strength and weapons, he knew there had to be a worthy smith with supplies. He ventured on towards a busier part of the city. Humans in various styles of armor were walking along the streets. Each of them eying the dwarf with judgmental glares. After passing several streets, Balin found what he thought was the market. Buildings filled with goods from food and clothing to weapons and armor stretched along the street. Still, he did not find a smith. Balin approached a group of citizens who were sitting outside a market building. Balin puffed his chest as he approached them. A dark-haired woman, smoking something that smelled fowl, turned to him, and smiled. "A dwarf." The woman said, looking at her companions. Each of the three women wore the same hard expression that had greeted them at the city gate. Unlike Gweneth, these women were thin with softer features. Though, by the city's reputation, he knew these women had proven themselves by the Trial. "So, you are one of the travelers who wish to become proven are you not?"

"Aye." Balin said. "I am searching for a smith to purchase supplies for a new axe."

The women seemed stunned by the dwarfs' words. "We do not forge here in Nupross." One of the other women said as she tossed her red braided hair over her shoulder. "We use the weapons passed down by our ancestors." The dark-haired woman drew her blade, revealing an ancient sword with markings not seen for centuries. Balin scoffed as the woman held the blade to him. "Are you amused by something dwarf?" The red-haired woman asked.

"Aye." Balin laughed, tugging his beard. "As fine as these weapons are… obviously forged by master smiths, it has no place on the battlefield." The dark-haired woman sheathed her blade and spat on the ground near the dwarfs' feet. "If there is one thing, we dwarves know." Balin said, pointing to the hilt of the woman's blade. On the handle of her sword was a symbol, a dwarven stamp of approval. "We know our weapons. If you ladies could obtain me an axe or short sword, I would be happy to repair those blades and give them new life."

"You mock us, dwarf." The red-haired woman hissed after taking a hit of her smoke. "You are an outsider. Unproven. Unworthy of even seeing our steel."

Balin shrugged dismissively to the woman. "How would you breathe life into our blades, dwarf?" The dark-haired woman asked. "They have slain plenty, and their edges are sharper than your dwarven wit."

"Aye." Balin said. "Yer blade is sharp, but could it be better?" The women passed curious glances to one another. "I find it strange you do not forge your steel in a city known for its strength."

"Many arms vendors make stops in Nupross." The dark-haired woman said. "We are always provided excellent steel… when we require it."

"Have you ever wielded a sword forged by a master dwarf." Balin asked, twirling his whiskers. The women said nothing. "I need a weapon and you have nothing to lose from my offer. Let me show you the difference a dwarven kept blade can make."

The dark-haired woman smiled at the dwarf as she took a hit from her smoke. "I have not known a dwarf before." The woman said, licking her lips. "Very well, dwarf. I will bring you what you need to forge yourself a weapon worthy of the Trial, and you will use your dwarven skills to improve my family sword." Balin nodded as he crossed his arms. "And… since my curiosity is being peeked." The dark-haired woman said softly. "If I am impressed by your craft… you will be rewarded by… my curiosity."

"You are quite a negotiator." Balin said, smiling at the woman. "Your name, las?"

"Brenna." The dark-haired woman said. "I am Brenna. Twice proven. I will see you… and your party at the Inn. It will not take long to gather what you need. We Nupross… have more weapons than citizens."

"Of that." Balin laughed. "I do not doubt."

Chapter 11

Yavanna sat by the fire, watching the duck Hadriel had caught cook over the fire. The Daemon angrily paced around the forgotten temple of the Divine God. A long-forgotten relic of the past now surrounded by a thicket of shrub, forest, and vines. Thankfully, Hadriel possessed the ability of flight. Without an aerial view, it would have been impossible to find the crumbled ruins of the temple. Hadriel mumbled curses as he paced around a collapsed wall. He had flown them to the temple, on Chrisopher's orders. Days had passed and the Daemon was growing impatient with waiting. He had made his opinions clear about the mysterious Christopher. Yavanna would try and calm the Daemon, explaining his wisdom and strength. Still, it did nothing to ease the Daemon's nerves.

Along with the frustration of making camp at an old relic of the past, Hadriel worried about Gidione, his mother's sister. If the Goddess simply decided to strike them down, she could without a second thought. As powerful as Hadriel was, he knew the pair would stand little chance against a Goddess. "Will you sit down." Yavanna snapped, growing tired of his mumbling and pacing. "I am not enjoying the idea of being here anymore than you."

"I find that hard to believe." Hadriel said as he sat down heavily next to the elf mage. "You seem eager to follow any order given by that strange man."

"Christopher is wise beyond even your years, Hadriel." Yavanna said through a heavy breath. "But that doesn't mean he wouldn't' send us into danger. I saw how he killed Ratrek and my Tempest mage."

"They were in the way." Hadriel said, eyeing the elf. "So, your Grandmaster says."

"Something is happening." Yavanna said, looking at the roasting duck. "I don't know what, but something is coming, and he is watching closely."

"Who is he?" Hadriel asked after taking a calming breath and rotating the duck. "He seemed to care little for the Tempests or the fact that the city was left in ruin."

"Tempests have different leaders in different locations." Yavanna said. Her mouth was watering as she watched the duck cook over the fire. They had lived off berries and bugs for the past two days. Luckily, a flock of ducks had flown over, and Hadriel had managed to catch a decent meal. "I was the leader over the Murdok headquarters, but we are gone now. Christopher is in control of all Tempests. Yet only the leaders of the Tempests even know about him."

"Why the secrecy?" Hadriel asked. "With so many hands at his disposal, finding the Savior's seal would have been easier."

"He saw those not powerful enough as a waste of time." Yavanna said, forcing a smile. "The Tempests have yielded little results over the past centuries. No one has been closer to the truth than Chrisopher."

"So, he is aware of Jakob and Feya?"

"Yes." Yavanna said, turning to the Daemon. "He knows them. Has talked to them. He is watching their progress closely. Which is why he was so angry about Feya's capture." Hadriel pulled the duck from the fire and separated the meat, handing a leg to the elf mage. Yavanna accepted the meat quickly and bit down into the steaming duck. Yavanna chewed with her mouth open, in an attempt to cool the meat as she ate. Hadriel laughed as he watched the elf struggle with her feast. "Don't laugh." Yavanna said, trying not to smile. "I grew tired of bugs and berries. Not all of us can go weeks without eating."

"Very true." Hadriel smiled. "I think I would sooner starve than eat whatever beetles you ingested." Yavanna stopped chewing and narrowed her eyes at the Daemon. "But that's me." Hadriel grinned, wiping juices from the elf mages lips with his thumb. Yavanna turned away in embarrassment, wiping her face with her sleeve.

A strong fluctuation of magic broke the pair from their meal. Hadriel quickly stood and turned, knowing the familiar magic that had just arrived at the temple. He could feel his heart pounding in his chest, working its way up his throat. Taking a deep breath, he tried to calm himself as he watched his aunt step around the crumbled wall. Gidione's eyes narrowed, and her face contorted into a scowl as she saw the Daemon and elf mage. She combed her fingers through her long white hair and sighed. "What brings an elf and my sisters spawn to this temple?" Gidione hissed as she watched the elf toss what remained of her duck onto the ground. "I doubt." Gidione said slowly, eyeing Hadriel. "You would come here... unless you wished to be found."

"It is not common for the Gods to step foot on the mortal world." Hadriel said, crossing his arms. Gidione tilted her head and closed her eyes in frustration. "We are here to see you, dear aunt Gidione."

"Do not presume to think of me as family simply because my sister shot you from her womb." Gidione snarled.

"Fair enough." Hadriel said with a shrug. "We aren't here to cause you problems."

"Then why are you here?" Gidione said, resting her hands behind her back. "Do you wish to side with the Divine God, Daemon? Choose your kin over this world."

"Eh." Hadriel said, bobbing his head. "More... wanting to know if you would help us."

Gidione's face flushed red as she looked down at her nephew. "Help. You." The Goddess said softly. "You think me a traitor like my sister?"

"It's all a matter of perspective." Hadriel said, trying to hide his nervousness behind a false air of confidence. "Mother thought she was doing what was right... you see otherwise."

"You are just as much an abomination as her half breed child." Gidione hissed. "What help would you ask of me? Speak quickly and you may leave here with your life."

Hadriel's eyes widened as he turned to the elf mage. Yavanna shrugged, not entirely sure what to tell the Goddess. "You see." Hadriel said, scratching his cheek. "I don't really know how you can help." Gidione's face turned a new shade of red as she dropped her hands to her side. "We were... asked to come see you."

"By whom?" Gidione snarled.

"A vagrant." Hadriel said, forcing a smile. "He seems to think you can... bring a positive change to this world."

"I plan to." Gidione said with venom in her voice. "By striking down those who wish to protect the Abomination."

"It is hard to protect someone you haven't found." Hadriel said. "Centuries of searching and still I haven't found him."

"So, you claim." Gidione said.

"I wouldn't be speaking to you if I had." Hadriel said in almost a whisper. "The world is becoming more dangerous, Gidione." Hadriel said after taking a long breath. "Lucile has reclaimed her pet. Who knows what she is planning. She was always... ambitious."

"I am aware." Gidione said dryly. "I have spoken with the Devil."

"So, the Gods are aware?" Yavanna asked, breaking her silence. "She could threaten, not only the mortal realm, but your realm as well."

"Lucile has no reason to attack Elysian." Gidione hissed, looking down at the elf. "You mortals should be more focused on getting back in the good graces of the Gods, instead of searching for a false savior."

Hadriel licked his lips as he thought. Christopher had said that Gidione would not side with them. He only needed to give her a reason not to distrust them. "What if…" Hadriel said, rubbing the back of his neck. "Unsealing him is the only way to find him?" Gidione turned to Hadriel with a look of distain on her face. "He has been without his magic for a thousand years. If he is unsealed, it is likely going to take time for him to cope with the sudden shock of magic. That might be the only chance you have to strike."

"You would doom the one you have been searching for?" Gidione asked. "I see through your words, Daemon. I am not a fool."

"No." Hadriel said. "But I speak the truth. What other way do you have to find him? The seal on the Basilisks is growing weaker, meaning the Divine and Ancestral are growing weaker. If they are no longer bound to the earth magic that seals him, perhaps they would become whole once again."

"You speak as much madness as Lucile." Gidione said, looking away from the Daemon.

"So, you know what she is planning?" Hadriel said, a soft smirk crossing his lips.

"Matters of the Divine do not concern traitors." Gidione said. "I expect you two to be gone from here when next I return." Hadriel bowed his head, secretly feeling relieved. "Enjoy your… bird." Gidione said. The Goddess turned as a portal opened behind her. "All three of you are considered abominations in the eyes of our kin." Gidione said without looking at the Daemon. "Do not expect mercy if we should meet again, nephew."

"Better finish your duck, Yavanna." Hadriel said, pulling at his hair after Gidione stepped through the portal. "Christopher didn't say we needed to wait a second time."

The march of several warriors echoed through the empty streets leading up to the Nupross Inn. Jakob rushed from his room and ran down the stairs. Before reaching the bottom step, the door slung open, revealing Gweneth and a small militia behind her. Jakob slowly stepped off the last step as Gweneth gave a venomous smirk to the young man. She stepped aside, as did the small army waiting outside the Inn. An older man with salt and pepper colored hair walked towards the door. He was dressed in leather armor with a cape made of animal pelt. By his entrance and the army accompanying him, Jakob surmised this man was the chief of Nupross.

Jakob took a short breath, trying to calm his nerves from the strange morning wake up. The chief entered the Inn and looked at Jakob with his only good eye. Jakob noticed a thick scar running from the top of the chief's forehead to the bottom of his chin. The chief eye Jakob. The young man was barefoot, shirtless, and only wearing his pants. The chief stepped closer to Jakob and pulled his sword from his belt. The sword remained sheathed as the chief pointed the tip of his sheathed blade towards Jakob's stomach. "You have known battle." The old man said, pointing to Jakob's scar with his sword. Jakob nodded his head as he looked into the chief's only working eye. "What foe have you this trophy."

"An Angel." Jakob said. "He had been hunting me and my friends for some time. Whenever we bested him, he fled."

"Until he could flee no longer." The old man said with a half-toothed smile. Jakob nodded. The chief laughed, followed by several of his men. "The weak do not survive in Nupross. We are forged by blood. Those who shy away from death are not welcome here." Jakob's face became hard as the chief eyed him for several heartbeats. "But I can see you are not one to run from death."

"No." Jakob said calmly. "I am too close to my goal. Too close to be keeping a promise to a friend."

"For one to be a strong warrior." The old man said. "You must have strength, honor, wisdom, and the respect of those who follow you." The Nupross warriors began slamming their fists against their chests. "I am Chief Nupross." Jakob tilted his head in confusion. "I am ten times proven. One must sacrifice to be chief of the most powerful city in all the realm. I have sacrificed my body, my soul, my very name to be the protector of my people."

"You have done the Trial ten times?" Jakob asked.

"The Trial proves you are worthy of the title you wish to hold." Chief Nupross said. "As chief, I offer myself to the Trial after every one hundred are proven."

"Bold." Kylo said from atop the stairs. Jakob looked back and sighed at what he saw. Kylo was naked, aside from his revealing trousers. "Should a chief really throw himself into the fire so often?"

"It is an honor to relive the Trial. Though, it is not as often as one might think." The chief said, as he eyed the hunter. "You are the Nephilim Gweneth told me about.' The chief said, turning to Jakob with a soft smirk. "You travel with many of Divine blood, I hear." Jakob gave the chief a single nod. "Angels, Nephilim, Elves, Daemons, and dwarfs."

"And a Faerie." Feya said, shoving Kylo aside as she stepped down the stairs.

The chief's eyes widened as he saw the Faerie. Feya's wings fluttered as she stepped next to Jakob. "I have seen much in my life. My eyes have never seen a Faerie. Truly this trial will be one to be sung about."

"So, we will be participating in the Trial?" Jakob asked.

"Indeed." Chief Nupross said. "You aim to go to the Lake of Endless Fog. The resting place of our fallen souls."

"Greetings grandfather." A woman said from atop the stairs. Jakob sighed as he turned, seeing a dark-haired woman descending the stairs.

"I see Brenna has taking a liking to your group." Chief Nupross said, turning to Jakob. The young man swallowed hard as he turned to face the chief.

"Don't look at me." Kylo said, scratching his stomach. "I, unfortunately, knew an empty bed last night."

Brenna showed her sword to her grandfather. The chief studied the blade and admired the alterations that had been made to their family sword. Jakob took a stunned breath, realizing who the chief's granddaughter had spent her night with. "Fine craftsmanship." The chief said, handing the blade back to his granddaughter. "I see we must procure ourselves a dwarf smith for ourselves."

"I wouldn't mind us keeping the one we have found." Brenna said, eyeing the stairs as Balin stepped into view. the dwarf was stunned at the sight of so many warriors around the Inn. "The sword he forged for himself is truly a masterpiece as well. Perhaps the merchants have been… neglectful in acquiring worthy weapons for our people."

"Aye." Balin said, causing Jakob to sigh in frustration. "A proper tribe of warriors such as yourselves should have a master smith."

"Are you offering your services, master dwarf?" Chief Nupross said with a raised brow. "If you survive the Trial, we could build you a forge."

"A tempting offer." Balin said, puffing his chest proudly. "But my place is by the side of my friends. We are on a mission of importance."

"I see." The chief said, rubbing the stubble on his chin. "And what mission would be of such importance a dwarf would deny a forge or a beautiful woman?"

"Unsealing the Savior." Feya said.

"Ah." Chief Nupross said. Murmurs and laughter came from the crowd of warriors standing behind the chief. "The Savior of the mortal realm. The one to return the Gods resource to the world and send the Devils back to hell."

"So, some believe." Feya said, crossing her arms. The chief could not hide his curiosity by the Faerie's words. He gestured for her to continue. Feya turned to Jakob and the young man shrugged, allowing her to make this decision for herself. "The Savior is sealed away by the Gods and Devils. They fear him."

"Why would the Gods fear the one to defeat the Devils?" Gweneth asked from the chief's flank.

"Because they don't belong on this world." Feya said. "When the Savior is unsealed, the true Gods of this world will return."

"We do not judge those of opposing beliefs." The Chief said. "Strength is what matters to we Nupross. Show us your might. Show us your ability to survive, and you will be allowed access to the Fog." Jakob bowed his head to the chief. "On the condition… that Brenna joins you at the Fog." Jakob looked up at the chief, his face was hard as he eyed the young man. "The Fog is the resting place of our fallen. Even if you survive, you are ignorant of our ways. Brenna will see that you do not do anything to disturb their rest."

"I will join them in the Trial as well." Brenna said. "If I am to be the one to guide them to the Fog, let me be tested by the Trial beforehand once again."

"A worthy reason." Chief Nupross said. "The Trial will take place when the sun is high tomorrow." The warriors began slamming their fists against their chests. "Find glory in victory, Travelers. Or find victory in death."

"Let us hope it isn't in death." Kylo said as he gracefully strode back to his room.

Jakob watched as the chief and his warriors departed from the Inn. Brenna remained standing next to Balin, sensually rubbing his shoulders. "Let us discuss your strategy, Jakob." Brenna said. "And see what we are working with for the Trial."

Sebastian struggled to catch his breath as he fell to one knee. He had volunteered to travel with Elizabeth to find a new home for Trung and the injured boy, he didn't expect to find a Devil waiting with her troops in the village. The old mage lifted himself to his feet with his staff as a sudden surge of pain struck his chest. The old pain that had been absent for weeks. The Draugar infection. The pain of his shattered left arm was nothing compared to the pain of betrayal he was seeing. The Devil stepped towards the wounded old man, kicking him back onto the dirt. Elizabeth stepped beside the Devil, smiling at the old mage as she stroked the Devils waist. The old mage gasped for air as he felt the bone in his arm dig into his muscle. He watched, stunned, as Elizabeth stretched her neck and released her magic. Sebastian felt cold running through his veins as he saw the young commander who had traveled so far with them… was a Succubus. The Devil combed her fingers through the purple hair of the Succubus as her bat-like wings expanded and flexed. Tears began to pour from the old mages eyes as he watched a Demon toss the injured boy into the mouth of Senshe. The beast was much smaller than he was in Murdok, but still just as vicious.

"Did you enjoy the life I granted you?" The Devil said as she stood over the mage. "Lilith asked me to enchant that lute, giving your grandson a clearer mind as he searched for my nephew." Sebastian scowled at the Devil and Succubus. He noticed another Devil off in the distance, watching Basilisk devour the young boy. A devil with hair as yellow as the noon sun with a single braid strained red with blood. "Do no fear, mage." The Devil said as she tossed her hair over her shoulder. "We will not be slaying your grandson... or the others in your party." Sebastian could feel his heart pounding through as the Devil brushed her finger along his chest. "I still need them to find my nephew. But..." The Devil said with a venomous grin. "You are no longer needed. Letting you turn will add a sense of fury and fear amongst your party. They will know the Devil Lucile. They will fear me, and I will grow even more powerful. The fools that led us to this foul world will fall and I will assume the role of Ancestral... before claiming the throne of all Divine."

The Succubus laughed as Sebastian felt the Draugar infection flowing through his body. His hands began to burn as the flesh on his fingers started to rot and turn stone-like. Heat rushed through his body as he felt his life begin to fade. "Do not worry Sebastian." The Succubus said. "You will see Jakob again. Though, he will be forced to slay you as a Draugar." Sebastian groaned in anger and pain as the skin on his back burned away. A metallic taste lingered on his tongue as blood streamed from his mouth. "Do be sure to give him the staff, my love." The Succubus said sensually to the Devil Lucile. "It will let the others know... that the Draugar they slay... is Sebastian."

"Ergren." Lucile said, looking at the Devil over her shoulder. The yellow-haired Devil turned and appeared next to Lucile instantly. He bowed his head and held his fist by his heart. "Turn the large one. make him a Draugar worthy of Gadreed's might." The Devil Ergren smiled as he pressed his tongue against his fangs. He lifted a finger, causing Trung to levitate and be pulled towards him. Sebastian watched helplessly as the Devil shoved his finger into the heart of the simple man. Trung screamed in pain as his body hardened like stone. Trung's body enlarged as two arms formed from his shoulders. His eyes shot out with fire as his cries turned into roars. Sebastian reached out his hand and opened his mouth to scream but was taken by the darkness as his soul no longer inhabited his body.

"A perfect pair." The Succubus said, examining the two Draugar's awaiting their commands. "This is sure to cause enough turmoil to draw out the Abomination."

"Indeed." Lucile said as she leaned down to kiss her Succubus. "You have done wonderful, Lilith. Now, tell me, you have seen my nephew before?"

"Yes, my love." Lilith said, not wanting the Devil to pull her lips from hers. "He travels the world as a vagrant named Christopher. The Faerie has discovered he is your nephew. He is the Abomination child." Lucile smiled as she stroked Lilith's cheek. "The Nephilim and Faerie say he is powerful in the ways of earth magic. We must be careful if we find him."

"We do not need to seek him out." Lucile said, turning to Ergren. "The time is not right. We must strengthen our forces against Tor before we try to move on my nephew."

"This is why you keep the mortals alive?" Ergren asked.

"Yes." Lucile said, licking her lips as she looked at the Devil. "They have gotten closer to finding him than any Divine in a thousand years. Let them continue on their journey and find him." Lucile turned to her Succubus and pulled her in for another passionate kiss. Their tongues me and Lilith moaned with pleasure as Lucile gifted her more of her magic. "You must return to them." Lucile said, pulling away from the Succubus. "You will tell them of my attack on the village."

"Must I?" Lilith pouted. "Is these Draugar not enough? They could think me dead. Killed in your attack."

"I still need your eyes." Lucile said, her tone turning harsh. "I do not know what they plan to find at the lakes of Nupross, but it is information I need to know." Lilith sighed but agreed. She took a long breath and flexed her neck as she took the form of Elizabeth once again. "You will go on foot, claiming to have lost in battle against my forces." Lilith looked up at the Devil. "So, you must look the part." Lucile smiled as she struck the Succubus with her taloned hand. Ergren struck Lilith across the face, nearly removing one of her ears. Lilith didn't scream or cry as the beasting continued. She only smiled, willing to suffer whatever Lucile demanded as long as she was her Devil.

Lilith struggled to stand after the beasting from the pair of Devils. Ergren turned to the Draugar, ordering them to head towards the Great City of Nupross. With the added command of allowing Lilith to reach the city first so the Succubus can warn Jakob of his grandfather's death. Lucile smiled as she gave her farewell kiss to her beaten Succubus. Lilith savored the Devil's taste before turning to stagger her way back to Nupross. A few hours ride now turned into over a day's walk. The Draugar remained where they stood, waiting for the time for them to begin their own journey towards the Great City. Lilith turned on last time to see Ergren handing the turned Sebastian his staff. The Succubus smiled, hoping to savor the anger and heartbreak she would witness from Jakob and his party and the sight of the slain mage.

Chapter 12

The air was humid and felt thick with every breath. Plant life not seen on the continent since the Gods War flourished in the climate of Les Island. The trees stood taller than any building and were nearly as wide. Vines hung from the branches like temple chandeliers. Each vine with its own shade of violet and orange with the smallest of flowers guiding the eye up the tree. Strange foliage covered the ground. Strangely colored grass and shrugs with leaves as large as dwarves made traversing the thicket nearly impossible. The sound of rain hitting the treetops was soothing. The thick roof of vines and leaves kept the coming storm from muddying the forest floor. As peaceful as the rain, wind, and soft sounds of wildlife were… Christopher was listening for a different sound. He turned, eyeing an ancient tree with blue and grey bark. He narrowed his eyes as he stood motionless. The bark seemed to move and shift. Halfway up the tree the blue-grey bark changed into a soft brown. A male figure dropped down, bow and arrow in hand. Several other male figures dropped from the tree in front of Christopher. The first male fluttered his wings, a silent order to the others to surround the stranger.

Christopher watched without moving his head as he was surrounded by a Faerie patrol. The vagrant focused his gaze on the first male Faerie. His soft brown skin was covered in black tribal markings of the Forest Basilisk. The Faerie male approached Christopher, sliding his bow over his shoulder, and returning his arrow to his quiver. The Faerie stood tall in front of Christopher with a face harder than stone. Suddenly, the Faerie smiled and offered his hand to the vagrant. Christopher extended his hand, grabbing the Faeries forearm as they other armed Faerie approached and welcomed their long unseen ally. "It has been ages, Canna." Christopher said, smiling up at the Faerie.

"Centuries." Canna said, wrapping his arm over Chrisopher's shoulder. "I sense you have mastered your earth magic." The Faerie said. 'But I see from your appearance… you have not managed to unseal your power."

"No." Chrisopher said. "I haven't. Gadreed's descendant is on the path, and I believe he will be the one to discover my name." Canna smiled as he nodded. The Faerie whistled, causing several other Faeries to drop from the surrounding trees. "There is a Faerie on the continent." Christopher said. Canna looked at his men before eyeing the vagrant. "She is not a typical Faerie. She is fair skinned and short in stature."

"She does not sound like any Faerie I have heard of." One of the other Faeries said, combing his fingers through his long green hair. "What tribe does she hale from?"

"Water." Christopher said. "But I do not believe she knows the truth." Canna and the other Faerie looked at Christopher with curiosity. "Gadreed's shield offers her protection. It says she is of the water tribe, but she does not have the complexion of Oothra's tribe and Gadreed's runes are incomplete."

"Strange." Canna said, rubbing his smooth chin. "You have a theory?"

"Her magic…" Christopher said, looking at the group of Faerie. "Is sealed, but… when I have been around her, I sensed Shinrahn."

"Impossible." Another of the Faerie shouted. "Shinrahn has created no tribe. His tribe are the Basilisks, he has no need to create a Faerie tribe of his own."

"It is possible." Canna said, silencing the other Faerie. "Shinrahn did awaken almost a year ago for a short time."

"Then perhaps he senses the coming situation." Christopher said. "Which brings me to why I am here."

"Yes." Canna said. "You were never one for a friendly visit, were you?"

Christopher smiled as he stepped away from the Faerie. "Senshe has awakened, and Lucile has come to reclaim him."

"We know." Canna said with a heavy breath. "We pray for the day that his body may be put to rest."

"The egg is still safe then?" Christopher asked.

"Indeed." Canna said, looking out into the thicket of the forest. "Senshe's soul waits for his body to finally return to the earth so he may be reborn anew." Canna turned to Christopher with a somber expression. "Will Gadreed's host be able to slay Senshe? Or will you be forced to do it yourself?"

"It was Jakob who woke Senshe." Christopher said, after a long pause. "I do not believe he is ready to take on Senshe. Our best chance to free him from his hell would be to slay Lucile herself."

"If she doesn't bury you first." Canna said with a smirk. "After all these centuries, do you plan to challenge the Divine?" Christopher's silence was answer enough for Canna. The Faerie and his tribe had helped raise the child of prophecy since Senshe was taken. They had played, trained, and prepared for the day that Christopher would return order back to the mortal world. Return order back to the Basilisks and Faerie. "What is your next move?" Canna asked, resting his hand on Christopher's shoulder. "You are always several moves ahead, but I am sure Senshe's awakening has shifted your thinking."

"I have sent Jakob and Feya to Nupross, to the Fog." Christopher said. "It is my hope Feya's magic can be unlocked. Or, that Meer can confirm her true origin."

"I have not seen the Bringer of Storms in centuries." Canna said, looking to the sky hidden above the trees. "I yearn for the day that we may repair this world. I wish to see the skies filled with the true Gods. The Seas being controlled by Oothra. And Shinrahn…"

Christopher looked at his longtime friend, seeing the pain in his eyes and hearing the hurt in his voice. "I see no young." Christopher said in a poor attempt at humor. Canna forced a smile as he rubbed his eye.

"We have no need for children." Canna laughed. "Or women to produce them." Christopher smiled, knowing well that the gender of each tribe of Faerie are determined by the Basilisks they serve. Canna, and the other Forest tribe Faerie, were all male. "What need to immortals have to bear children?" Canna said with a smirk.

"The Divine seemed fit to shove me from their loins." Christopher said dryly as he eyed his friend.

"There are…" Canna said, embracing the Savior child. "Exceptions. Sometimes." The Faerie held Christopher close to his chest as he would his own child. Canna rubbed his hand along Christopher's shaven hair and felt the burns along his arms with his other hand. "I am ready for your suffering to end as well, my friend." Canna said. "You deserve your freedom." Christopher sighed, hoping for the day he will truly know who he is. "Come." Canna said, gesturing to the forest. "Let us enjoy your company… before you disappear again."

A large crowd had gathered around to watch those entering the Trial. Cheering, along with some taunting, came from the Nupross natives as they looked on at Jakob's party. Several insults were slung towards Arys. The once slaved Angel seemed to pay little attention to the crowd as he felt his magic flow through his body freely. Jakob had removed the Angel's collar, allowing the Angel to fight and defend himself at full strength. Or what strength he had left. Many men cheered for Ava, promising to make her return worthwhile if she survived. The elf girl ignored the lust filled cheers as she gripped the bow Jakob had given her. Brenna stood by Balin, wielding her freshly maintained blade, eager for the title of three times proven.

Jakob turned to Feya, noticing her eyes were fixated on the sky above Nupross. The clouds were turning dark as the midnight sky over the Draugar infested section of the city. The entrance to the Draugar sector was sealed off by a large wall with a single gate. The only way to reach the gate was over a wooden bridge that crossed over a seemingly bottomless pit. A strong safety measure in the event of a Draugar escape. "The storms are speaking to you." Chief Nupross said softly as he stepped towards Feya and Jakob. "The souls of our fallen are going to be watching."

"A week is bad enough." Feya whispered to Jakob. "But if a storm comes…"

"A coming storm." Chief Nupross said, looking to the sky. "Signifies the Trial will be difficult. That the souls of the fallen will test you quickly and mercilessly themselves." Jakob sighed as he turned to the chief. The old man didn't look away from the storm as he closed his eyes to listen to the rumble of the storm. The chief inhaled the cool air of the coming storm as a strong gust of wind blew over the city. "One day." The chief said. "The thunder commands it. You will be tested like I haven't seen since my father was seven times proven."

"So, we survive a day?" Balin asked, looking to Brenna. The dark-haired woman smiled and winked at the dwarf. "What is so different about a Storm Trial?"

"All life fears a good storm." Brenna said. "But a Nupross storm… is vastly different. Your subconscious fears will feed the Draugar and make them more powerful and resourceful." Jakob and Feya turned to the dark-haired woman slowly. "Have you faced a Draugar, warrior?" Brenna asked Jakob.

"A few." Jakob said, turning his attention back to the darkening sky.

"There are more than a few." Chief Nupross said with a large smile. He shouted a command to the guards by the gate as they opened the pair of wooden doors. "Fight. Triumph. Survive." Chief Nupross shouted. Cheers and chest pounding filled the air around the gate. "We Nupross have bested the Trial with nothing but our honor and our steel. Let us see if you will be welcomed to the Fog with your magic, young Jakob."

Jakob felt the bridge shake as his foot stepped onto the first plank. Thunder roared as if the storm was announcing the start of the Trial. Lightning struck the Draugar infested streets like rain as the party made their way across the old wooden bridge. Jakob stepped through the threshold of the gate and saw a city long forgotten. Toppled buildings, collapsed roads, nothing like the thriving city on the other side of the pit. Between the rumbling of the thunder, groans could be heard through the streets. Arys was the last to step through the gates before they were closed and locked behind them. The group turned and saw the chief and Gweneth looking out over the city from atop the gate. Jakob turned back to the ruined city, gesturing for the group to follow behind him.

The young man led the group through several streets, working their way strategically through alleys and buildings. Brenna was silent as they navigated the Draugar city. She was two times proven and knew the streets, but this Trial was Jakob's. He and his party wanted to visit the lake of Endless Fog. A high-pitched squeal shot through the empty street. Jakob tugged at Feya, pulling her against a nearby wall. The others followed suit as Jakob peeked around the corner. A lumbering creature appeared from a half-collapsed home. The Draugar was larger than the ones Kalross had summoned. The creature had one long horn and skeletal wings incapable of flight. "Spirits." Brenna whispered as she peeked around the corner with Jakob.

"A Demon." Arys said, without breaking their formation. "He must have fallen to your people some time ago… and was turned by the Draugar horde of the city."

"I wasn't aware the Demons could turn.' Anna said, turning to Arys.

"Neither was I." Arys said with a heavy breath.

"Some of the turned have been here since the Gods War." Brenna said, returning to Balin's side. "Back when the Devils and Gods were at their peak." Brenna said, smirking at the forgotten Angel. "What is our plan, Jakob?" The dark-haired woman said, still wearing her smirk.

The creature stood in the center of the street, seemingly looking at nothing. The Draugar tilted its head and made several clicking sounds from its throat. Groaning began to fill the air as several other Draugar appeared from their hiding places. Draugar with the form of fallen men and women of Nupross stepped around the Demon Draugar as he turned towards Jakob's corner. The Demon Draugar roared as a beam of dark magical energy shot from its mouth. Jakob leapt from the corner, brandishing his shield. The beam struck Gadreed's shield and was absorbed into the Divine steel. *Do you require my assistance?* Gadreed asked in Jakob's mind as the dark magic faded. Several of the humanoid Draugar ran towards the party. Feya gripped her charm as she took flight over Jakob. Followed by her pixies, she commanded them to attack the incoming Draugar. *Jakob?* Gadreed asked as Jakob wrapped his hand around the hilt of the sword. "No." Jakob whispered. "Can you just… give me some power without taking over?" Jakob swung his shield against an incoming Draugar. The creature staggered back as Brenna and Balin lunged their blades into the chest of the creature. As the Draugar wailed in pain, it turned to ash, falling to the ground. *Very well.* Gadreed said as Jakob pulled the blade free of its sheath.

Two Draugar fell and turned to ash before hitting the ground from Feya's pixies. Brenna swung her leg, toppling another as Balin severed its head. Arys and Anna combined their magic to force the Demon Draugar to the ground. The creature struggled against the pull of the gravitational magic and prepared to launch another dark magical beam. Ava quickly took aim and struck the Demon Draugar in the jaw, freeing it from the Draugar's skull. Kylo drew signs in the air, trapping several Draugar in unseen shackles. Gadreed's magic shot through Jakob's body. His arms began to ache from the heat of the Angel of War's magic running freely through him. A single swing of the blade through the air is all it took. The shackled Draugar were split and turned to ash as the Divine magic sliced through their bodies. Jakob turned and nodded to Anna as he pointed to the Demon Draugar with his sword. The Daemon gave a single nod, shifting her fingers into another sign. The creature was lifted into the air as Arys used his magic to pull the Draugar towards Jakob. Kylo drew a line as Jakob swung his blade. The former Demon's arms separated from its body as Jakob felt the force of his blade strike the Draugar's body. Heat left the walking corpse as every inch of flesh turned to ash from touching Gadreed's blade. *The Head.* Gadreed screamed in Jakob's mind. The young man quickly turned and severed the creatures head from its neck.

What Draugar remained turned to ash as the Demon Draugar turned to dust on the ground. "Spirits of the fallen." Brenna said through heavy breaths and a wide smile. "You lot know how to put on a show." Jakob didn't respond as Feya landed beside him. She held out her hand, commanding her pixies to return back to her side. Lightning struck the ground for several heartbeats. Each crack of the strike seemed to summon more of the Devils minions. "The fallen are preparing for another wave." Brenna smiled. "You lot might earn your braids yet."

"Aye." Balin said, puffing his chest and resting his sword on his shoulder. "These minions are nothing compared to Angelus."

"Jakob." Ava screamed as she ran from her perch. "Jakob." The ground shook as one of the buildings collapsed behind the elf. Debris and steel fell from the structure towards the fleeing elf. Kylo stepped forward, drawing signs with each step. Suddenly, Ava was lifted from the ground and pulled towards the hunter. The elf slammed into Kylo as the hunter turned to protect her with his body. Jakob lifted the shield, summoning a magical barrier around the party. The building finished its descent, slamming into the barrier and the earth. Ava buried her face in Kylo's chest as she tried to catch her breath. "Something…" Ava muttered.

The ground shook again as a monstrous Draugar appeared from under the fallen building. "Gods Hammer." Balin shouted as the giant creature stood tall over the party. "What in the realms name is that?"

"A Colossus." Arys said with a look of horror. "A beast created by the Gods during their raid against the Basilisks.' Arys stood motionless as he looked up at the beast. "When the last Colossus had fallen… the Gods called on the Devils to aid in their war."

"What?" Brenna hissed. "What nonsense do you speak Angel?"

"We don't have time to give you a history lesson." Feya shouted. "We have… bigger problems. How do we slay it?"

"I don't know." Arys muttered. "Only the Basilisks have bested these beasts."

Jakob shifted the hilt of Gadreed's sword in his hand. He took a long breath as he looked up at the Colossus Draugar. "Jakob." Feya said, placing her hand on his. Jakob turned, meeting the Faerie's bright blue eyes. "I…"

"Wait." Jakob said, turning to face the Faerie. "I couldn't protect you once already. Let me make up for that first… then I will deserve to hear what you have to say." A soft smile crossed Jakob's lips as he looked at Feya. "Gadreed." Jakob sighed. "I need you."

"Who the fuck is Gadreed?" Brenna hissed as she turned to Balin. The dwarf turned to his friend in an attempt to protest. Flashes of Senshe breaking free of the mountains of Murdok shot through the dwarf's mind. Just as Balin was about to speak, shoving his way past Brenna, flames engulfed Jakob's blade. The young man's head tilted back, only for a moment, as Gadreed assumed control. Divine writing appeared down

Jakob's arm as a halo formed around Jakob's neck. Four wings, seemingly made of golden dust, formed above Jakob's back. "Spirits." Brenna shouted as she stumbled to the ground. Balin pulled the dark-haired woman back before helping her stand as Jakob's transformation completed.

Feya pulled her hand away from Jakob as the flaming runes of the Divine appeared along Jakob's forearm. His once short brown hair seemed to glow and turn white. Feya gasped, realizing she hadn't taken a breath for several heartbeats as she watched Jakob change. The transformation was different. She knew Gadreed had taken more control this time. Another sign that Gadreed's soul was overwhelming Jakob's. Ava gripped Feya's arm tightly and shook her head as their eyes met. Feya sighed as she slid her hand into Ava's. She looked at Jakob who had turned into the Angel of War. Gadreed lifted his sword, placing both hands on the hilt. "Holy Bidental." The Angel of War shouted, stretching the handle of his sword. Gadreed's blade, Gods Wrath, changed. Its hilt became that of a spear. The blade widened and became jagged as a duplicate blade formed at the base of the staff. Both were engulfed in flames of war fueled by the Angel of War himself.

"I feel…" Jakob said, his heady fuzzy and his vision blurred. "I feel strange." The young man looked around, seeing he was surrounded by an endless sea of still water. "Gadreed?" Jakob said, his voice echoing in the emptiness. He recognized this world. The world where Gadreed would speak to him in his dream. The place his soul went when the Angel of War assumed control.

"I am sorry, Jakob." Gadreed's voice said from nowhere. "What we face is one of the last soldiers from my army." Jakob slowly stood on the water, causing a gentle ripple through the water. "I will need more power to bring down the Colossus." The Angels voice said softly. "I'm sorry Jakob, but your soul will weaken from this fight. I had to assume more control in order to defeat this Colossus."

"Will I die?" Jakob asked, thinking about his friends and the enemy they were about to face. "Will it hurt?"

"I will end him as soon as I can, Jakob." Gadreed said softly. "But... yes, it will hurt." Jakob looked down at the water. There was no reflection. Only an unknown world could be seen through the still waters. Jakob sighed, wishing he could hear Feya's voice. Hear what she wanted to say. Even though he knew what she was going to say, he wanted to be able to tell her... "I must go, Jakob. Be strong... for her."

A magical gust shot from Gadreed, causing the party to stagger. His wings expanded and shoved off, launching the Angel of War into the air. The Colossus roared, shaking the ground and shattering windows. Gadreed shot towards the beast like an arrow leaving a bow. The Angel spun his bidental as he prepared to strike. The beast turned to the incoming Angel, launching Divine energy from his eyes. The Angel flew between the beams as they shot into the earth.

Feya and the others scattered, seeing the Colossus prepare to swing his massive fist. "What in Gods Hammer are we supposed to do against that?" Balin screamed as he and Brenna ran behind cover. Feya took flight, carrying Ava as she headed towards Balin. Kylo, Anna, and Arys made their way to find a vantage point of the Colossus's legs, hoping their magic could aid the Angel of War. Arys slung curses at the beast, wishing he still had his wings. The idea of watching his friend fly into combat, unable to properly help, infuriated the forgotten Angel. Gadreed turned and struck the Colossus's head. A burst of magical energy shot through the city, crumbling any nearby structures. "Damnit." Balin screamed as he and Brenna ran from the building that was once their cover. "They could level Nupross." Balin screamed to Feya. "Like Murdok."

Gadreed dug his blade into the flesh of the Colossus and flew down, slicing the beast's eye. The creature bellowed in pain as orange liquid poured from its eye. The beast managed to strike the Angel of War with a panicked swing of its hand. Gadreed fell from the sky but managed to land on his feet before launching himself back into the fight. The Colossus began taking a long slow breath as a magic circle formed in front of its mouth. Gadreed quickly turned, pulling the three magic users with him. The Angel of War landed forcefully in front of Feya and Balin as he dropped Anna, Kylo, and Arys onto the ground. Gadreed surrounded Jakob's party with his wings forming a magical barrier around them. The Colossus shot a blast of Divine Fire at the cowering party. Brenna cursed as the flames surrounded the barrier. Gadreed seemed unfazed as he turned to Feya. The Faeries eyes shined bright blue with worry as she looked up at Jakob's face. She reached out her hand, gently caressing his cheek. Gadreed nodded and released the shield once the assault had ceased. "Shield them." Gadreed said, looking at Arys.

"Yes, my friend." Arys said, placing his hand on Gadreed's shoulder. "I am sorry I wasn't there…"

"Irrelevant." Gadreed hissed. "If Jakob is to survive, I need you to protect the others." Arys nodded his understanding as Gadreed took to the skies once again. The Angel flew high above the Colossus. A magic circle, half the size of the city, formed over the beast. Green flames traced the intricate lines of the magic circle as Gadreed prepared his attack. The beast began to slowly inhale, ready to repeat its previous assault. Gadreed forced his hands together, sending a ripple of magic through the city.

"Anna." Arys screamed. "We must use every protection spell we can." Anna looked to the Angel, feeling the power that was building from the Angel of War. "Anna." Arys screamed.

"Y-Yes." Anna said, slowly nodding her head. She formed a sign with her hands. Flashes of her past rushed through her mind from feeling the immense power of Gadreed. The party became coated in a dark magical aura. Arys gave a single nod as he held up a sign. A barrier formed around the party as a magical dust took the shape of wings behind Arys.

Kylo slid a ring on each member of the party. "I don't have protection magic." The hunter said. "But the rings will offer you some protection." Kylo slid the last ring onto Ava's finger and gave the elf a wink. "Don't go thinking anything crazy now."

"Shut it." Ava hissed as she tightened her ringed fist. Kylo laughed as he looked up at what could be the end of their journey.

The storm that once was supposed to challenge the Trial members now raged with fury above the Angel of War. Lightning from both the sky and Gadreed shot down, destroying anything in its vicinity. The sky blackened as streaks of multi-colored lightning continued to cut through the air. The beast released its breath, launching a stream of Divine Fire at the Angel of War. Feya gripped Ava's hand tightly in her own as time seemed to slow around them. "Eye of Heaven." Gadreed shouted, his words seemed to pierce the world as the bright green flames of the magic circle became still. "OPEN!" A waterfall of fire fell from the magic circle. Roars and cries of long forgotten warriors seemed to be screaming from the fires itself. The Divine Flames of the Colossus vanished as even the air turned too hot to breath.

The Colossus cried in pain as the flames encased its body. Buildings and the earth itself seemed to melt from the head fueled by the souls of fallen soldiers of war. The furry of wars long past on worlds whose names had been lost to time rained down on the beast that once served Gadreed himself. A crack echoed through the skies as magic shot freely through the world. The black clouds that once filled the sky were now gone as the sun shined bright on its blue canvas. The scorching air instantly cooled to freezing temperatures as ash began to flow from the Colossus. Feya's eyes widened as she saw what had become of the beast. A statue of stone, covered in the ghosts of fallen warriors. The Colossus statue groaned and fell, turning to ash.

Brenna cried by Balin as everyone looked on in horror after seeing another display of the power of Gadreed. Chief Nupross ran to his granddaughter's side. He and the army of Nupross rushed the Trial after witnessing the arrival of the Colossus. Feya watched as Gadreed slowly descended in front of her. His face was hard and emotionless. The face of one who dealt death. The Nupross people stepped back as Gadreed landed in front of them. A surge of magical energy shot through the earth as he took a step. "We… are proven." Gadreed said. Feya reached for Gadreed's hand and looked up at the Angel of War. Gadreed wiped a tear from Feya's eyes and smiled at the Faerie. Feya sighed, knowing that Jakob was still in there. Still alive.

Chapter 13

The Forest Faerie tribe of Les island threw a feast in honor of Christopher's return to the islands. Beautifully crafted homes built near the top of the trees stretched as far as the forest itself. Rope bridges hung from branches, allowing the young and flightless, and Christopher, to traverse the treetop village. Despite their earlier conversation, Christopher noticed several groups of children in the village. Canna walked with Christopher, introducing the prophesied savior to the young of the village.

Even with the festivities and food around him, Christopher felt a sensation run down his spine. He felt the fury of the Angel of war and had a subconscious fear that Jakob was in trouble. Canna gave him a curious look, snapping Christopher from his thoughts. He looked down and saw several young Faerie asking him to display his earth magic. The vagrant gave the children a soft smile. He could see that the children, all male, bore a resemblance to both the Forest tribe and the Sea tribe. "What use are children to immortals?" Christopher whispered to his friend with sarcasm.

"I told you.' Canna smiled. "There are exceptions. When the women of Oothra come, demanding the bear a child, you do not turn them away."

"I see the women of the Faerie haven't changed." Christopher said, ruffling the blue-green hair of one of the small boys. "I mustn't stay long."

Christopher said. "As much as I wish I could… I can sense I am needed elsewhere." Christopher sighed as he forced a smile to his friend.

"I felt it too." Canna said. "I haven't felt Gadreed in centuries either." The Faerie crossed his arm after shooing the children away to go play. "The Ocean tribe will be cross with us for hosting you without notifying them." Canna smiled. "You know you have had those pining for your affection from those demanding women."

"Canna." A scout Faerie yelled as he landed on the bridge. The young Faerie knelt in front of Canna and Christopher, holding his hand to his heart. "A portal has appeared off the southern shore. Dark Magic. Devil Magic."

"Come." Canna said, grabbing Christopher by the waist as he took flight. "Assemble my men." Canna ordered the young Faerie. "Let us remind these intruders why they should not step onto the islands." Canna flew through the thicket as though he had memorized every tree and branch. Only moments had passed before Christopher could smell the salty air. "What would drive them here?" Canna asked as he flew above the trees.

"Desperation." Christopher said. "They know Jakob and Feya are close to the truth. Perhaps they are scouting to see if the Faerie have weakened over the centuries."

Canna flew through the trees and entered the emptiness of the white sand beach. He straightened and fluttered his wings as he gently sat Christopher on the sand. The purple-black portal was hovering just over the shallow water of the beach. White runes encircled the portal. Christopher swallowed hard. He had not expected to face a Divine until his power was unsealed. The vagrant turned to Canna, knowing he could not back down from the fight. Les was his home after Senshe had been taken and the Faerie were his family.

The portal shook with magic power as a small figure stepped through. A male, short with violet hair that touched his stomach. Two horns stretched around his skull from his forehead to the back of his skull. A halo of blue fire hovered above his horns as the Devil stepped into the cool water of Les island. Christopher took a slow breath as he watched the Devil approach. The Ancestral Devil himself… Tor. The Ancestral Devil was thin and short in stature compared to the other Devils. He seemed ungroomed and sickly as he approached Christopher and Canna. Christopher could hear the soft footsteps of the other Faerie lying in wait in the thicket behind them. "Your forces." Tor said with a heavy breath, followed by a coughing fit. "Will not be required."

"Why are you here, invader?" Canna hissed. "Is it not enough for you to have stained our world with your presence?"

"I have come." Tor said through his coughing spell. "To speak to my grandchild." Christopher's face hardened at the Devils words. Tor struggled to walk through the water as he made his way further onto the beach. "If something doesn't change…" Tor said with a heavy breath. "I will not live much longer."

"Sounds good to me.' Canna snarled. "You and the others have tainted our world with your magic and presence."

"I know." Tor breathed. "Eeus, my love, is stubborn and has us bound to this world. We are of one race… and she does not want to admit our failures here." Christopher said nothing as he watched the Ancestral Devil approach. Even with his magic sealed, he could sense the Devil was weak and vulnerable. "Lucile plans to dethrone me… she is gathering an army of my own children, and her pet Senshe."

"Senshe is no pet." Canna hissed.

"Seems to be your problem, old man." Christopher said, tilting his head. "What concern is that of ours."

"Lucile intends to ignite a war to bolster fear in her name." Tor said through struggled breaths. "She aims to leave this world… but not before seeing to its destruction."

"Lucile is just as unable to abandon this world as you are." Christopher hissed.

"True." Tor said. "But she aims to have the Goddess Gidione overthrow my beloved. If she succeeds, she will slay Gidione and assume control of all Divine. Gods and Devils will unite under her, giving her the strength to destroy this realm before departing." Tor scowled at Christopher as their eyes met. "I did not orchestrate the execution of your father, child." Tor said. "I was aware of Alvarome and Kirames's plan to seal us from this realm." Tor looked at the forest, shielding his eyes from the high sun with his taloned hand. "We are slowly dying thanks to this world. A magic we were never meant to wield. Lucile killed Alvarome and now commands his forces against me. All Devil kind with to leave this damned realm, but Eeus has our magic funneled into the earth, binding us, trapping us… killing us."

"Then kill her." Christopher said. "It would seem you are aware of what needs to be done. So why not do it and keep control of your kin?"

"You have not known what it means to love, child." Tor hissed, wiping blood from his lip. "I have promised to follow her to any realm and follow every order."

"Then you are weak." Canna shouted, fluttering his wings. "A god amongst gods, damning their people to extinction. I can think of no better song than to hear the cries of your kin perishing."

"It is a song I do not wish to be heard." Tor coughed. "Let us not pray for the demise of one another, child." Tor said, eyeing his grandson. "I am here… with a proposition."

"Then speak quickly, old man." Christopher hissed. "Or you may know death before stepping back into Onitara."

Tor scowled at Christopher as he struggled to catch his breath. "Slay Lucile." Tor said. "Strike her down in my name. Senshe will fall and his body will be at rest." Another coughing spell took over the Ancestral

Devil. Blood and mucus shot from his nose and mouth as breathing became a struggle. "When... when she is slain." Tor said, rubbing his chest. "I will tell you how Anna can unseal your power."

"You spit lies from your lips, Devil." Canna said. "You have done nothing but stain this realm. Forced the memories of the true gods from the minds of mortals. Why should we believe you now?" Canna turned to Christopher, seeing his friend glaring at the Devil. "It would seem... if you are slain, the seal itself could be undone."

"Untrue." Tor coughed. "Eeus and I hold the brunt of the seal, but if I am to be slain... another will assume my burden. Payment in blood and magic was used to seal your power child. The beasts might awaken from my death... but you will remain as you are. You have lived a long life as all Divine do, but your true immortality will not unseal unless your name is spoken."

"Then speak it." Christopher snarled.

Tor smiled softly and shook his head. "It is not I that knows your name, child. It is your sister who holds that key. Only she was there when Senshe coiled himself around the mountain at your birth." Tor said, eyeing Christopher. "I have heard whispers of Hadriel speaking with the Goddess Gidione. You know you will need her... but if you help me deal with Lucile, I will be able to aid you."

"You think I am a fool?" Christopher said, raising a brow.

Tor shook his head. "You could not have survived this long if you were a fool. I grow tired of this realm and the toxic magic that plagues my soul. Help me, young one, and I will help you speak your name."

Jakob had spent the rest of the day after the Trial in his room. His arm ached and burned. His back was sore, and his legs trembled under the weight of his own body. The young warrior was nauseous from his time as Gadreed. Thankfully, he was still standing and conscious. He had gotten stronger and become more accustomed to Gadreed's power. Jakob no longer felt the need to sleep for hours, or even days to recuperate.

Night came quickly, even after the events of the day and his body protesting, Jakob still wasn't tired. He was ready for tomorrow. Chief Nupross had accepted their performance at the Trial. Defeating a Demon Draugar and Colossus Draugar was enough to give them each the title of Proven. Now, the only thing he had to do was wait for morning. Brenna would escort them to the Lake of Endless Fog. The resting place of the souls of their fallen, so the Nupross believe. Jakob wondered what truly was waiting for them at the Fog. It was hard enough to believe that there would be some sign or relic to aid in unsealing the Savior, but what was even harder to believe was that Christopher was the one they had been searching for.

Taking in the silence and solitude of his room, Jakob had asked Gadreed to share the truth with him. The Angel of War did in fact know that Christopher was the Savior. He had shared information on why the Devils and Gods remain in this realm, despite the toxicity of the world. And… that the Faerie were created by the Basilisks themselves. The idea was unbelievable. Feya, a powerless Faerie, was one of the demi-gods of this realm. Gadreed also shared that Feya was not like any other Faerie but would not go into further detail. Not for lack of prying from Jakob. The Angel simply did not understand her origin. Gadreed believed Christopher is aware of Feya's difference to the Faerie race. With that theory, Gadreed assumed whatever awaited them in the Fog would hold the answers.

Remembering what was lying in wait at the Broken Spear, Jakob feared what threat could be waiting within the waters of the lake.

Jakob sighed and sat on the floor beside his bed. The door slowly opened as Feya announced herself while entering. She was silent as she gracefully stepped across the room and sat beside the young man. Jakob could feel his heart pounding in his chest, waiting for her to speak. Instead, Feya leaned towards him, resting her head on his shoulder as she hugged his arm. It had felt like an eternity since he had simply *been* with Feya. Her familiar scent and hair brushing against his nose. Her soft skin pressed against his. He tilted his head onto hers and felt at home.

"I'm sorry." Jakob whispered, welcoming Feya's hair against his face. "I'm sorry I wasn't there when Cole…"

"It doesn't matter." Feya said. "I knew you wouldn't abandon me. I knew you and the others would come for me."

"It does matter." Jakob said. "You… when you were taken, I felt as though I had lost my family all over again. I made you a promise when you joined me all those months ago. you have been with me through so much when anyone else would have left. You don't know how important you are to me Feya." Jakob said, pulling the Faeries chin with his fingers as his brown eyes met her shining blue. "I don't think… I even knew before…"

"Jakob." Feya said, pressing her finger against his lips. "I have a lot to say. I made myself a promise, while back at the Palace. I need to say it… before I lose the nerve." Jakob nodded and watched as the Faerie stood from the floor, brushing dust off her white and grey dress. He had never seen her dressed in such a way before. He was used to seeing her in her typical shirts and pants suited for combat or comfort. As Feya paced around the room, silently rehearsing what she wanted to say, Jakob saw exactly how beautiful she was. How blind he was to how he truly felt about her. "I love you, Jakob." Feya said sharply, like a mother disciplining her child. "I have loved you… for so long. I know the rumors about Faerie. How we are pests about our emotions. I have tried to… hold back my feelings, but when you gave me this." Feya said, looking down at her charm. "I could feel our bond. That is why… I had to kiss you. To know for myself." Feya sighed as she covered her face with her hands. "I love you. I want… I want to be with you. I want to *bond* with you." Feya said, slowly dropping her hands and hiding them behind her dress. "If… if you feel the same."

Jakob sat for a moment as he looked at Feya. His body was numb, and his heart felt as though it had stopped. He wasn't sure how, but he had managed to stand without feeling the pain from today's fight. He stood in front of her and caressed his hand along her cheek as he watched a tear build in her eye. "Feya." Jakob whispered. Their breaths mixed as he pulled her close. His lips met hers as he wrapped his hands around her waist. Feya wrapped her arms around his neck, keeping his lips pressed against hers. "I love you, Feya." Jakob said, resting his forehead against hers. "But, do you genuinely want to bond with me? I know… I know how important that is. It would mean everything to me to be with you… forever. But I don't deserve…"

Feya pulled his lips to hers to silence him. "You mean everything to me Jakob." Feya whispered, laying her head against his chest.

Jakob wrapped his arms around her, pulling her close. He twitched as a sharp pain shot up his spine. Feya looked up at him, seeing the pain in his eyes from Gadreed's control. "Stay with me." Jakob said, feeling her heartbeat against his chest. She smiled and closed her eyes.

"Always."

Kylo sighed as he shoveled eggs into his mouth. He closed his eyes, savoring the flavor of the breakfast Anna had prepared. The hunter had hardly slept last night, thinking about the Trial. Seeing the Demon-Draugar was an odd sighting. The Colossus was even stranger, but what had really surprised him was the Jakob wielded. The idea of Gadreed existing inside him was worrisome. Gadreed, The Angel of War, Astaad had written tales about him in his journals. Tales of the strength the Angel possessed… he had now witnessed firsthand, and it terrified him. The hunter eyed Ava as she sat down at the table, taking a seat opposite him. He let out another sigh as he forked a piece of ham into his mouth.

The elf girl was stunning and seemed unmoved by his morning tales of his journey. From what he had gathered from his short time with Jakob and his party, Ava and the party leader were once connected. Though, since his joining, he has noticed a distance between the pair. The hunter had made… suggestions to the young elf girl, only to receive hard stares and fowl curses. Kylo smiled as he watched the elf butter her bread. "Did you sleep well?" Anna asked her sister as she sat at the table. Ava nodded as she took a bite of her bread. "And you, Kylo?"

Kylo smiled, combing his fingers through his red-gold hair. "Well enough." Kylo said, closing in eyes as he smiled. "Though, I have never had a good night's rest in an empty bed."

Anna chuckled as she took a bite of her eggs. Ava narrowed her eyes as she glanced over at the hunter. "Then go find yourself a companion." Ava said with a mouthful of bread. "No need on lingering around us if you feel that lonesome." Kylo smiled as he cut his ham while Anna tried to hide her laughter. "What business do you have traveling with us anyway? We appreciate you rescuing Feya, but if Christopher hadn't paid you… you wouldn't have even known about her."

"Very true." Kylo said, propping his chin in his palm as he looked at Ava. "But I find myself fascinated with this little group. Honestly, as a hunter, I never imagined I'd find myself traveling with so many interesting individuals. Daemon's, Angels, a host to the Angel of War, and now I learn that the lot of you have met the Savior. Of course I'm going to be sticking around."

"If you must." Ava breathed, finishing the last of her bread. The elf girl spooned herself a helping of eggs onto her plate, looking to the stairs for the others to finally wake. She looked up the stairs, seeing Feya's bedroom door slightly open. Ava knew the Faerie had gone to see Jakob. She was actually happy that she was finally able to tell him, and that he obviously felt the same. Ava did have love for Jakob, but after killing Thrayn, she realized her love what not what either of them needed. He protected her and Anna, just like he did with the others. But Feya. Feya was the one who genuinely loved him. Ava turned back to her food, seeing Kylo still eyeing her from across the table. She grunted and began eating her eggs. "Stop looking at me." Ava said as she chewed. "Or you won't live long enough to see the Fog."

"Jakob." A voice called from the Inn entrance. The trio turned, seeing Gweneth rushing up the stairs. "Jakob." The Nupross captain shouted. "Your comrade Elizabeth has returned… she is injured and being followed by Draugar."

The Nupross captain ran back down the stairs, quickly followed by Feya and Jakob. Balin followed behind, struggling to fasten his belt as he stumbled through the door. Kylo stood from the table, sliding on his rings as he made his way to the door, telling the elf sisters to remain inside. "Lively morning." Brenna said, gracefully stepping into the kitchen wearing nothing but her shirt.

"He forgets you are a healer." Ava said, turning to her sister. Anna stared out the window as she watched the Nupross guards help Elizabeth to the Inn's steps. The Daemon narrowed her eyes as her expression hardened, watching the others tend to Elizabeth. "Wh-what's wrong Anna? Aren't you…"

"No." Anna whispered, turning to Ava. "There is something I need to tell you about Elizabeth."

Feya held Elizabeth's bloodied and bruised body as Jakob and the others waited for the approaching Draugar. Jakob gripped his sword tightly watching as the two figures stepped into the Great City. Gweneth and her warriors formed a line to prevent the Draugar from entering further into the city. Feya examined the wounded commander, frantically searching for Anna to arrive. "Jakob." Feya said, moving the commander's bloodied hair from her face. "She is seriously wounded. We need to get her inside."

Low groans came from the Draugar as they inched closer through the gate. Balin gasped at the sight of the larger of the two. Four arms and a bulging body. The dwarf gritted his teeth as he took notice of what few human features remained on the Devil's minion. "Trung." Balin hissed, looking at the lumbering Draugar. A piece of the simple man's shirt still remained on his half-rotted body. Jakob's breathing became quick and erratic as he looked at the tall slender Draugar… carrying a staff. "G-Gods Hammer." Balin said, his voice trembling. "Is that?"

"Gramps?" Jakob whispered, looking at the slender Draugar. Feya's ears perked up as she turned to see the Devils minions. Tears began streaming from her eyes as she looked at what remained of Sebastian. Feya slowly turned her head to Jakob, seeing his sword trembling in his hand. "G-Gramps… no."

"Jakob." Feya whispered, loud enough that only she could hear. "Bas."

"It doesn't matter who they were." Gweneth shouted, drawing her sword. "They are Draugar now and we… we are proven." Cheers and battle cries came from the Nupross warriors. "If you do not help us strike down these Draugar… I will not permit you to see the Fog."

Jakob stood motionless as his Draugar grandfather inched closer, groaning, and roaring from his throat. The day he prayed would never come was finally here. His grandfather, last member of his family, was an undead monster. His only purpose now is to follow the orders of the Devils. Destroy. Murder. Infect. Jakob could feel his grip slipping as his heart thumped loudly in his ears. "Jakob." Balin said, gripping his short sword. "I-I know how you must feel, but Bas… Bas is gone." Jakob turned to his friends, tears falling from his eyes like rain. "He knew this day was coming but lived everyday with a smile. The least we can do… is stop him… as Kal promised." Jakob glanced back at his undead grandfather. The Draugar stumbled, dropping his staff as he approached. "Let his soul be with Kal once again." Jakob wiped his eyes with his free hand as Balin spoke. "If it be easier for you lad, I'll do it."

"No." Jakob said, tightening his grip around the hilt of the sword. A single red flame surrounded the blade. "Gramps is gone. Only this monster remains… I'll do it."

"Aye." Balin said, wiping his eye with the palm of his hand. The dwarf could feel his heart turn heavy as he eyed the walking corpse that was once Sebastian. "Let him rest now. Kal must be quite lonely without him."

Jakob pointed his blade towards the approaching Draugar. The Devils minions were only steps away from striking range. Kylo stepped next to Jakob, using his tongue to clean his teeth. "They aren't powerful." Kylo said, drawing a symbol in the air. "Trung is meant to look more powerful than he is. Simple intimidation. I've dealt with creatures like this before." Kylo finished his aerial drawing, slashing all four of the lumbering Draugar's arms from its body. The creature roared in pain as Kylo drew a vertical line, finishing the Draugar by splitting it in half. Trung's undead corpse fell, turning to ash before striking the ground. Feya whimpered as she watched her friend from the Palace turn into a dark stain on the ground. Jakob took a slow breath as his grandfather stepped closer, seemingly unaware of the danger. The Draugar continued its approach, not raising a hand for an attack.

"Gramps." Jakob said, his voice cracking as he breathed. The Draugar stepped closer, walking into the blade with its chest. The creature groaned as he tilted his head to Jakob. "I'm sorry, Gramps. I wish… I wish you could have seen what would become of this world." The Devils minion groaned, stepping further against the blade. "Feya finally told me, Gramps. And… And I told her that I love her." Jakob said, smiling at what little features remained of his grandfather. Balin readied his sword as the Draugar lifted its hand, stepping closer to Jakob while his sword was shoved further into its chest. Ash began flying from the body of the Devils minion. Jakob stood in shock as the Draugar gently rested its hand on his head. Tears shot from Jakob's eyes as the creature rubbed his hair as it turned to ash. "G-goodbye… Grampa Sebastian."

"Gods Hammer." Balin said, watching the Draugar stain the ground with ash. "He… He didn't attack. Just like back in Graham."

"Your grandfather must have had a strong will, Jakob." Kylo said, resting his hand on Jakob's shoulder. "Too strong for even the Devils to taint his soul."

Jakob fell to his knees, scooping handfuls of his grandfather's ash into his hands. "I'm going to find him, Gramps. Christopher is the Savior. We are going to unseal him, bring back the Basilisks, and kick the Gods back to their realm. Just like you wanted. I-I just wish you could have seen it all." Feya wrapped herself around Jakob as he knelt with the ashes. She could feel his heart pounding in his chest as the ash fell from his fingers like sand. "I told Feya." Jakob whispered to the ashes. "As long as I have her… I won't be alone. So, don't worry about me. Just go be with Kal. Tell her we are close to the truth. I won't let the work the two of you have done be for nothing."

"I'm sorry Jakob." Feya said, interlocking her fingers with his. Both of their hands became stained with ash. "But he is at peace now. No longer infected. Free to be with the spirits. To be with Kal again." Feya leaned her head against his as the wind carried the ashes away. "He can tell your mom and siblings about how great of a man you have become."

Jakob smiled as he stood from the ground. He offered a hand to Feya, lifting her beside him. They embraced each other once again as his tears fell on her shoulder. "Thank you, Feya. He was strong, even in the end, he didn't truly turn." Feya wiped the tears from Jakob's eyes, kissing his cheeks afterwards. Jakob turned to Balin and Kylo, before focusing on Elizabeth. The ring Kylo had given him burned his finger as he looked at the wounded commander. No longer did he see the dark-haired niece of the Governor in Graham. What he saw… was a purple haired woman with small horns and violet bat-like wings. "You." Jakob hissed, picking up his sword. Elizabeth sat up from the ground and scowled as the four of them turned to her. "Who are you? What did you do with Elizabeth?" Feya turned to Jakob with a look of confusion. "When did you kill her?"

"You see her then?" Kylo said without looking at Jakob. "You see her true form?"

"Yes." Jakob said coldly.

"What in Gods Hammer are you talking about Jakob?" Balin said, stepping in front of the warrior. "Elizabeth is injured. We need Anna to treat her."

"That is not Elizabeth." Kylo said, looking at the dwarf. "The Elizabeth you all knew died some time ago I would assume. The person in front of us… is a Succubus." The hunter removed one of his rings and tossed it to the dwarf. Balin, in his confusion, slid the ring on and faced Elizabeth. He too saw the form of a Succubus. "She likely killed the Elizabeth you met before she joined your party."

"Elizabeth…" Balin muttered, pulling the ring from his finger. Elizabeth smiled and snapped her finger, taking her true form. A Succubus. Long flowing purple hair and half-dressed. Her injuries faded away as she flexed her bat-like wings. "Why?"

"Of course, the Nephilim smelled me." The Succubus said. "Lucile will be most upset." Jakob narrowed his eyes at the Divine creature. "I am Lilith, proud servant and lover of my Devil Lucile." Jakob sent his magic through Gadreed's sword. Divine writing and flames formed around the blade. "No need for all that, Jakob." Lilith said, giving a venomous smile, pressing her tongue against her fang. "If Lucile wanted you dead… I would have killed you already. You still have your part to play in the game, Jakob."

"I am no player in your master's game." Jakob hissed, pulling Feya behind him. "I will kill your master if she tries to interfere."

Lilith chuckled as she bit her lip. "You are already a key player, Jakob. As is your little Faerie. Do not worry, we have no intention of killing or stopping any of you… not yet at least." Lilith smiled. "Well, Lucile decided the old mage had played his part… so he was discarded."

"You… You bitch." Balin hissed. "I can't believe…"

"What's wrong, Balin?" Lilith said, winking at the dwarf as she rubbed her breasts. "I would think this form would be more appealing to a man." The Succubus extended her wings, sending a powerful wind behind her. The Nupross warriors fell from the magical wind as the Succubus took flight. "Travel safely young Jakob and Feya." Lilith said. "I'm sure I will be seeing you very, very soon."

"I'll kill you." Jakob screamed, pointing the flames of his sword towards the hovering Succubus. Lilith laughed softly as she stroked her breasts, laughing as she disappeared into the sky.

Chapter 14

Gidione sat in the garden of roses in her temple on Elysian. The Goddess plucked pedals from a thorned black rose as she looked down at Emanuel. The Angel had returned from his travels on the Mortal world. Though, he had returned without the information on Gadreed's host. Instead, the Agnel returned with new from Onitara. "What do you mean you spoke with Lucile?" Gidione hissed, pulling a pedal free from the rose. "You come back to me with useless information about the Devils instead of where this Jakob and Faerie are."

Emanuel lifted his bowed head as he stood from his kneeling position. "My Goddess." The Angel said. "Surely you understand what Lucile is plotting. I know of your history with her. I believe you knew of her intentions."

"Tread carefully, Angel.' Gidione snarled, angered by the Angel's boldness. Gidione, though unlikely, believed her relationship with the Devil Lucile was secrete. Since her sister's betrayal with the Devil Alvarome, Gidione refused to be categorized the same. "I am a Goddess, one of the true rulers of all realms. With whom I share a bed with is no concern of yours, Emanuel."

The Angel bowed his head. "My apologies, my Goddess. I did not mean to upset you. I only wish for you to be up front with me… more than you did with Angelus." Gidione scowled as she looked down at the Angel. "Lucile's plan." Emanuel said, lifting his head to look at the Goddess. His eyes were cold, and his face was hard. "She aims to assume control of the Devils and become the Ancestral. On the other end of her plan, she wishes you to assume control of the Gods and become the new Divine." Gidione sighed and closed her eyes, tossing the rose to the ground. "She seems to be growing in both strength and support in her realm, my Goddess."

"And?" Gidione hissed, picking a fresh rose from her garden. She began gently pulling the pedals as she glared down at the Angel. "What concern does a goddess have with the affairs of the Devils?"

"We are two sides of the same coin, my Goddess." Emanuel said calmly. "Eeus will declare war on the Devils if her beloved is slain." Gidione tilted her head, uninterested in the Angel's concerns. "Perhaps." The Angel said as his wings shifted behind him. "You should share in Lucile's… ambition."

Gidione stood, dropping the rose. "You speak of treason." Gidione hissed as she stood over the Angel. "You speak of betraying our people. Balance. Order." The Goddess scowled as past memories shot through her min. "Just like Kirames."

"My Goddess." Emanuel said. "Surely you understand the situation. Even if Lucile herself was not planning to assume the title of Ancestral, we Divine are growing weaker by the year. Eeus's hold on this world is weakening us. Keeping us from finding a suitable realm to rule." Gidione, in anger, struck the Angel, forcing him to his knees. "She will be the death of us all."

Gidione snarled as she extended her hand to her side. She opened her palm as a golden trident formed in her hand. The Goddess spun the shaft, pointing the trident tip to the Angel's throat. "You aim to betray our Divine God." Gidione said. "With such words leaving your mouth, I should send you to oblivion."

"If you must." Emanuel said, feeling the hot steel pressed against his throat. "But you must ask yourself, my Goddess. Why did Kirames and Alvarome turn on the eldest Divine?" Gidione scowled as she pressed the trident closer to the Angel, drawing blood from Emanuels throat. "It is because… they saw the insanity of their games. We are to rule the realm, replenishing our magic with both fear and praise. Instead, they drain the worlds of its magical resources. Destroying the world itself and forcing us to go in search of new realms. Until… we found a world where its gods were too mighty to slay."

"You are afraid, Angel." Gidione snarled. "So, you would prefer treason. Leaving your life in the hands of a Devil with selfish ambitions."

Emanuel closed his eyes as he took a long breath. "We are doomed already, my Goddess." The Angel said. "Better to put what faith I have left in someone who wishes to free us from this fate." Gidione's arm trembled in anger as she looked down at the Angel. HE opened his eyes slowly as he met Gidione's gaze. Emanuel took a gasped breath as the Goddess shoved the trident in his neck, piercing through his spine. Emanuel dropped to one knee as he coughed up blood. Gidione pulled the trident of the Angel's flesh and watched as Emanuel collapsed in the garden. "F-Farewell… my… Goddess."

"What have you started sister?" Gidione whispered, looking at the Angel's corpse. "How could anyone deny the wisdom of Eeus?" The Goddess began thrusting the trident repeatedly into the Angel's back. "It is your fault, Kirames." Gidione screamed, slamming the trident into the corpse. "You have caused a rift between our kin. You have birthed the one who would see us killed. You chose those beasts over you… over your own sister."

"My. My." A voice mocked from behind the Goddess. Gidione, shoving her trident into the back of the Angel, turned and saw her brother. "Now, what could that poor fool have done to merit such abuse?"

Gidione scowled, wiping her hands free of blood. "He was a traitor, Tedros." The Goddess said, glaring at the corpse. "He spoke of betraying our Divine God."

"As do many." Tedros said, propping himself against one of the garden pillars. Gidione turned, her eyes shined like fire as she met her brother's gaze. "Kirames was not the first to speak of Eeus's weakness." Tedros said, smiling as he sat comfortably by a rose bush. The God plucked a rose with yellow and white pedals from the shrug, sliding the stem behind his ear. "She was only the first to act."

"All of you speak madness." Gidione cried as she sat back in her flower coated throne. "What has become of us?"

"Defeat." Tedros said. "Eeus has finally known failure but chooses not to admit it. That is why we are stuck in this toxic world of Faeries and monsters."

"We can deal with the Basilisks after we find the Abomination." Gidione said. "That is Eeus's orders. He is the threat."

"Is he?" Tedros asked, lying back in the shade as he closed his eyes. "It's been a thousand years, and he hasn't been seen. This world is our true adversary. Each year it eats our power away. Soon, even mortals will be able to slay a God."

"More madness." Gidione hissed, not looking at her brother.

"You didn't slay that elf or Hadriel." Tedros said coldly. "Was it because he is family? Or was it because you fear death?" Gidione remained silent, refusing to acknowledge her brother's taunts. "Being half mortal, which is what kept them linked to magic I'm assuming, has allowed them to keep their strength and power over Divine magic. Not affected by the toxic power we pure Divine face."

"You plan to join Lucile?" Gidione hissed.

Tedros laughed softly as he adjusted to be more comfortable. "Of course not." Tedros said. "But I don't intend to fight her either. Siding with the victor, that is how I plan to survive the coming war."

"You think those mortals will unseal the Abomination?" Gidione asked softly. "You're probably right, considering I am the only one trying to stop them."

"Either they unseal our nephew." Tedros said. "Or Lucile has her way. Doesn't matter, both outcomes lead to war." Tedros took a slow breath, enjoying the flower-scented air. "Either way… I will live I the world ruled by the victor."

"Worthless coward." Gidione shouted, standing from her throne as she made her way out of the garden. "All of you… worthless traitors."

"It's a shame." Tedros said, watching Gidione return to her temple in frustration. "That you never got to know how wise our sister was."

Hadriel felt the steel of the elf guard's blade pressed against his chest. Neither he nor Yavanna received the welcome they expected when they arrived in the Great City of Meridian. Now, the pair found themselves in the presence of the Meridian King. An elf by the name of Tanniv Master of the Realm. The Daemon didn't understand why a mortal would grant himself such a title. The Great City was nothing compared to the sparkling wounder that it was when the invasion began. A Great City, seemingly built with nothing but glass, now reduced to filth. None of the miraculous structures from before the war had survived in Meridian. No sky touching glass buildings. No masterfully crafted works of art along the city streets. The streets themselves, once paved with beautifully colored stones, now nothing but dirt and shit. *How could any mortal who rules over such a domain claim himself a master of the realm?* Hadriel cursed in his mind.

Aside from the filth and grime of the once Great City, the castle was beautifully built. Not a structure from before the war. No. this was elven craftsmanship. It would seem all the wealth this once Great City had now belonged to whomever this Tanniv character is. An obvious elf elder. *Probably of high birth.* Hadriel thought. *It doesn't matter.* The Daemon smiled as he gripped the guard's blade. The steel melted under the heat of the Divine Fire around the Daemon's hand. The surrounding guards drew their weapons but stepped back from fear. "Who are you that still wields the Gods Resource?" King Tanniv hissed, twirling his fingers through a strand of his long blond hair.

"Who are you…" Hadriel asked, crossing his arms. "Who claim to be a master of the realm?" The king clicked his tongue as three of the guards swung their blades at the stranger. The swords collided with an invisible shield, shoving the guards back as they fell to the stone floor. "I am Hadriel. Son of Kirames. I am a Daemon, and the Gods Resource is mine to master."

Murmurs filled the king's hall after Hadriel's overly dramatic introduction. Yavanna sighed as she glanced at the guards around her. "A Daemon." The elf king hissed. "I thought your kind were wiped out long ago, after your mother was executed."

Hadriel smiled as he looked at the curious crowd of guards and servants. He could hear the murmurs and gossip growing between the separated classes. "I take it you are the only one in this kingdom of filth that possesses magic." Hadriel said mockingly. "So, you decided to grant yourself a powerful title and fancy throne." The elf king snapped his fingers, ordering the guards to cut down the Daemon and elf mage. Hadriel lifted his hand as a magic circle formed along the floor of the chamber. All but Hadriel and Yavanna were pulled to the floor by a powerful gravitational force. Screams of panic echoed through the castle as Hadriel stepped up to the king's throne. The Daemon smirked as he sat his foot on the king's head, knocking his silver crown to the floor. The immense pull of the magic bent and contorted the silver crown. The guards roared in anger as their king was forced to kneel to the outsider. "I have no time to play king with you, elf." Hadriel mocked. "This city is old, and you appear old enough to know where its secrets are hidden." Hadriel dug is foot into the king's flowing blond hair, pressing the elf's forehead against the cold stoned floor. "Legends say this city is where Alvarome made his pact with the Faeries." Hadriel said, kicking the king and forcing him onto his back. The Daemon's golden dust wings formed above his back as Divine writing burned along his arms. "You will take me to the resting place of the Cambion Lavender."

"C-Cambion?" Tanniv said as he trembled from both the magic and fear of the Daemon. "I-I…"

"Take me to the catacombs." Hadriel hissed, slamming his foot into the king's chest. "I know you are aware of them. How else could you have afforded to build this castle… in a city of trash." Yavanna sighed as she covered her face with her hand. She hid her face to hide the smile forming across her lips. *At least he gets things done.* The elf mage thought to herself. *Still, I wonder what this Cambion is… and what is so important about them?* Hadriel released the magic circle. The guards quickly stood and fled from the chamber, abandoning their king to the mercy of the strange pair. "Let's get going, your majesty." Hadriel said, lifting the king by the collar. "I have other places to be, aside from your disgusting kingdom."

In honor of Jakob's victory and becoming Proven the Nupross people held a ceremony for his fallen grandfather. A large bonfire was lit, and a feast was set to welcome Sebastian and Trung into the Fog. A Nupross custom that Jakob welcomed. He was unable to give a proper memorial for his siblings or mother. *At least we can honor you, Gramps.* Jakob thought to himself as he watched the fire rise high into the air. Feya tugged at Jakob's hand, interlocking her fingers with his as she pulled him towards a bench near the edge of the bonfire. Every Nupross warrior placed a sword in the soil around the fire in honor of Sebastian and Trung. The old mages staff was displayed by the main dining table for the feast. Feya propped a wooden spoon and spatula by the staff, knowing Trung's only passion was cooking.

Jakob wrapped his arm around Feya as the pair watched the fire grow in height. Balin stepped up to the growing flames, tossing fragments of metal into the tower of orange and yellow. The dwarf knelt to one knee and held his hammer into the fire until it began to glow. Balin drew his short sword and slammed the hammer against the base of the blade. "An old dwarven custom." Balin said, still kneeling by the fire. "I have given the fire iron and steel, along with giving the experience of my hammer." Balin said as he looked up at the tower of smoke. "May you forge a better life in the next world." The dwarf said softly as he stood. "How are you holding up, lad?" Balin asked as he approached Jakob and Feya. "I know I'm going to miss the old man."

"Me too." Jakob whispered. "He was the last of my family, but I hope he can tell the others… that I am going to succeed."

"He will." Feya said, resting her head on Jakob's shoulder. "We have to. Kal and Bas spent their lives searching for the Savior. Now, we know who he is."

"I still can't believe that vagrant is the one we've been searching for." Balin said, taking a seat next to Jakob. "To think… we ate breakfast with the Savior of the world."

"I don't understand why he didn't just tell us." Jakob said. "He knew what we were doing, and he knew Kal and Gramps were searching for him."

"Guess he has his reasons." Balin breathed. "Ya don't live a thousand years being hunted by the Divine by telling everyone who you are."

"True." Feya said. "But… he is clearly keeping an eye on us. He is the reason we came to Nupross. Do you think he is coming?"

"Who knows anymore." Balin scoffed. "First, we learn the vagrant is the Savior. Then we learn Elizabeth was a Succubus." Jakob's eye twitched from hearing that name. *Elizabeth.* The young man thought. *I'm going to kill her.*

Jakob stood from the bench, keeping Feya's fingers intertwined with his. "Let's go eat. You know Gramps never missed a meal."

The *Feast Table* was nearly as long as the city street. Hundreds of people sat and enjoyed the delicacies offered along the table. Chief Nupross requested tales from Jakob's journey be told. Many of the group shared stories of their travels and conflicts with the Divine. Cheers of admiration shot through the table as Anna and Balin shared the story of how Angelus was slain. Kylo sat in silence as he took in the details of every story told as he enjoyed his wine. The hunter was asked little of his own adventures, though, he tried to tell his tales when he could. Hoping to impress the young elf girl who seemed so eager to forget his existence. Though, his story of the Arachnes did spark interest from a few nearby Nupross ladies.

Jakob's mind continued to focus on Elizabeth's betrayal. He wondered how long the real Elizabeth had been dead… if she even made it out of Graham. *Was she killed before joining us? Or was that the Succubus that asked to join?* Jakob thought to himself. It didn't matter now. What mattered was getting to the Fog. Then, when he see Lilith again, he would kill her. *For Gramps.* Jakob turned to Feya, watching the Faerie help herself to another portion of roasted pork. He smiled, remembering their night together. She said she wanted to bond with him, but after the Trial, all they could do was confess their feelings before falling asleep. He knew how important it was to Feya to be pure. The bonding was the equivalent of marriage to her people. She turned to him; her mouth full of pork as sauce dripped from her lips. Jakob smiled, wiping her face clean with his thumb. "What do you think will find at the Fog?" Feya asked, still chewing her pork. He looked deep into her eyes, feeling the love he had for her pounding in his chest. But he still had a fear deep inside him. A fear he didn't know how to express to her.

"It wouldn't surprise me if it's just Christopher." Jakob laughed. "He seems to appear out of nowhere."

"It better be more than just him." Feya smiled. "We had to fight off a Colossus."

"I agree." Ava said, smiling as she watched the pair. "Know him…" Ava sighed, looking down the large table. "He is probably sitting at the table somewhere."

"I'd kill him." Kylo said, taking a bite of chicken. "We could have used him against that monster."

"Oh." Ava said mockingly as she reached for a potato. "I thought you were an expert hunter. Figured creatures like that was nothing to someone like you."

"I appreciate you recognizing my skill." Kylo said as he closed his eyes and smiled, causing Ava to sigh. "But even someone as skilled as I was happy to see the Great Angel of War in action."

"Speaking of Gadreed." Feya said softly, turning to Jakob. "Are you alright? After…"

"I'm fine." Jakob said. "Just a little sore." Jakob took a bite of his greens and ate silently for a moment as he thought. The more Gadreed was used, the sooner his soul would weaken. The fear Jakob felt about bonding with Feya, was wondering how long he would have with her. The young man wondered if it was right, or selfish of him to want to be with her. promising a life with her when he didn't know how long his life might last. "You think Yavanna and Hadriel made it out of Murdok?" Jakob asked, turning to Ava and Anna. The sisters sat silently and shrugged, not wanting to remember the devastation of Senshe's attack. "I'd hate to think…"

"I'm sure their fine." Feya said, resting her head against Jakob. "Hadriel is strong and seems to keep Yavanna close."

"Your probably right." Jakob said, enjoying the feeling of having her next to him again. He savored her smell as her hair tickled his cheek. Jakob tilted his head, pressing his face into the Faeries thick blue hair. "I love you." Jakob whispered. "Thank you… for being here." He kissed her head before pulling away and turning to his friends. "Thank you all for being here with me."

"Of course, lad." Balin said, lifting a mug of ale. "I think of us all as family now, lad. You are not alone. Just remember that." Jakob smiled and acknowledged his friends. All the others held up their own glasses to remember Sebastian and to solidify their bond. "I have to ask, Anna." Balin said after taking a drink of his ale. "You had suspicions of Elizabeth?"

Anna nodded slowly. "Yes. Though, I thought it was just my body becoming accustomed to my Devil magic. That's why I didn't say anything. I didn't want to be wrong." The Daemon sighed as she took a sip of her wine. "I wish I was."

"We all do." Feya said.

Chapter 15

Every chamber of Lucile's temple was packed with devoted followers. A small army of Demon's and Succubi, along with several Devils, had arrived in to show support for the ambitious Devil herself. Several Devils were Demon's, giving speeches of support to Lucile. Cries of freedom from their bondage on earth sang through the halls. Lucile had managed to recruit some of Tor's most powerful War Devils to her side. Even Tor's former right hand, Mammon, had joined as one of her advisors. Lucile was not shy about her feelings towards the Devil. He held the second highest position in their race. Right hand to the Ancestral Devil. Still, mammon was outspoken about Tor and Eeus's acts against their kind.

The Devils did not truly fear their Ancestral as the Gods feared their Divine. Their race relied on the fear of mortals to fuel their magic. The Devils knew, even without the Gods, fear could still rule the hearts of mortals. Unlike the other worlds, earth was toxic to any Divine race. Mammon had disclosed to Lucile that many high-ranking Devils expressed their concerns about earth. Alvarome was one of those voices. "It is simple and not needing debate." Mammon had told Lucile. "Those were your brother's words to Tor. This world is a plague. Merciless and unforgiving to us. We are not meant to exist here. And, if the Basilisks don't destroy us, earth itself will."

Lucile listened to Mammon's words from her throne. Lilith sat at her master's feet, ecstatic to be back at her Devils side. No longer forced to follow the mortal party in search of the Abomination. Lucile had not shared with any of her followers the information Lilith had gathered. Now, she knew who the Abomination was. His name. His appearance. And, by the tales told by the Faerie, his power of earth magic. Sharing the details of the Abomination could hinder her plans. The Devils still wanted the blood of Alvarome's child. She, on the other hand, believed her nephew would be of better use if alive. "As foolish as my brother was." Lucile said, biting her lip. "He was wise in his own ways." Mammon bowed his head to Lucile silently as his fire orange hair fell over his face. "You are one of the eldest of our kin, Mammon." Lucile said, drawing the attention of all her guests. "You hold many secrets…" Mammon took a slow breath as he lifted his head. Lucile smirked as her face took on a venomous expression. "I know of the great secret Eeus and Tor keep from our people. The great lie that has allowed them to reign over us." Lucile stood from her throne and stepped down towards the Devil elder. "Prove your devotion to me. prove you side with our people over that fool Tor. Share the truth… why is the Ancestral and Divine so fearful of the Abomination?"

Mammon swallowed hard as he heard the silence grow through the room. Hundreds of murmuring voices became silent instantly in anticipation of his words. The Devil elder looked over his shoulder at the horde of Lucile's followers. "The Abomination." Mammon shouted, to reach every ear listening in the grand chamber. "Is a reminder of the reason Tor and Eeus fled from Addilan." Whispers began to pass from one to another. All in attendance, aside from a handful of Devils, remembered Addilan. The realm of both God and Devil. "In the beginning." Mammon said, turning to the horde, ready to preach to the mass of Lucile's loyalists. "Addilan was a place of power. That power… was held by the Alpha's. beings of immeasurable magical capabilities. They… were our fathers and mothers. The Alpha's devised the Balance. A way to fuel their unsurpassable power. The Alpha, Krow, separated his power and blood… and created Eeus and Tor." Confusion shook the audience as their whispers turned to shouts. Lucile smiled and held up her hand to silence them immediately. Mammon sighed, wiping sweat from his brow before continuing. "Eeus and Tor were charged with bringing praise and fear. They created us, the Devils and Gods, to play this game. We had our roles, our responsibilities, to fuel our own magics. From the Balance, the Alpha's would gain power from both races. This led to Eeus plotting against the Alpha's, causing the mortals of Addilan to lose their faith. Eeus and Tor were hunted but fled the realm before facing the wrath of the Alpha's. this… is why we search for new realms."

"And why would the Abomination be such a threat to Eeus and Tor?" Lucile said as she sat back on her throne. "Tell us, Elder."

"The Abomination child's birth should have been impossible." Mammon said to the horde. "Though we can produce offspring from mortals and lesser Divine, we Gods and Devils should not be capable of offspring between one another. The child of Alvarome and Kirames… would be of both pure bloods. The blow that Krow himself had given to create us. The Abomination… is also believed to have been gifted earth magic from the Faerie… making him as strong as the Alpha's Eeus fears so greatly. If not… stronger."

"Then why keep us here?" A Devil shouted from the chamber. Questions were thrown at the elder. Voices were so loud that no words were heard clearly.

"The Basilisks are just as powerful as the Alpha's." Mammon said, glancing at the coiled beast through the chamber window. "Eeus likely does not wish to acknowledge their strength… as she did the Alpha's of Addilan so many millennia ago."

Lucile stood from her throne and began clapping her hands at the elder's tale. The horde was silent, nervous, as the Devil stepped next to the aging Devil. "Such a tale." Lucile said, pressing her tongue against her fang. "Let it be known." The Devil shouted to her horde. "That I, Lucile, have conquered at beast equal to the might of the Alpha's. I, and I alone, am to be the one to lead us to a world away from the games of the Divine God." The horde began to cheer Lucile's name as Senshe roared outside the temple walls. "Do you see the lies Tor and Eeus have filled our minds with brothers and sisters?" Lucile said. "They have no claim over us. They have no right to doom us in this toxic realm and let those who would still remain loyal to them…" Lucile swung her taloned hand across Mammon's throat. Three large gashes shot blood from his wounds as the aging Devil reached for his neck. Lucile kicked the aging Devil down the steps from her throne. Lilith cheered and laughed as Mammon rolled to the bottom step. "Will be fed to Senshe, like this aging fool." The horde continued to praise the Devil Lucile as three Demons slid the lifeless body of Mammon towards the chamber door. Senshe slithered towards the building, waiting for his gifted meal. "I only require two more players." Lucile whispered to Lilith as the Succubus wrapped her hands around the Devils waist. "I only need Gidione's mind to weaken… and to find my nephew."

"Would Tor's right hand not have been put to better use?" Lilith asked as Lucile caressed her cheek. The Succubus enjoyed the feel of her Devils blood-soaked talons along her face. "Aside from being a snack for Senshe, I mean."

"Mammon was weak." Lucile said, sliding her taloned finger under Lilith's chin. "A fool from a generation too simple minded to make a difference in my plans. I need loyal and strong allies… like you."

"Anything for you, my love." Lilith moaned as her lips were pulled to meet Lucile's. "Anything you desire. Anything you request. All you need do is ask it of me."

Jakob helped Feya step over a fallen tree as they trekked further into the thickening fog. The brush was thick and untouched. *No one*

ventured to the Lake of Endless Fog. Jakob remembered Brenna telling them. The Lake of Endless Fog sat at the center of several other smaller bodies of water around Nupross. Each lake seemed to have its own purpose for the Great City. Some were overflowing with fish, making fishers a key role in the community. The other bodies of water, more ponds than lakes, had several types of plant life growing. Rice, tomatoes, beans, and anything else one could wish to find on farms. Somehow, food was in abundance in Nupross. There were no farmers or farms. The lakes provided for the city and the lakes never disappointed. When one lake was depleted from a harvest, it would replenish itself after only a few days. Jakob and the others knew that magic had to be in the waters of Nupross. Magic not of the Divine. The Divine races never seemed, even in history, to use their magic for agricultural uses. Their magic was focused on power and control. Faeries were people of the earth. The people, created by the Basilisks, to support and keep the world in balance. Nupross's magic had to be flowing with the magic of the true gods.

The sound of water could be heard as the Fog grew thicker with each step. Jakob's mind flashed back to his youth. The smell of the water and the stillness of the woods reminded him of his grandfather. Back to the days after his father was cut down by those dwarfs. Sebastian would take Jakob on hunting trips and taught him to fish. He taught him how to survive without his father. How to take care of his mother and siblings. Jakob turned to look over his shoulder. Feya was walking beside him as Ava and Anna followed close behind. Balin marched in the rear of the group, wielding his short sword nervously in the Fog. Jakob took a slow breath, wishing his grandfather walking along with them. Feya took his hand and gave him a supportive nod, understanding his silent thoughts. He smiled and turned back to follow Brenna as she pushed the brush from the path. Feya fanned her hand through the fog, wishing the growing white cloud would vanish. "How much farther?" The Faerie asked as Brenna became more of a shadow in the growing white.

"The fog is thick here." Brenna said, stopping to regain her sense of direction. "We are close." The Nupross woman too another step, realizing they were now out of the forest. Waist tall grass surrounded them as they stepped free from the thicket. The ground was muddy and slick. Balin cursed as he slipped and fell into the mud. He slung dwarven curses at the fog as he wiped his beard clean of the muck. "Be easy, my little dwarf." Brenna chuckled. Jakob stepped closer, seeing Brenna had stopped advancing in the fog. A stone alter stood in the tall grass. The alter had a gold bowl sitting on its peak. Writings, not Divine or mortal, were carved on each stone. The fog seemed to be thinner around the stoned alter, allowing everyone to see the writings and hieroglyphs. "The offering pillar." Brenna breathed. "It is said that to speak to the souls of the dead, one must give an offering worthy of their attention."

"What are we supposed to give?" Ava asked, examining the bowl made of solid gold. "We don't even know where we are here." Anna passed her sister and touched the ancient artifact, hoping memories would return to her. The Daemon's fingers grazed the cold bowl, but nothing happened. Anna sighed as she turned to Jakob. "I guess it isn't from the Devils." Ava said.

"Of course, it isn't." Brenna hissed. "This is a sacred place of my people. We do not worship creatures of darkness."

"She meant no offense." Jakob said, eyeing Brenna. "It is just something we needed to check." The Nupross woman narrowed her eyes at Jakob before turning in the direction of the lake. Jakob knelt down in the grass, searching for any sign of what they are supposed to do. Buried partially in the mud, he found something. Jakob lifted the object that was suck in the ground, wiping it clean with his shirt. a dagger, made of gold and diamond. The hilt resembled scales. The blade was carved in such a way it resembled a serpent's eye. A shining diamond set in the center as its iris. "What do you think?" Jakob asked, handing the dagger to Feya.

The Faerie ran her fingers along the back of the blade, feeling the detailed carvings. "Christopher said…" Feya whispered. "I have to prove who I am to the fog." She looked at the bowl silently as she held the dagger. Feya tightened her grip on the handle as she placed the blade against her left palm. Jakob grabbed her wrist as he silently questioned what she was doing. She gave him a soft smile and slid the blade across her palm. Her eyes squinted from the pain of the blade slicing through her flesh. She tightened her fist, dripping blood into the golden bowl. Her blood hit the bowl with a hiss as it evaporated into nothing. Jakob stood nervously next to Feya, watching the blood sizzle away as it hit the gold.

The sound of water rushing around the lake caused everyone to turn. A low growl followed the sound of falling water. A shadow formed through the fog, larger than any tree in the forest. Suddenly, a powerful gust of wind blew away the white fog from the alter. The gust hit with such force, Jakob and the others struggled to stand on the muddy ground. Feya fluttered her wings, pushing herself against the wind. "Spirits." Brenna muttered as she looked up at the figure from the fog. A large creature with an elongated narrow head with a single horn on the back of its skull stood over them. The creature's narrow frame stood atop two stubby legs. The beast extended its wings, each twice as long as the trees were tall. Brenna collapsed to her knees at the sight of the beast that appeared from the lake. "Balin." Brenna whispered, reaching for the dwarf while eyeing the beast. "What is that?"

The creature lowered and tilted its head, turning its eye to Feya. A low growl came from the beast's throat as it glared at the group gathered around the alter. "Child of Shinrahn." The creature said, its voice rumbling in their heads. Its mouth didn't move as it spoke to them in their minds. Jakob was stunned by the low rumble of the creature's voice in his ear. The creature's wings folded as it stepped out of the water, using its wings as arms to aid its stumpy legs. "What brings you to me, child?"

Feya swallowed hard as she looked up at the blue-grey beast. "I-I don't know." Feya trembled. "I was instructed to come."

The beast roared like thunder, causing lightening to strike the lands around Nupross. "I am Meer the Bringer of Storms. Guardian of the Skies and master of the Storm Tribe. Who send you, child of Shinrahn?"

"The Savior." Feya shouted, closing her eyes tightly from fear of the creatures glaring golden eyes. Kylo stepped beside Jakob, looking in awe at the great beast. "The child of Kirames and Alvarome." Meer's head raised as he sat heavily on the muddy ground. "I was sent here… but I don't know why."

A low crackling sound came from the creature's throat as it looked at the fog. Every sound emanating from the beast reminded Jakob of a storm. "He lives?" Meer asked. Feya nodded slowly as she opened her eyes. "What do you seek?"

"We want to unseal his magic." Jakob shouted. "He has been traveling the world in search of his name. Now, he sent us here. Why?" Meer lifted his head and clicked his jaw, eyeing the party of mortals at his feet. The beast released a long powerful breath, blowing the fog and trees like an ocean storm. "Why would he send us to you? Can you help us unseal his power?" Jakob turned to Feya before looking back at the Basilisk. "Is it true the Faerie serve the Basilisk?"

"So many questions…" Meer hissed, lowering his head and eyeing Jakob. "A shame you mortals have forgotten your true masters. Do you not know your purpose, child of Shinrahn?" Feya shook her head and stepped closer to the beast as he lowered his head. "Let me answer the question plaguing your soul, child." Meer pressed his snout against Feya, causing her eyes to roll over white. Her body tightened as blue tattoos formed around her waist and arms. White scale-like designs formed within the tattoos as her mind linked with the Basilisk.

Feya stood in a world of fog, surrounded by clouds of white. She looked at her tattooed arms in shock before realizing Jakob and the others were gone. She turned, hearing the sounds of beast's roaring. The fog cleared, revealing Senshe, before he was taken. He was coiled in the middle of a vast thick forest. His head hovering over the trees. In the trees… was a society of Faeries. All the Faeries were male, tall, with varying shades of brown complexion. Senshe roared and the fog returned. A gust of wind blew past Feya, disturbing the fog. She could now see Meer soaring through the sky, followed by several Faerie. Another all-male tribe with greyish skin and varying blue toned hair. Feya combed her hands through her hair in confusion. *Is this how Gadreed speaks to Jakob?* She asked herself. Meer roared and the fog returned once again. Suddenly, Feya was standing over a vast ocean. A creature appeared from the water. Its body was made of the ocean itself. Countless boats followed behind the great beast. All the Faerie were female. *The water tribe.* Feya thought. Blue skin and yellow hair. Feya took a slow breath as she watched the Faerie dive into the water, altering their bodies to swim along with the Basilisk Oothra. *But... I don't...*

"You are not of the Water Tribe, child." Meer said, his voice echoing through the emptiness of the fog. "You are of Shinrahn, King of the Dragons. His only Faerie." Feya shook her head in disbelief. She remember her Da and Ma. She remembered the village in the trees. *But... Da...* "Is but a fabrication." Meer said in her mind. "Shinrahn created you for a purpose. Giving you a mixture of the Faerie culture. Every Faerie tribe has their own culture and responsibilities. But... Shinrahn has had no tribe. Until... you." A vision of a great red and white Dragon appeared through the fog. An army of male Faerie around him as they stood atop a great mountain. *No.* Feya realized. *A volcano.* "There are many of us who rule this world." Meer said. "Each with our own Faerie to aid us in the balance when the birth of mortals came.

"But." Feya whispered, watching the vision of a Basilisk with pink and white scales bless the birth of countless mortal children with her army of female Faerie. "I have no tribe?"

"Wrong." Meer hissed. His voice boomed like thunder in the distance. "You are the first of Shinrahn's tribe. He is the master of this realm. It is his magic that fuels this world. From him, all earth magic is possible. In you is his power. It needs only to be released."

"But we Faerie..."

"All Faerie still possess their power." Meer roared. "You are the only one who seems to be without your power. You were only able to walk freely amongst the mortals if you were powerless. A Faerie with magic could sway the mortals back into worshiping the invaders."

"What do you mean?"

"The Divine races require praise and fear." Meer said. "This you know. They have wiped the memories of us from their minds, a simple sighting of us… know we exist would return our power."

"Then why not reveal yourself?"

"The Devils have become powerful over the centuries." Meer said, his voice low and rumbling. "We have even lost one of our own to their magic. Shinrahn commands that we wait for the one of both bloods to aid in the coming war. For he is o power that the Gods and Devils fear most."

"So…" Feya mumbled. "What is my purpose?"

"To unseal the one who will restore balance to this world, child." Meer said, his shadow forming through the fog. "I see you have faced many trials on your journey." Meer said. Feya began to see her memories appear in the fog. The battles with Angelus. The Demon that killed Kal. The many nights camping with her friends. "This one…" Meer said as several flashes of Jakob appeared. "Is important. Not only to you, I see, but to the balance. He is of Gadreed. One of the few allies we had from the invaders."

"I know." Feya said, reaching for the images of Jakob. Her hands grazed his face, causing the fog to return. "What am I to do, Meer? I am powerless. I've had to learn what little magic I can… and had to rely on others to save me."

"Relying on those you travel with does not make you weak, child." Meer said. "They are there, not only by fate, but because of your bond. I will awaken what power I can in you. Though, I cannot promise much. Shinrahn's power is unlike any magic I possess." A golden aura surrounded Feya as Meer attempted to unlock her power. She felt a rush of energy and magic flow through her. "You know the invaders water magic." Meer said. "I can grant you knowledge of the storm... my magic. Practice it well, young one. for it is more dangerous than the spells you have mastered." Feya felt a rush n her head. She could *feel* her surroundings. The wind. Rain. The storms themselves. She looked at her hand as a spark shot between her fingers. "Seek the one called Lavender." Meer said. "There you will reunite with the Daemon Hadriel."

"Hadriel?" Feya said, realizing the Daemon hadn't fallen in Murdok. "And... Lavender?"

"A Cambion." Meer said. "The only being born of both the Forest Tribe... and a Succubus." Feya's face contorted from disgust at the idea. Her mind turned back to Elizabeth and her betrayal. "Lavender's mother was an ally to Alvarome." Meer said. "The Cambion will be of use to you... when she unlocks the Daemon Anna's memories." Feya's eyes widened as Meer's golden gaze appeared through the fog. "Awaken."

Feya gasped for breath as she fell back into Jakob's arms. "Feya." He shouted, falling to one knee as he held her. "What happened?" Jakob helped Feya to her feet, looking at the tattooed lines along her body.

"Where is Lavender?" Feya asked the Basilisk as she stepped closer. "Where is Hadriel?"

"Meridian." Meer said. Everyone passed glances between one another. Jakob eyed Kylo, who had been silently staring at the great beast. "I will ready a way for you to reach Meridian. Return to me tomorrow with what supplies you may require." Feya nodded her understanding as she turned to Jakob.

"We are going to Meridian." Feya told the others. "There is someone there that can unlock Anna's memories."

"Meer." Kylo shouted, ending his long-standing silence. The hunter stepped forward, clinching his fists. The Basilisk turned its large head to eye the approaching Nephilim. Kylo's stare was hard and angry as he looked into the golden eye of the beast. "What do you know of an Angle named Astaad?" Feya quickly turned to the Basilisk, worried the hunter would make a foolish mistake. A rumble came from the beast's throat as he lowered his head closer to Kylo. "Was it you that stuck him down?"

"I have slain many invaders." Meer said, his voice shaking the earth. "Why would I know the name of one who took up arms against me?" The Basilisk sniffed the air as he moved his eyes closer to the hunter. "Offspring of the trickster." Meer said. Kylo's face turned red with anger as the beast spoke. "The one who aimed to hunt my brethren."

"He was no trickster." Kylo shouted. "He was a proud hunter. The greatest hunter of all the Divine. In his pride, he refused to hunt weakened beasts. But you struck him down anyway."

A low roar reverberated in the beast's throat. "So you say." Meer hissed. The Basilisk turned his attention to Arys. The Angel slowly bowed his head as the golden eye glared at him with hatred. "How far have you fallen, weakened invader." Meer hissed at the Angel. "Nearly slain by wondering this world which has never belonged to you."

"I raised no sword against you or this realm." Arys said, continuing to bow his head. "My kind have done atrocious things to this world."

"Indeed." Meer said, revealing his rows of jagged teeth. "I am unable to bring a weakened Divine." Meer said, turning to Feya. "This one… must remain in Nupross." Feya turned to Arys with a worried expression. The Angel smiled and nodded his head.

"Then in Nupross I will remain." Arys said.

Meer snapped his jaw as he lifted his head. "Return tomorrow, Feya." The Basilisk said, standing on his stubby legs. The fog returned around Meer as he stepped back into the lake. "I will be waiting."

Tanniv escorted Yavanna and Hadriel down a hidden stairwell underneath his palace. The elf king carried a torch with him, angered as the strange pair used their illumination magic to light their own way. Tanniv cursed under his breath, annoyed how easily the pair could use the Gods resource. It was clear to Hadriel that Tanniv was the only elf in Meridian that could use magic. Though, he wasn't talented in the art. Yavanna followed behind Hadriel, touching the walls, and admiring the detailed glyphs along the stones. The catacombs were old. Incredibly old. Obviously predating the Gods War. She couldn't read the glyphs. A language long forgotten in the mortal world. The elf mage noticed several stones were newer than some along the wall. When asked, Tanniv explained that the stones that were once there were made of gold, silver, and jewels. Pulled and replaced to fund his desire to play king.

The tunnel of stairs became colder as they descended. The stairs led into a large room, each wall housing a single door. The room was empty and stripped of any valuables. Two of the doors were standing open. The third was sealed with a magical lock. "The only room I haven't been able to enter." Tanniv said, stepping beside the locked door. "I've used every ounce of magic, but I haven't made any progress."

"A king bested by a mighty door." Hadriel smirked as he shoved the elf king aside. The Daemon knelt down to examine the lock. He closed his eyes and took a slow breath as he sensed the magic. "Statis magic." Hadriel said, pressing his finger against the lock. A small golden magic circle appeared around the lock, shocking the Daemon's finger. Hadriel laughed as he stood and turned to Yavanna. "Seems her *rest* is just that."

The Daemon said, smiling as he turned to the elf king. "Lavender lives… sleeping on the other side of this door."

"How do we open it?" Yavanna asked, examining the lock. "Is it Divine magic? Or earth?" Tanniv looked at the pair in confusion as they exchanged theories. "We've hit a dead end if it's not Divine magic."

"She doesn't expect to live in there forever." Hadriel said as he rubbed his chin, examining the door. "She must have some plan… some way someone is supposed to get her out." Hadriel sighed as he poked his finger against the door repeatedly. Small magic circles appeared each time, shocking his finger with each jab. "God's help us if we need to know the Savior's name."

"That would imply she knows it." Yavanna said as she gently pulled Hadriel's poking finger from the door. "I didn't even know this woman existed. I didn't even know there were Cambion's in the world."

"As far as I know." Hadriel said, propping himself against the elf mage. "She is the only one. must have been a striking Succubus to get with a Faerie.' Hadriel said, smirking at the elf. "What about you, your majesty?" The Daemon said, turning to the king. "Ever been with a Succubus?" Tanniv sighed as he leaned against a nearby wall, unwilling to join in Hadriel's humor. "I'm sure your busy tormenting your castles help."

Yavanna jabbed her elbow into the Daemon's side, trying to hide her growing smile. "This isn't helping us with the door, Hadriel." Yavanna said, summoning a magic circle. The elf mage hovered her hand over the door, revealing the writing hidden within the Stasis spell. Yavanna stepped back, watching the words rotate around the door. "Blood… of… the bringer… of balance… is…" Hadriel laughed as Yavanna was reading the words. He bit his thumb, causing blood to flow into his hand. He pressed his bloody palm against the door, making the rotating words stop. "What are you…"

"Typical." Hadriel said, healing his hand and cleaning if free of blood. "Everything tied to my brother always requires blood."

"But why did you do it?" Yavanna asked, shoving the Daemon. The golden circle remained around the door. Hadriel tilted his head in confusion. "It said the bringer of balance. That is definitely not you."

The door unlocked and slowly opened. Hadriel smiled as he turned to Yavanna. Dust fell from the doorframe as the creaking door opened wider. "No." Hadriel said cheerfully. "But I am *of* his blood."

"Not the child I was expecting to see." A voice said from the darkened room. "Is there a reason you are the one waking me… Hadriel?" The woman said as she stepped into the doorway. She was a head shorter than Hadriel. Shorter than typical Divine races. The sides of her head were shaven, revealing her long Faerie ears. The hair at the top of her head was long and yellow with a purple braid draped over her shoulder. Her skin was a light shade of grey and her eyes shined like amethyst. "This better be important Daemon." Lavender said, digging her finger in her ears. Yavanna noticed the many piercings with small chains linked between them the Cambion had on each ear. "I planned on waiting for your brother. A girl needs her sleep, you know?"

"I expect you've slept enough, Lavender." Hadriel said as he crossed his arms. "But we are here because of my brother." Lavender was unfazed, still digging in her ear with her finger. The Cambion flicked whatever was on her finger towards the elf king. Tanniv scoffed and made his way back up the stairs and out of the catacombs. Lavender smirked as she adjusted her tight-fitting leather top. Her entire outfit displayed her Succubus blood to Yavanna. Her stomach was fully exposed, revealing her well-toned form. Her top barely covered her breast, making the elf mage feel a sense of inadequacy, while her pants left little to the imagination. If it wasn't for her ears and the flutter of her wings, Lavender could have easily been mistaken for a full-blooded Succubus. Her wings resembled Feya's but still held their Devil features. "We found my brother. Though, he seems to enjoy wondering the world." Lavender smiled as she stretched her arms and stepped out of the dark room. "We were hoping you had some idea of how to unseal him."

"Where is the other?" Lavender asked. "Alvarome's daughter, does she live?" Hadriel nodded. "Then…" Lavender said as she stepped back into her chamber. "I will need her before anything can be done." The Cambion stepped back out of the dark room, holding a slab made of gold and bordered with red wood. "Alvarome gave me this and told me to wait for Anna's return." She handed the golden slab to Hadriel. The slab was smooth with no writings or markings on either side. Hadriel gave a curious look to the Cambion as he returned the slab to her. "This hold the name of your brother. It was given to me after Alvarome sent Anna to this age. The fool." Lavender said, shaking her head. "That is how he was killed, you know." The Cambion said. "He used an earth spell to shoot her here. He was weak and vulnerable. That's how Lucile managed to slay him."

"History doesn't interest me." Hadriel said. "Unsealing my brother does."

"your plan of finding him?" Lavender asked. "You said you know where he is."

"My friend here." Hadriel said, gesturing to Yavanna. "Has a master that has been searching for him. Claims that, once his name is spoken, he will come to us."

Lavender took a slow breath and closed her eyes. "You're a fool." The Cambion said. "I can smell him on you." Lavender said dryly. "You have been near him. Or, he has attacked you. You smell of Alvarome and earth magic."

Hadriel tilted his head as he looked at the Cambion. His eyes darted around the room as he thought. After a moment, his eyes met Yavanna's. she looked away, making him realize who the Savior was. "Shit." Hadriel hissed. "Christopher?" He asked the elf mage. Yavanna nodded her head slowly as she eyed Lavender. "I was scolded by my younger brother it seems." Hadriel said, turning back to Lavender.

The Cambion looked around the catacombs slowly, perking her ears. "Let us head to the surface." Lavender said. "We are about to have some important guests."

Chapter 16

Gidione watched as the pair of Angel's she had brought gathered the citizens around the palace. She eyed the once beautiful city that was now reduced to typical mortal filth and scowled. The Angel's struck down a few of the city guards that were trying to protect their king. Gidione rolled her eyes as one of the Angel's dragged the crying king to her feet. *Who had ever heard of an elven king?* The Goddess thought to herself as she looked at the trembling man. Gidione stared at the Angel, a silent order for her to get the king on his feet. The Angel lifted Tanniv by the back of his neck before shoving him towards the Goddess. "What a disgusting kingdom you reign over, elf." Gidione hissed. Tanniv said nothing, trying to avert his eyes from the Divine being. "You also seem to be housing a traitor to the Gods. A crime punishable by death." The Angel held her trident to the king's throat as she pressed the steel against his skin. Tanniv panicked and pleaded for his life as the cold steel cut his flesh. "Where is the Daemon?"

"The catacombs." Tanniv said, trembling and pissing his pants. The Angel scoffed at the display of weakness from the elf king. "He and another mage came here. Disrupting my kingdom and forced me to take them to the catacombs." The elf leaned his head back, trying to distance himself from the trident. "There was a woman down there…" The elf continued. Gidione tilted her head and ordered the Angel to help the elf stand. "She looked like a Devil… but she had no horns. I don't know what she is… but I want her out of my kingdom."

"Your kingdom?" Gidione said, smiling fiendishly at the elf. "This trash is your kingdom? I remember Meridian being a place of beauty and art. You have tainted this once glorious city." Gidione grabbed the elf by the collar, lifting him into the air. "Who is this woman from the catacombs?" Gidione hissed, shaking the elf. "Surly such a… powerful king…" Gidione laughed, seeing the fresh stain on the king's pants. "Knows all in his walls."

"I do not know, my Goddess." Tanniv said, trying to loosen Gidione's grip. "The intruders… they awoke her and…" The king fell silent as a magical pulse was shot through his chest. Gidione sighed and tossed the elf's lifeless body to the ground.

"Was that necessary?" Hadriel shouted as he stepped out of the palace. Yavanna followed nervously behind him as Lavender watched from the gate's threshold. "Killing a useless king seems beneath you Gidione. Doesn't seem like the work of a God."

"Hadriel." Gidione scowled, wiping her hands clean of the king's blood and filth. "Eeus demands your head." The Goddess said. "She sees through the lies you spew. You aim to aid the Devils in their attempt to upset the balance."

"I believe we are well passed upsetting the balance, Gidione.' Hadriel said. "I assume you spoke with Eeus about our little conversation."

Gidione scowled at the Daemon. She had spoken to the Divine God about their talk. About killing Emanuel. About his ideas of betrayal. Eeus had given her clarity and direction, approving of her actions against thoughts of treachery. Tor had become weak in body and mind. He has gone in search of the Abomination child. He knows about the uprising against him and has done nothing to stop the Devil Lucile. Gidione was not punished for slaying Emanuel. She was praised by the Divine God for her loyalty. *Tor is too weak to do what must be done.* Gidione remembered the Divine

God telling her. *Hadriel has sided with the Devils. The mortals aim to rebel against the Gods.* That was the wisdom given to Gidione from Eeus. The Goddess knew Lucile had to be stopped. Her fist step was to take care of anyone planning to aid her. Hadriel and the mortals want to find the Abomination. Lucile is watching and waiting for them to find him. She knew Hadriel's blood had to be spilled. Gidione narrowed her eyes at the grey skinned woman standing near the palace. "So." The Goddess hissed. "You do exist. A Cambion. Filth born of Devil and Faerie blood."

"Succubus actually." Lavender said, smiling as she scratched her stomach. "And I don't think it was blood they exchanged to make me."

"You will die as well." Gidione shouted. "No one defies the Divine God." Lavender shrugged, adding fuel to Gidione's growing anger. "Bring me their heads." Gidione ordered her Angel's. The Angel's readied their weapons as Hadriel called on his power. Lavender stood motionless, propped in the doorway. The Cambion looked out at the Meridian gates… waiting. Hadriel turned to her curiously as the Angel's slashed their way through the crowd of cowering elves.

Thunder boomed from nowhere. Gidione looked up to the clear blue sky. A magical force formed behind her. the Goddess turned and saw a portal towering over the city walls. A loud roar like thunder came from the portal. Hadriel began laughing as Jakob and the others stepped out of the black and grey portal, like ants exiting a cave. Gidione shouted commands to her Angel's, ordering them to intercept the mortals coming from the massive portal. The female Angel bowed her head and flew towards the portal. Suddenly, another roar shook the earth as a lighting strike brought the Angel back to the ground. Gidione forgot to breath as she watched a massive beast exit the portal. "Holy shit." Hadriel shouted as the beast roared once again. Lighting fell from the sky like rain during a heavy storm. The crowd of elves ran for shelter as lighting engulfed the city. The Angel stood from the ground and flew towards the attacking beast.

A powerful downward wind forced the Angel back to the earth. Jakob turned and nodded to Feya after her display of magic. She made a sign with her hand, causing a star-like symbol to form over her hands as she called lightening down on the injured Angel. Blood shot from the Angel's wings as they separated from her body. Jakob gripped his sword and summoned Gadreed's magic into the blade. He did not call on the Angel himself. He knew, after the Trial, it was too dangerous to call on him. Jakob tossed the sword towards the Angel as she lifted her head. The sword met its mark between the eyes of the Divine warrior. "You have grown weak invader." Meer roared as the Angel collapsed dead in the dirt.

Gidione stepped back nervously as she looked up at the enemy of the Divine God. Her remaining Angel flew towards the great beast. Weaving through lightening to close the gap. Meer leaned his head back. The sound of thunder booming in his throat. As the Angel approached, Meer leaned forward and opened his mouth. A white magic star formed around the Basilisks mouth as a blizzard shot towards the Angel. Wind, ice, and snow hit with hurricane-like force against the incoming Angel. His wings froze, causing him to fall. Jakob extended his arm, calling the sword back to his hand. He swung his blade, as did Balin, severing the Angel's limbs. "Aye." Balin shouted. "These be weaker than Angelus." The dwarf laughed.

"Or perhaps we are stronger." Jakob said, turning to the Goddess. "Still... we haven't faced a God."

"What say you, dear aunt?" Hadriel shouted, looking down at the Goddess from the palace steps. "Has the Divine God given you the strength to fight a Basilisk?"

Gidione snarled and lifted her arms, summoning a magic circle around the Basilisk. A powerful gravitational force pulled at the party and Meer. Jakob was socked, as was Gidione, when nothing happened. Meer tilted his head and snapped his jaw. Suddenly, Gidione fell to the ground, screaming in pain. Her ears began to bleed. A powerful sound was shot in the mind of the Goddess. Her own private storm raging within her mind. Gidione screamed as she pulled at her bleeding ears. "Filth." Gidione screamed. "Monsters. Traitors. Abominations. I will see you all..." Meer snapped his jaw again, sending another shockwave of sound in the Goddess's mind. She screamed as her eyes cried blood. "Monster." Gidione screamed.

"Foolish child." Meer's voice echoed through the Great City. "You are weak. My presence was enough to dispel your power. You have lingered too long in our realm. Your power has faded." Gidione's screams of pain and anger continued. "You are no threat to us. You are not the ones we watched in the shadows. Send your armies of Angels and Gods so we may feast before the war begins. Our magic and presence alone will be enough to end your invasion."

Gidione roared from her knees as she looked at the Basilisk with bloody eyes. Lavender rushed towards Feya from the palace. She fluttered her wings and took flight, weaving between elves while slinging a final insult towards the screaming Goddess. The Cambion landed in front of the Faerie and handed her the golden slab. "Give it to Anna, quickly." Lavender ordered Feya before tugging at the Faeries shorter ears. "Huh." Lavender said, watching Feya walk over to Anna. The Cambion turned to Kylo, who was eyeing her suspiciously. "She's a Faerie? With those ears?" Meer stepped over the party, making his way closer to the Goddess. "Don't kill her." Lavender shouted to the beast. "We may need her… for now." A low roar came from Meer's throat as he eyed the Cambion with his golden stare. Lavender turned to Jakob and Balin and smiled. "But don't let her leave."

"Aye." Balin said, smiling as he turned to the Goddess. Meer roared, launching a powerful wind at the Goddess. She collapsed to the ground as Jakob and Balin shoved their steel into each of her legs. "Can't let you go yet, little lady." Balin grunted, shoving the blade through Gidione's flesh. The Goddess screamed and cursed in pain.

"You." Gidione hissed, glaring at Jakob. "Host of the traitor Gadreed. You will die. He… will die."

"Not today." Jakob said, narrowing his eyes to the fallen Goddess. He turned watching Feya return the slab to Anna. When the Daemon grabbed the golden slab, she fell forward. *That's it.* Jakob told himself.

Memories flooded Anna's mind. Her horn grew longer, and her eyes shined bright. Her hands became taloned as she began unconsciously scratching symbols onto the slab. Ava watched nervously as her sister wrote along the gold. Her taloned fingers began to bleed. Anna suddenly snarled and grabbed her horn. She broke off half of the horn from her skull and finished writing on the slab. "A-Anna?" Ava whispered as she watched her sister mutilate herself. The elf looked at the slab as Anna silently handed it to Feya. The Daemon collapsed in Ava's arms and remained unconscious. Her horn began to heal, and her talons vanished as she slept. "Anna." Ava panicked.

Feya looked at the slab, unable to read what Anna had written on the gold. "W-what does it say?" Feya asked, hoping Anna would wake. "Anna, please, what does it say?"

"She doesn't know." Lavender said. "It is written in the original tongue of the Divine." The Cambion turned to face the fallen Goddess. Feya and Ava looked at Jakob, who was standing over the Divine being. "She can read it." Lavender said with a smile. "That's why we need her alive." Gidione cursed as she formed a magic circle around her hands. Meer lowered his head and roared, dispelling her magic. Gidione felt weak and sickly the closer the beast stood to her. Meer snapped his jaw onto the Goddess's arm. Gidione screamed one again as the Basilisk pulled her arm free from her body. "Shit." Lavender whispered.

"Aye." Balin said, lifting Gidione's remaining arm. "No need for this then..." The dwarf said, slicing his blade through the Goddess's wrist. Gidione screams became silent as her head fell back and she drifted into darkness.

Meer had escorted everyone back to Nupross through another portal. Everyone, including the fallen Goddess. Lavender and Meer used their magic to bind the Goddess in chains. Unbreakable and toxic to those of Divine races. Though the Goddess was missing an arm and both hands, Meer knew her body would regenerate. Being bound in chains coated in earth's magic would be toxic and restrict her own magic and healing. The Basilisk remained at his lake, not wanting to gain the attention of the Nupross natives. The Cambion and Kylo tossed the Goddess into an empty room, imprisoning her withing the four walls with a mixture of Faerie and Divine magic. Hadriel remained in the room with Gidione, watching her chest slowly rise and fall as she slept. He himself had never seen a God fall so quickly to a Basilisk. Meer had made it clear, just by him being there, the Goddess was weakened. This fact made Hadriel curious of what would happen when, not only when his brother's magic was released, but what would happen when the Basilisks were released.

Pustules and bruises formed along Gidione's body as she slept, a side effect of being bound by Faerie magic. Even as he sat in his aunt's prison, he felt his power weaken. The Cambion's spell that enchanted the room affected all of Divine blood. "She will read the slab." Lavender had said to him, after tossing the Goddess onto the bed. "Or she will die. Either way is fine with me." As much as his aunt despised him, Hadriel hated seeing her in this condition. He knew, once his brother's power returned, more would be like this. Like Gidione. Gidione was one of the youngest Gods. Yet, she was a powerful God. To see her fall, with such ease, sent a shiver through his spine. The Daemon hoped Gidione would simply read the slab. Read what Anna had etched in her tranced state. He knew it was a name. The name the world had ben searching for since the Gods War ended. A dead language used by the Gods in a forgotten age when the Divine God was young. So devoted to proving her loyalty to Eeus, Gidione delved into every aspect she could about the history of the Gods. Hoping to please

Eeus and avoid execution like her sister. Though, Hadriel knew there were parts of their history Eeus would not permit the young Goddess to learn.

"Knowledge is power." Hadriel whispered to his sleeping aunt. "But it can be a curse as well. A lesson you have learned today, dear aunt."

A gentle knock came from the open bedroom door. Hadriel turned and saw Kylo and Anna standing in the doorway. "Still in here I see." Kylo said, stepping into the room. Each took a long breath as they stepped into the prison, feeling the magic dampen their power. "She still asleep?" Hadriel nodded as he turned back to Gidione. "I can't believe Eeus still plans to lay claim to this world." Kylo said, sighing as he sat on the floor beside Hadriel. Anna followed suit, sitting next to the hunter. "Meer could have killed her without a second thought. Honestly, I'm surprised he didn't, but he was just one Basilisk. What does Eeus plan to do against them all?"

"Perhaps her mind has withered, like Gidione's body seems to be." Hadriel said. "Those chains could be the death of her themselves. No need for weapons or attacks. Meer was right." The Daemon laughed as he turned to Kylo and Anna. "We have become weak. When their magic is unleashed back into the realm…"

"It itself could kill us." Anna said, rubbing her horn. What about when Christopher is unsealed?" The Devil Daemon said. "What do you think will happen when his power is returned?"

"Let us hope we are not in his vicinity." Kylo said. "For our own safety.'

"I agree." Hadriel said with a heavy breath. "I have seen Christopher's power. And… how quickly he will use it. Discarding those he considers useless." He turned and eyed the pair sitting beside him. "How useful will we be… when he is at full strength?"

"Indeed." Kylo sighed. "I have seen his power as well. Even as he is now, he could kill a city in a matter of moments. No one would even know he was there."

"I do not fear him." Anna said softly. Kylo turned to her curiously with his typical smirk. "I don't." Anna repeated. "I have more memories. I remember... I remember when he was born." Hadriel leaned forward to face his fellow Daemon. He was there as well. Though, he was not as close as Anna. Hadriel stood guard in the city of Murdok while Anna went with their parents to the Broken Spear. He remembered seeing Senshe coiled around the great mountain, protecting the world from the shockwave of magic soon to follow the birth. That act weakened the Basilisk, which later lead to his defeat at the hands of Lucile. "I remember the name carved on the mountain." Anna said. "That was probably what I was supposed to find before..."

"Before Jakob destroyed the city." Hadriel hissed.

Anna sighed as she slowly nodded. "I remember... Faeries. Brown skinned with long ears. They didn't look like Feya. But... they were Senshe's Faeries."

"Amazing." Kylo said with sarcasm. "Is there a point to all this?"

"I assume." Anna said, raising a brow and smiling at the hunter. "Christopher was raised by the Faeries. Probably all the Faerie races. I don't believe his true interest is sealing away the Gods and Devils." Hadriel's leg became restless as he tapped his foot against the floor. "I don't believe he wishes us dead. If so, he would have done it already. Ultimately, they haven't really needed us."

"You scribed the runes on the slab." Kylo said with narrowed eyes.

Anna shrugged. "True." She said with a smile. "Still, if I was raised in this world as he was. Raised by the rightful rulers of this realm. Knowing what I was... I wouldn't want to fulfil the prophecy we were taught. I would seek revenge."

"You think he wants to kill all Divine?" Hadriel asked with a worried look. "And you still don't fear him? Do you forget our lineage?"

"I believe he will kill those who the Basilisks see as enemies." Anna said softly. "They do not see us as such. If they did… Meer would have killed us. Because Jakob and Feya are the only ones they truly need."

"Speaking of the big lizard bird." Kylo said. "Why did he bring back Gidione when he claimed Arys was too weak to travel through the portal?"

"Because he's dead." A voice said from the doorway. Anna and the others turned to see Ava standing in the hallway with tear filled eyes. "Gweneth and Brenna just… just told me." Ava said, wiping her tears with the palm of her hand. "He died not long after returning from the lake. It's not fair." The elf girl cried. "He was finally free." Silence. Silence was the only response the three Divine blooded occupants could give. Feya stepped into the hallway, trying to comfort the elf. Ava fell into the Faeries arms, unable to hold back her tears from her fallen friend. Arys had been bound to Thrayn longer than Ava had. He had known the same suffering as her. The same humiliations. Still, he was kind, gentle, and caring to her. He deserved to enjoy his freedom, not die in the streets only days after gaining it. Feya escorted Ava to her and Jakob's room, hoping to ease the elf's mind. Anna knew Jakob was still in his room in a meditative state, conversing with Gadreed about Gidione and the golden slab.

"I don't know if we can survive the coming war." Hadriel said, watching the Faerie and elf as they left. "If we decided to fight…" Hadriel said, shaking his head. "Perhaps it best we shelter ourselves, after Christopher is unleashed into the world."

"No." Anna said calmly. "He is my brother. I will fight alongside him. He suffered this realm for so long… while I was simply launched into this age."

"I agree." Kylo said. "I am the son of Astaad, the greatest hunter to ever live, I will not sit by and watch my world fall into chaos."

"You think we can stop the chaos?" Hadriel laughed. "If it wasn't for Meer, Gidione would have killed us."

"Do you wish to fight against them then?" Anna asked, eyeing Hadriel. "Are you seeing Gidione and wishing to see our kin victorious?"

"No." Hadriel breathed with frustration. "That is not what I'm saying. Still, they are our… family. I wish them sealed away, returned back to our realm. Not butchered or eaten."

"Then…" Anna said. "Gidione should help us. Help us unseal Christopher. Stop Lucile and convince the Gods to abandon Eeus."

Hadriel laughed as he shook his head. He looked up at his aunt as she began gasping for air. "She will never do that." Hadriel said. "She has blinded herself to reason… as has many of the Gods."

"It will take the death of the Ancestral Devil and Divine God to sway them." Kylo said. "Though, the Devils seem to be dealing with their own problems." Gidione's struggled breathing calmed down after a few moments. The trio sat and watched the Goddess. She began to mumble in her sleep. Soft whispers of panic from the fallen Goddess broke through the silence of the room. Each word, each plea in her unconscious state hit each ear like a drum. Every whimpered sentence always mentioned the same person. *The Abomination.* "Anna." Kylo said after swallowing nervously. "Why can Christopher use this world's magic? He is of our blood. Shouldn't that magic… be impossible for him to master?"

Gidione suddenly screamed as she slept, reliving the pain of Meer pulling her arm from her body. Anna took a long slow breath, trying to summon what magic she could in the shielded bedroom. She managed to form a magic circle and let the Goddess sleep a dreamless sleep. A small act of kindness to her beaten enemy. "It was a gift." Anna said as she turned to Kylo. "While Kirames was still carrying Christopher, the Faeries of each tribe would visit her. with the blessings of their Basilisks, they fed their magic into the unborn child. He is immune to its toxic effect on our kind. A being of both God and Devil… blessed by the Faerie." Anna shrugged after standing from the floor. "At least, that's what father had told me. I believe there are reasons why were are not affected either. Like Kirames and Alvarome. Even Gadreed." Anna sighed and turned away as she stepped towards the door. "I'm going to go check on Ava. She needs to rest… as do the two of you."

"You found his name." Gadreed said. His spectral form hovered above the still waters of Jakob's mind. The Angel of War became silent as he retreated into thought. "And now we rely on the willingness of Gidione to translate the text. A predicament I did not foresee."

"I take it, from your tone, we will be unable to convince her to help." Jakob said, twirling his finger, disturbing the still water. Gadreed sighed as he spectral form sat on the water. "Not surprising." Jakob said. "How well did you know the Goddess?"

"Too well." Gadreed sighed. "I swore to protect, not only Kirames, but Alvarome. Gidione… was less than supportive."

"Clearly." Jakob said with a heavy breath. "If it wasn't for Meer, we might have been killed."

"Unlikely." Gadreed said as his wings expanded. "The Gods themselves are growing weaker, as are their subordinates. Unlike the Devils. Thankfully." The Angel of War said, closing his eyes and crossing his arms. "When I perished, my magic was at full strength."

"How was that?" Jakob asked, stretching his legs while sitting on the water. "How did you not succumb to this worlds magic."

"At first I had." Gadreed said. "But when we allied ourselves with the Basilisks a protection spell was cast by the Faerie. That same spell exists in the shield, which is why I am careful of whom I grant its protection. As a being of my blood, no matter the distance, you too are protected by the spell. As are the Daemon's. Though, they may not be aware." Jakob took a slow breath as he listened to the Angel. "The spell does more than protect us from the magic of this world Jakob." Gadreed said, slowly looking up at his host. "It was insurance. If we ever raised weapons against the Basilisks or Faerie, the spell would break and deplete our immortality."

"But." Jakob said softly. "If that is the case, how did Gramps become turned? Shouldn't your blood have protected him from turning?"

"The Draugar infection is more disease than magic." Gadreed said. 'A Divine disease that slowly kills the body, allowing the Devil's dark magic to freely consume the infected host." Gadreed looked into the eyes of his host, seeing the pain spreading across his face. "I am sorry, Jakob, for the loss of your grandfather."

Jakob sighed as he rubbed his eyes. "I remember the stories Gramps use to tell me when I was young." Jakob said as he faced the Angel. "The same stories most of us in this world grew up hearing and believing." Jakob's eyes met with Gadreed's as he thought of his grandfather, his life, his family. "Now, everything is so different. And it seems we had to learn the hard way, seeing as you wouldn't just share the information with us."

"Indeed." Gadreed said plainly. Jakob sighed, realizing that was the only response the Angel would give on the matter. "The elf." Gadreed said suddenly. "I see you have moved from one companion to another." Again, Jakob sighed as he rubbed his eyes. "Yet you have not mated. Why?"

"You suddenly have an interest in my personal affairs?" Jakob smirked. "I wouldn't think the Angel of War would care for romance."

Gadreed laughed softly, surprising the young man. It had been the first *human* emotion he had seen from the Angel. "I had a beloved as well, Jakob." Gadreed said. "But that is not my concern. You have not bonded with her. though, I know your connection with her. I am simply curious as to why."

"Is there… a point?" Jakob asked. "It's not like…"

"You fear you will leave her." Gadreed said. "And that I will consume your soul." Jakob shrugged as he nodded. "An understandable fear, but a fear that should be shared with the Faerie nonetheless." The spectral Gadreed stood from the water and offered his hand to Jakob. "And let me tell you… how Feya can save your soul."

Gidione sat on the edge of the bed, glaring at the party of mortals that had mutilated her. The pain still resonated in her mind from the neural attack from the Basilisk. Her body ached and burned from her severed limbs. She took a long slow breath to calm herself, a façade to mask the pain. The Goddess refused to show weakness or fear as she eyed the mortals who had trapped her in these four walls. After waking from her dreamless sleep, she had made several attempts to free herself. She angrily asked for her chains to be removed. Arguing that the room was sufficient to hold her. the argument was ignored. Jakob insisted the chains remained on the Goddess, despite the clear rot forming along her body.

Balin stood by the door, watching the Goddess as he held his short sword. Gidione hated the sight of the blade. The blade that severed her hand. Tensions were high in the room. Jakob could feel Gadreed watching through his eyes. It was obvious from her expression that Gidione could feel the Angel's eyes as well. The Goddess turned away from the eyeing mortals and looked out her dust coated window. The three Divine blooded party members were outside, easing the minds of the Nupross chief. The Goddess smirked, seeing the fear in the mortal chief's eyes from knowing a Divine was in his city. Gidione's smile widened as she slowly turned away from the window to face the mortals. "Don't flatter yourself, las." Balin said, sliding his finger along the blade of his short sword. "They wanted you dead once we dragged you here." Balin winked at the Goddess as she scoffed and turned her head. "They just making sure the natives don't barge in here to finish ya off."

"They fear Meer." Jakob said, watching the Goddess with hard eyes. "They do not fear you."

"A foolish mistake." Gidione hissed, twisting her body in the hopes the chains would fall. "After I deal with the lot of you... Eeus will see to this city and the beast's destruction."

"Doubtful." Jakob said, his voice changing as his eyes began to glow. Gadreed had pushed forward through his mind, assuming control of the coming interrogation. "Even you, Gidione, fell with ease to the power of a Basilisk."

"You hide behind your treason, Angel of War." Gidione hissed. "You turned on the Divine God. Turned on our people. For protection against this worlds power."

Gadreed's form took control. His magical wings formed above Jakob's back as his hair turned long and white. "Still so young and naïve." Gadreed said. "Too blinded by proving your loyalty that you do not see your master's betrayal."

"You are the only traitor here, Gadreed."

"Still so ignorant you refuse to see what is right in front of you, Gidione." Gadreed said. Gidione snarled, seeing the room's magical properties had no effect on the Angel or his host. "You have seen a Basilisk firsthand. You have seen the lasting affect this world has on our kind. The Devils have known this. Lucile turned on Alvarome, simply to take his place amongst those who wish to leave this realm." Gadreed looked into the hate filled eyes of the Goddess. "This... I know you are aware of. She has reclaimed Senshe, sent her spy, and you know more than that." Gidione glared at the Angel, remaining silent. Gadreed shrugged as he took in a frustrated breath. "Read from the golden slab." Gadreed said. Feya gripped the etched gold in her arms as she watched the Goddess spit on the Angel.

Gadreed was unfazed as a smirk crossed the Goddess's lips. Gadreed shoved his foot against Gidione's chest. "You will read the slab, Goddess." Gadreed snarled as Gidione groaned in pain. "To aid in Lucile's plans, which I know she has disclosed to you. Or, because if you do, I will release you. Then you can return to Elysian and warn your Divine God that the Abomination is now visible to the world."

"You wish me to aid the very being that would bring destruction to us?" Gidione coughed. "Eeus…"

"Do you believe Eeus is capable of slaying the Abomination? Slaying the Basilisks?" Gadreed shouted, slamming his foot against the chains. The earth magic burned hotter against the Goddess's flesh, burning away her delicate fabric robe. Blood oozed from the chains as the metal slowly burned into her flesh. "You have your doubts." Gadreed said coldly. "You have seen her condition. You have seen the might of only one Basilisk. How much faith will remain when the skies and earth are filled with the true gods of this world?"

Gidione remained silent as Lucile's plan rushed through her mind. She would not admit it to the Angel of War, but she had her doubts. She knew of Lucile's followers. Senshe. Devils. If Tor was in a similar condition to the Divine God, he would stand little chance against a rebellion from within. She thought back to her brother, wondering how many other Gods felt the same as him. "He would kill us." Gidione said with narrowed eyes. "No matter my decision… he will kill us."

"And what happens if you stay in this realm?" Lavender asked, snatching the golden slab from Feya. The Cambion tossed the gold on the bed next to the Goddess. Gidione turned away, refusing to look at the words written on the slab. "The way I see it." Lavender said, crossing her arms mockingly to the Goddess. "You're going to get weaker and weaker… until even mortals can slay the Divine God."

"Filth." Gidione muttered. "You are all filth." The Goddess rolled onto the bed, turning away from the mortals. "I will not aid the enemy of my

Divine God. I will die her loyal servant. Leave me… so I may perish in peace."

"Whatever you say." Lavender smiled. "But think about this. If I was the Abomination… my fury would be aimed at Tor and Eeus. No need for your entire race to die… when they could be his ally."

Chapter 17

The night came quick after speaking with Gidione. The Inn was as silent as the dead, despite no one being able to sleep. The occasional soft groan could be heard from the hallways. Gidione's attempts to hide the pain from the toxic magic binding her. Kylo had seen Anna leave her room and headed towards the kitchen. The Daemon had looked at the hunter with concern filled eyes. After their talk with Hadriel and hearing of Gadreed's interrogation, they knew the war was coming and closer than ever. Little was said between the Daemon and Nephilim, but he knew she was headed to speak with Hadriel. The half God had spent these past hours sulking in the kitchen, alone with his thoughts. Kylo stepped towards the bedroom Anna and Ava shared and gently knocked on the door. Ava invited him in with a whispered voice.

The elf girl was covered by multiple blankets in her bed. Her hair was disheveled. Half of her head was covered by one of the thinner blankets. Ava looked at him silently as she wiped tears away with her many coverings. "Sorry." Ava whispered, continuing to wipe her face. "I thought you were Feya."

"Sorry to disappoint." Kylo said, smiling as he sat on the edge of the bed. Ava turned her body under the covers to face him as he sat silently on the bed. The hunter's eyes darted from one end of the room to the other, not looking at the elf. After several moments, he combed his fingers through his hair and sighed. "I'm sorry." Kylo said softly. "I'm sorry about Arys. I know you were happy you had all gained your freedom from that dwarf." Ava didn't respond, pulling one of her sheets over her mouth to keep from crying. "How long… how long did you two know each other?" Kylo asked.

"A long time." Ava said with a trembling voice. "I was at the Palace since I was a child. He had been there since Thrayn's father was alive."

Kylo took a long breath as he slowly turned to the elf. "I can't imagine what it was like."

"Can't you?" Ava said, sliding the cover from her face. "You have paid for your fair share of attention from women. Seems you would have been a customer instead of a savior if Christopher hadn't found you."

The hunter sighed and looked away from the elf. "You're probably right." Kylo admitted, a soft smirk crossing his lips. "Seeing that place. Seeing Feya and the others." Kylo shook his head slowly. "Hearing the cries I heard through the night." He turned to her with shame filled eyes. "I'm sorry Ava."

Ava sighed and got up from the bed. She was still wearing her dress as if sleep was not an option for the night. "It's not your fault." Ava said, combing her fingers through her long blond hair. "Sex sells, and clearly men are incapable of resisting the market." Kylo chuckled as he rubbed the back of his neck. Ava tilted her head to meet the hunter's eyes. "Why come to me?"

"I wanted to give my condolences about Arys." Kylo shrugged. "But… I also wanted to apologize to you personally. You're right about me. I'm just some Divine blooded brat, looking for the pleasures of this world and hiding behind my father's name."

"I don't remember having enough conversations with you for you to know that." Ava said with a smirk.

"It was easy to tell what you thought of me." Kylo smiled. "It's always easy to tell what people think of me, because… it's what I think of me."

"Well." Ava said, sitting back against the headrest of the bed. "You did try to seduce me immediately after Jakob and I were over."

"Guilty as charged." Kylo said, leaning forward and rubbing his head. "It's just… the more I spend with your people, the more I get to know all of you, even though I haven't been here long, I've grown fond of you all." Ava's smile was soft and genuine as she watched the hunter sit nervously on the bed. His foot was gently tapping on the floor from anxiety and embarrassment. "I just… like I said. Seeing that place. It made an impact on me I guess."

"The son of the great Astaad should be doing more than slaying beasts for coin to buy a night of passion." Ava said, mocking the Nephilim. Kylo smiled and nodded his agreement. "You know…" Ava said, looking out the window beside her bed. "Even through his decades of slavery with Thrayn and his family, Arys was the most warm-hearted person I ever knew. Honest. Loyal. Protective. That is why I morn him so much. Everyone at that Palace deserved their freedom, but none more than Arys."

"He fought bravely with Gadreed." Kylo said. "Helping defeat that Colossus; I could see the pride he felt fighting beside his friend."

"Yes." Ava said softly. "He seemed… happy."

Kylo turned and smiled at the young elf. "You were, and are, amazing yourself Ava. I don't know if you know that, but that was an excellent shot during the Trial." Ava rolled her eyes and turned back to the window. "It's true." Kylo said, fixing his gaze on the floor. "Anna and Hadriel are Daemon's. Feya a Faerie. Jakob has Gadreed. Sebastian was a powerful mage. Balin… is Balin, from what I have gathered." The hunter shrugged as he laughed. "But you have no magic. No real reason to follow this rag-tag group of self-proclaimed saviors. Yet, you follow and fight. You do all you can to help."

"I don't do much." Ava sighed. "Shoot an arrow here and there, but the closer we get to the end… the more useless I realize I am."

"I wouldn't say that." Kylo said.

"Why not?" Ava scoffed. "I retreated back to what I ran away from. Using my body to keep Anna and I safe. When it comes to fighting… I'm nothing compared to the rest of you. Just a whore. Meant for nothing but sex and problems."

"You are strong, Ava." Kylo said. "What you overcame. What you endured for your sister. You have shown everyone who travels with you the strength needed to save this world. That better world needs to be created." Kylo turned to the elf shaking his head. "Do not think so little of yourself or what you have lived through."

"Well." Ava said. "Then I suppose I can accept your apology and forgive your lust filled acts towards my fellow females." Kylo smiled and nodded his head. "So why do you stay, son of a hunter?"

Kylo leaned back in the bed, resting his arms behind his head. "I guess… I want to do something meaningful. My father respected these beasts, enough to not hunt them in their weakened state."

"They don't seem weak to me."

"Indeed." Kylo said. "It makes me wonder what my father was actually doing and thinking."

"So, you hope to find out what he was actually doing?" Ava asked, easing closer to the hunter.

"I don't know." Kylo breathed. He smiled and turned to Ava. "But traveling with this lot lets me be around you." Ava stopped her approach and tilted her head. "I'd like to change your view of me." Kylo said, looking up at the dirty ceiling. "You're the only woman that has made me want to do that."

"Why is that?" Ava asked, looking at the hunter as he stared off into nothing.

"I don't really know." Kylo shrugged. "Your bravery. Your beauty. Your compassion for you new family." He turned his head slightly, letting his eyes meet her emerald green gaze. 'But I am looking forward to finding out."

Ava chuckled and looked away, trying to hide her flushing red face. "I think you should try to get some sleep." Ava said, smiling as she looked at the hunter. "I don't want Anna to come back and get the wrong idea."

"I don't think she would get the wrong idea." Kylo laughed, standing from the bed. "You've been notorious about turning me down since we met."

"Very true." Ava said, standing from the bed and walking the hunter to the door. "You were a womanizing bastard with an ego the size of a dragon." Ava laughed opening the door.

"Were?" Kylo asked as he stepped into the hallway.

Ava began closing the door as she leaned against the wall. The door was cracked open, just enough for her to look at him one last time. Her smile was wide, and her cheeks were pink as she sighed. "Things can change." Ava said. The hunter smiled wide as he gave a gentle bow of his head. "Goodnight Kylo." Ava said, slowly closing the door. She pressed her forehead against the wood, listening for his footsteps in the hallway.

"Goodnight... Ava."

Jakob sat silently in his bedroom waiting for Feya. He was filled with nervous energy. Not only from the day's dealings with the Goddess, but he was ready to talk to Feya. They had shared a bed but not each other. Though, he knew she wanted to, as did he. Despite the strangeness of taking relationship advice from a long dead Angel, he knew Gadreed was right. It was time to lay everything on the table with her. what his worries were and what Gadreed had told him. Jakob's mind was flooded with thoughts. Anna had shared the concerns of the Divine blooded members with him earlier. They were valid concerns. A still lingering question of what Christopher would do once his power was unsealed. He was unable to give an adequate response. Christopher was a mystery. They had only met a handful of times, but he was no threat to them. He gave advice and filled in gaps to history. All Jakob could do was pray that the Savior would see the good his Divine blooded allies have done.

He knew Anna and the other Divine blooded members were talking in the kitchen. Unable to sleep and aimlessly snacking away the hours as they talked with Balin and Brenna. Jakob could hear bickering in the kitchen about adequate seasonings or cooking techniques about whoever was behind the stove. He couldn't help but smile. Through everything, Balin was always the same. Elizabeth's betrayal seemed distant now. Jakob rationalized it as a dwarven trait. Perhaps having such long lifespans helped them overcome those feelings. It was no secrete that Balin sought Elizabeth's attention. Jakob couldn't imagine the emotional pain of learning the truth. Still, Balin acted like Balin. He even found himself a woman. One that seems to be interested in their journey and remaining by him. The betrayal Jakob felt for the disguised Succubus still remained in his heart. Knowing the Devil's servant toyed with them and his grandfather. Giving false hope to an already doomed man.

The bedroom doo opened slowly as Feya stepped in. she was carrying a small tray with two cups of tea and several teaming buns. She smiled as she slid the door shut with her foot before removing her shoes. Jakob watched in admiration as Feya placed the tray on the bedside table. She began digging through her clothing, searching for something more comfortable to sleep in. she was wearing a soft blue dress Ava had given her. short enough to showcase her legs but still modest enough for the young Faerie. Jakob was unable to remove his eyes from her. the blue of the dress was almost white, perfectly accenting Feya's fair complexion, blue hair, and sapphire eyes.

"Sorry it took so long." Feya said softly. "Balin insisted I try the stew he and Brenna are making."

"A little late for stew." Jakob said, walking over to the Faerie.

"I don't think they plan on sleeping." Feya sighed. "Everyone is on edge. Nervous." Jakob stepped behind her and wrapped his arms around her. she lifted her hands, caressing his arms. Jakob leaned in, kissing her cheek. "What's on your mind, Jakob?" Feya whispered as she turned to face him.

The young man held her close, loving the feel of having her in his arms. "There… is a lot I want to talk to you about." Feya gave him a soft smile and pulled him to sit on the bed. Silently, she handed him his cup of tea before taking her. Jakob blew on the steaming drink then swallowed hard. He was ready for this, but also unprepared. He took a sip of the tea, letting the hot liquid calm his nerves. "I love you, Feya." Jakob finally said without looking at her. His eyes remained fixed on the steaming drink. "I want you to know that. No matter what you decide after this… I want you to know I love you." Feya said nothing but Jakob could feel her eyes on him. He could almost hear her heart beathing beside him. "I know the bonding is a lifelong commitment. I want you to know that I would want nothing more than to bond with you. To be with you until my dying breath." Feya moved closer to him, resting her hand on his shoulder. "My… my fear." Jakob said, stumbling to find his words. "Is that my dying breath may be sooner rather than later. This coming war. Gadreed possibly overtaking me. I don't want to hurt you. I don't want to leave you."

"Then don't leave me." Feya said, leaning forward to meet his eyes. "Seems simple enough."

Jakob turned and smiled at her. "You know what happens every time Gadreed takes control." Jakob said with a trembling voice. "My soul gets weaker. And soon, he will be in full control."

"There's something else, isn't there?" Feya said. Jakob nodded slowly. Feya could feel his arm trembling. "So, tell me."

"Promise me, if I tell you, it will not be the reason you want to be with me." Jakob said, pulling away from the Faerie. He looked at her with hard, tear-filled eyes. She agreed with an unreadable expression. "Gadreed told me how he, and the others with Divine blood, are capable of surviving earth magic. Protection given to us by the Faeries." Feya tilted her head as she listened. She took his hand, a simple act that gave strength to the nervous young man. "Gadreed said, either the Basilisks or the Faerie, could save me. that the bonding between Faerie is almost a magical promise."

"I don't understand." Feya said. "Is it a protection similar to what the Faerie did for Gadreed?"

Jakob shook his head slowly. "The bonding is apparently unifying souls. A promise between two people to be with each other forever."

"I know." Feya said softly. "And that's why I want you to…"

"Gadreed told me Shinrahn could save me." Jakob said quickly. "That you are his only tribe member, and me being your bonded… you could convince him to save me." Feya became silent as she tried to understand. "Shinrahn is the Dragon King. Giver of all magic. Giver of life. Thanatos, the Basilisk of Death, and Carrier of Souls, will be needed to save me. Shinrahn is the only one capable of summoning him."

"I still don't understand." Feya said. "How can I convince Shinrahn? What does Gadreed think will happen to you?"

"I don't know." Jakob said.

Feya sat silently for several heartbeats. She scowled and turned to Jakob as she stood from the bed. "Jakob." Feya said with a harsh tone. "I love you. I want… I have wanted for so long to be with you. If bonding with me can save you, keep you with me, then…"

"I don't want you to bond with me just to save me."

"Shut up." Feya hissed. "Do you think if Thrayn would have let someone rape me that I would have been bonded with them?" Feya took several frustrated breaths as Jakob's eyes met hers. "No." She snarled. "Bonding is more than sex. I love you. I have loved you for so long. When… when we bond, it is more than a physical thing. I want to bond with you because I love you. And if that saves your life, that just means you are not going to leave me."

"I love you, Feya." Jakob said, standing from the bed and taking Feya's hands in his. "If you are sure you can bare to be with me forever…"

Feya pressed her lips against his. "There is nothing I want more." Feya said as she gently pulled her lips from his. She shoved him onto the bed and slid her arms free of her dress. Her body became free of the soft blue fabric as she crawled on top of him. Her lips met his once again as she pulled at his belt. He could feel the cold of her amethyst charm against his chest as she slid his hands along her waist. She pulled her lips away as she slid and found him. Joy. Pleasure. Peace. Love. They felt everything the other was feeling. They knew what each of them felt for one another. Feya moaned as the blue lined tattoos began to glow. A thin tattoo formed between her breasts. The line moved and reshaped itself into runes as Jakob's lips kissed every part of her. Every sensation was shared between them. Feya closed her eyes as she moaned, moving her hips to feel more of him. A white light shined from her eyes as they slowly opened. Her wings fluttered and began flowing white as a cooling dust hovered around them. Jakob didn't know what was happening, but he didn't care. They were one. she was his, and he was hers. She leaned down, kissing him as her body shook. Their hands explored each other. Jakob sat up, sliding Feya on her back as he pulled her back to him. Feya smiled as she bit her lip. "I don't plan on sleeping tonight either." The Faerie said, wrapping her legs around Jakob's waist. Her sapphire eyes returned as her tattoo completed its rune.

"Neither do I."

The kitchen was filled with laughter, thanks in most part to Brenna and Balin's bickering by the stove. Anna and Hadriel had welcomed the pair as an interruption for their sulking. Remembering how Gidione looked, hearing her pain filled groans in the halls was difficult on the Daemon pair. Hadriel most of all. As hateful as the Goddess was, she was still his family. He prayed. Something he hadn't done in centuries. He knew his prayers would not be answered, not by any God or Devil. The Daemon wanted his aunt to see reason. To side with them. If she simply read from the slab, she could return to Elysian, warn the Gods, and convince them to remain in hiding. Lucile would be a good distraction for Christopher. She would be the one bold enough to approach him. Her arrogance would give both he and his aunt enough time to save as many of their people as possible. He knew it was a foolish prayer. Gidione and the other Gods would never turn on their Divine God. Death was in both directions for their races. Death by earth's magic or death by war. Unless the Gods surrendered their hold on this world.

Brenna cursed as Balin slapped her hand away from the boiling pot. She had tried to add more salt, despite the dwarf's instructions. Anna laughed behind her teacup as she watched the dark-haired woman toss salt in the dwarf's beard. Hadriel forced a smile, trying to hide the thoughts still plaguing his mind. Anna noticed his façade and slowly sat her cup on the table. "We can talk to her." Anna said as she leaned slightly forward on the table. Hadriel lifted his head to look at the half elf. "Let's just have our stew first." Anna said with a smile. "They've been fighting over it long enough… we might as well eat and ease our minds." Hadriel smiled and nodded his head.

"The whole city can hear you lot." Lavender said as she stepped into the kitchen. She eased behind Anna, pulling a chair to sit beside the Devil Daemon. The Cambion took the teacup and let herself drink before handing the cup back to the Daemon. "After what you all have been up to, I expected something harder than tea." Lavender said, looking into the Daemon's emerald eyes.

"I'm sure there is something more to your liking if you look for it." Anna said, lifting the cup to her lips.

"I know there is" Lavender said, winking at the Daemon before turning to the cooking couple. "Hey dwarf." The Cambion yelled. "No dwarven shine with our meal?"

"Aye." Balin said, kicking a nearby cabinet open. Several plates and pots fell from the cabinet, revealing a large brown bottle of unmarked drink. "Picked this up in town. not as good as dwarven shine, but drink is drink."

Brenna ladled the stew in several bowls she had picked up off the floor. She sat a bowl in front of each guest before tossing several spoons onto the table. "You will find Nupross whiskey bolsters your senses more so than dwarven shine." Brenna said, narrowing her eyes to Balin with a soft smirk. Balin twirled his whiskers between his fingers, laughing as he took his seat. "Our drink is perfect to ready oneself for fighting… or fucking." Brenna said.

Lavender slowly turned her head to Anna, flicking her finger on the Daemon's cup. "Would you join me?" The Cambion said with a wide smile.

"Fighting or fucking?" Anna said with a raised brow.

Lavender smiled, biting her lip and revealing her fangs. "I'll let you pick. Though, I do have a preference."

"Gods." Hadriel hissed. "You don't even try to hide your Succubus blood, do you?"

"Why would I?" Lavender laughed, not pulling her eyes from Anna. "I've been… absent for some time, and this is quite a sight to wake up to."

"Such a charmer." Anna said mockingly. "But I don't think tonight is the night to be thinking of such things."

Lavender laughed as her ears perked up. "It would seem your leader and the Faerie disagree." Hadriel sighed as he poured the tea onto the floor and began filling his cup with whiskey. Balin laughed, holding his hand to his ear to listen upstairs. "I'm sure the dwarf and the warrior woman will be departing after a drink and feast as well." Lavender said, leaning closer to the Daemon. "I have no room… you could always invite me into yours."

"Fuck." Hadriel hissed, swallowing the aged drink. "This is an Inn, Lavender. You can find a room."

"You must be as pure as freshly fallen snow, Hadriel." Lavender said, sitting back in her chair. "I can't imagine anything wanting to fuck such a bore." Lavender looked around the room, tilting her head towards the entryway. "Where is your elf friend? She seemed to be the only one capable of dealing with you."

"She found herself a room." Hadriel huffed. "Yavanna had no need to try to spin words for a bed and sex."

"What a shame." Lavender said, turning to Anna. She smiled, seeing the Daemon wearing a soft smirk. "Even the elf mage would not bed you."

Hadriel and I are planning on speaking with Gidione." Anna said. "I don't think our conversation would go over well if…"

"If a Cambion was between your legs." Lavender smiled.

"Your kind are relentless." Hadriel hissed, finishing off his drink and pouring another.

"I was going to say intoxicated." Anna said, looking at the drinking Daemon. "Do you think it wise to keep drinking, Hadriel?" The half God shrugged as he tilted the cup up, swallowing its contents in one swig. "Should we offer our Goddess a drink as well?" Anna mocked as Lavender poured them each a glass of whiskey.

"Aye." Balin said, puffing his chest and holding up his cup. "Drink makes everything easier. The God might even read the slab by mistake if taken from drink."

"The Gods can't get drunk." Hadriel said, topping off his third cup. "Their magic keeps them in clear mind."

"Aye." Balin said. "But some thought the Gods were also unkillable. Yet, we have a half corpse upstairs."

Hadriel became silent and his face hardened. His foul demeanor spread across the room, causing unease amongst the diners. "She is still my family, dwarf." Hadriel said, closing his eyes and taking a drink. "I know what must be done, and I am prepared for it. I just… don't want to see our kind erased."

"Aye." Balin said after a long silence. "I meant no disrespect, my friend." The dwarf said, setting his cup on the table. "I know this must be difficult for the lot of ya, being of Divine blood and all. I believe the vagrant knows what he must do. Do not forget, he is of your blood as well."

"Aye." Anna said. "I believe you are right, Balin. He is our kin. It is not the fault of the lesser Divine that we have remained in this world."

"Isn't it?" Hadriel hissed. "They follow Tor and Eeus, knowing death is the only outcome. Lying to themselves believing they could defeat the Basilisks."

"All soldiers follow orders." Lavender said. "That is true in every race on every world. Faerie follow the orders of our elders. The elders follow the instructions of our Basilisk. Our Basilisks… follow the law of Shinrahn."

"I suppose that's true." Hadriel said with closed eyes. "A shocking point of view coming from a Succubus."

Lavender smiled as she shrugged her shoulders. "This tongue is used for more than pleasure." The Cambion said, standing from her chair, carrying her bowl of stew. "Your welcome to find out." Lavender whispered in Anna's ear. "I'll find myself a room. You are always welcome to find me." Anna couldn't help but smile as she listened to fading footsteps of the Cambion. She looked over at Balin and Brenna who were chuckling to themselves as they watched the half Faerie leave.

"Fucking Devils." Hadriel sighed, downing the rest of his drink.

"Anna is very popular with the ladies it seems." Brenna said, resting her head against Balin. "Some of the women in town have taken notice of her and now a half Faerie. Perhaps you should work on your demeanor, Hadriel. If what Lavender says is true." Hadriel sighed and sat his head against the hard wood table. "There are plenty of fine strong women here in Nupross."

"Again." Anna said. "I think we have more to worry about. Do you still want to speak to Gidione?"

Hadriel slowly lifted his head form the table, rubbing his eyes. "Yes." The Daemon breathed. "Let's get this over with." Hadriel huffed as he turned to Anna. "So you can discover everything the halfling's tongue is good for."

Chapter 18

Feya opened her eyes to see the familiar fog from her encounter with Meer. She called out to the Basilisk but received no response. She frantically turned, hoping to find any sign of life. Feya called out for Jakob, only to hear her words echoing through the thick sheet of white. Taking a step, her feet dug slightly into the ground. The feeling of cool water began covering her feet before being pulled away. Feya knelt down to feel the ground. "Sand." Feya said to herself with a whisper. She stood, holding a handful of sand in her hand. Small frothing waves surrounded her feet. The water relaxed her as she let the sand slowly fall from her palm.

A sudden gust of wind blew through the fog, erasing the once white coated world. Sand and ash blew in the Faeries eyes. She knelt back down, tossing water on her face to wash away the sand and ash. As she opened her eyes, she saw a great black mountain. There was no sign of life. No birds in the sky. No animals roaming through what little plant life thrived. She turned, looking out at the ocean. That's when she saw them. The islands. Home of the Faerie. A rumble shook the majestic mountain. Fire and magma shot from the mountains peak. Cracks shot down the stone, releasing steam and fire. Feya backed into the water as a piece of mountain collapsed, crumbling to ash as it hit the sandy beach. Feya looked at the collapsed mountain in shock. The fire and smoke had stopped. A large piece of white shined from the crumbled mountainside. The white moved, revealing the bright blue iris of an eye. Another rumble shook the island as the mountain finished collapsing to ash.

Feya felt magic flowing through her body. Her wings felt powerful. She took flight, slowly lifting herself from the water. She reached for her chest and realized she wasn't wearing her charm. "Blood of my blood." A thunderous voice boomed from the mountain. As and dust still filled the air around the now crumbled volcanic mountain. Two large tails, covered in white sparkling scales, lifted through the clouds of dust. Each tail had four spikes the size of trees on each end with glass-like dorsal plates running up the creature's body. Feya flew higher, watching as the creature's four great wings blew the dust and ash away. "Feya." The booming voice said. The voice was calling to her. the creature was calling to her. the beast's large blue eyes were fixed on the flying Faerie. Feya swallowed hard as she slowly approached the beast. It stepped free of the mountain on its four massive legs, shaking its head free of debris. "I knew I could rely on you."

"Who are you?" Feya asked, flying close to the beast.

The beast snapped its jaw, revealing its massive fangs. "I am Shinrahn."

"Shinrahn." Feya whispered. She was compelled to fly closer, resting her hand on the Basilisks snout. By touching the Dragon King, she could feel her magical power increase. Memories of her creation flooded her mind. She pulled her hand away as tears fell from her cheek. "Ma… Da…"

"I am sorry, my child." Shinrahn said in Feya's mind. "I am the only blood you have. To insure your success on the continent, I had to implant your memories of home and the belief that the Faerie are powerless."

"Why?" Feya asked.

Shinrahn lifted his head, allowing Feya to sit comfortably on his snout. "To keep you safe." The Dragon King said. "For the mortals believe the Faerie are to blame for the state of this world. For you to have survived, they must see you as weak."

"But… I haven't unsealed Christopher." Feya said. "Why do you speak to me now?"

"You have awakened, my child." Shinrahn said. "You have found your bonded, he was the one who awakened your power." Feya sat on the Dragon, shaking her head in confusion. "It was known to us that the ones who would restore balance to this world would come in this age. I sent you to travel the continent and find the prophesized individuals."

"You mean Jakob?"

A low rumble came from the Basilisks throat. "Yes. Gadreed's host and your bonded. You have also gathered the Daemon's and the child of Astaad."

"Kylo?" Feya asked, running her hand along the shining scales of the Dragon. "But…"

"His blood still has its part to play." Shinrahn said. "Now, when you wake, you will have your power, my child. You will be connected to this world's magic. My magic." Feya sat silently on the Basilisk. Her heart and mind filled with questions, concerns, and fears. "Speak child." Shinrahn said. "I am here to give you the confidence you need to see this through."

"Jakob is going to die." Feya said, trying not to cry. "Gadreed believes you can save him." She adjusted herself to kneel to the Dragon. "Please, if you can help him…"

"There is no need for you to beg or show weakness to me, child." Shinrahn said. "I am your Basilisk. You are my tribe. As you have been for millennia." Feya's heart skipped at the Basilisks words. *Millennia?* A soft growl echoed in the beast's throat as he turned towards the sea. "To win this war, Gadreed will be needed. His soul will overtake your bonded, and Gadreed will assume his form." Feya bit her lip, trying to stop herself from screaming in grief. "Do not weep, my child."

"How can I not?" Feya cried, standing on Shinrahn's snout as she balled her fists. "He is my bonded. My love. You are telling me he is going to be lost to me."

Feya could feel the rumble of Shinrahn's breath under her feet. "I have never known the feeling of being connected to a tribe." Shinrahn said, lowering his head for Feya to step onto a large cliff. Feya took a slow step, thankful the rock hadn't collapsed. "You are connected to more than just your bonded child. We, as a tribe, are also connected. As I am to my brethren."

"Like Senshe?"

"Yes." Shinrahn said as smoke left his nostrils. "I still morn his loss. His soul waits for his body to perish so he may be reborn anew."

"Reborn?" Feya asked.

"Yes, my child." Shinrahn said, lifting his head. "Basilisks do not seek magic for immortality as the invaders do. They are born, they live, they die, and are reborn anew. All while holding on to the memories of their previous life. We are in a never-ending cycle of life, death, and rebirth."

"And what about Jakob?" Feya whispered, fearful of the answer.

Senshe huffed a heavy breath as he turned to face the Faerie. "You have chosen a mortal as your bonded. Death was always the outcome for the mortals. They live. They die. Their souls live in the spiritual plain of this world.

"Spiritual plain?"

"Yes." Shinrahn said, turning his head so his shining blue eye met Feya's. "The realm of souls. Ruled by Thanatos, my brother."

"If you created me." Feya said. "And your brother is the ruler of the spiritual plain… can't you save Jakob?"

"Thanatos is particular about the rules of death concerning the mortals." Shinrahn said. Feya looked down at the stone, scratching her legs in frustration until they began to bleed. "It is unheard of for Faeries to fear the death of their bonded. Though, most do not form a passion strong enough for the bond to take as you have." Feya looked up at Shinrahn with tear filled eyes. "Very well." Shinrahn said, extending his four wings. "I will do what I can, but I can make no promises. You are the only of my tribe. It is likely, if your bonded was to perish, Thanatos's tribe would come. They would honor you by guiding him personally to the spiritual plain."

"That is where you could stop them?"

"That." Shinrahn said. "Is where I can try." Feya sighed but a small smile crossed her lips. The smallest glimmer of hope in a dangerous future. "The time is drawing nearer, Feya." Shinrahn said. "You and your friends have done well. All the pieces are now in play. All that is left is to unseal the child of two blood and release my confinement of this mountain."

"Do you know where Christopher is?"

"He was here, on the islands.' Shinrahn said. "Tor, the Ancestral Devil, appeared to try and make a deal with him." Feya's breathing stopped momentarily. The idea of the Ancestral Devil coming for Christopher, coming to the islands, was unbelievable. *Did he know Christopher was the Savior all along?* "Since his meeting, the child has gone to Atence. Far in the desert tundra of the continent. It is there that the blood of Astaad will fulfil their role. It is there that the war for this world will begin."

"So, Kylo is going to be heading to the desert tundra?" Feya asked. As she took a breath the white fog began to engulf the island and sea. She became surrounded by the cloud-like white as Shinrahn became camouflaged within the cloud. "Shinrahn?"

"When the seal is broken, bring your party to the islands." Shinrahn said through the fog. "All of them. Come to the volcanic island and call upon me." Feya watched as the shining blue of the Dragon's eye faded from sight. "And I... will answer."

The desert winds blew through the tundra with hurricane force. Christopher walked through the storm of sand, surrounded by a shield of magic. The glass-like sand was hungry for flesh, making life impossible in the tundra. Atence was a place Christopher despised visiting. Located in the center of the desert tundra, somehow a large forest surrounded the city. Aside from the ferocious storms of the desert, the forest around the city posed its own threat. Beasts still lingering from the Gods War roamed freely. The Great City was protected by its lingering magic and massive walls. An antient library was located in the center of Atence, built with bricks made of Scalestone. A sone that has not been found anywhere else in the world. The only known location of this rare gem is the library itself. Scalestone itself stores earth magic, keeping the Great City safe from the fierce storms of the tundra. The library is never used by the population of Atence. Shelf upon shelf of magical grimoires, all sealed from mortal eyes. Christopher had used the library and its knowledge for centuries. Sophillia's library. The Basilisk of knowledge. The only way to open an Atence grimoire is to believe in the Basilisks. A faith long lost to mortals since the invasion of the Gods.

Christopher groaned in frustration, unable to see the path he was taking thanks to the raging sands. He was amazed that mortals still traveled to the Great City surrounded by sand. The notorious storms were only calm for hours at a time throughout the year. Trade with Atence seemed suicidal. Yet, merchants made the journey in search of wealth. He couldn't understand their thinking as he watched the storm through his shield. Christopher missed the beauty of the islands. Since Tor made his unwelcomed visit, Christopher decided it was best for him to leave his

Faerie family. He knew the war was soon to begin. The desert was a safe place, relatively speaking, for him to be if he was to be unsealed. No one, not even Shinrahn, knew what would happen when his magic was unleashed. There was no life, no civilization for miles in the tundra. Atence was the only place that could support life. The vagrant hoped to find a cave or some kind of shelter. They were not uncommon in the tundra but were incredibly difficult to find. The sandstorm was relentless, making searching for shelter impossible. He groaned to himself again and considered heading for Atence. *The library should contain some magical disperse.* He thought to himself. *But there is still no guarantee the citizens would survive.*

The shield hit an object hidden within the sand. Christopher lifted his hand, expanding the shield's protection. A wagon was revealed, stocked with sand filled crates and tattered fabrics. The skeletons of the wagons merchants and horses were scattered around. From the condition of the fabrics, and judging the storm, Christopher assumed the merchants died only days prior. The raging sand stripped the flesh free from their bones. *Elf.* Christopher told himself as he examined the bones. *And... dwarf.* He knelt down to see the skeletal remains of the horses. *Meridian Steeds.* The vagrant said, running his fingers along the bone. *Strong horses. They probably assumed they could pull them through the storms. Idiots.* Christopher returned to the wagon and began examining what goods had survived. He dumped the contents onto the ground, freeing the merchandise from the sand. He found destroyed clothing and armor. A few blades that were decently crafted. *Probably the dwarf's work.* Christopehr told himself, examining the wagon. *Foolish not to bring a proper wagon.*

As Christopher ruffled through the wagon's contents, he found a black chest. It was sealed and well crafted, unlike the standard wooden crates used by most merchants. He looked at the three heavy locks and tilted his head. Christopher pulled the chest closer and snapped his fingers, breaking the locks. As he opened the chest, he noticed there was no sand in the box. Shining gems were separated by small boxes in the crate. *Amethyst. Sapphire. Moonstone. And... Scalestone?* Christopher pulled the rare stone from the box. There was only a small piece of the Scalestone. Still, it was unbelievable. As his eyes lifted, he saw a compartment on the trunks top. Christopher untied the laces and opened the hidden pocket. A broken arrow fell from the compartment. The shaft was made of antient dwarven grey wood. The tail feathers of the arrow were from the long extinct moon crow. A bird believed to signify the coming of death. Christopher scowled at the feathers. He had met Faerie of every tribe. Except the Soul Tribe. Thanatos's tribe. It was rumored they wore jewelry made of the rare feathers. His eyes became drawn to the arrowhead. He pricked his finger on the arrowhead as he examined the detailed carvings along the steel. *Elysian steel.* Christopher realized. *I can think of only one who would use such arrows.* Christopher smiled as he tossed the broken arrow into the sand. *These fools could have made a fortune selling the contents of this trunk. Why come here?* Christopher closed his eyes as he rubbed his chin. The distraction of exploring the wagon was welcomed. He grew tired of walking through the endless sand filled winds. *How long have you been following me?* Christopher thought as he sensed a familiar magic in the sand. Divine magic. An Angel's magic.

The ground beneath Christopher's feet shook. He turned, sensing dark magic approaching from behind him. The sand began to slow as if something large was blocking its path towards him. Christopher narrowed his eyes, waiting for whomever was approaching to reveal themselves. A large shadow stretched across the desert tundra. Christopher looked up, seeing golden eyes looking down at him. He released a long breath as footsteps could be heard in the sand. The vagrant strengthened his shield as he watched the tall, red-haired woman approach. She laughed softly as she stepped closer. There she stood, only paces away from him. A magic circle formed along the sand, forcing the winds into stillness. Christopher closed his eyes and took a slow breath. "Hello Lucile." The vagrant said as the Devil stepped even closer. Half dressed. Flaunting her womanly features, even in this weather. The Devil smiled a venomous smile, pressing her tongue against her fang. A purple-haired Succubus stepped form behind the Devil, moaning as she licked her lips at the sight of him.

"Hello… nephew."

Hadriel stood in front of Gidione's door. The Daemon was silently thinking of what to say to the Goddess while regretting drinking so much of the Nupross whiskey. Regrettably, Balin had convinced him to bring up what remained of the drink as an offering to the Goddess. Hadriel sighed as he turned to Anna. She smiled and shrugged, causing the three glasses in her fingers to clink. The half God knocked before opening the door He peeked inside before stepping into the Goddess's prison. Part of him expected to see Gidione lying dead on the bed or floor. Instead, the Goddess was sitting up, leaning against the dust coated headboard. Gidione eyed the approaching Daemon's as they welcomed themselves into the room. Anna slowly closed the door as Hadriel displayed the bottle to Gidione. A soft smile crossed his lips as he noticed the hand Balin had severed had regrown. Yet, the arm removed by Meer remained gone and her wound still bloody. "Care for a drink?" Hadriel said, wishing he had a better opening. Gidione scoffed, turning her head away from the halfblooded creatures.

"We just want to talk to you, Gidione." Anna said softly. She pulled a chair close to the bed and sat the glasses on the bedside table. She motioned Hadriel closer as she reached for the bottle. Hadriel slowly handed the drink to Anna, not taking his eyes off the battered Goddess. Anna began pouring them each a drink, noticing the golden slab lying face down on the bed. "I see you haven't tossed the slab out of the window." Anna said, offering the Goddess her glass.

Gidione mumbled insults as she licked her lips. The Goddess angrily snatched the drink from the Daemon and downed the whiskey in a single gulp. She began coughing, unfamiliar with the burn of alcohol in her throat. "I can't open the window." Gidione said through her coughs. "Filthy Cambion made sure I couldn't escape."

"I don't enjoy seeing you like this Gidione.' Hadriel said, nervously scratching his finger with his thumb. He swallowed hard, not knowing exactly what to say to the Goddess. "Why will you not help us? Your sister…"

"Kirames was a traitor.' Gidione hissed, grabbing the bottle from the table, and pouring herself another drink. "I will not betray our kind as she did."

"She wasn't betraying anyone." Anna said before taking a sip of her own drink. "She was trying to save everyone. Even you must see the damage this world is doing to the Divine races. It is time for our kind to leave."

"It doesn't seem to affect you half-bloods." Gidione snarled. "You hope that the Abomination will destroy us while sparing you. You think your protection from this worlds magic will save you from him?"

"I have met him." Anna said. Gidione's eyes widened as she looked into Anna's emerald eyes. Anna smiled softly as she looked at the defeated Goddess. "He wants to return rule to the Basilisks. I have never heard him speak of wiping out the Divine."

"He will though." Hadriel said. "That is why you have to help us. If you read this slab, you can return to Elysian and warn our people to remain there." Hadriel sat on the bed near Gidione's feet. He slowly placed a hand on his aunt's leg. She pulled away, not wanting him to touch her. "Eeus refuses to admit defeat, but she must. You know what will happen to our people if they are killed." Anna turned to Hadriel curiously. "They will return to Addilan. They will be trapped and judged by the Alpha's. the very one's Eeus and Tor fled from."

"You speak madness." Gidione said, taking another drink. "You are all mad. You. Those mortals. Lucile."

"How can you be a Goddess and not understand our history?" Hadriel said angrily. More so than intended. "Lucile will push her armies onto earth.

She will push them against the Gods. I may not know her… as intimately as you, but I do understand her mind." Gidione said nothing as she looked at the clear liquid in her cup. "She wants you to assume the role as Divine, doesn't she?" Hadriel whispered shaking his head. "She sees you as a toy. As weak. She wants to use you to get her way."

"And you think you ask differently, you filth." Gidione laughed. "You ask me to go against Eeus. Read those runes and release the Abomination. Are you not using me to get what you want?"

"We are." Anna said. "But what we ask of you is to release him and call your people to retreat. Have them convince Eeus to release her hold on this world."

"You think he cannot come to Elysian?" Gidione chuckled. "He is of both bloods. He can travel wherever he senses our blood."

"Why would he?" Anna asked, tilting her head. "He aims to return the balance of *this* world to the Basilisks and Faerie."

"Would you travel to another realm to slay the ones who executed your parents?" Gidion muttered.

"Your sister." Hadriel said softly. "And my mother. Did you lose all love for her, Gidione?" The Goddess said nothing as she turned away from the Daemon's. "Stop acting like a child, Gidione." Hadriel snarled, standing from the bed. "The war is going to come. He will be unsealed. If not by us, then by Lucile. Either way, you will die here. Is this really where you want to die? In a dirty Inn surrounded by mortals?"

"If you unseal him." Anna said, leaning closer to the Goddess. "You could change everything for our people. Save our people."

"He will want to kill Eeus." Gidione said, refusing to look at the Daemon's. "You are asking me to permit my Divine Gods death."

"She is dead either way." Anna said. "By Christopher or from this world."

"You are all protected from this world." Gidione said. "We can do the same."

"It's been a thousand years, Gidione." Hadriel breathed. "If it were possible, Eeus would have done it. What is it you're afraid of?"

Gidione took a breath as she turned to Hadriel. Her eyes were not filled with hate as he was used to seeing from her. instead, he saw fear and defeat. "You do not understand. Lucile does not understand. You are asking me to believe that my Divine God has lied to me. that all I was raised to believe is wrong. That she, in all her wisdom, is leading us to destruction. You cannot ask that of me."

"She did it to the mortals of this world." Hadriel said, looking into the Goddess's eyes. His eyes shared her fear. Fear of Christopher and the war. Of what outcome would befall them when he is unleashed. "Their memories and history were altered. Their beliefs are lies. Their true gods forgotten. All in an attempt to feed her power." Hadriel sat back on the bed, taking Gidione's hand in his. She didn't' pull away. Her eyes never left his. She saw him as she was always supposed to. As her nephew. She looked into his eyes. Looked at his sharp features. She saw Kirames in him. A tear slid down her cheek as her sister's face stared back at her. "Eeus has destroyed every world she claimed to rule. It has to stop. We can find a world devoid of gods. We can build a perfect realm for our kin." He tightened his grip around her hand. He felt her fingers embrace his grip as she looked down at his hand. "But we can't if she leads us to our deaths." Gidione looked back at Hadriel's face. Kirames's face. He reached behind his back, pulling the slab towards them. He turned it over and slid the gold in front of her. Gidione swallowed hard as she looked at the runes, not releasing Hadriel's hand. "Read it, Aunt Gidione." The Goddess's breathing became quick as her lips dried. She licked them as tears slid down her cheeks. Endless thoughts struck her mind. Lucile's plan to ally herself with the Abomination. The mortals plan to release him. The power the Basilisks hold, even without the seal being broken. What Eeus would do to her if she discovered her betrayal. She bit her lip as she turned to face Anna. *Have you truly failed me, Divine God.* Eeus thought to herself. The Daemon smiled, placing her hand on hers. Gidione took a slow breath as she faced Hadriel. He nodded to her as his own tears fell from his eyes. She looked down at the runes. They were written in antient glyphs from a time when Eeus was young. She knew the language from her studies. She sighed as she read the slab to herself. Lifting her eyes to Hadriel, the Goddess sighed as her lips quivered. "It says…"

Table of Contents

Definitions:

- **Mage**: A mortal who is still able to call on magic despite the Gods recalling their power after the Gods War.
- **Daemon**: A being of half Divine blood (God/Devil) and Mortal blood (Elf, Human, Dwarf).
- **Malachim**: A lower-level Angel typically assigned tasks such as messengers or resonance.
- **Archangel**: A mid-level Angel often doing groundwork for the Gods. Most are seen as deliverers of the Gods judgement.
- **Seraphim**: Highest ranked Angels. Divine beings with great power and also known as Angels of War.
- **Nephilim:** A Mortal being born with one parent being Mortal and the other parent being a lower Divine being. (Demon, Succubus, Angel)
- **Cambion**: A Being with one parent being of the Divine Race and the other of the Faerie race.

Organizations:

- **Tempests**: An organization founded after the Gods War. Founded by mortals who wished to find the child of Kirames and Alvarome and restore magic back to the Mortal Realm.
- **Cleansers**: An organization of mercenaries that hunt those who preach or practice magic. Their belief is that all those who believe in the Child of Both Blood and the use of magic will bring about the wrath of the Gods.
- **Sisters:** An Organization of all female followers. Worshipers still dedicated to praising and spreading the word of the Gods. The Sisters are known to denounce the Savior and preach to those who listen about the glory of the Gods. The Sisters believe the Savior is merely a half breed and one that does not deserve the same praise as the Gods themselves.

Races:

- **Human**: A race in the Mortal Realm with the highest population of any other Earth race. Humans are capable of magic but are often seen using enchanted items (Weapons, armor, jewelry)
- **Elf:** Elves are one of the oldest races in the Mortal Realm. They were the most adept at magic with enchantments until the Gods War. Even without magic, the elves' lifespans are many times greater than humans.
- **Dwarf**: Dwarves are another of the oldest races in the Mortal Realm. They were granted blessing by the Gods in

exchange for the dwarfs to forge their weapons during the Gods War. Dwarves live centuries longer than even the Elves.

➤ **Faerie**: A mysterious race that remains isolated on their islands. Most of the Mortal Realm blames the Faerie for the loss of magic and even bringing the Devils to the Mortal Realm.

➤ **Gods**: Divine beings from another Realm that once blessed the Mortal Realm with their magic (Gods Resource). After the Gods War, the Gods pulled their magic from the Mortal world, leaving the mortals with what little of the Resource that had stained the earth to use.

➤ **Angels**: Beings that serve under the Gods. Often sent on missions in the Mortal Realm since the Gods have not stepped into the Realm since the Gods War. There are various levels of Angels, and each is given a specific purpose by their God or Goddess.

➤ **Devils**: Beings from an outer realm that use what mortals refer to as *Dark Magic*. The Devils are the enemy of the Gods and gain their power from the fear the Mortal Realm has for them.

➤ **Demons**: Beings that serve under the Devils. Demons are always male and are sent on missions in the Mortal Realm. They are usually known for summoning beasts (Draugar) and annihilating cities to spread fear and panic, powering their Devil masters.

➤ **Succubus**: Beings that serve under the Devils. Succubus are always female and are sent on missions of espionage and resonance in the Mortal Realm. Succubus are known for their sexual nature. Replenishing their power by taking the magic of those they sleep with. Succubus are also known as tricksters as they can take the form of anyone whose blood they drink.

➢ **Basilisk**: Antient beings that once ruled over the Mortal Realm. Great creatures of power that even the Gods and Devils feared. They were known as lords of the skies and passed their magic into the Mortal Realm as long as the people of their realm believed in them.

➢ **Alpha:** The ruling race of the world Addilan. They are the creators of the Divine Races (God/Devil). The Alpha's ruled their world, creating the Divine races to keep balance as they gained power from the beliefs of their religious followers.

Great Cities:

➢ **Meridian**: One of the great cities that predate even the Gods War. Its population is primarily Elven and is led by an Elven King. Meridian is no longer visited by outsiders thanks to the rule of the Elven King. The city is no longer a shining example of the Great Cities and is now a poverty-stricken city.

➢ **Murdok**: Another of the great cities that predate the Gods War. It is known as the Dwarven City due to ninety percent of its population being only dwarven.

➢ **Nupross**: One of the great cities near the large lakes of the continent. Mostly populated by humans whose ancestors could be traced back to the Gods War. Travel to Nupross is strictly regulated as the city's population wishes to keep their city *pure.*

➢ **Atence**: The most diverse of the great cities. Populated by almost all mortal races (except Faerie). The city is surrounded by large woodlands that are inhabited by strange beasts and creatures from the Devils Realm.

Creatures:

➢ **Fenrir**: Wolf-like creatures that have magical elemental properties. Most known Fenrir use Ice or Earth magics.

➢ **Snyth**: Bird-like creature that stands on two legs with large taloned feet. It has a feathered reptilian-like tail.

➢ **Draugar**: Creatures created by Demons. They are mortals infected with dark magic and transformed into husks with dark magic. Draugar will reproduce by infecting those they kill. Draugar's lifespans are shortened the more they reproduce. They have a hive-like mind and die after their magic is fully depleted.

➢ **Arachnes**: Creatures that's lower body is that of a giant spider while its upper body is that of a humanoid. Arachnes's were mostly wiped out after the Gods War. The few that have been spotted have been female. They are venomous with magically infused webbing. They are known to hunt horses and other large livestock. Typically, the only mortal deaths from Arachnes's are farmers or lone merchants.

- **Colossus:** Fabled as 'Giants.' The Colossus were created as soldiers of war for the Gods during their invasion of earth. The Colossus were commanded by the Angel of War Gadreed in the early years of the war with the Basilisks. During the war, all Colossus were slain by the armies of Basilisks and Faerie.

Basilisks:

- **Shinrahn:** King of the Dragons. Master of all Earth magic. Feya is Shinrahn's only Tribe Faerie.
- **Senshe:** Life of the Forest. Master of plant and Forest magic. Senshe's Tribe is the Forest Tribe (All Male Faerie).
- **Akirakesi:** Bringer of Fire. Master of Fire magic. Akirakesi's Tribe is the Fire Tribe (All Male Faerie).
- **Oothra:** Master of the Seas. Master of Ocean magic. Oothra's Faerie Tribe is the Water Tribe (All Female).
- **Thanatos:** Dragon of Death and Carrier of Souls. Master of Life and Death magic. Thanatos's Faerie Tribe is the Soul Tribe (All Male Faerie).
- **Meer:** Bringer of Storms. Master of Storm and Weather magic. Meer's Tribe is the Storm Tribe (All Male Faerie).
- **Materna:** Guardian of Life and Love. Master of Fertility magic. Materna's Tribe is the Fertility Tribe (All Female Faerie).
- **Cordilra:** Breaker of Mountains. Master of Earth and Stone magic. Cordilra's Tribe is the Earth Tribe (All Female Faerie).

- ➤ **Sophillia:** The Wise. Master of Knowledge and Keeper of Grimoires. Sophillia's Tribe is the Scholar Tribe (All Female Faerie).
- ➤ **Mithae:** Purveyor of Pleasure (Twin Sister of Pyron). Master of Pleasure and Entertainment. Mithae shares her Tribe with Pyron. Pleasure Tribe (All Female Faerie).
- ➤ **Pyron:** Purveyor of Pleasure (Twin Brother of Mithae). Master of Pleasure and Entertainment. Pyron shares his Tribe with Mithae. Pleasure Tribe (All Male Faerie).
- ➤ **Tier:** Protector of Beasts. Master of Summoning magic. Tier's Tribe is the Beast Tribe (All Female Faerie).
- ➤ **Guerison:** Master of Medicine and Alchemy. Master of Healing magic. Guerison's Tribe is the Nurture Tribe (All Female Faerie).
- ➤ **Akua:** Guardian of Rivers and Lakes. Master of Water magic. Akua's Tribe is the River Tribe (All Male Faerie).

Faerie Tribes:

- ➤ **Forest Tribe:** Aid the Forest Basilisk in maintaining the Earths forests. Masters of Plan and Forest magic. The Forest Tribe members are named after the exotic plants found in Senshe's forests. (Male Faerie)
- ➤ **Fire Tribe:** Aid the Fire Basilisk in controlling Earths Volcano's and cleanse dying forests with fire for the Forest Tribe to bring new life. Fire Tribe members are named after the types of Fires the tribe masters. (Male Faerie)

- **Water Tribe:** Aid The Ocean Basilisk in maintaining the Seas. Master of Ocean magic and have the ability to alter their bodies to swim in the worlds oceans. Ocean Tribe members are named after the various types of Ocean stones. (Female Faerie)
- **Soul Tribe:** Aid the Death Basilisk in escorting the souls of fallen mortals to the Spiritual Plain. Masters of Death and Spiritual magic. It is believed the Soul Tribe are given names based on the type of Spiritual magic they possess. (Male Faerie)
- **Storm Tribe:** Aid the Storm Basilisk on controlling weather and the seasons of the Earth. Masters of Strom magic. The Storm Tribe are given names based on the different types of storms they produce. (Male Faerie)
- **Fertility Tribe:** Aid the Fertility Basilisk in blessing new life. Master of Fertility magic. The Fertility Tribe are given names based on motherly emotion. (Female Faerie)
- **Earth Tribe:** Aid the Earth Basilisk in forming mountains and controlling the movement of the Earth. Master of Earth and Stone magic. The Earth Tribe are given names based on the various stones of the Earth. (Female Faerie)
- **Scholar Tribe:** Aid the Wise Basilisk in archiving magic into Grimoires. Masters of various magics and Grimoires. The Scholar Tribe are given the names based on their preferred method of archiving knowledge. (Female Faerie)
- **Pleasure Tribe:** Aid the Twin Dragons Mithae and Pyron. Masters of Pleasure and Entertainment. The Pleasure Tribe members are often named after various games, arts, and pleasures. (Male [Pyron] and Female [Mithae] Faerie)

- ➢ **Beast Tribe:** Aid the Protector of Beasts. The Beast tribe are responsible for the preservation of the worlds creatures. Masters of Summoning magic. The Beast Tribe are often named after various furs or features of the worlds beasts. (Female Faerie)
- ➢ **Nurture Tribe:** Aid the Master of Medicine and Alchemy. Masters of Alchemy and Medicinal magics. The Nurture Tribe are given names based on medicinal herbs. (Female Faerie)
- ➢ **River Tribe:** Aid the Guardian of Lakes and Rivers. Masters of Water magic. The River Tribe are named after the various creatures who live in bodies of fresh water. (Male Faerie)

Made in the USA
Columbia, SC
12 June 2024

37080739R00188